G000146514

THE PEACE OF CARNAGE

By Philip Trewinnard and published by New English Library

THE RAPE OF ST CLARE
THE PEACE OF CARNAGE

THE PEACE OF CARNAGE

Philip Trewinnard

NEW ENGLISH LIBRARY

Copyright © 1987 by Philip Trewinnard

First published in Great Britain in 1987 by
New English Library, Mill Road, Dunton Green, Sevenoaks, Kent.
Editorial office: 47 Bedford Square, London WC1B 3DP.

All rights reserved. No part of this publication may be
reproduced or transmitted in any form or by any means,
electronically or mechanically, including photocopying,
recording or any information storage or retrieval system,
without either the prior permission in writing from
the publisher or a licence, permitting restricted
copying, issued by the Copyright Licensing Agency,
7 Ridgmount Street, London WC1E 7AE.

Typeset by Hewer Text Composition Services, Edinburgh.
Printed in Great Britain by Biddles Ltd., Guildford and King's Lynn.

British Library Cataloguing in Publication Data
Trewinnard, Philip
The peace of carnage.
I. Title
823'.914[F]   PR6070.R4/

ISBN 0 450 40375 0

For Jean,

for the in-between years.

Part One

UNIBORE

1

A WARM winter's day in July, and all over Paradise the busy chatter of AK47s signalled the start of another lightning *coup d'état*. Throughout the archipelago of palm-green islands and aquamarine lagoons, the long-suffering masses, accustomed to the tempestuous rise and fall of tyrant upstarts, turned cautious ears towards the capital, Port Paradise, and went nervously about their daily toil.

The sporadic crump of mortar fire crept slowly closer to the capital, and shells began to whistle over Tranquil Bay from the old French destroyer, *Richelieu*. Everywhere, people stopped whatever they were doing and peered anxiously towards the sky. Fishermen diving from the coral reef; raucous women haggling over breadfruit in the marketplace; trishaw drivers idling outside waterfront bordellos; infants treble-piping *Pater noster* to a holy sister in the shade of rustling palm fronds; everyone fell silent and looked up into the cloudless heavens at the sound of asthmatic jet engines approaching from the east.

A vintage Canberra bomber, pride of the nation's air force, wheezed its way across the pineapple plantations, aimed a two-hundred-pounder at the presidential palace, missed by half a mile and flattened the only public convenience between Mombasa and Australia. Nimble foreign tourists dived for cover as windows blew in at the Royal Victoria Hotel nearby; glass and rubble cascaded down upon the acacia trees and fuchsia beds of Curzon Square; and old-timers, freshly powdered with the ochre dust, stood sadly round the smoking crater, aching for relief.

Come mid-morning, silence fell. An uneasy stillness settled everywhere. Throughout the islands, people clustered round transistor radios to await news of who was in and who was out. At half past eleven, Radio Paradise came back on the air with clarion blasts of martial music. A new messiah was born: Lance-Sergeant Hudson Butcher, seventh son of an impoverished plantation worker, forty-two-year-old instructor with the élite Corps of Guards. Not a man to dither over constitutional niceties, Sergeant Butcher, with an assured sense of destiny and a fine sense of priorities, had shot the army chief of staff by noon, elected himself President by half past, and was busy at his desk in Government House by ten to one, opening numbered bank accounts in Liechtenstein and pinning field-marshal's insignia to his epaulettes.

After a working lunch with his new politburo, military aides and assorted cousins answering suddenly to the rank of colonel, he addressed an anxious, waiting nation over Radio Paradise. Reading from his own impromptu text, lovingly prepared months in advance by kindly neutral well-wishers in the Cuban foreign ministry, he proclaimed the dawn of a glorious new era of equality and freedom, and blamed the failure of all such glorious new eras that had gone before upon the evil machinations of the Great Satan in Washington DC.

Their tiny nation, he declared, was yet another victim of the imperialist conspiracy of banks and multinational corporations. Now the hour of retribution and deliverance was at hand. In a voice tremulous with emotion, he unleashed a torrent of blistering invective against the White House, the State Department, the CIA, Congress, Wall Street, General Motors, Union Carbide, Coca-Cola, Donald Duck and a host of other household favourites; and, in conclusion, declared every one of the nine hundred and sixty-odd US citizens in Port Paradise – from Ambassador Hiram Colby to the humblest Catholic missionary – *persona non grata*, and gave them all forty-eight hours to clear out, bag and baggage.

While American families were gathering like bewildered refugees at Port Paradise airport in the pink-grey light of a subtropical dawn, all hell was breaking loose at the United Nations.

A sultry summer's night in New York, and blood was simmering at the UN building in Manhattan. All afternoon and half the night, the General Assembly had been locked in virulent debate over an American resolution to censure the government of Hudson Butcher for its inhuman treatment of US nationals in Port Paradise. Reason and diplomacy had evaporated in the fierce heat of sulphurous exchanges. Arguments raged like forest fire, tempers blazed and vitriol flew.

In the small hours of the morning, with violence threatening to erupt on the floor of the assembly itself, the Secretary-General took the vote. The resolution was lost by sixty-two votes to fifty-seven, with thirty-eight abstentions; while a counter-resolution tabled by the Paradise Islands, blaming Uncle Sam for virtually everything that was wrong with The World As We Know It, from Hong Kong 'flu to the slump in the Afghan tourist industry, was passed on a wave of Third World support by a majority of thirty-six. The session was dissolved in uproar at ten past two, and the Security Council agonised till dawn before agreeing on a comprehensive course of resolute inaction.

US Humiliated at UN, proclaimed the headline in the late editions of the *New York Times*.

Third World Backs a Butcher, the *Boston Globe* declared.

Two hundred miles away in Washington DC, Senator Eugene Erdreich, vice-chairman of the Senate Foreign Relations Committee, had decided that enough was enough.

'Who does that Paradise asshole think he is, anyhow?' he asked his old crony, Congressman Irwin Cato of Oregon, over lunch in his office that day.

'Christ knows,' said Cato, opening a jumbo tub of Captain Gunn's Nebraska Broiled Turkey Balls while Erdreich poured the wine. 'Who is he?'

'And what the hell kind of a Mickey Mouse country does he think he's running? They've had more presidents in thirteen years of independence than we've had in two centuries. They've got a worse human rights record than Attila the Hun. And half those dumb sons of bitches who voted for him at the UN last night don't even know where those pisspot little islands are.'

'Right. You're damn right.' Cato dunked a turkey ball in the ketchup and chewed in silence for a moment. 'Where are they, matter of interest?'

'Christ knows,' said Erdreich. 'Who cares? They exist, that's all that matters.'

Cato got up and removed a dog-eared atlas from Erdreich's bookcase. The two men pored over it for a while, hunting for the tiny archipelago. Erdreich abandoned the search after discovering to his amazement that New Zealand was in two pieces.

'The hell with Paradise, anyhow,' he said, resuming his lunch. 'I am sick to the teeth, Irwin, sick to *the teeth* of having to sit and listen to Third World jackasses foul-mouthing our great country at the UN. And if you ask me, more and more plain, simple, decent, freedom-loving people across this nation are beginning to question why we have to go on paying twenty-five per cent of the UN budget and getting ninety-five per cent of the world's abuse in return.'

Generally speaking, Senator Erdreich regarded all those simple, decent, freedom-loving people across the nation as a mass of morons and could not have given a two-bit damn what they thought about *any*thing. But there were occasions, it was only fair to say, when there was not a hick or half-wit in the land so humble that his opinions were not deemed worthy of the senator's most assiduous attention. These occasions came round regularly, once every four years, and were called *elections*.

'If you want my opinion, Irwin,' he concluded, 'it's high time we began to ask ourselves whether the United Nations really needs America and whether we need *them*.'

'You mean . . . quit?'

'I mean just exactly that.'

'Pull clean out? Of the entire United Nations? The whole organisation? Just like that?'

'Could be a real vote-winner,' urged the senator. A turkey ball slipped off his fork and slithered down the atlas, leaving a spoor of grease and ketchup across the Hindu Kush.

Cato whistled softly. 'Jesus. I don't know. That's, that's a hell of a step to take. I mean. . . .'

'America first, Irwin,' said Erdreich with patriotic fervour. 'Next year is election year, remember. These are difficult times for this administration. We need an issue like this to unite our great country. And strengthen moral fibre. And appeal to the pride of the people.'

'And get the President out of the shit.'

'Exactly.' Erdreich nodded gravely. 'So think about it, Irwin. Think about it.'

So Irwin Cato thought about it. And over the following weeks he discreetly sounded out opinion in the House of Representatives, while Erdreich discreetly sounded out the Secretary of State, and the Secretary of State sounded out the President, and the President sounded out his foreign policy advisers. And they all decided that the United Nations was one can of worms that might be worth opening up for further scrutiny. So at the end of July the President appointed a special presidential advisory commission into UN agencies (SPACUNA) under the chairmanship of a diligent White House sycophant called Eddison Packard, and instructed them to find out precisely what did happen to the quarter of a billion dollars or so that Uncle Sam poured down the UN drain each year, and to assess whether or not it might be wasted more productively on some other, less pathologically anti-American organisation.

After three months of hard graft in New York, getting wrecked and laid every night at UN expense, Packard and his colleagues concluded that the organisation was doing its best in a difficult world and that, on balance, the United States was better off *in* it than out of it. They then began to turn their attentions to the multifarious UN agencies around the world to see if they, too, were giving reasonable value for money. And it was at this injudicious moment that the United Nations International Board for Ontological Research and Education (UNIBORE) chose to pipe up and advise its one hundred and fifty-two member-governments of a thirty-eight per cent increase in their budget contributions from July the first.

'And what exactly does Unibore *do*?' enquired the President who had never even heard of it before.

'No one seems to know,' replied the Secretary of State. 'Packard's on his way to London right now to find out.'

2

PACKARD ARRIVED unannounced at Unibore's headquarters at Halcyon House, Pall Mall, just after ten, one misty grey morning at the end of October. Entering a marble lobby about half the size of Grand Central Station, he flourished a letter of credence signed by the Secretary of State in person and was promptly conducted to Doctor Byron Cleveland's office on the fifth floor.

Byron Cleveland had been the United States' delegate to Unibore for almost three years. He was a forty-two-year-old ontologist from Lynchburg, Virginia, a writer, academic and – before taking up his post at Unibore – senior lecturer in ontology at Yale. That was virtually all that Packard knew about the man, and it was not a propitious beginning. Academia in general was something of a closed world to Eddison Packard. In common with about half the American nation, he was a lawyer, and his experience of dealing with intellectuals was limited to prosecuting or defending them (preferably prosecuting). He did not regard himself as a prejudiced man, but his fair, unbiased opinion of academics as a species was generally on a par with his opinions of junkies, pacifists, child-molesters, gays, draft dodgers, press reporters and people on welfare. And there was nothing about Byron Cleveland's appearance that, on first impression, prompted him to modify that view. The guy looked a wreck. (But then, to be fair, Byron always looked a wreck by daylight.) He had a sallow city pallor, a wild thatch of coarse blond hair, foggy blue eyes and rimless glasses reinforced at the hinges with Band-Aid. He needed fibre, vitamins and exercise. He needed a new suit. (But Byron always needed a new suit. He had been alternating the same pair of wash-and-wear jobs in genuine wool-look polysynthesised tweed for the past seven years.)

And the office reflected the man. Behind its elegant Georgian facade, Halcyon House had been gutted and rebuilt to accommodate Unibore's one hundred and fifty-two delegates and untold legions of clerical staff in tasteful comfort – at a cost approaching the gross national debt of several of its most indigent member-nations. But Cleveland's office was a tip. Littered (knee-deep, was the phrase Packard would use when he reported back to Washington) with books, papers, and every kind and colour of garbage – files, letters, computer print-out, plastic coffee-cups, old *Herald Tribune*s, sweet wrappings, Kentucky Fried Chicken cartons and soiled Kleenex. The only thing in the place that looked remotely tidy was the top of his desk. And that looked suspiciously desolate.

'The President,' Packard explained, ensconcing himself in a soft leather armchair, 'has asked me to assess the general levels of efficiency of all the United Nations agencies to which we are currently affiliated. So this is primarily a fact-finding mission.'

Byron nodded and smiled. He did not know who this Packard character was but he did not take too kindly to White House menials barging into his office first thing on a Monday morning without warning. And this particular menial looked a sight too healthy for Byron's liking – lean and combative, with aggressive, ratty features, treacherous dark eyes and the sort of inscrutable X-ray stare that customs officers clamp onto scruffy itinerants flying in from Bogotá. He did not care much for the sound of that word *efficiency* either. It smacked suspiciously of dangerous concepts like waste-elimination and value-for-money, and other anti-cultural obsessions that had suddenly become fashionable among governments everywhere.

'As you're no doubt aware,' Packard went on, 'the State Department has recently been notified of a thirty-eight per cent increase in its contributions to Unibore as from next July. Which means that the American taxpayer is being asked to shell out thirty-five million bucks a year to keep this organisation afloat.'

'Is that so?' said Byron, who could not even make head or tail of his own telephone bill let alone Unibore's biennial budget forecasts. 'I had no idea. You want to talk to the comptroller-general about it?'

'Maybe later,' said Packard. 'But first I'd like to ask you one or two questions about what goes on here.'

'Sure. What can I tell you?'

'Well, what does Unibore actually *do*, for a start?'

'Do?' Byron hesitated. He was not often asked that kind of question. Unibore did nothing, that was the whole point of it. It was an organisation of thinkers. Metaphysicists. Paid by their governments to sit in London and contemplate the human condition and come up with lots of exciting new abstract ideas for solving all those intractable problems besetting The World As We Know It. 'Ontology is a field of metaphysics,' Byron explained. 'It studies the nature of existence . . . the essence of life . . . in the abstract.'

'To what purpose exactly?' asked Packard.

'Purpose?' Byron took a deep breath and stalled. What the hell did he mean, to what purpose? Unibore was there to provide a refreshing oasis of inertia in a wilderness of global panic. While every other United Nations agency was rushing round getting hot and bothered and interfering in all kinds of hideous world crises that were probably better left alone,

Unibore was quietly soldiering on at Halcyon House, pondering upon all sorts of fundamental questions. Like the purpose of existence, the meaning of the universe, and how to justify a budget of a hundred and forty million dollars a year.

'Well, put it this way,' said Byron. 'Whenever war, famine, disease, poverty, ignorance or despair darkens the surface of our planet, Unibore is there, in spirit, giving it a lot of very careful thought.' He opened a drawer in his desk. 'I have some literature here that might be of help.'

'I was given a publicity handout by the UN in New York,' Packard replied, opening his attaché case and producing a student's wall-chart in primary colours entitled *Everything You Always Wanted To Know About UNIBORE*. 'But there are one or two items of terminology here with which I'm not familiar. For example, you have five disciplines of ontological research, according to this chart: peace ethics – which I believe is your specialty . . .?'

'Correct.'

'And dialectical ontology, metaphysical sociology, abstract politics and theoretical realities.'

'Right.'

'Well, what do they all mean?'

'Mean?' Byron removed his glasses and chewed thoughtfully on an earpiece. He had never actually considered it before. 'I suppose,' he ventured at length, 'you could define dialectical ontology as a kind of . . . Hegelian way of looking at abstract existence. Whereas metaphysical sociology is more of an ontological way of approaching noumenal phenomena.' He put his glasses on again and began to mould an imaginary vase with his hands on the desk in front of him. 'Abstract politics, conversely, is basically just a noumenal way of approaching sociological dialectics. And I guess theoretical realities is really little more than a positively negative way of approaching concrete abstracts.'

Packard remained silent. He was not sure whether Byron had finished or was merely pausing for breath.

Bryon smiled. 'There's a whole lot more to it than that, of course,' he added reassuringly. 'But that's pretty much it, in a nutshell.'

'Nutshell,' Packard echoed quietly. And noticed how oppressively warm the room had become.

Byron's secretary crept in, carrying two cups of coffee and a plate of biscuits on a small tray. She handed one cup to Packard, left the tray on Byron's desk and crept out again.

'Doctor Cleveland,' said Packard, loosening his tie a fraction, 'may I ask a pathetically simple layman's question?'

'Go right ahead. Please. Any question.'

'This must sound a little trivial to the ontological mind, but what exactly does this organisation produce? What is the end product tangiblewise?'

'You mean . . .' Byron helped himself to a Jaffa cake. He really could have done without obscure questions of this kind before lunch. '*Any* tangible product . . . endwise?'

'I mean,' said Packard, beginning to sweat a little round the collar, 'what do you guys actually have to show for a budget of one hundred and forty million dollars a year?'

'Well, of course we're not like – say – the World Health Organisation,' Byron replied. 'I can't just take you out and show you a malaria-free zone for your money, or a new cure for Green Monkey disease.'

'OK, so what *can* you show me?'

Byron did not know how he was going to get this across to a philistine klutz like Packard, but there was *no* tangible end product to Unibore's work. Apart, of course, from a phenomenal abundance of printed matter. He tried offering that, as a last resort. 'Papers,' he said, and tried to make them sound at least as exciting as a cure for Green Monkey disease.

Packard looked hopeful. 'What sort of papers?'

'Academic papers.' Byron tried to explain it as simply as he could. Unibore's delegates sat in Halcyon House, thinking (ontologically) about the world and its problems. And from time to time they consigned the fruits of their contemplations to paper. These papers were duly typed out by secretaries, jargonised into UNenglish by experts, word-processed by young women from places like Tolworth, and churned out in prolific quantities on finest-quality blue-tinted paper. Copies were then distributed all over the world to anybody who might conceivably be interested. There were papers of all sorts and for every kind of consumption, for academic consumption, public consumption, government consumption, UN consumption, diplomatic consumption, student consumption, religious consumption, and even papers for virtually no one's consumption.

'And does anybody of the least importance,' enquired Packard, 'take any notice of these papers?'

'Difficult to tell,' Byron replied. 'We simply offer an alternative way of looking at a given situation. So whatever influence we have tends to be purely subliminal. And how can you assess a subliminal influence?'

Packard was both fascinated and appalled in equal measure. 'Tell me, Doctor Cleveland, is anyone actually in control of what goes on in this . . . institution? Is anybody accountable to anybody?'

'Well, naturally,' Byron replied. 'We're a thoroughly democratic organisation. Every summer we have an annual general conference when we review the year's work and elect thirty-five of our member-delegates to an executive board. And once every five years we elect a new director-general. The director-general is accountable to the board, and the board is accountable to the delegates.' And the entire organisation, Byron omitted to add, was managed with sedulous inefficiency by a bureaucracy of thousands, accountable to nobody. 'As I guess you know by now,' he went on modestly, 'our present director-general, Otello Fabrizi, is retiring next summer, and I have had the honour to be elected his successor.'

Packard's face remained neutral. 'No kidding?'

Byron felt wounded. He imagined the news would have been all over Washington by now. 'I take over on the first of July.'

'So tell me,' said Packard, not unpleasantly, 'as director-general-elect of this prestigious academic body, do you seriously consider it a worthwhile way of spending one hundred and forty million dollars a year, keeping a hundred and fifty-two ontologists and Christ knows how many secretaries sitting on their butts in Pall Mall all day long, churning out blue-tinted subliminal influences?'

'Oh, hell no,' Byron replied swiftly. 'That doesn't cost anything like a hundred and forty million. I doubt if it even costs half that.'

'Then where does the other half go?'

'On research fellowships, mainly, and educational bursaries of one sort or another.'

'Bursaries and fellowships for whom?'

'For students of ontology worldwide.'

'And they do what you do?'

'Pretty much,' said Byron.

'Pretty much,' echoed Packard quietly, and savoured the words as if anxious to extract every last drop of ontological goodness from them. He finished his coffee in silence and placed the empty cup on Byron's desk. 'Tell me, Doctor Cleveland, what sort of things do you write about in your capacity as United States' delegate?'

'You haven't seen any of my work?' Byron was surprised. 'I mail copies of everything to the State Department once a month.'

'Sure, but you know how it is . . . the pressure of work.' Packard shrugged apologetically. 'But if I could maybe take a leisurely browse through some of your more recent offerings, I'm sure I'd get a clearer picture of what actually goes on here.'

'I'm sure you would,' Byron agreed, opening another drawer beneath that vast, deserted desk-top. 'In which case I can recommend my very latest work on conflict in Central America. That should give you a pretty straightforward idea of what ontological analysis is all about.'

3

PACKARD HAD spent half a working lifetime grovelling about backstage in the theatre of American politics, drafting speeches and inventing election pledges, and he considered himself a master of weasel words and a craftsman in the art of writing gobbledegook. But never, in twenty years dedicated to the propagation of public misinformation, had he come across anything so wonderfully incomprehensible as *Conflict in Central America – an Analysis by Sociopolitical Trilectics* by Byron J. Cleveland.

'Tell me,' said the Secretary of State, when he had had a chance to wade through the first eighty-seven pages himself, 'what exactly *are* sociopolitical trilectics?'

'I'm afraid I can't even tell you approximately, sir,' Packard confessed.

'And positive negativisms?'

'No idea.'

'Concrete abstracts? Noumenal phenomena?'

Packard shook his head. 'Nobody seems to know. I telexed Doctor Cleveland for clarification, but all I got back was about half a mile of debate on the meaning of "clarify".'

'And what did that say?'

'We don't know, sir. No one in the White House or the State Department can make any sense of it.' Packard had even referred it to UGLIBECC, the President's new Unit for Governmental Language Improvement and Betterised Enhancement of Communications Comprehensibility. But nobody there had heard of noumenal phenomena or concrete abstracts either.

'Is Cleveland putting us on, do you think?' the Secretary of State wondered.

'No, sir. I'm sure he's for real.'

'Who gave him the job in the first place?'

'You did, Mr Secretary.'

'On whose advice?'

'Professor Aaron Goldbaum's.'

'Who is Professor Goldbaum?'

'The world's leading authority on noumenal phenomena.'

'You can't be serious.'

'Yes, sir. He won the Nobel prize for metaphysics in 1947 for his research in that field.'

'And have you asked *him* for his opinion of Unibore?'

'No, sir. That's not possible. He's been in a psychiatric institution for some years now.'

'And what about all these bursaries and research fellowships that Unibore hands out? I don't want this administration to be seen as anti-educational.'

'Well, sir, about eighty-five per cent of the funds go to postgraduate students from the poorer countries to enable them to study ontology in the West. The other fifteen per cent gets swallowed up in administration costs.'

'And how the hell is that supposed to help the starving millions?'

'Subliminally, I guess,' said Packard.

The Secretary of State tossed *Conflict in Central America* into his wastebasket. 'OK, get onto the General Accounting Office, Ed, and have them rush me a flash report on Unibore's financial affairs. Then get Byron Cleveland over here for some straight talking.'

'Well, I guess it depends how you conceptualise *straight talking*, Mr Secretary,' Byron began, when he was summoned to Washington in the second week of December.

'I conceptualise it thusly,' the Secretary of State replied. And clobbered him straight over the head with the news that the United States government would be terminating its membership of Unibore with effect from the first of July.

At the age of forty-two, Byron Jefferson Cleveland had made United Nations history. He had just been director-general-elect for the shortest time in the thirty-four years of Unibore's existence.

4

BYRON WAS still reeling with shock in the third week of December, when Washington's decision was conveyed officially to Halcyon House in London, where it left most people reeling with indifference. Partly because it was impossible to take anything the White House said at face value at the start of an election year, but more especially because it was Christmas. Christmas was the busiest time of the year at Unibore and usually began around Guy Fawkes Night, when anything that could be described as useful work was postponed until after the skiing season to give everyone a chance to get on with the serious business of hanging paper chains and planning office parties. Even so, it did occur to the director-general, Otello Fabrizi, that since the US government contributed no less than twenty-five per cent of the organisation's gross income, it might be prudent to ask the comptroller-general, David Schellenberg, to consider what the financial consequences might be if Washington withdrew.

However, by the time Schellenberg had done his Christmas

shopping and got around to calculating what twenty-five per cent of two hundred and eighty million dollars amounted to, five more nations – the UK, France, West Germany, Canada and Japan – had announced that they, too, were reconsidering their membership of Unibore in the light of the latest swingeing budget increases and widespread allegations of financial mismanagement. And since their combined contributions amounted to a further third of the organisation's income, Otello Fabrizi hastily summoned an unusual general session of the executive board and asked Schellenberg to spell out in words of round figures precisely what effect all these precipitate withdrawals might have.

The board assembled at the end of the second week of January to hear Schellenberg's prognosis. It was not the most auspicious day. It was Friday the thirteenth, and Unibore's new and prodigiously expensive heating system – which had been going wrong ever since the first nip of frost the previous November – had chosen the bitterest morning since 1947 to pack up altogether. The thirty-five delegates of the executive board sat shivering in their cashmere and furs in a wide arc around the director-general's podium, looking more like prospective candidates for a trans-polar expedition. Their eyes drifted uncomprehendingly over the pages of summary accounts that the comptroller-general's office had generously provided for their edification. From his elevated throne beside Otello on the director-general's podium, David Schellenberg – a dour accountant with the build of Orson Welles and the features of a bloodhound – surveyed them glumly over half-moon spectacles.

'I very much regret to inform learned delegates,' he began, 'that this organisation is poised upon the precipice of an acute financial crisis.' He paused momentarily while interpreters began muttering into their microphones in the adjacent room and delegates fiddled with their earpieces. 'We are approximately thirty million dollars in debt,' he continued, 'half of which is owing to United Nations central funds. We have no reserves left to draw on and one third of our member governments are behind in their contributions. The outstanding total amounting to some sixty million dollars.'

Delegates caught their breath and exchanged looks of startled innocence, as if they did not know perfectly well that this had been going on for twenty years or more. The word 'disgraceful' tiptoed darkly from the lips of Air Vice-Marshal Engineer of the Paradise Islands, none of whose many governments had ever paid one penny piece of their contributions in thirteen years of independence.

'If the six member governments concerned *do* decide to withdraw or withhold their contributions,' Schellenberg went on, 'we shall lose a little over half our projected income for the next two financial years. In which case we shall have no option but to reduce expenditure by the same proportion . . . By an amount roughly equivalent, as it happens, to what is spent each year on educational bursaries and fellowships.'

Schellenberg was merely trying to be helpful, but education was a sensitive issue at Halcyon House. Throughout the developing nations of the world Unibore was the only major source of funding for ontological research, and to hint at even a modest paring of this munificent budget was to venture into a minefield where none but fools or heroes dared to tread. The words had scarcely left Schellenberg's lips before the first hint of thunder began to rumble from the Third World delegates and the Soviet bloc.

'It is neither here nor there to *me* how learned delegates elect to wield the surgeon's knife,' Schellenberg assured them soothingly. 'But if no one is prepared to reconsider the education budget, then the only alternative is to focus our attention on administrative costs here at Halcyon House.'

Otello Fabrizi shifted uneasily on the podium beside him. Wherever humanly possible one wanted to *increase* administrative costs, not diminish them. They needed every clerk and typist they could get their hands on these days, to justify the exorbitant financial demands on member governments.

'Do you have any particular areas in mind?' Otello ventured cautiously.

Schellenberg glanced over the sheets of statistics in front of him.

'According to the accounts, we spent seven million pounds last year on delegates' salaries. Four million on clerical staff. Eight hundred and sixty thousand on cars, chauffeurs, taxis and airline tickets. Two and a half million on subsidised housing and private education. And a further million and a half on delegates' expenses, which included the following items, considered indispensable to ontological research . . .' Schellenberg paused to select another page of facts and figures, and continued tonelessly, 'Compact disc players, video recorders, television sets, fridge-freezers, washing machines, snooker tables, golf clubs, a grand piano, several thousand seats for Covent Garden, God only knows how many tickets to Wimbledon, and a three-week Polynesian cruise for a family of five and their Filipino nanny.'

He looked around the delegates to see if anybody wished to challenge him on anything so far, but they were all riveted by these revelations and itching to know the identity of the profligate South Sea cruiser. Schellenberg, however, was not prepared to say.

'If these figures,' he went on diplomatically, 'do not suggest areas where one or two small economies might be in order, perhaps I could draw your attention to the telephone and telex accounts for Halcyon House, which last year amounted to something in excess of six million pounds. To put that figure in perspective, it is the equivalent of every single person in the building speaking to Milton Keynes for two hours every morning for a year.'

The full significance of which was lost on most members of the executive board. For it was a mystery to anyone with even a rudimentary knowledge of Buckinghamshire, that *any*body – let alone the entire building – should wish to speak to Milton Keynes for two hours every morning. However . . .

'Far be it from me,' concluded Schellenberg, 'to suggest where the axe should fall. But let there be no illusions. If those six member governments withdraw from this organisation and the appropriate expenditure cuts are not made, we shall be unable to meet our liabilities much beyond July. Unibore's affairs will then be placed in the hands of a receiver, and the United Nations would be entitled to sue this board for financial mismanagement . . . and claim from every delegate, personally, the repayment of all monies owed to UN central funds. In which event, you would each be liable to a surcharge of approximately a quarter of a million dollars, as debts now stand.'

There was a long, stupefied silence. Schellenberg was in his element, luxuriating in the cold, merciless logic of statistics. 'The alternative,' he continued, smoothing his hands lovingly over the files of brutal arithmetic on the table in front of him, 'would be to spread the burden of cuts overall. To trim the education budget by, say, fifty per cent; make a quarter of the clerical staff redundant; freeze all salaries for two years; sell the lease on these cripplingly expensive premises in Pall Mall, and move out of London to somewhere very much cheaper . . . Such as Milton Keynes, for example.'

He might as soon have suggested moving Unibore to the Dogger Bank for all the enthusiasm he inspired. They all sat and stared up at the podium as if he were talking in some arcane moon language. The only delegate to speak was Academician Konstantin Rhoskov of the USSR who turned, somewhat puzzled, to his neighbour, Nina Kabanova, the Bulgarian delegate. "Милтон Кейнес?" he whispered, wondering if this might be some obscure relation of the illustrious British economist. 'Who *is* dis "Милтон Кейнес?"

5

THE HEATING was back on again by mid-afternoon and the warmest place in the building was the chauffeurs' restroom, next to the basement boilerhouse. It was a homely little hideaway, like a stokers' mess in the bowels of a ship, crawling with hot, serpentine pipes and rich in the aroma of fuel oil. Providence and the Portobello Road had equipped it with a dart board, a worm-eaten snooker table and some comfy old armchairs, full of broken springs and geriatric moths.

It was getting on for quarter past three, and driver (grade 1) Gladstone Shilling, chauffeur to Byron Cleveland, had just brewed up a fresh pot of tea for the lads and was settling himself into his own personal private armchair with his cricket boots and a little pot of Meltonian whitener. Outside, a savage north wind was howling round the basement car park like a trapped animal, spitting sleet in all directions. Gladstone loathed winter. It was a barbaric European institution, when all good men and true had to hang up their cricket boots, get lost in the fog, and risk life and limb carrying the wife's bags through the January sales.

It had always been something of a mystery to Gladstone why so many geniuses in Halcyon House spent such an inordinate amount of time and thought and expensive blue paper trying to fathom out what life was all about. He could have told them that in one sentence. Apart from earning a living to keep the missis happy and ensure that the kids went to school in a decent pair of batting gloves each year, life was about enjoying the sunshine and playing/practising/discussing/organising/watching/thinking/reading/writing or simply dreaming about cricket. It was as simple as that; and Gladstone, who was a charitable fellow, felt sorry for anyone who could not see things that way. As for all that intellectual claptrap about peace ethics . . . if only the nations of the world would do the decent civilised thing and agree to resolve their differences on a strip of new-mown turf, armed with nothing but willow and leather, then wars would become obsolete at a stroke. (With, of course, the added bonus that Jamaica would be the new world superpower overnight.)

Gladstone was no mere theorist either. He preached by example, as founder, president and secretary of the only United Nations cricket club in the world – the Woodpeckers. He also had the honour of being their captain, manager, opening batsman and leading pace bowler. In fact, were it not for Gladstone's tireless energy and dedication, the Woodpeckers would almost certainly have stopped pecking long since and expired of terminal apathy. As it was, he had managed to build up a flourishing and talented eleven (sometimes ten, occasionally only eight or nine) with their own small ground in south London and a busy schedule of fixtures all through the season, from Easter till September.

Come the bleak, dark months of frost and ice and civil strife in every store in Oxford Street, however, there was nothing much that a good man and true could do except clean his kit, put a shine on his balls and plan next season's fixture list. And he was doing just this – whitening his boots and wondering if he could cram three matches into the Easter weekend this year without bringing the missis out on strike again in protest – when his fellow chauffeurs began arriving for their afternoon tea in varying states of agitation.

First to burst in was Ernie Dodds, Academician Rhoskov's driver, with the bewildering news that David Schellenberg was suing everyone in Halcyon House for a quarter of a million dollars. Hard on his heels came Sid Tideyman, the director-general's chauffeur, with the still more bewildering news that the executive board were being moved to Milton Keynes. Then Archie Dent – driver to anyone who was daft enough to get into a car with him – lurched in before skidding off in search of another accident, and announced that Unibore had gone bankrupt. And a moment later, Les Nuttall, shop steward and chief car-washer, arrived hot-foot from a hostile exchange of monosyllables with the head of personnel and informed them all that no one's job was safe beyond July.

The lower levels of Halcyon House (geographically speaking) were something of a bargain basement for gossip and speculation, and extravagant rumours of one sort or another were ten a penny. But in twelve years of service, Gladstone had never heard anything quite so extravagant as the claim that Unibore was bankrupt. Somewhat discomfited by what he'd heard, he mentioned it to Byron Cleveland as he drove him home to St John's Wood that evening. Byron, unable to deny the rumours, told him frankly what Schellenberg had told the board that morning. (Byron was always frank with Gladstone; in fact, he looked upon him as a kind of auxiliary psychoanalyst, with the particular advantage that Gladstone was always on call and did not charge fifty pounds an hour.)

The minutiae of Unibore's financial problems were neither here nor there to Gladstone. Nor was the spectre of impending redundancy or the loss of his free Jaguar. His sole concern was the survival of his cricket club. If Unibore were, in a manner of speaking (in Gladstone's manner of speaking, at any rate), to pack up shop and disappear down the plughole, what would become of the Woodpeckers? A question he put there and then to Byron – who did not even understand the basic principles of ping-pong let alone cricket, and was totally stumped for a helpful reply.

Gladstone drove home to Ladbroke Grove in a state of deepening depression. It was choir practice that night, but he could not face all that 'joy o'erwhelms me, humble sinner' number over and over again. So he dropped his wife off at the local church hall and repaired in deep gloom to the saloon bar of the Umpire and Mango, where he found his old friend and mentor, Everton Pascall, supping a pint and browsing through that month's edition of *Balls and Bowlers*.

Everton was one of the wise elders of the Umpire and Mango and a wellspring of sound advice. He was, furthermore, an active member of the Woodpeckers CC Supporters Club (in fact, their *only* member) and as deputy reserve wicket keeper for the London Transport second eleven from 1961 to 1964, could justly claim a distinguished playing record in his own right. Listening patiently to his young friend's account of Unibore's plight, Everton was reminded of a somewhat analogous situation in his own experience. It was, he told Gladstone, not unlike the occasion when the local borough council suspended its grant of thirty pounds per annum to the North Kensington Ramblers Association.

Gladstone said he couldn't see the slightest connection.

Well, a few years ago, Everton explained, Kensington and Chelsea council, who had been subsidising the ramblers association with a modest subvention for many years, had peremptorily withdrawn the grant on the grounds that the association was no longer finding enough rambles to justify the money.

Gladstone said he wasn't surprised. Nobody in his right mind would want to go rambling round Ladbroke Grove. One needed countryside to do that sort of thing; somewhere pastoral, full of haywains and cowpats and ploughmen tolling the knell of parting day. And there wasn't much of that to be found in North Kensington.

Nevertheless, Everton continued patiently, rightly or wrongly that was what the council had decided. So, to make them change their mind, the association had organised a number of very useful community projects.

Gladstone was beginning to feel that they were straying rather from the point at issue. 'What kind of projects?'

'Well, for instance,' said Everton, 'we organised a bus survey. Countin' the buses goin' up and down Ladbroke Grove and all round the borough.'

Gladstone frowned. 'What for?'

'Well, 's useful.'

'How?'

'Helps the community put pressure on London Transport to improve the service.'

'Yeh, but whassat got to do with ramblin'?'

'That's not the point, man. The point is the association was undertakin' useful projects for the community. And when the council saw that, they changed their minds and gave us back our grant.'

Gladstone swallowed a long soothing draught of stout and pondered on the analogy. 'So whassat got to do with Unibore?'

'Well, think of Unibore as the ramblers association,' said Everton. 'And think of the American government as Kensin'ton and Chelsea council. Right?'

It was straining credulity somewhat but Gladstone did his best. 'All right. Then what?'

'Then aksk yourself why the Americans want to pull out.'

'Well, that's obvious,' said Gladstone scornfully. 'Everyone knows that. Because that facety Butcherman on Paradise been givin' 'em a hard time at the United Nations.'

'Yeh, but they can't *say* that's the reason,' said Everton. 'They're tellin' the world it's because Unibore's a total waste of money.'

'So?'

'So just tell your governor, all he's got to do is follow the example of me ramblers association.'

'And start countin' buses?'

'No, man, use your head, yeh? Get Unibore doin' somethin' useful. *So* useful that Washin'ton won't have no excuse for pullin' out. Right?'

'But Unibore's not *supposed* to do anythin' useful,' said Gladstone wearily. 'That's the whole point of it. It's a think tank, full of geniuses, all philosophisin' and makin' weighty cogitation. It's a heavy number, man.'

'Well, OK,' said Everton. 'Why can't they cogitate and philosophise about useful things?'

'And what do *you* call useful, hah?' Gladstone asked suspiciously.

Everton had to think about that. 'Dunno. Maybe they could hold some kind of conference or somethin'. Like a summit conference, for peace, or whatever. Somethin' so important for the whole future of mankind that not even the government of the United States would dare to stay away from it . . . not in election year, with all the propaganda them sneaky Russians would start stirrin' up.'

The trouble with Everton, Gladstone reflected in bed that night (aloud to his wife, who had fallen asleep some twenty minutes earlier) was that he had such a simplistic view of the world. But that came from being a wicket keeper, of course. All wicket keepers in Gladstone's experience had a parochial outlook. It had something to do with being so close to the ground for such long periods of time, he supposed. It gave them a worm's eye view of everything.

Even so, there was a grain of ingenuity hidden away in all that chaff about the ramblers association, and Gladstone pondered on the matter at some length that weekend. After all, Unibore would not actually have to *hold* a peace conference. It would just have to go through the motions of arranging one or *threaten* to arrange one. That surely would be enough to worry the American government. At all events, he considered it worth mentioning to Byron Cleveland as he drove him to work on Monday morning.

It was difficult for any but the most trained observer to detect any sign of meaningful life in Byron much before teatime on Mondays. While Gladstone nudged the Jaguar gently through the rush-hour traffic and shared aloud the fruits of Everton's considered wisdom, Byron remained slumped in the front seat beside him, a study in whey-faced torpor, contemplating the mucky, slush-wet pavements and the bustling office workers splashing their way down Regent Street. But it was all going on inside that large, untidy head of his. Gladstone's words were triggering off a chain of intricate thoughts that flashed around the complex microcosm of Byron's brain like a dozen pinballs in the same machine at once.

The idea was indisputably a stroke of genius. There were drawbacks, of course. Not least the fact that Unibore was quite bankrupt enough as it was, without taking on the responsibility for a major world peace initiative. But desperate situations called for bold, decisive action; and like so many of his truly ingenious ideas, this was one of epic simplicity.

'A United Nations . . . international . . . peace . . . symposium,' he mused aloud as they drew up outside Halcyon House. And the acronym UNIPEAS swam into focus in his mind.

'Juss a lickle brainwave what come to me in the bath last night,' Gladstone confessed modestly.

But slush-gazing Byron was not listening any more.

6

'I HAVE just had,' said Byron, crashing into Otello Fabrizi's seventh-floor office uninvited and unannounced, 'the most truly ingenious idea.' He collapsed into Otello's favourite leather thinking chair. 'And yet, one of *epic* simplicity.'

Otello was seated at his desk – a walnut affair the size of a small banqueting table – drafting a letter to the press. 'Idea . . . ?' He continued scribbling.

'To bail us out of the crisis.'

'And that is?' Otello glanced up – more out of polite curiosity than any sense of expectation, for his successor-elect was always having truly ingenious ideas; several in one morning was not unusual.

'A Unibore . . . peace . . . symposium. UNIPEAS.'

Otello frowned. 'UNI what?'

'PEAS,' said Byron. And perceiving that Otello was still tuning in from another wavelength: 'I'm sorry, was I interrupting something?' He looked around, as though he half expected to find a naked typist hiding behind the curtains.

'Nothing that can't wait,' said Otello, laying aside his fountain pen and removing a pair of faintly blue-tinted reading glasses. 'A letter to *The Guardian* about the Godalming Marbles, that's all.'

Otello was a gentle, silver-haired Sicilian; elegant, benevolent and wholly imperturbable. An amateur archaeologist and one of Italy's finest classical scholars, he had made something of a *cause célèbre* of the Godalming Marbles – those world-renowned buttocks and pudenda from the great statue of Venus, purloined during the excavation of Nero's *fornicatorium magnum* in 1908 by the notorious aesthete and art vandal, the seventh Earl of Godalming. Lord Godalming had smuggled the marbles back to England to augment his prodigious collection of marmoreal erotica at his ancestral home at Horsham Towers, and upon his death had bequeathed the lot to Guildford museum, where Venus's celebrated nates languished still, looking faintly absurd detached from the body for which they had been so exquisitely sculpted. Otello had been campaigning zealously for their repatriation to Rome for many years.

'So, what is this Unipeas?' he enquired.

'A United Nations ontological peace conference,' said Byron. 'Sponsored exclusively by Unibore.'

Otello looked worried. 'A *peace* conference?' That sounded a little too controversial for his liking. 'Wouldn't that be too political? In breach of our charter, I mean. Everyone here is appointed on academic merit, remember. Our work is supposed to be above all nationalistic bias and petty self-interest.'

This was undeniably true in theory. Although, in practice, Halcyon House was riddled silly with all manner of repressed Nazis, crypto-Maoists, Zoroastrians, Xenophobes, Pan-Slavists, anarchists, paedophiles and God only knew what; and the only guaranteed way to get anything done was to make a generous charitable donation to certain Third World delegates (preferably in used banknotes) on the vague understanding that it would be put to some worthwhile cause . . . such as keeping the bank clerks of Zürich in gainful employment.

'No, you don't understand,' said Byron patiently. 'This wouldn't be a *political* peace conference.'

'It wouldn't?'

'Heavens, no. I'm not talking about more SALT talks, or START talks, or STOP-START SOFTSOAP talks. Forget all that posturing and numbers-juggling that goes on in Geneva or Stockholm. I'm not talking about defence secretaries or roving negotiators sitting down to twenty-course lunches in Vienna and spieling out the same tired old horseshit they've been spieling out ever since Yalta.'

'Then what *are* you talking about?'

'A meeting of the finest ontological minds in the world, to examine the causes of conflict in every trouble-spot on the earth today.'

Otello looked puzzled. 'What for?'

'What do you mean, what for?' Byron wondered if he had

caught Otello on a bad day. The Godalming Marbles had become something of an obsession with him of late. 'To try and find that elusive path to true, lasting, global peace. What else?'

Which merely confirmed Otello's worst suspicions. 'But would that be wise, dear boy?'

'Wise?'

'No government in its right mind wants lasting global peace. It could cause no end of trouble.'

'What could?'

'Global peace.'

'How so?'

'Well, think of the damage it would do to the armaments industries for a start.'

'But — '

'Entire corporations would be crippled overnight. Stock markets would collapse. Millions of workers would be thrown onto the welfare queues.'

'Otello — '

'And the Third World would simply disintegrate into anarchy.'

'I'm talking about *peace*.'

'Of course you are. But peace can be a lethal thing, believe me. It leaves armed forces with nothing better to do than foment revolution and stage *coups d'état*. And it leaves the man in the street with nothing to take his mind off the mess his government is making of every other aspect of the nation's affairs. All things considered, lasting global peace could be the biggest single threat to the stability of the world.'

'Oh, Christ, Otello, come *on* . . .'

'My dear Byron, in this highly sophisticated technological age, the art of pragmatic statesmanship is not to secure world peace but to keep a healthy level of conflict on the boil on somebody else's territory. Ideally, between underdeveloped countries, where the uneducated masses can dissipate their energies fighting each other, and pose no serious threat to the established world order.'

Byron was fast losing patience. 'But Otello, for Christ's sake, I didn't say anything about *achieving* peace.'

'You didn't?'

'Hell, no. I didn't say anything about achieving *any*thing. I'm simply talking about *talking* about peace.'

'Ah, well, that puts a different complexion on the matter,' said Otello, brightening a little. 'If there's going to be no point in having this conference then you could be onto something.'

'Of course there'll be a *point* to it,' said Byron. 'The point will be to try and embarrass the State Department into changing their minds about quitting Unibore.'

Otello thought about that. There was some ingenuity in the idea, certainly. It would be political suicide for any American administration to turn its back on a world peace initiative in an election year. His gaze wandered thoughtfully over a small bust of Cicero on his desk. He took a sapphire-blue silk handkerchief from his top pocket and flicked dust off the face of the venerable sage. 'One major drawback occurs to me at the outset.'

'What's that?'

'Washington would never let you get away with it. You'd be recalled at once.'

'Which is why I figured it should be *your* idea,' said Byron. 'I want *you* to propose it to the executive board.'

'Me?' That caught Otello unawares. Unibore's long-term future was not really his personal concern; he was retiring at the end of June and returning to his chair at the University of Messina, where he was professor of classical ontology. Nevertheless, he had his pride like anyone else, and would have very much preferred to go down in history as the skipper who piloted Unibore safely through the maelstrom, rather than the captain who stood helpless on the bridge while she sank in a hundred fathoms of ignominy with the loss of all hands. 'Well, I'm highly flattered, of course,' he said. 'But I should be stealing your thunder. I mean, look on the bright side: suppose this conference were a success?'

'Then that would be *your* success and yours alone,' said Byron generously. (And omitted to point out the converse, should Unipeas prove a fiasco.) 'And just think: this could be the start of an annual world event. The Unibore peace symposium . . . as founded by Otello Fabrizi.'

That prospect had faintly dynastic overtones which rather appealed to Otello. At the age of fifty-nine he had begun to wonder what, if anything, future generations would remember him for. The return of the Godalming Marbles would be as proud an accolade as any to retire with, but it would have precious little cachet outside Italy. Whereas, to achieve immortal fame as the progenitor of a noble line of Unipeas . . . that had *global* implications. Possibly even universal.

'Your name,' Byron went on, 'could go down in the pantheon of international peacemakers: Bertrand Russell, Pope John the Twenty-third, Jesus Christ, Otello Fabrizi.'

'Oh, come come come,' chuckled Otello, fanning himself with his epistle to *The Guardian*, 'a sense of proportion, dear boy, a sense of proportion, please . . .' He lapsed into thought again and idly dusted Cicero's alabaster pate with his silk handkerchief. 'In any case, we should have to sell the idea to the executive board first. And then to an extraordinary general conference.'

'A mere formality,' said Byron confidently. 'Like asking condemned men to sign their own reprieves.'

'Or better still, an extraordinary general luncheon,' said Otello, in a flash of inspiration. 'We haven't had one of those for ages. Stuff them all with lobster thermidor and Krug, and push an emergency resolution through on a show of hands.'

7

UNIPEAS TOOK Halcyon House by storm. At an extraordinary general luncheon in the seventh-floor conference room the following week, Otello's brilliant (but epically simple) new idea was acclaimed amidst emotionally charged scenes of unprecedented unanimity and enthusiasm. Paean upon paean of lavish praise was recorded in the minutes:

'Strikes deep at the vile black heart of hegemonistic expansionism.'
Li Zhao Yang (China)

'A mortal blow against adventurist aggressor imperialism.'
Konstantin V. Rhoskov (USSR)

'A gigantic step backwards in the race for doom.'
Dermott Plunkett (Ireland)

'Yet another stroke of sheer genius.'
Byron J. Cleveland (USA)

Unibore, however, was an organisation that thrived mainly on inertia; and there was intense competition among delegates to avoid getting roped in for anything that involved the remotest suggestion of extramural activity. So, having voted Unipeas into existence, the entire membership quickly voted to absolve itself of all responsibility for organising the event and bestowed that privilege on the executive board instead. The board then voted unanimously to bestow it upon the director-general. And Otello, in turn, voted unanimously to bestow it upon a committee that did not even exist. At which stage it was difficult to pass the buck very much further down the line without shoving it right out into Pall Mall and into the back of a passing taxi. Otello proposed therefore that a conference liaison and administration committee (CLAC) be set up under his chairmanship to organise Unipeas in accordance with delegates' wishes, and asked if three executive board members would kindly agree to sit on the committee with him. Byron was the first to volunteer; followed by the Bulgarian delegate, Nina Kabanova; and lastly, Air Vice-Marshal Jericho Engineer of the Paradise Islands. CLAC was then voted officially into existence by the extraordinary general luncheon and given full authority to do all the donkey work and refer every decision back to the board for ratification.

CLAC had their first meeting the following morning in Otello's office, and it became clear at the very outset that they were labouring under a common handicap: not one of them had ever organised anything more complicated than a Christmas party before, with the possible exception of Air Vice-Marshal Engineer, who had organised the bombing of the only public convenience between Mombasa and Australia the previous July; but that was a special case. CLAC's very first decision, therefore, was to seek the advice of Unibore's new director of public relations, Melanie Boewater.

Melanie Boewater was a one-time high flyer from the glittery cosmos of PR. Her career had crash-landed prematurely after marriage to a wealthy commodity broker and seven prolific years of childbearing, and she was now launching herself back into professional life at the age of anything between thirty-eight and forty-four (estimates varied like the weather). Melanie was delighted to get stuck into this new challenge, and her first recommendation was that CLAC should have an exclusive office of their own – or better still an entire suite; somewhere spacious and dignified commensurate with the prestigious nature of their work. Otello thought this was an excellent idea, but owing to the chronic over-employment of clerical staff at Halcyon House, office space was at a premium. So he appointed a Special Office Change-round Committee (SOCC) to examine ways of squashing an even greater concentration of people into an even smaller area so that CLAC could have a few rooms to themselves.

SOCC made a detailed appraisal of the situation and in so doing chanced upon a forgotten colony of typists, clerks and half-finished knitting tucked away in a quiet corner of the fourth floor, performing no useful function, but growing old gracefully and causing harm to no one. SOCC promptly booted the whole lot out, lock, stock and knitting, and dispersed them around the building, cramming them into any available nook and cranny they could find. CLAC then requisitioned all five offices thus vacated, installed themselves in the largest, and purchased a boardroom table the size of a small tennis court to fill up some of the desolate empty space.

CLAC now felt ready to concentrate their creative energies on more detailed matters of organisation. Fortunately, Melanie Boewater had an instinctive flair for organisation. That is to say, she was a past mistress at keeping dozens of PAs scurrying about with clipboards all day long, while she zoomed round town in a BMW having lunch with people. The essential thing to bear in mind, she stressed, was *image*. All the organisation in the world would be to no avail if Unipeas did not have the correct public *image*. So it was important, right from the word go, to give the world the indelible impression that Unipeas was a major international event. To that end she felt it should have its own distinctive logo or symbol, which would germinate in the public imagination.

CLAC thought that was a splendid idea, and Otello suggested that they might also choose a distinctive Unipeas colour to go with it – such as imperial Roman purple. They could then redecorate the CLAC offices (and possibly the entire fourth floor while they were at it) to put everybody into the right 'summity' kind of mood. The committee thought that was a splendid idea too, and Melanie immediately commissioned a freelance artist to design a Unipeas symbol and suggest some suitably peace-inspiring colours.

The artist returned the following week with a selection of logos and delicate pastel hues for the committee to choose from. CLAC agreed finally on a modification of the United Nations symbol: a globe embraced by two olive branches, with UNIPEAS circumscribed around the equator. But Otello was not happy with the pastel colours. He wanted something more assertive. Majestic. Imperial even. Like Roman purple. So the artist suggested imperial Roman purple, and everyone thought that was a brilliant idea. Melanie immediately commissioned a firm of interior decorators to repaint the entire fourth floor, recarpet it in finest purple Wilton, and paint 'CLAC' and the Unipeas symbol in gold on every door they could find. And while she was in the mood she ordered a lifetime's supply of purple and gold stationery from Liberty's to match the walls and carpet.

CLAC now had a magnificent suite of offices the size of Victoria station, but nobody to occupy them. So, anticipating that the committee would need all the assistance they could muster once the great engine of organisation got under way, Otello appointed a Temporary Office Staff Secondment Panel (TOSSPAN) to weed out supernumerary staff from other departments around Halcyon House and install them in and around the empty purlieus of the CLAC wing. TOSSPAN then made a detailed appraisal of the situation and, after mature consideration, moved back all the typists, clerks and knitting that SOCC had turfed out in the first place.

CLAC now had a magnificent suite of crowded purple offices, full of people who had nothing to do, apart from their knitting. So Byron suggested that since Unipeas would almost certainly generate a tremendous volume of paperwork (with any luck), it might be a good idea to train the typists in the use of word processors. CLAC agreed that that seemed an eminently sensible idea, and every secretary with an IQ of six or more was promptly packed off on a suitable training course.

At this juncture it dawned on Nina Kabanova that there was not a single piece of word processing equipment anywhere on the fourth floor for the newly trained girls to use. Which struck everyone as an extraordinary state of affairs, given the superabundance of paperwork that Unibore churned out each day. Otello therefore appointed a Special Committee to Assess Software and Hardware (SCASH) and requested them to furnish the CLAC secretariat with an adequate quantity of whatever equipment they deemed most suitable. SCASH made a thorough appraisal of the situation, and allowed dozens of sales executives to buy them lunch and give them free tickets to the Cup Final, and finally purchased a substantial tonnage of highly sophisticated technology, none of which anyone – least of all the newly trained typists – had the faintest idea how to operate.

At this point the comptroller-general, David Schellenberg, intervened, turning up uninvited at a CLAC meeting one morning to enquire who exactly was going to be footing the bill for Unipeas and all this Wilton carpet and inoperably complex technology. Whereupon the rest of the committee looked on Melanie Boewater, Melanie looked at Otello, and Otello looked at a loss. It was finally agreed to designate the entire question an Important Budgetary Matter (IBM) and refer it back to the executive board, who referred all IBMs, as a matter of course, to the comptroller-general, who passed the whole problem on to the nearest available dogsbody – in this case, a junior accountant called Hugo McGuffy.

McGuffy was a small, round, furry fellow from Dundee, covered in freckles and spectacles and ginger hair. He obligingly took the budget to pieces, wrote down dozens of sums on bits of paper marked URGENT, and ultimately recommended that CLAC should try and palm off the bill for Unipeas onto somebody else, such as the United Nations, or Texaco, or the NatWest bank. CLAC thought that sponsorship was a truly brilliant idea, and McGuffy was immediately appointed Official Conference Cost Accountant (OCCA), installed in his very own freshly painted purple office on the fourth floor, and provided with typists, knitting and a word processor that nobody even knew how to plug in.

The first thing that McGuffy needed to know was where Unipeas was going to happen, how many people were going to be involved, and how long it would all be going on for. Trying to strike a balance between what was credible in terms of a world-scale conference and what was economically feasible, CLAC agreed that it should last for one week and that each member country should be invited to send up to three delegates. They decided, furthermore, that there should be a grand public inauguration day at which an extremely famous person would perform some sort of official opening ceremony.

By happy chance, Air Vice-Marshal Engineer knew just the sort of extremely famous person everyone had in mind: the President of the Paradise Islands, Field-Marshal Hudson Butcher, statesman and scholar. A strained silence followed, as if someone had just nominated Hermann Göring for a Nobel peace prize. Otello conceded that President Butcher was certainly an extremely well-known person, but suggested that the final choice should be left, perhaps, until other matters, such as a date and a venue, had been settled. Jericho agreed and promised CLAC that in the meantime he would ascertain from Port Paradise whether the President had any spare weeks available in his punishing schedule of public engagements for the forthcoming year.

Moving on to consider the question of a venue, the committee ruled out any sort of conventional conference centre at the outset. A historic country house, Byron felt, would be more the sort of thing; somewhere with lots of thought-provoking wood-panelled ambience, and acres of treeful grounds where delegates could ruminate in pastoral tranquillity. Melanie agreed; it would also help to make inauguration day a fun day out for the whole family and a major fund-raising event for Unibore. They could have a fête, she suggested. A funfair even. With sporting contests, fancy-dress parades for the kids, egg-and-spoon races, a barbecue in the evening and a grand Unipeas firework display. While they were at it, McGuffy chimed in, they should think about merchandise as well. There were colossal profits to be made in that area – exclusive Unipeas sweatshirts, teeshirts, coffee mugs, ball-point pens, balloons, sunhats, bikini briefs, teaspoons . . . the list was endless.

Otello viewed commercialisation of that nature with profound distaste; he felt that it cheapened the noble spirit of Unipeas. But accustomed as he was to making pragmatic moral compromises in troubled times (few academics, anywhere, had been held in such high esteem by the Duce, the Vatican and the Red Brigades, all in one lifetime), he deferred to majority opinion and left the whole tacky business in Melanie's capable hands. At the same time he instructed CLAC's idle battalion of clerks and typists to furnish themselves with all the relevant travel books and gazetteers and to draw up a list of suitable historic houses within reasonable travelling distance of London.

Melanie then appointed a special merchandise panel (SMERCHPAN), composed of herself and all her favourite PAs with clipboards, to commission a suitable range of official Unipeas commemorabilia. SMERCHPAN spent the following week examining the sample wares of dozens of shifty-looking characters in tinted glasses and Ford Capris, and finally commissioned one Demosthenes Metaxis of Metaxis Leisure Enterprises (Camden Town) Limited, to supply an exclusive line in Unipeas sunwear, funwear and commemorative gimcrackery. The question of a souvenir brochure was also raised, but much as CLAC wanted the general public to take a closer interest in Unibore and all its good works, it was felt that, on balance, the less they were told about what went on at Halcyon House the better, in case the press started raking up all that philistine claptrap once again about value for taxpayers' money. So everyone agreed that Melanie should compile a big glossy booklet, packed with colour pictures of delegates sedulously working themselves to death for the greater public good, and supplemented with a scanty text, composed for the greater part of wholly uninformative waffle.

McGuffy, meanwhile, was beavering away trying to attract sponsorship from a wide variety of commercial institutions, from British Airways to Coca-Cola, and looking at ways of offsetting some of the conference costs by diverting funds from Unibore's existing budget. This was not as difficult as it appeared at first sight. Being a lapsed Calvinist who had been brought up to believe that where money was concerned, thriftiness was next to godliness, McGuffy had great faith in the economic principles of rationalisation and merger. And if there was one major event in the Unibore calendar that was an obvious candidate for a spot of rationalising and merging it was the annual general conference.

The annual general conference took place during the last week of June, when all one hundred and fifty-two delegates and coachloads of randy typists took off for the seaside for a week to make whoopee and long speeches, and congratulate themselves over and over again on another successful year's inactivity. It was the most extravagant beano of all the many beanos in the Unibore year, and McGuffy suggested to CLAC that it might not be a bad idea, given the current financial crisis, to shorten the a.g.c. that summer by just a wee fraction (about four-quarters was the sort of wee fraction he had in mind) and merge it with Unipeas. By that means, much of the cost of the symposium could be absorbed within Unibore's existent budget.

CLAC concurred with the indisputable logic of this proposal but felt that it was more than their lives were worth to tamper with anything so sacrosanct as the a.g.c. They therefore declined to give a ruling one way or the other and referred the whole matter to the executive board.

By and large, the idea of economising by rationalisation or merger was anathema to the learned delegates at Halcyon House, and anyone daft enough to suggest merging two perfectly good separate beanos into just one would normally have been looked on as a heretic. There were exceptional circumstances, however, and after careful consideration the board agreed that it was a small price to pay, to forego a little annual general whoopee for just one year, to safeguard the long-term future of Unibore. So McGuffy's proposal was formally adopted as board policy and the conference was pencilled in for the last week of June – subject to the approval of member-governments – with the preceding Saturday, Midsummer Day, provisionally nominated as Unipeas inauguration day.

The only serious reservations the board had at this stage concerned the name Unipeas itself, which everyone agreed was a concise enough acronym for a United Nations International Peace Symposium but failed, they felt, to convey the essential dignity and gravitas of the event; and as far as the Australian delegate, Isobel Maddox, was concerned, merely conjured up images of a multinational vegetable corporation. Besides, it made no mention of ontology, and the word *symposium* had overtones of intellectual bacchanalia. *Conference*, they decided, was preferable, and *congress* better still. So, after careful consideration, they agreed that Unipeas should thenceforth be known as the World Ontological Peace Congress. Which satisfied everyone except Melanie Boewater, who now had to bring in signwriters to obliterate UNIPEAS from every door on the fourth floor and paint WOPEC in its place, and order another truckload of crested stationery from Liberty's, and instruct Demosthenes Metaxis of Camden Town to stop churning out UNIPEAS sunwear and funwear and to start churning out WOPEC merchandise instead.

CLAC now had virtually everything they required to organise a successful international conference. They had a date, a budget, offices, clerical staff, sophisticated technology, expertise and the full support of the United Nations. All they lacked was a venue. So it came as an acute shock to them to discover that after weeks of assiduous research and enquiry, the secretaries had failed to find even *one* country house within fifty miles of London that was willing or able to open its doors for a week to four hundred and fifty academics, or even to *one* hundred and fifty, for that matter. They had exhausted every possible channel of enquiry, from the Historic Houses Association to the National Trust, but the only buildings that were even remotely suitable were either booked up throughout the summer months or lacked the facilities to cope with such large numbers. After all that time and effort, the best that CLAC's secretaries were able to offer the committee was a choice of the Wembley conference centre, Earls Court stadium or the Royal Albert Hall.

8

THERE WAS an air of deepest gloom and despondency in the saloon bar of the Umpire and Mango that night.

'It's no use you just jabberin' on akskin' me who, what, when, where, how, why,' said Gladstone irritably. 'I'm tellin' you, Everton man, there's nowhere south of Birmin'ham that's big enough. And that's a plain fact. Wopec's a dead duck. Finished. And so's Unibore. And so's me Woodpeckers.'

'No, listen, man. Calm yourself,' said Everton soothingly. 'There's no way on earth the United Nations is goin' to let Unibore go down the tubes just 'cos of some fenky-fenky politicians in Washin'ton.'

'I na give a stuff about the UN,' Gladstone retorted. 'Whabbout me Woodpeckers, hah? That's the burnin' question of the moment. Damn it, some of us given the best years of our lives to that club. I got letters of testimonial from Wesley Hall . . . Vivian Richards . . . you name 'em.' He thumped the table angrily and a gill or so of best bitter slopped over the brim of their tankards in sympathy. 'Christ, man, I jus' don't see the point in bein' born sometimes.'

Everton was enthroned in his customary listening chair beneath a framed photograph of Sir Garfield Sobers and other deities. It was a solid, high-backed, magisterial seat from which he had dispensed much wise counsel over the years. 'Well, what do you mean, there's nowhere south of Birmin'ham that's big enough?' he said, mystified. 'What's wrong with the Albert Hall?'

'Hasn't got the ambience,' Gladstone replied. 'Got to have ambience.'

Everton frowned. 'What for?'

'For philosophisin'. Got to have the right vibes, man. 'S heavy stuff.'

'Well, if the Albert Hall's good enough for gospel, it must be good enough for cogitation,' reasoned Everton.

Gladstone shook his head. 'No way. They want some place in the country. They need peace and quiet. Somewhere with a bit of history and, you know, like . . . majesty and . . . you know . . .'

'Ambience.'

'Yeh, right.' Gladstone nodded gravely. 'Ambience.'

Everton had a long, studious think about this. Unipeas, Wopec, whatever they wanted to call it, was his brainchild after all. No caring father could stand idly by and let his progeny wither and perish in the cradle for lack of anything so rudimentary as a home.

'Whabbout Chequers?' he ventured.

'Don't talk so daft,' Gladstone scoffed. 'That's only for prime ministers.'

'OK, OK,' said Everton patiently. 'Well, how about . . .' He tried to remember some of the stately homes he had visited in recent years with the North Kensington Ramblers Association. 'How about Blenheim?'

'They don't want to know.'

'Woburn?'

'Don't want to know either.'

'Carnage?'

'Whattage?'

'Carnage Castle.'

Gladstone's face rumpled. 'Never heard of it.'

'It's about an hour's drive from London. Near a place called Lydhurst.'

'What's it like?'

'It's sort of like the castles you see in kids' picture books. All walls and towers and cold dark dungeons.'

'Yeh?' Gladstone brightened a little. 'Reckon me governor might be interested?'

'Worth a try,' said Everton. 'If you ask me, that place has got ambience pouring out of every keyhole.'

9

ST VALENTINE'S DAY, and the snow lay deep and crisp around Carnage Castle. A renegade wind, icy-toothed and raging from the east, howled through the thirteenth-century battlements and sent powdery snow fleeing in blind turmoil across the frozen moat, smothering the bronze equestrian on guard before the gatehouse:

GENERAL SIR SACKVILLE STERLING-PALLGRAVE
G.C.B., K.B.E., D.S.O., M.C.
1879–1976
Dulce et ducorum est pro patria bellum gerere.

Two miles away in the quiet hamlet of Allshott, the estate manager, Clarence Brownjohn, was sitting in the squalid kitchen of his tied hovel, mopping up the last smears of congealed bacon fat from his breakfast plate with a crusty wedge and glowering at the stark white world outside. He swilled the bread down with the dregs of a pint mug of gravy-dark tea and dumped everything that was washable into the sink, where several days' supply of crockery and cutlery lay submerged, at peace, beneath a protective layer of opaque grey-green scum. Having made this daily concession to domesticity (once a week, on Sundays, he would launch a major assault, with scalding hot water, Brillo pads and Teepol, restoring the status quo, so that the entire scummy cycle could start all over again), he put on his hobnailed boots, brown leather gaiters and army greatcoat, and set off for Carnage in the Land Rover.

There was little traffic on the road; only the early-morning bus to Lydhurst, crawling timorously through the freshly fallen snow, and a ten-ton gritting wagon stranded in a snowdrift with a flat tyre. Brownjohn glued a Gold Flake to his lower lip and lit it with a petrol-fired Ronson. A few Volvos crunched past him in their smart new tyre-chains, *parmp-parmping* impatiently on their horns, rushing chinless stockbrokers to Lydhurst Junction to catch the eight forty-three to Charing Cross. Brownjohn waved them on their way with a brace of upraised fingers. Bloody arrivistes. With their mock Tudor mansions and pony-club daughters and moronic red setters and gleaming Range Rovers kept safe and snug in their centrally heated garages. Parvenus. Aaagh. He coughed and hawked, and spat a fat green oyster of phlegm out of the window at a passing Peugeot.

Two miles out of Allshot he arrived at the main entrance to the Carnage estate and turned in through the great wrought-iron gates. A notice, half obscured by snow, read:

Department of the Environment
Carnage Castle
Grounds open 10 a.m. to sunset daily.
Castle open 10 a.m. to 6 p.m., Easter to Sept 30th.

Brownjohn drove on up the winding avenue of frozen poplars shivering in the east wind, touched his cap respectfully to the statue of General Sir Sackville, turned in through the medieval gatehouse and parked in the castle courtyard by the domestic offices. The offices were built into a block of fourteenth-century lodgings ranged along the west wall. Aubrey Wormslow, quondam batman to the General and now resident dogsbody to the Department of the Environment, was just inside the entrance, pushing a broom ineffectually up and down the narrow passageway. ''Day, Clarence,' he said cheerfully.

'Aubrey,' grunted Brownjohn, flicking cigarette ash over the newly swept flagstone.

'Edwina's had a communication,' said Wormslow, a scrawny fellow in his sixties, with a toupee of shiny henna-red hair and bushy white sideburns. 'From J. Hector Lammas himself.' Wormslow looked rather impressed. Brownjohn did not. Edwina Sheffield MA was the Department of the Environment's resident warden at Carnage, and J. Hector Lammas was her superior at the DoE's directorate of ancient monuments and historic buildings in Savile Row.

'What was it?' enquired Brownjohn tartly. 'A Valentine card?' For J. Hector Lammas seldom wrote these days unless redundancy or dismissal were involved.

'It's a letter,' said Wormslow, 'about Unibore.'

Brownjohn scowled and coughed and hawked and swallowed another fat green oyster. 'Never 'eard of it.'

'They've been in the news lately. Something to do with America, if memory serves.'

'I don't believe in news,' grunted Brownjohn truculently. He was proud to say he had not read a newspaper since the Berlin airlift. 'Not good for people, too much news.' And he clumped away down the passage to Edwina's office.

'You'd never know who was dead if you didn't have news,' reasoned Wormslow, feeling slighted by this brusque indifference to his little scoop.

'Who *wants* to know?' retorted Brownjohn, and disappeared from view into Edwina's office.

'Well, it's nice to keep up with who's dead,' said resentful Wormslow, but to himself, alone with his broom.

Edwina's office was over six hundred years old and cluttered with obsolete Ministry of Works furniture of much the same vintage. It bulged at the sides and rattled with draughts and reeked of her scruffy mongrel, Walpole. Edwina was a sprightly forty-six and did *not* reek of scruffy Walpole. Nor, contrary to popular lore concerning middle-aged spinsters and their dogs, had she grown to look like him. Far from it; if anything, she had begun, chameleon-like, to blend in with her surroundings – sagging and bulging, rattling with wind, and cluttered with sturdy old Ministry of Works-ish tweed suits and sensible brown brogues.

She was bashing out a letter on an arthritic Imperial

typewriter when Brownjohn entered. 'Aubrey tells me you've had a Valentine's day missive from J. Hector,' he said, lowering himself into one of several crippled chairs that had found a permanent home in that little junk-shop of a room.

Edwina riveted a full-stop to the page, abandoned the typewriter and passed him the letter from Lammas. 'I'd call it a friendly ultimatum, myself.'

Brownjohn stretched out his legs in front of the electric fire with a deep sigh of relief, as if he had just ridden five leagues through the blizzard, and putting on a pair of grubby spectacles, read:

> Dear Miss Sheffield,
> Following the Secretary of State's directive of March last (my memorandum 85/19) requiring this department to seek ways of increasing the revenue from the establishments in our care, you will, I am sure, be delighted to learn that the United Nations International Board for Ontological Research and Education has approached me with a view to staging an international conference at Carnage Castle in June, the precise details and nature of which have yet to be discussed.
>
> I have assured their director-general, Professor Fabrizi, that you and your staff will give him your fullest co-operation, and I should appreciate it if you would telephone my office and let me know when it would be convenient for Mr Clack to visit the castle and inspect the facilities.
>
> I will not, of course, need to remind you that the future of the Carnage estate and the jobs of everyone employed there depend largely on the success of your attempts to make it pay its way and become a profitable enterprise in its own right.
> Sincerely yours,
>
> J. Hector Lammas

'Who is this Mr Clack?' asked Brownjohn, puzzled. 'One of ours or one of theirs?'

'Haven't the faintest,' Edwina replied. 'But no doubt we'll soon find out.'

CLAC arrived the following week, whooshing up the avenue of poplars through the half-thawed slush in mud-spattered convoy – Melanie accompanying Otello in his official Rolls-Royce Silver Shadow; McGuffy and Nina Kabanova in Byron's

Jaguar, with Gladstone at the wheel and Bob Marley on the cassette player; and bringing up the rear, in his super-reinforced bomb-proof Mercedes, the twenty-two-stone bulk of Air Vice-Marshal Engineer, stately as a barrage balloon, in full dress uniform, dripping in scrambled egg and beribboned with decorations for incredible valour. They drove through the medieval gatehouse into the north courtyard and parked outside the great hall, where Edwina Sheffield and gaitered Brownjohn came out to greet them. After introductions in the great hall, Edwina showed them into a drawing-room the size of a small cathedral, where Aubrey Wormslow handed round cups of steaming Nescafé and a plate of stale ginger nuts purloined from the DoE's dark and hibernating cafeteria.

Edwina had no idea what an ontological congress was or what it entailed, but could think of few buildings less suitable for a conference of four hundred and fifty delegates than Carnage Castle; for while there was hardly a room in the place that could be called intimate, neither was there a single room that could seat so many at one time. But this did not seem to trouble Professor Fabrizi or his colleagues; so as soon as they had drunk their coffee, she took them on a guided tour of the castle and recounted something of its history.

The oldest parts – the sixty-foot curtain walls, great hall and solar – dated from King Stephen's reign and stood upon the site of a ferocious battle a hundred years before, where the Anglo-Saxons had been decimated by their Norman conquerors. The Normans thereafter called the place 'Le Bois de Carnage' and gave that name to the castle, which was built a century later. With the fall of Stephen and the rise of the Plantagenets, the land for many miles around passed into the hands of a formidable warlord, one Henri de Palgrave of Anjou, whose family were to remain the masters of Carnage for the next eight hundred years. They became one of the richest and most powerful dynasties in the south of England, acquiring vast estates and all the grubby serfs and villeins that came with them, in the finest traditions of the British aristocracy – by pillage, extortion, fraud, arson, buggery, treason, regicide and the slaughter of kind old monks. But then, fortune favours the bold, as Attila the Hun used to say.

In time the family outgrew their spartan medieval quarters, and in 1546 Sir Robert Pallgrave, ten times great-grandson of

Henri de Palgrave, Angevin warlord extraordinaire, prodigiously enriched by plundering every monastery within a hundred miles for King and country, began to build a palatial new home within the castle walls, abutting on the keep tower and connecting with the medieval block around the great hall. Almost bankrupt as a consequence, he restored the family's fortunes by marrying off his grandson to a scion of the infamous Sterlings of Effingham – the nearest approximation that the Elizabethan slave trade ever had to a multinational corporation. The names of the two great families became coupled from that day forth, and for the next four hundred years or so they did practically nothing of historical interest but breed generation after generation of stolid military leaders, culminating in that indomitable twentieth-century warmonger, General Sir Sackville Sterling-Pallgrave.

Sir Sackville, however, was destined to be the last of that long, historic dynasty. Childless, witless, and dragged to the precipice of bankruptcy by the rapacious demands of the Inland Revenue, he died at the age of ninety-seven, daft as a brush and down to his last two Bentleys. Everything else had gone – the thirty-thousand-acre estate he had inherited from his father; the Titians, the Tiepolos; the Ming, the Dresden; the Sheraton, the Hepplewhite; the Louis Quinze silver; the three and a half tons of antiquarian books and first editions. All carted away to Sotheby's to pay off his vertiginous mountain of debts. Without an heir in the world, he bequeathed everything he had left – one desolately empty castle, two Bentleys and a hundred and fifty acres – to the Ministry of Defence as a permanent memorial to the glory of war. But the Ministry of Defence was not accustomed to receiving bequests of this kind; and bereft of its art treasures or any endowment for its maintenance, Carnage was a monstrous white elephant, wholly unsuitable for any military purpose. So, after abortive attempts to turn it first into an army museum, then into an intelligence headquarters, and finally into an RAMC convalescent home, the ministry leased it free of charge to the Department of the Environment to do with as they saw fit, until such time as the climate of public apathy allowed them to flog it off to the Arabs.

The DoE, flush with funds at that time, decided to open the prestigious pile to the public, retaining the services of all those estate workers who had served the late General, and installing

Edwina Sheffield as resident warden. But the venture was to prove a dire commercial failure. No one beyond the environs of Allshott and Lydhurst had heard of the place, and without so much as an El Greco in the parlour or a predatory carnivore prowling round the rhododendrons, it had little to recommend it to coach parties or the casual weekend visitor. So in recent years it had begun to cost the DoE a small fortune. By which time a recessionary economic climate had ushered in an era of trenchant public spending cuts and the secretary of state had started leaning heavily on the department to eliminate waste and reduce overheads. The department, in turn, leant heavily on the directorate of ancient monuments and historic buildings, and J. Hector Lammas leant heavily on Edwina Sheffield. Profitability or privatisation, that was the unequivocal message from above. Carnage had two years to put its affairs in order and start paying its way. Failing that it would be closed to the public and sold off to the highest bidder. And it was at that critical juncture in the history of Carnage that Unibore had come along.

CLAC were delighted with the place. It was exactly what they had had in mind all along. Ontological discussion, Byron explained to Edwina, was not well suited to the formal atmosphere of the conference hall. Ontologists liked to keep a variety of arguments on the boil at any one time, debating issues in small groups, ever changing, never settling, wandering from room to room, from argument to argument, maintaining a constant interflow of new ideas, pooling fresh thoughts, like tributaries feeding a stream of endless metaphysical discovery. Carnage was perfectly suited to a conference of that nature. It had an abundance of rooms, all rich in history and atmosphere – the great eating room, where the Prince Regent had once dined; the long gallery above, where Charles I had played bowls; the Hapsburg chamber, where Austrian emperors had slept; and the library, with its magnificent painted ceiling depicting the Fall of Man . . . the sole surviving work of a sixteenth-century Venetian pederast, burnt at the stake for necromancy and bad taste. Furthermore it had excellent catering facilities, only recently installed by the DoE in the old kitchens and buttery. Outside there were a hundred and fifty acres of grounds – expansive lawns, flower gardens, riverside walks – which would provide an idyllic setting for the inauguration-day fête and fireworks display. All this, and only one hour's drive from

London, or fifty minutes on the train from Charing Cross. It was, concluded Melanie, as they returned to the drawing-room at the end of their conducted tour, the ideal venue in almost every particular.

Edwina was highly gratified but still had no clearer conception of what an ontological congress was supposed to achieve. 'Forgive my asking,' she said to Otello, while Wormslow passed around more cups of lukewarm Nescafé and mildewed ginger nuts, 'but what exactly is this conference going to be about?'

'About?' said Otello, who thought that that much had been clear from the very outset. 'Why, peace, of course. World Peace. Didn't Mr Lammas tell you?'

There was a long, uncomfortable silence.

'Peace . . . ?' said Brownjohn, as if he was not sure that he had heard correctly.

'Indeed,' said Otello. 'Wopec will be the first international congress of ontologists for world peace. And, we hope, only the first of many.'

Brownjohn glanced across the room at Aubrey Wormslow. The scrawny little batman seemed to wince and stagger for one moment, as if he had taken a pile-driver in the midriff. He gazed, incredulous, at the puzzled professor, and then turned and tottered back through the great eating room, like a man transfixed, to the sanctuary of the cold empty kitchens.

Wormslow remained in a state of mute shock all day. It was inconceivable. A peace conference? At Carnage? In the General's very own home? In the birthplace of a whole dynasty of men who had dedicted their lives so selflessly to the perpetuation of global conflict?

Bleak and bitter night outside. But high up in her bedroom in the West Tower, Edwina lay naked on the duvet, pink and glowing from a scented bath and basking in Sahara-hot breezes from two judiciously positioned fan heaters.

'It's sacrilege,' muttered Brownjohn, draping his long johns over the back of her dressing-table chair. 'Profanity. I knew they were a dodgy bunch, the minute they walked in.'

'We need them, Clarence. More than they need us. They could prove to be the goose that lays our golden egg.'

'Arrivistes. Parvenus. Aaagh . . .' He coughed and hawked

and swallowed a tasty green bolus. 'The lads won't like it, I can tell you. Wormslow, Strongman, Kershaw. All the General's men. Won't like it one bit.'

'Well, they'll just have to lump it,' said Edwina, spraying herself all over with an atomiser of Passion de Calypso. 'Because there's sod-all they can do about it.'

'It's not them I'm worried about,' said Brownjohn darkly. 'It's the General himself. I can't see the Old Man taking this one lying down, straight I can't . . .'

Seventy yards away in the south wing, Aubrey Wormslow was standing at the foot of the General's empty bed in the Hapsburg chamber, holding a candle in one hand and sheltering its delicate flame with the other.

'We just wanted you to know, sir,' he whispered, 'that this business is none of our doing . . . Clarence, me, Strongman and the boys. Nothing we can do, sir. We wanted you to know that.'

He waited, shivering, for some token of kindly reassurance. Outside, a savage gust of wind pounced hungrily on the windows and rattled the ill-fitting casements. The candle flame cringed in terror and expired with a puff of smoke. The bedroom door swung open very slowly on creaking butts. Wormslow bowed to the empty bed. 'As you wish, sir.' Creeping out of the room, he closed the door and retired to his lonely quarters high in the south-west tower. With heavy heart he filled his Lenny the Lion hot-water bottle, hung his toupee on a nail to air, and undressed for bed. The General was not happy. Not happy at all. No good was going to come of this Wopec business, he could feel it in his water. It was doomed, doomed from the very start.

Outside, keeping his eternal vigil at the gatehouse, the bronze warlord sat indomitable astride his puissant charger in a greatcoat of frozen snow, his face set stolidly against the Arctic gale.

Indoors, snug in his basket in Edwina's kitchen, dreaming boneful dreams, smelly Walpole twitched a scruffy ear and sensed an unquiet spirit raging out there somewhere in the cruel night.

Part Two

WOPEC

10

NO ONE in Washington knew what to make of Wopec. It seemed to have erupted out of nowhere, like a carbuncle on the State Department's derrière, and for the time being the White House was remaining obdurately tight-lipped while the President's advisers tried to work out the deeper implications of it all. But the very principle of the thing was anathema to Senator Eugene Erdreich, vice-chairman of the Senate Foreign Relations Committee. It was a vicious and calculated attack on the whole future of world conflict.

'Whose insidious idea was it in the first place?' he asked Packard over lunch at Mussolini's, the fashionable new brasserie on Wisconsin Avenue.

'The director-general's. Otello Fabrizi.'

'Treacherous Sicilian bastard.'

'I wouldn't get too worked up about it, Gene,' said Packard, who had seen at first hand what went on at Halcyon House and was very impressed with their general level of incompetence. 'They've got less than four months to get this thing off the ground. They don't stand a cat in hell's chance.'

'You don't reckon?' The senator looked up hopefully from his twenty-four-ounce T-bone.

'My guess is Wopec will burn out in a blaze of apathy and disorganisation by April.'

'Maybe we should tell Byron Cleveland to help it on its way to the ash can.'

Packard knocked back half a glass of Californian Cabernet and began to pick his teeth with the nail of his little finger. 'You mean sabotage?'

'Christ, no.' Erdreich looked nervously around the restaurant in case there was anyone with scruples in the vicinity, and continued quietly, 'No, no, Ed. I'm just talking about a little discreet, active, non-cooperation. Like, ah, filibustering the agenda committee, or, ah . . .'

Packard nodded. 'You mean sabotage.'
Erdreich thought about that. 'OK, then. Sabotage.'
Packard shook his head. 'Ah ah.'
'What do you mean, ah ah?'
'Cleveland wouldn't buy that.'
'Why not?'
'Ethics.'
'What ethics?'
'Professional ethics. The academic ethos and all.'
'Ethos, my ass. You'll be telling me he's a man of honour next. Jesus, what is he? Some kind of pervert?'
'No, but you've got to remember he's the . . .'
'I mean, fuck ethics, Ed, this is politics,' Erdreich went on angrily. 'He was appointed by this administration and he'll damn well do what the administration tells him to do.'
'But he *is* the director-general-elect, Gene, and . . .'
'Christ almighty, isn't it bad enough we've got a hundred and fifty-two macrocephalic assholes over in London right now thinking about peace, without dragging ethics into this?'
'Sure, but you've got to think ahead, Gene. The guy's taking over from Otello Fabrizi on the first of July.'
'That two-faced Sicilian son-of-a-bitch.'
'You can't reasonably expect a guy in Cleveland's position to start wrecking . . .'
'I don't reasonably expect *any*thing. God damn it to hell, Ed, all I'm asking Cleveland to do is his patriotic duty.'
'But he's not a diplomat, Eugene,' said Packard patiently. 'He's an academic. He's a pretty smart guy.'
'Then fire the bastard and put some dumb slob in the job who can be relied on to screw the whole thing up.'
'But why fire the guy when he's about to take over as director-general?' reasoned Packard. 'Look, suppose we can't back out of these Wopec talks. Suppose we're obliged to hang on in with Unibore a while longer. Then at least we'll have the consolation of knowing that our representative is going to be running the outfit for the next five years.'
Erdreich had to concede that Packard had a point. 'Well, OK. I guess,' he murmured grudgingly. 'But I still want questions asked in the State Department about how a peace-mongering jackass like Cleveland got appointed to that job in

the first place. This world's a dangerous enough place as it is, without letting guys like him run amok.'

11

IT WAS a painful mystery to the Cleveland family back home in Lynchburg, Virginia, how Byron had ever managed to acquire this unwholesome interest in peace. His father was an air-force colonel, wounded out by sheer weight of medals. His mother was an admiral's daughter, and three of his great-grandfathers had fought to the last bullet at Gettysburg. Yet little Byron had been an inexplicably gentle and unaggressive child, and despite the assurances of eminent psychiatrists that he would grow out of it in time, had never shown much interest in violence or destruction. While his elder brothers were performing deeds of derring-do with Special Forces, and big sister was slaving in her laboratory to bring biochemical warfare within the reach of even the poorest nations of the world, Byron – to the family's enduring shame – had done nothing with the first thirty years of his life but write books and amass degrees in the humanities.

But then, in his thirty-second year, he had begun to show signs of a remarkable recovery. It was all thanks to a perky young psychotic called Rosheen, whom he met one weekend in a singles bar in Madison, New Jersey. It was bed at first sight. The two fell head over heels in lust with each other and soon after, in a moment of concupiscent madness, married. Whereupon Byron's tranquil life took on a whole new dimension. Rosheen was the twenty-three-year-old daughter of a Madison City police captain – a man with a splendid record of gratuitous violence, the Cleveland family were delighted to learn, and never short of a kind word to say in memory of the late great Heinrich Himmler. Rosheen, happily, had inherited her father's volcanic temperament, and her sincere love of mayhem did Byron a power of good. A wilful wench, accustomed to having her own way in all things and inclined to start smashing up everything in sight until she got it, Rosheen eventually prised out the latent aggression that lay buried deep in Byron's psyche, and scenes of heartwarming domestic brutality ensued for several years. But sadly, it was not to last. As his father had always suspected, Byron lacked staying-power. After three years of invigorating strife, he grew weary of gluing the furniture back together again every Monday and buying new crockery, and withdrew like an anchorite to a clapboard summerhouse in the garden of their Virginia home to pursue his literary work in peace.

Rosheen – nothing if not a game trier – did everything that could be expected of a loving wife to breathe a little life-saving turbulence back into their ailing marriage. She pruned his roses to the roots; reversed over him in the station wagon; put warfarin in his hominy grits; set fire to the summerhouse while he was sleeping inside; went to bed with most of his best friends . . . and even a few of his best enemies. But to no avail. Byron remained as docile as a stuffed sheep. Nothing, it seemed, could provoke him. So, driven to distraction by this unprovoked outbreak of mindless peace, Rosheen finally packed her bags and made off with one Moses 'the Rod' McRory, a six-foot-seven-inch footballer with the Cincinnati Cyclones.

Eternally thankful to Moses McRory, but suddenly burdened with everyone's sympathy (including that of his father-in-law, who said that this kind of thing could never have happened under the good old Third Reich), Byron sold what was left of their Virginia home and moved north to Connecticut to take up a lectureship in ontology at Yale.

At that point in time divorce had not even been discussed, for Byron had no wish to cross swords with his father-in-law (a fanatical Catholic in all but Christian principles) and Rosheen, it seemed, had vanished for good. Rosheen, however, had *not* vanished for good. No sooner had Byron been appointed United States' representative to Unibore at the end of his third year at Yale, than she decided that she was fed up with being a groupie with the Cincinnati Cyclones and would rather be a groupie with the London diplomatic corps instead. He had scarcely had a chance to settle into his new apartment in St John's Wood before he found her hammering on the door one warm spring night with a Boeingful of excess baggage, vowing to be a good and faithful wife for the rest of the week, and imploring him tearfully – *mea culpa, mea culpa* – to let her stay. A soft touch for any damsel in distress, and spurred on by the seminal instincts of one who had not been laid for the past six months, Byron relented. And lived bitterly to regret it.

For the next two years, his life was purgatory. It was not that Rosheen was evil; she was *not*. Or even that he didn't like her; he *did*. He was actually quite fond of her in an antipathetic sort of way. It was just that he was even more fond of a quiet life. Whereas she liked raising Cain, in every room in the apartment, as often as possible, at all hours of the night, with *her* kind of people – heavymetal-playing, joint-rolling, coke-snorting, sofa-sprawling, off-stripping, spouse-swapping, soon-fighting, loud-bawling, boo-hooing, up-chucking, wrist-slashing, out-crashing, deep-sleeping, and usually still there in the fridge-empty, sick-smelling, head-hammering morning.

He would not have minded quite so much if he had had a clapboard summerhouse to retreat to, like the one in Lynchburg. But they didn't even have a garden. They were in a third-floor two-bedroomed flat with wafer-thin walls, surrounded on all sides by octogenarian Viennese insomniacs with sensitive ears and aggressive lawyers. And as time went by, Byron grew increasingly fed up with having to take bunches of flowers and bottles of whisky next door to the Feinbaums, and downstairs to the Weitzmanns, and upstairs to the Mendelsohns to apologise for Rosheen's corybantic revels, when all *he* ever wanted to do in the evenings was curl up to a little Mingus or watch old movies on the box.

So it was a tremendous relief to Byron when, after two years of this, Rosheen abruptly fell in love . . . or the nearest approximation to it that her fickle emotions could aspire to. The victim of her affections was the outgoing French delegate to Unibore, the Baron Guy de Montcalme-Challois, who was retiring at the age of sixty-three to his château of Saturnalia on the Côte d'Azur. Byron was so grateful – to Rosheen for going and to the baron for taking her – that he threw a farewell party for them both at the Café Royal and invited every delegate at Halcyon House.

If his joy seemed just a trifle unconstrained, it was because his own emotions had been thrown in turmoil at this time, as well. That same spring, while delivering a speech on peace ethics to a

World Council of Churches conference in Cambridge, he had met and fallen for a twenty-three-year-old schoolteacher from Salvation, Mississippi. Her name was Annabelle Cartwright, and she was in England for the conference with her father, the Reverend Noah Cartwright, a minister of the Southern Independent Baptist Church. Annabelle was blonde, beautiful, gentle, sensitive, uncorrupted, sweet-natured and everything that Rosheen was not. Having burnt his fingers to a frazzle once already, Byron no longer believed in love at first sight. But he and Annabelle had tumbled headlong into an emotion of *some* sort, he could not deny, and for the rest of that year endless wittering, cooing letters flew to and fro across the Atlantic on the wings of Cupid, and hours of pound-a-minute phone-time were clocked up in the exchange of amorous, heartfelt nothings. There was only one problem, of course, and that was Rosheen.

In theory, there should have been no problem at all. Events should have followed a natural, predictable course. The dirty old Baron deBauchery – besotted with Rosheen's nubile body and desperate for a male heir – should have proposed marriage; the gold-digging Rosheen should have asked Byron for a divorce; and Byron would have obliged just as fast as a man can phone a lawyer. But in practice, the wily baron seemed in no great hurry to legitimise the domestic status quo and let another wife (she would be his sixth) get her greedy paws on the family fortune. Moreover, by October the high-performance cash register between Rosheen's ears had clocked the news that Byron-baby was going to be the next director-general of Unibore and earning twice his current salary come July. He could, therefore – in theory, at any rate – be clobbered for twice as much alimony, if she could only stave off a battle in the divorce courts for another year or so.

Naturally, Byron had no insight into the way Rosheen's mind was working. He could only guess. But by Christmas she had fallen ominously silent about the whole subject of divorce; in fact, he had not heard a peep out of her for three whole months. Which would have been a blessing *sans pareil* under normal circumstances, but not at a time like this. There was nothing, of course, to prevent him from suing her for divorce in the conventional manner – on the not unreasonable grounds of her adultery with about three hundred people of his personal acquaintance, not to mention the entire Cincinnati Cyclones football team. But that way madness lay. Rosheen would simply have counter-petitioned on the most scandalous grounds that she was capable of dreaming up. For she had a wondrously inventive imagination when it came to filth, and a welter of mendacious ordure would have been flung around in open court, besmirching all and sundry and getting splashed across the pages of every newspaper from coast to coast, becoming common knowledge in Salvation, Mississippi, overnight. This would have been bad enough – sullying the unblemished reputation of the Reverend Noah Cartwright's only beloved daughter; but to make matters worse, Byron had told Annabelle a little white lie . . . or if not exactly white, then at least a tolerable shade of grey. Fearing that no Southern Baptist preacher's daughter would have allowed herself to get involved with a married man, he had told her that he was divorced *already*. Because it had seemed to him at that time that he virtually was, all bar a few signatures and the lawyers' fees. And Annabelle, in turn, fearing that the good reverend would not approve of her involvement with a divorcé, had told her father nothing about the ex-spouse at all.

In consequence, Byron's life had become progressively more complicated as the year wore on, with Annabelle under the fond illusion that she was on a petal-strewn path to matrimony, and Rosheen keeping obstinately silent, like a sleeping cougar, down there at her Château deBauchery in Mougins. Finally – just to put the icing on the cake – Eddison Packard and SPACUNA came slithering into his life that autumn, like a nest of cobras, and by Christmas the State Department had put his whole professional future on the chopping block. Totally unable to cope with this gathering snowball of trauma, Byron adopted the time-honoured ontological approach to all crises and did nothing – in the hope that the whole problem might simply vaporise of its own accord and blow away in the next strong wind.

The birth of Wopec, however, put a completely new complexion on things. For, once the State Department had deferred any final decision to withdraw from Unibore while they tried to work out the political ramifications of it all, Byron felt free to stop worrying himself to death about his future as director-general for a month or two and start worrying himself to death once more about his future with Annabelle. (Basically speaking, as long as Byron was worrying himself to death about *some*thing he was as happy as a lark.)

He had told Annabelle very little about the Wopec conference thus far. (Being an unshakeable pessimist at heart, he was reasonably confident that the thing would never get off the ground.) But once a formal agreement had been signed with J. Hector Lammas for the use of Carnage Castle, even a resolute defeatist like Byron had to admit that Wopec seemed to be safely airborne at last. So, on the night of the official signing ceremony, after an ad hoc CLAC dinner at La Gavroche to celebrate, he telephoned Salvation to give Annabelle the good news.

It was five-twenty in the evening in Mississippi when he phoned, and Annabelle was pottering about in the kitchen of her sprawling clapboard home, unwinding after an attritive day with her class of demonic six-year-olds. Mentally speaking, she was not at her most athletic . . . which one had to be to keep pace with all the leaps and somersaults of Byron's cerebral process at *any* time, but more so than ever when he was under the influence.

'Baby, I have only word for you,' he burbled, none too coherently. 'And that is Wopec.'

'Opec?'

'And Carnage.'

'Byron,' (silly question) 'have you been drinking?'

'Have and still am, sweetheart. We've been out celebrating. We have finally got a venue, would you believe.'

'Who have?'

'*We* have . . . CLAC have . . . Unibore have. We've got Carnage.'

'You've got what?'

'Carnage Castle. Didn't I tell you? This titanic medieval pile about thirty miles out of London. We clinched the deal today with J. Hector Thing. We've got it for the last two weeks of June.'

'Got it . . . for what?'

'Didn't I tell you? The Unibore world peace congress.'

'You mean your big brainwave you didn't want to talk to me about? The conference? It's definitely going to happen?'

'As of today, angel, the twenty-fourth of June is officially Wopec Day. We have fifteen weeks to lift off, and counting.'

'Byron, that's just *won*derful!'

'Isn't it just? So that's what we've been celebrating tonight. And that's what I'm doing here on the sitting-room floor, with a bottle of Bourbon and a pot of coffee at half past eleven on a Friday night, wishing to hell you were here too.'

'Wait a minute . . . You mean Washington's going to have to about-face now and stay with Unibore after all?'

'Sweetheart, that chicken-brained administration is dumb enough to try most anything, but I don't think even *they* could be so stupid as to stay away from a world peace conference in election year.'

'Darling, this is the most fantastic news! I can't wait to tell Noah. He'll go wild when he hears.'

'Well, what did I tell you? Genius will out. Stick with the action, baby, you could be married to the director-general yet.'

'I could what?'

'I said you could be . . .' Byron suddenly realised what he had said. Instinct told him to burble on, and on and on and on, and hope that she would let it pass. But his tongue, ever his least dependable ally, mutinied in the breach and left him dangling in silence for what felt like half the night.

Annabelle had not the least intention of letting it pass. 'Byron,' she said coyly, 'is that your idea of a proposal?'

'Of a, did you say, ah, pardon me?' He tried to ease himself into a more upright posture to cope with this small emergency, and suddenly felt a fierce hot pain spreading across his chest. He wondered in a fleeting moment of panic if it was simply heartburn or the onset of his first coronary thrombosis. But clamping a hand to his sternum he discovered that he had just spilled half a mug of steaming black coffee down his shirtfront. 'Ahhh, shhhhhh*oot*!'

'Byron?'

'Sweetheart, I'm sorry, I've just poured coffee all down myself.'

'Don't prevaricate.'

'Honey, I'm not prevaricating, truly. I'm burning myself to bits here.'

'You mean *scalding*, darling,' said Annabelle. 'You can't burn yourself with hot coffee.'

'Wanna bet?'

'Byron, you haven't answered my question.'

'What question?'
'Was that your idea of a . . .'
'Angel, can we talk about this some other time?' said Byron in some discomfort. 'I'm dripping in hot scalding coffee and the carpet's flooded all around me.'
'How come? What are you drinking the stuff out of, a barrel?'
'Baby, please, I'm not kidding. I love you to pieces but I really am in a mess here.'
'You're prevaricating.'
'Rosheen, I am *not* prevaricating, I'm lying here in . . .'
'The name's Annabelle. Harry.'
'Christ, I'm sorry. You see the mess I'm in?'
'I can't see you at all, darling, you know that. And maybe it's just as well.'
'Annabelle, I am *not* playing. I'm being poached alive here in burning scalding coffee.'
'Who is Rosheen?'
'Rosheen? Rosheen who?'
'Byron . . .'
'Oh, *that* Rosheen. That's, that's my secretary.'
'Your secretary's called Louise.'
'Ah, sure, but Rosheen's my *other* secretary. I have a special *new* secretary, just for Wopec.'
'Ah hah. And is she there with you?'
'Annabelle, sweetheart, what are you suggesting? Rosheen is a dog. I mean she's, she's fifty, and married, and has a very serious alcohol problem. How can you even *think* things like that?'
'You still haven't answered my question. Was that or was that not a proposal of marriage?'
Byron began to flounder. 'Darling, this is something that is far too important to trivialise over the phone this way. It really is something that we should discuss face to face.'
'Why?'
'Why? Because . . . because I'm a bit old-fashioned, I guess, and I just can't cheapen and demean something so intimate by bawling about it over a five-thousand-mile phone line with half the world's operators out there right now listening to every word. And in any case, I keep telling you, I'm being gently casseroled to death here in boiling coffee.'
'Byron, you always say we'll talk about this at some other

time. *When* is some other time, for heaven's sake? When am I going to see you again? Christmas?'

'Hell, no. No, no, no, no. Just as soon as Wopec is out of the way. July. We'll take a vacation in July. Anywhere in the world you want. That is a promise.'

'And you promise we'll talk about *us* for once? Those things that are too important and intimate to trivialise and cheapen over the phone?'

'I promise, promise, promise. Cross my soaking-wet, coffee-stained, newly braised heart.'

'Well, all right,' said Annabelle reluctantly. 'I'll let you go change your shirt then. I want to give Noah the great news about Wopec, anyhow. He just walked in the door.'

'OK, baby, I'll call you next week.'

'Promise now?'

'Promise.'

'Night-night then.'

'Night, sweetheart.' Byron dropped the phone back in its cradle and keeled over onto the floor in a pool of sweat and continental roast. Close one. Too damn close for comfort. But pretty smartly handled, even if he did say so himself. He poured himself another cup of coffee, retired to the bedroom, stripped off and put on a bathrobe. Maybe it was time to give the arch succuba herself another prod and push things along a little. They had not actually spoken to each other for a good six months now and much water might have flowed under the proverbial *pont* down there on the Côte d'Azur since their last exchange of incivilities.

12

IT WAS ten to one in the morning in Mougins, and upstairs in his bedchamber at the Château Montcalme, Guy Louis Guillaume, seventeenth Baron de Montcalme-Challois, lay fast asleep on top of the housemaid. Downstairs in the *grand salon* –

the finest example of rococo excess in the whole of Provence – Rosheen Rynagh Bridget, fifth daughter of Eamon O'Halloran, Madison City police captain, sat curled up in a fauteuil with a bottle of Jameson's and two hundred Disque Bleu, watching *Mutilator Rape-ghouls*, a brand-new video hypernasty that had arrived that very morning from her sister Siobhan in Trenton.

She was just ten minutes into the tape and the plot was thickening nicely. A bus full of schoolgirls had broken down outside the Happy Axe Motel in an isolated part of the New Mexico desert. The motel owners, two drug-crazed hippies, were welcoming their unsuspecting little blue-eyed guests with home-made hot dogs in spicy LSD sauce, while their wall-eyed mother was cackling in the kitchen, pressing another screaming resident feet-first into the sausage machine . . . when the telephone began to ring. Spitting obscenities, Rosheen pressed the pause button on the remote-control unit, leaned out of the fauteuil and snatched up the phone. '*Oui?* Allo?'

'Hi, sweetie. Guess who?'

'I don't know, Byron, give me a clue.'

'It's me.'

'Well, you sure had me fooled there. What do you want?'

'Just thought I'd call to say hi and wish you a happy St Patrick's Day, whatever.'

'It's not St Patrick's Day.'

'It's not?'

'No. What do you want?'

'Are you sure?'

'Of course I'm sure.'

'Well it must be getting kind of close.'

'It's on the seventeenth. Now what do you want? I'm busy.'

'I just thought we might have a talk, that's all.'

'What about?'

'Divorce.'

'We've been talking about divorce for centuries.'

'But not since October.'

'Ever since the day we were married.'

'Sure, but circumstances change, honey. Now that you're living down there with Guy . . .'

'Byron?'

'Sweetie?'

'How long have I been living down here with Guy?'

'Oh, I don't know, about, ah, a year, I guess.'

'A year I've been living down here. One year. That's twelve months, fifty-two weeks, three hundred and eighty-whatever-it-is days. But you have to call up at one o'clock in the morning, when I'm right in the middle of a very important thing on television . . .'

'Baby, it's not even midnight.'

'Well, it's one a.m. in France, asshole. So *bonsoir*.'

'Well, no call to get mad. I am your husband after all.'

'You've got something new to say? It couldn't go in a letter?'

'What are you getting so wild about?'

'You've lost the use of your right hand, have you? You can't pick up a thing called a *pen* and make squiggles called *writing*? You have to wake me up at some ungodly hour of the night when I'm busy watching them stuff this kid into the sausage-maker — '

'Jesus, I figured you'd be on top of the world tonight . . . St Patrick's Day . . . everyone having a ball out there . . .'

'I *was* on top of the world – till you rang. I was having a ball watching this picture. And leave St Patrick out of this.'

'Rosheen, angel, why are you getting so upset? I just feel we ought to push things along a little, that's all. We've been discussing this divorce for a very long time now. Since right back before the honeymoon even. That's ten years, you realise?'

'So one more day matters? You have to call me up at two a.m. on St Patrick's Day night? What's the rush?'

'You call ten years a rush?'

'You're getting married again. Is that it?'

'*Married*? Are you kidding? I'm trying to get *un*married, for Christ's sake.'

'You sound guilty, Byron.'

'*Me* guilty? Jesus, that's almost funny.'

'There's a guilty *je ne sais quoi* in your voice. Gotten some poor kid into trouble?'

'Rosheen, that is so puerile I don't even intend to grace it with an answer.'

'Been shoving that miserable stick of gristle up some innocent young sophomore, hah?'

'Honey, why are you being so unreasonable?'

'Who's being unreasonable? Who's phoning me at three o'clock in the morning?'

'But you never go to bed before three, anyhow. Correction: you never go to sleep before three.'

'Now who's being puerile?'

'Rosheen, I just want to get this divorce over and done with and out of the way, that's all.'

'Byron, I don't think that's a very nice way to speak of terminating our marriage, I really don't. Think of the vows you made. There is a spiritual side to this as well, you know.'

'Oh, come on, don't give me that crap. Our marriage finished years ago in all but law.'

'So what do you need a divorce for?'

'I just want to make a proper, final, legal break. For ever.'

'Ah hah. And what's in it for me?'

'What do you mean, what's in it for you?'

'I'm thirty-three years of age. I have no job, no income, no prospects — '

'You've got Guy.'

'While you're about to hit the peaks of success.'

'One of the richest guys in France.'

'I helped you get to that peak, Byron. I gave my all to you, selflessly, for the best years of my life.'

'That's not saying much, sweetie. You also gave your all to the Cincinnati Cyclones and Christ knows how many of my best friends.'

'You ungrateful bastard. I gave you everything that a loving woman could give a man.'

'And most times it had to be cured with penicillin.'

'If you want to wash your hands of your marital responsibilities, Byron, that is just fine by me. But you're going to have to pay me fair compensation.'

'Well, you just crawl up your ass, Delilah. You deserted the matrimonial home to go live with that geriatric Frog paedophile.'

'Leave Guy out of this. This is between husband and wife. You're going to be earning two hundred thousand bucks from the first of July.'

'*Two hundred thousand* . . . Rosheen, honey, have you gone clean out of your tiny mind?'

'Byron, I know what you'll be earning as D.G. because Mirella Fabrizi told me what Otello was getting. And that was eighteen months ago. So don't give me any of that "I-only-pull-in-nine-eighty-a-month-after-taxes" horseshit, because it won't wash.'

'You want to see my salary checks?'

'I've seen your salary checks, fuckwit. I used to write your expenses claims, remember? If you're in such a hurry to toss our marriage into the trash can and me with it, OK. I'm not going to be difficult. I won't stand in your way. Just make me a reasonable offer and we'll say adios.'

'And what do you call a reasonable offer?'

'I don't know. Think of a social security number and double it.'

'Rosheen — '

'Call me when you've got a figure in mind. Meantime, *bonne nuit.*'

'Rosheen?'

'Rosheen?' The line went dead. 'Well, sweet dreams to you too, Medusa.' He put the phone down and knocked back the last of his whiskey. Funny, he could have sworn it was St Patrick's Day.

He climbed into bed and lay awake for a while with the light on, contemplating the ceiling and wondering what to do about Rosheen. Perhaps, he could have her put down by some clean humane method. Or better still, by the Algerian underworld. Maybe some kindly Arab would baste her with cement and leave her to marinate for a few years off the Cap d'Antibes. Or simply lace her Badedas with nitric acid and let her dissolve without trace in the bath one night. Byron thought about that. Now that was a brilliant idea. He wondered that some whodunnit writer hadn't thought of that before. The perfect murder. If Rosheen were to keep her hands out of the water until the last possible minute, she might even be able to pull the plug on herself and disappear effortlessly down the wastepipe in one long stream of sudsy effluent, and add another few gallons of pollution to the Mediterranean Sea.

13

THE IDEA of hosting a Wopec dinner party at Carnage Castle came to Otello in the bath that weekend. It was to be no ordinary dinner party; but then it was no ordinary bath.

Otello did most of his inspired thinking in the bath. In the Fabrizi household the bathroom had a significance that extended far beyond its mere functional value. It was to them, as it had been to the ancient Romans, a sociable place to gather; somewhere convivial to relax, for health and *conversazione*. At their villa in Messina the Fabrizis had a magnificent bath-house modelled on one built for Pompey the Great. At their official Unibore residence in Highgate, however, they had been obliged to settle for something more modest. Nevertheless, Otello had done his best within the structural limitations imposed upon him. He had ripped out all the existing plumbing, torn up the floor, knocked down a couple of bedroom walls and installed a new sunken bath in ersatz marble, three metres long, and half as wide. In the middle of it stood a small fountain, surmounted by a brass effigy of Neptune, with sea-nymphs at each corner from whose mouths the bath water flowed, or would, at a mere twist of the nymphs' arms, spray forth an invigorating shower in any or all four directions. Padded cork cushions had been provided so that family and friends could sit around the sides and immerse their feet or inhale the vapours of refreshing mineral salts that Mirella added in generous measure to the water; and weekend bathing parties with as many as a dozen guests were a common occurrence in the Fabrizi household, with a running buffet of pasta and salads, a copious flow of Frascati, and endless Verdi piped in from the drawing-room.

On this particular Sunday morning, however, Otello and Mirella were alone, up to their ears in bath foam, meditating over a pre-lunch Martini, with the Royal Philharmonic fluting and harping Mozartly in the background.

'It seems,' Mirella reflected at length, 'to lack a certain something. I don't quite know what. A certain . . . augustness, perhaps.'

'The conference?'

'No. Wopec Day. The inauguration ceremony. It lacks grandeur. Dignity. It should be a day the world will never forget. Wopec is the apotheosis of your career, remember. It marks your retirement, when all's said and done.'

'Coincides with, rather than *marks*, I think,' said Otello modestly. 'Wopec is primarily about world peace, after all, not my retirement.'

'Possibly,' said Mirella, who did not see it that way at all. 'But there's no point in organising anything on that scale unless you're absolutely sure that the world is going to remember you for it in centuries to come.'

'But I don't think I should care to be remembered for an excess of conceit,' said Otello.

'Better than being forgotten for an excess of self-effacement.'

'Well, I don't mind a modicum of vanity here and there,' Otello conceded (anything for a quiet life). 'But there are limits. What did you have in mind?'

Mirella came from a highly successful family of political opportunists and sardine exporters and did not believe in modicums of *any*thing. Vanity and ambition were the stuff of life, and modesty was one of those vulgar manifestations of inverted arrogance so beloved of Anglo-Saxons. She was a forceful woman who pursued her ambitions through others, notably her husband and their children. Otello, for his part, did not lack courage or determination (no Italian living had fought more resolutely for the return of the Godalming Marbles, for example) but he was constrained in his personal ambitions by an ingrained Sicilian diffidence and conservatism. Ever since the day they were married, Mirella had had to coax him gently towards every little goal in life that she selected on his behalf.

'I'm not suggesting anything too flamboyant,' she said. 'Just a gesture of farewell to remind the world that you're retiring, that's all. A small garden party, perhaps, here at the villa.'

'Not exactly *august*, would you say?' Otello remarked. 'Or even very dignified.' For although Mirella liked to refer to it as their *villa*, it was in fact a conspicuously ordinary terraced house – Georgian and handsome, to be sure, but really not the sort of place where people gave garden parties. Whilst they had a back yard of sorts, filled with flourishing plants in terracotta jars and colourful cache-pots, it boasted barely a postage stamp's worth of lawn (and an Italian postage stamp at that) and reeked of tomcats.

'Then a ball,' Mirella suggested, undeterred. 'A grand ball.'

'Don't be so absurd,' Otello scoffed. 'A *ball*?'

'Why ever not?'

'In Paris, possibly. In Vienna, very probably. But here in Highgate?'

'Not *here*, prune. At Carnage Castle. A grand ball. For heads of state. A glittering international finale to the inauguration day ceremonies.'

'Really, a sense of proportion, *cara mia*,' said Otello. As a classicist he was obsessed with a sense of proportion in all things. 'Can you imagine even a handful of heads of state being prepared to come to England for a ball at Carnage Castle just to celebrate my retirement? Some buffoon like Hudson Butcher of the Paradise Islands, perhaps, but . . .'

'Well, all right,' said Mirella, who was rather adept at getting her way by overpitching her demands in the first place and gradually retreating towards her chosen goal as though she were making hugely generous concessions. 'A ball for ambassadors, then. Your personal farewell to the London diplomatic corps.' She despatched the last of the Martini in her glass with an exuberant flourish and reached out to pour herself another.

'But we're not the sort of people who give balls,' said Otello – attracted, nonetheless, to the idea of hosting some sort of function to say farewell to all their many friends in the diplomatic world. 'Balls are rather old fashioned and *belle époque*-ish.' More to the point, they were prodigiously expensive and he would have a devil of a job trying to slip the bill through on his expense account – especially at a time of acute financial crisis.

'What do you mean, we're not the *sort*?' Mirella retorted, groping through the foam that engulfed her, fumbling for a bottle of gin that was lurking somewhere on Neptune's fountain. 'You can be so infuriatingly humble sometimes.' (It came from his mother's side; five generations of Sicilian muleteers.) 'Just because we've never had a good excuse to give a ball before.'

'Not a question of needing an excuse. I'm simply not a ballish type of person.'

'But I thought the inauguration was supposed to enhance Wopec's image?'

'Well? What's so enhancing about dancing?'

'Damn sight more enhancing than speeches and fêtes and firework displays.'

'Things like that appeal to the general *public*. Which is the whole point of inauguration day. Well, *half* the point of it, anyway. Besides . . .' He fell silent.

Mirella poured herself a tumblerful of gin and added a dewdrop of vermouth. 'Besides, what?'

'Balls are more in the Teutonic tradition. We don't *dance* farewell to people. Ours is the heritage of Bacchus not Strauss. A dinner party perhaps. But a ball is quite out of the question.'

'Very well, a banquet,' said Mirella, juggling with a jar of olives that slithered perversely in her foam-wet hands. 'A banquet at Carnage for the diplomatic corps.'

'Well, a *modest* banquet, perhaps,' said Otello uneasily. Because knowing Mirella she would want to invite the head of every legation in London and they would end up with about three hundred at table. 'The great eating room only seats fifty-odd, in any case.'

'Just for our special friends then,' said Mirella, spilling half the olives into the bath. 'Our favourite ambassadors.'

'The DoE of course, may not consent.'

'The who?'

'J. Hector Lammas and his *apparatchiks*. They may not approve.'

'Of a banquet? Why not? As long as Unibore are paying.'

'Even so . . .'

'Only a few dozen ambassadors and their wives, after all. And I suppose we should invite the guest of honour . . . whoever that's going to be.'

'No one's come up with any suggestions so far. Jericho Engineer did mumble something about asking Hudson Butcher, but I don't think anyone took that very seriously.'

'Have you thought of approaching the palace?' asked Mirella, groping about on the floor of the bath in search of the lost olives.

'The Quirinal?'

'Don't be obtuse, dear.'

'You can't mean the Vatican, surely?'

'I mean here in London, of course.'

'HM?' said Otello, dropping his voice abruptly, as if she might have been hiding behind Neptune, listening to every word.

'Not necessarily. An HRH would do just as well. You could start at the top and work down. There are hundreds to choose from, after all.'

'I suppose there are.' Otello had never really considered it before. 'It would certainly attract the media and bring the crowds in, I grant you that.'

'And add that vital touch of majesty and grandeur to the day,' said Mirella, 'which is what I told you it lacked in the first place.'

Otello hmmed and hahhed and stroked his snow-white beard for a while in contemplation. 'Not a bad idea,' he murmured at length. 'Not a bad idea at all. I might put that forward to the board at UGS 1 tomorrow.'

The executive board met once a week, as a rule, but with the organisation of Wopec now fully under way they had agreed to convene as often as necessary in unusual general session (UGS) to ratify CLAC's decisions and deal with whatever the committee did not feel competent to deal with on their own. The first of these sessions, UGS 1, was held the following afternoon, on Monday 13 March.

The first issue that Otello raised was the proposed banquet at Carnage Castle on the evening of Wopec Day. No delegate had any objections to this, as long as it was genuinely a party for the diplomatic corps. It did, however, prompt a strong recommendation from Doctor Dieter Landgrebe, the West German delegate, that with so many distinguished people likely to be at Carnage throughout Wopec week, a Director of Conference Security should be appointed to liaise with the local police and the appropriate department at Scotland Yard.

Involved as they were in work that was of crucial importance to nobody whatsoever, Unibore had never been a very security-conscious organisation. Halcyon House was crawling with old-age pensioners and ex-convicts in smart blue uniforms, with the doubtful claim *Aceguard* arched in gold across their shoulder blades, but that was not quite what Dieter Landgrebe had in mind. Otello himself – although hailing from a land world-famous for its subversive fanatics, from the Dolomites to the Malta Channel – regarded security matters in general as a tedious irrelevance that got in the way of more pressing United Nations business. Like organising banquets. He therefore proposed that the honour of being Director of Security should be bestowed upon his deputy, Byron Cleveland. Byron – whose practical experience of security amounted to double-locking his front door occasionally and nailing his windows shut to keep out the fresh air – reluctantly agreed to shoulder this additional burden, and the board quickly voted thirty-four-nil to approve the appointment before he had time to change his mind and lumber someone else with the responsibility.

Otello then moved on to the matter of choosing the Extremely Famous Person to make the inauguration speech at Wopec Day and plant the commemorative olive tree for world peace. His proposal that they should invite HRH and The Wife (*the* HRH), not any old HRH took everybody by surprise. Those delegates who had bothered to think about it at all had turned their thoughts to Nobel Peace Prize winners, like Lech Walesa or Mother Teresa of Calcutta – although the East Germans, it was true, had had someone less controversial in mind, like Fidel Castro. British royalty had never even crossed their minds, but as long as it was to be *the* HRHs, and not some lesser substitute, everyone was generally in favour. Their royal highnesses were apolitical, non-controversial, would bring the public flocking to Carnage on Wopec Day, and attract worldwide news coverage. After a brief discussion, Otello put it to a vote and the proposal was adopted by thirty-four votes to one. The only serious objection coming from Air Vice-Marshal Engineer of the Paradise Islands, who was stunned that any other mortal should have been offered first refusal before Field-Marshal Hudson Butcher . . . and the more so since he had been rash enough to give the great man the impression that the honour was virtually his for the taking. He drew some small consolation, however, from the thought that the HRHs were extremely busy people and might already be booked up for the last weekend in June; and further, from Otello's promise that if the royal couple were to decline the invitation, priority consideration would be given to inviting President Butcher in their place.

The board then moved on to consider the contentious question of a Wopec agenda. Agendas were something of a novelty at Halcyon House. They were occasionally trifled with but never taken very seriously. By and large, ontologists liked to think of themselves as intellectual pathfinders, blazing exciting new trails of philosophical light through the dark hinterland beyond the frontiers of conventional thought. The essential characteristic of ontological debate was that it had no beginning and no end. Speakers just rambled on interminably, digressing at whatever philosophical tangents took their fancy along the way. To formalise and restrict everything by imposing an agenda which predetermined what was to be discussed, who was going to discuss it and when, was a negation of the whole ethos of ontological discovery.

Wopec, however, was something of a special case. Most delegates accepted that if the outside world was to have even a sporting chance of following what was going on (and the event was nothing if not a million-dollar public relations exercise, after all) then they would need some sort of clearly defined agenda; even if it were not strictly adhered to on the day. (In fact, it would not greatly matter if no one took a blind bit of notice of the thing, just as long as it gave the media and the general public the wrong impression.)

Unaccustomed as they were to drawing up agendas, the board decided that the simplest and most democratic way of going about it would be to ask all member-governments to submit a list of issues that they wished to debate at Wopec, with the sole proviso that those issues should concern only clear cases of armed conflict or *potential* armed conflict between sovereign independent states. Member-governments were to be given four weeks in which to make their submissions, at the end of which period the board would consider all the issues and sort them into a practicable timetable. In the meantime, all submissions were to be kept securely under lock and key in a special agenda room in the CLAC wing on the fourth floor – not least because the secretariat's record for losing or shredding important documents was awe-inspiring even by Unibore's breathtaking standards of incompetence.

With the board in unanimous agreement on all these points, there was nothing further they could usefully do until the agenda submissions had been received. Otello therefore concluded UGS 1 and pencilled UGS 2 into the calendar for the second week of April.

Fifteen hundred miles away to the east, meantime, even older and wiser heads were beginning to focus their minds on the Wopec agenda.

14

It was early evening in snow-grey Moscow and crowded trams were hissing and clattering along the prospekts and boulevards, rocking the hard-working millions home to borsch and *Koronation Strəət.* Meanwhile, the vast machinery of national security ground on relentlessly deep within the Kremlin walls, where the foreign policy co-ordination committee was in late session and dozens of terribly frail old men were busy falling asleep over their cocoa.

At the head of a very long table, committee chairman Andrei Nikolayevich Feodorenko cleared his throat and referred to the next item on his schedule. 'We move on, comrades,' he croaked into his microphone, 'to item one hundred and forty-six on your order papers: Unibore and the Wopec agenda. Comrade Chernikov has just received the minutes of Unibore's first unusual general session yesterday afternoon, I believe.' He looked up and peered hopefully towards the other end of the table far away in the foggy distance, where, when last he'd heard, his deputy and close friend, Dimitri Sergeyevich Chernikov, was seated and still alive.

A kindly apparatchik prodded Dimitri Sergeyevich, who awoke with a start, adjusted his deaf aid and began to read out the latest estimate of Mujahedeen troop-strengths in Afghanistan. The kindly apparatchik silenced Dimitri Sergeyevich with another prod and directed his attention to the relevant minutes that Academician Rhoskov had recently transmitted through the London embassy. Dimitri Sergeyevich obligingly read them out, in the wrong order, in a solemn, ponderous monotone. When he finally came to the end, some twenty minutes later, there was a short intermission while his colleagues tried to remember what he'd been talking about and word was got through to Andrei Nikolayevich at the other end of the table that his dear friend had finished. Then Andrei Nikolayevich spoke into his microphone once more.

'First essential then, comrades, is to ensure that we secure total control over this Wopec agenda.'

'Control,' agreed Dimitri Sergeyevich, nodding with approval. 'Good. Good.'

'This will require careful co-ordination of our agenda submissions to avoid conflict with the policies of non-aligned nations.'

'Conflict,' echoed Dimitri Sergeyevich. 'Good. Excellent.'

'Academician Rhoskov will then be able to rely on the support of the Third World delegates and exercise control of all the agenda-making sessions.' Andrei Nikolayevich paused to allow applause to ripple its way around the table. 'It would be highly advantageous then,' he continued, 'if we were able to scrutinise in advance some of the issues that other member-governments are submitting. All the agenda documents, however, are to be kept locked away by the CLAC committee, and our only representative on CLAC is Sofia's delegate, N. R. Kabanova.'

'Locked away,' mumbled Dimitri Sergeyevich, beginning to lose track of what was going on. 'Delegate Kabanova. Good.'

'Which means, I'm afraid,' concluded Andrei Nikolayevich with considerable unease, 'that we may have to rely on the Bulgarians once again.'

Those words, *rely on the Bulgarians*, percolated slowly through to the subconscious of the dozing gerontocracy all around. Ancient sages began muttering in protest in their sleep, pleasant dreams of schoolgirl gymnasts dissolving swiftly into old recurring Balkan nightmares; and the mere thought of it took a year off Dimitri Sergeyevich's life.

15

THROUGHOUT THE whole of her first year at Halcyon House it had been a painful mystery to Nina Kabanova why none of her Eastern bloc colleagues would let her tackle any sort of job that required a delicate diplomatic touch. It was not that no one liked her, she was confident of that. Yet whenever an opportunity arose for one of them to act as spokesperson for the bloc, or conduct special negotiations, or undertake any sort of initiative that called for diplomatic skill, Bulgaria always seemed to be left out. It was as if, for some inexplicable reason, they were frightened that she might bungle it.

In her early months at Halcyon House she had ascribed this to the fact that she was new to the job and this was her first posting in the West. Then she began to wonder if it might be a question of her age – she was only thirty-nine, and barely out of nappies by Soviet standards; or misogyny perhaps, for she was the only woman delegate in the Eastern bloc, and Academician Rhoskov was not celebrated for his fondness of the fair sex. She did manage to pluck up the courage on one occasion to ask him why she was never given her fair share of opportunity; but he simply waved her away and told her she was imagining things. Worse, he even implied, none too subtly, that she seemed to be developing a persecution complex. At which point she let the matter drop; the KGB had an unpleasant habit of picking on people with persecution complexes.

Then she stumbled, quite by accident, on the brutal, naked truth. She overheard Helmut Meisinger, Berlin's delegate, sharing a joke with an East German embassy attaché at Rhoskov's new-year party. 'There are these three defectors walking down the road,' Meisinger was saying, unaware that Nina was standing just behind him. 'A Czech, a Pole and a Bulgar. The Czech says: "I'm defecting to the USA, then I won't have to queue for gasolene any more." The Pole says: "I'm defecting to England, then I won't have to queue for meat any more." The Bulgar says: "I'm defecting to the USSR. Then I won't have to queue for an exit visa!"'

At that, Meisinger and his friend fell about, helpless with laughter. When they'd recovered a little and wiped their eyes and massaged their aching sides, the attaché said: 'OK, here's a quickie for you, hot from the GRU cypher room. How could Lithuania smash China?'

'Dunno.'

'Import a Bulgarian dishwasher!'

Again the two men doubled up in fits of laughter. Incensed, Nina crept discreetly from the room, too shocked and embarrassed to protest. What sort of pathetic apology for humour did they call that? What sort of a comrade went around spreading malicious slanders of that kind about a friend and ally? Now if it had been the *Poles* they were laughing at, it would have been an entirely different kettle of fish . . .

On more mature reflection, however, she began to wonder if she had not over-reacted somewhat. After all, the Germans were a notoriously nationalistic lot. Perhaps Meisinger and his chum had some sort of running gag going between them. So, as an experiment, she decided to try the same joke – with just one essential modification – on the Roumanian delegate, Grigore Marcu.

'There are these three defectors walking down the road,' she told Grigore. 'A Czech, a Magyar and a Pole. The Czech says: "I'm defecting to the USA, then I won't have to queue for gasolene any more." The Magyar says: "I'm defecting to England, then I won't have to queue for beef any more." The Pole says: "I'm defecting to the USSR. Then I won't have to queue for a visa!"'

Grigore waited, solemn-faced, for her to continue. Then: 'Is that it?'

'That's it.'

Grigore looked puzzled. 'So why was this Pole in such a hurry?'

'It's not a news story, Grigore. It's a joke. Funny ha-ha.'

'Well, didn't he want to *pay* for his visa or something? Was he Jewish, this Pole?' Grigore began to smile. 'It's a Jewish joke?'

'Grigore,' said Nina limply, 'who would be so stupid as to defect to his own side?'

Grigore thought about that for a moment. 'A Bulgar?' And he promptly collapsed across his desk, helpless with laughter.

Nina was mortified. This was a revelation. So *this* was why no one would give her any responsibility: prejudice. Blatant, unashamed prejudice. Did they *seriously* think that all Bulgars were bungling incompetents? How long had this been going on? How long had Bulgaria been the unwitting butt of these despicable un-jokes? What in heaven's name had happened to the spirit of Pan-Slavism?

This, then, was why she had volunteered to serve on the CLAC committee and help organise Wopec. True, it was a job that all her comrades were practically hiding under their desks to avoid, but even so it did offer her at least *some* opportunity to show the powers-that-be what she could do. Moscow's eyes, they said, were everywhere, constantly on the lookout for hard-working young zealots among the party faithful. Loyal service never went unnoticed; and her devotion to duty, it seemed, had begun to pay off even sooner than she had dared hope. One Wednesday morning in the middle of March, just two days after the board's first unusual general session, she received a mysterious summons to a house in Holland Park to meet an official from the foreign ministry in Sofia . . .

His name was Kotsev. Stoyan Kotsev. A worried little man in his late fifties, with a crumpled face, pebble-thick glasses and no eyebrows. They drank black coffee, seated on opposite sides of a dining-table in an otherwise empty upstairs room. Kotsev chain-smoked, avoiding her eyes and talking at first in a sort of nervous shorthand.

'Wopec. CLAC.'

'Comrade secretary?'

'Vital, you understand, Warsaw Pact foreign ministers agree a common approach to the Wopec agenda in advance.'

'I suppose it would be, yes,' Nina replied, never having given the matter the slightest consideration.

'And their task would be very much easier if they knew exactly what issues other governments were submitting to Halcyon House.'

'Well, once all the submissions have been received, they'll be photocopied and distributed to every delegate.'

Kotsev shook his head. 'Missing my point.'

'Comrade secretary?'

'The foreign policy co-ordination committee need to see

other governments' submissions *before* they are distributed to everybody else. At least a week before.' Kotsev ground out the butt of his cigarette and lit another. 'Making myself clear?'

'Perfectly clear, comrade secretary,' Nina replied apprehensively. 'But with respect, it would be no easy task getting copies of all the relevant papers.'

'Why not? You have photocopying machines.'

'But all the agenda submissions are locked away in steel cabinets in a special room. The keys are with the director-general's secretary and I have no valid reason to ask for them.'

Kotsev was faintly amused. 'No one is suggesting that you *ask*, Comrade Kabanova.' He paused to let her digest his meaning, and in case it was still not clear, added: 'In the socialist struggle for world peace it is necessary sometimes for the individual to undertake acts of courage and initiative for the greater good of her comrades. And with the very utmost discretion.'

'Comrade secretary,' said Nina, 'I am ready to play any part in the socialist struggle that the party sees fit.'

'Good.' Kotsev nodded approvingly. 'This attitude is correct.'

'But I'm an ontologist not a safebreaker. I simply cannot walk into a locked room and open a locked cabinet. It's not possible.'

Kotsev smiled again. 'But surely you don't imagine we would expect you to undertake a mission of such importance on your own?'

'You mean . . . one of my colleagues at Halcyon House?'

'No, no, no,' said Kotsev emphatically. 'When I said *utmost discretion*, I meant it. No one else at Halcyon House is to know about this. Work of this nature demands the expertise of a highly trained professional. We shall be sending you one of our top men from Sofia. His name is Zlob.'

'Zlob?'

Kotsev nodded reassuringly. 'Have no fear. Zlob will know exactly what to do. Put your trust in Zlob. He will take care of everything.'

Zlob arrived on her doorstep the following week at half past eight in the morning. Nina had been up since six, as usual, jogging round Hyde Park with a rucksack full of phone books on her back. Returning to her Bayswater flat, she had just showered and was sitting down to a bowl of prune and seaweed compote in the kitchen, when the doorbell rang; and there he was – a tall, scrawny fellow in a shabby raincoat, with a lugubrious voice and a matching hangdog expression.

''Ullo,' he said glumly. 'You Kabanova N.R.?'

'I am.'

'I'm Zlob.'

She observed his sickly grey pallor, the boils on his neck, the pustules around his badly shaven mouth and a disconcerting vagueness about his eyes. He could not in all honesty be said to look like one of Sofia's top men; but then, good spies were not *supposed* to look like spies.

'I suppose you'd better come in,' she said, though it was hardly the most convenient time.

'Ta.' He picked up his luggage – a cheap-looking, plastic attaché case and a Drouzhba Dynamos F.C. grip-bag – and followed her inside into the kitchen.

'Coffee?'

'Ta.' He dumped his bags on the floor and sat down at the table, sniffling and snuffling – a thick gooey snuffle, suggesting a cold in full bloom. He looked deathly pale.

'Are you feeling all right?' Nina asked suspiciously. She had a strong antipathy to people bringing their filthy germs into her clean, healthy apartment.

'Yup. Ta. Fine now. Just a touch of airsickness.' He gave her prune and seaweed compote a bilious once-over. 'Flying always makes me sick. That's why I had to transfer out of the air force. Because I kept chucking up. All over the maps and bombs and everything.' He took out a packet of full-strength army-issue cigarettes and lit one, without offering them or asking if she minded.

Cigarette smoke made *her* feel sick, as it happened, but she did not want to strain relations at the very outset, so she suffered in silence and found him a chipped saucer for an ashtray.

'I was expecting you sooner than this,' she said, 'from the way Kotsev was speaking.'

He looked at his watch. 'Well, I only landed an hour ago. First flight in. Come straight here. Only got one pair of legs, you know.'

'I meant, before *today*. I was expecting you last week.'

'Oh, I see.' He fingered a ripe pustule on his neck. 'Well, I've been all over the place. I should've got here last Thursday, matter of fact. But some silly sod sent me to Stockholm instead. When I got there they said I was in the wrong place and sent me to Frankfurt. Frankfurt said I was supposed to be in Vienna. And when I got to Vienna they realised I should've been in London. I haven't done so much flying for ages. And was I sick? Cor, not 'alf. Been honking away like a good'un ever since breakfast last Wednesday.'

'Why was there so much confusion?' said Nina.

'Always is. They don't know whether it's lunchtime or Leningrad, that lot.'

'What lot?'

'The brains,' he said contemptuously. 'The masterminds. Our elders and betters.'

She passed him a beaker of strong black coffee. He said 'ta' and shovelled about half a kilo of demerara sugar into it. She sat down to finish her prune and seaweed compote. 'Is that all the luggage you've got?'

'Yup. Travel light, that's old Zlobby.' He prodded the Drouzhba Dynamos bag with his foot. 'That's me tools.'

'Tools?'

'Keys. Not many locks I can't get through, I can tell you. Should've been a burglar, me. I'd have made a fortune.'

'I don't imagine those cabinets are going to give you much trouble then.'

'Cabinets?' Sniffle snuffle. 'What cabinets?'

'Didn't they brief you about the cabinets in the agenda room?'

He frowned. 'What agenda room?'

'Where the documents are being stored.'

'Documents?'

'The agenda proposals.'

Zlob looked puzzled. 'I didn't bring any.'

'Hasn't anyone told you yet?'

'Told me what?'

'What's happening.'

'No.' He drew closer, anticipating a breath of scandal. 'What?'

'Don't you even know why you're here?'

'No.' Sniff. 'Why? Don't *you* know?'

'I was told *you'd* know.'

'Were you?' He nodded glumly, not in the least surprised. 'See what I mean? No one ever knows what's going on in this outfit. I get this every time, everywhere I go. It's either the wrong place, or the wrong job, or the wrong week.'

'Didn't Kotsev explain?'

'Who's Kotsev?'

'Well, what did they say before you flew out?'

'Don't mention flying.' He ground the cigarette to death on the chipped saucer. 'Was I sick? Dear oh dear, was I ever. Sick everywhere. Sick down me trousers. Sick on the carpet. God, was I sick.'

'But what did they tell you, Zlob, before you left Sofia?'

'Nothing. No one ever tells me anything. Except the wrong thing. I'm not really army intelligence, you see. I'm sabotage reserves, strictly speaking. I'm only on *loan* to army intelligence. Because of my special skills. But you're not supposed to know that. That's a state secret. Even *I'm* not supposed to know it.' Sniff. 'Just goes to show how much they don't tell us.'

'But this seems incredibly inefficient,' said Nina.

'No. Just averagely, I'd say,' Zlob replied, unconcerned. 'Averagely. I wouldn't put it any higher than that. You should hear *some* of the bungles I've been mixed up in. Dear oh dear oh dear.'

'But a large number of important documents have to be photographed. Didn't anyone brief you?'

'Somebody burbled something about the United Nations. Some crowd of intellectual know-alls.' He sniffed and wiped his nose on the sleeve of his crumpled, once-white raincoat. It was liberally encrusted with the dried spoor of many previous encounters. 'I don't like intellectuals, meself. Wherever you look, whatever's gone wrong in the world, there's a clever-clogs behind it. I think Stalin had the right idea about intellectuals, don't you? I do. Yup. I think history's been a bit hard on poor old Stalin.'

'Zlob,' said Nina, beginning to lose patience, 'there are hundreds and hundreds of crucially important papers that we have to copy.'

'Where?'

'Locked away at Unibore headquarters in Pall Mall.'

'How far's that from London?'

'It's *in* London. Right in the centre. Don't they teach you *any*thing in military intelligence?'

'Not a lot. 'Cos everything you learn there is a state secret. And you get shot for knowing state secrets. So no one wants to learn anything. In case they get shot.'

'Did you bring any special equipment?'

'Only me keys.'

'I mean photographic equipment.'

'Nope. Just me little Instamatic to get some shots of Nelson's Column for me mum. Why? Want to borrow it?'

'We have to copy those documents, I keep telling you.'

'Well, isn't there a photocopier where you work?'

'One on every floor but — '

'One on every . . . ? Blimey, you're laughing then. Dunno why they bothered sending me over. You could do the job yourself, easy as pie.'

'But I can't get into the store room. And if I were seen photocopying those documents there'd be a terrible scandal. It could wreck the entire conference.'

'What conference?'

'Didn't they meantion Wopec?'

'Is he the bloke in charge?'

'Zlob,' said Nina, wilting, 'surely they explained . . . this is a very, *very* delicate operation.'

'Daagh,' he scoffed, 'they always tell you that. Just to put the wind up you. They reckon it concentrates the mind.'

'I give up. I don't understand what's going on.'

'Nobody does. So you're with the majority, don't panic.'

'But this is nothing to laugh about.'

'Who's laughing? Just look to the future, that's my motto. Only another thirty years and I'll be retired. You get a really good pension in this line of business.'

'I think you should talk to someone as soon as possible.'

'All right. I'll take a toddle over to the embassy then.'

'No, no, not the embassy. They're not involved. Go to Kotsev. You know Kotsev?'

He shook his head. 'Is that near London?'

'It's a *he*. He's not far away. In Holland Park. I'll drive you.'

'I ought to warn you, in that case.'

'What?'

'I get car-sick as well.'

16

THE NEWS that their royal highnesses had had the audacity to accept Unibore's invitation to be guests of honour at Wopec Day reached the Paradise Islands on the evening of 24 March and was borne by messenger straight to the People's Palace of Culture, where President Hudson Butcher was attending a gala performance of Shostakovich's fifth symphony being given in his honour by the Ho Chi Minh Philharmonic Orchestra.

The great man himself was fast asleep at the time, enjoying the third movement, for it had been a long tiring day. He had been up since the crack of ten, opening goodwill gifts from well-wishers all over the government, and had spent most of the afternoon driving round Port Paradise in an open-topped Cadillac, acknowledging the cheers of the happy screaming masses who had thronged his route at bayonet point. So he was not best pleased to be shaken from slumber half way through Shostakovich Five that evening by a messenger who came crashing into the royal box with an urgent telex from London. He was even less delighted by the tidings therein:

REGRET HRH AND MISSIS TODAY ACCEPTED UNIBORE INVITE WOPEC INAUGURATION. BOARD DECISION IRREVOCABLE. AWAIT INSTRUCTIONS. JERICHO ENGINEER/UNIBORE

Visibly shaken by the news, the President stormed out of the concert hall, gave orders for the messenger to be flogged, and summoned an emergency politburo meeting aboard his private yacht, the *Kalashnikov* – a converted destroyer fitted out with luxurious staterooms, a swimming pool and the very latest line in heat-seeking missiles. She was kept moored at the mouth of Tranquil Bay, near the presidential palace, for a swift getaway in the event of any untoward political developments in the capital . . . such as a serious outbreak of democracy.

The politburo had been having an exhausting day too,

organising the equitable distribution of IMF development aid among their Panamanian bank accounts, and those who were not enduring the performance of Shostakovich's Fifth that evening were scattered about the archipelago, relaxing on their private plantations. No sooner had the President summoned the emergency meeting aboard the *Kalashnikov* than radio-phones began to warble throughout the islands. Banquets were hastily abandoned and supine houris left panting on the edge of ecstasy. Limousines sped away into the night; helicopters came chattering in across the still lagoons; and powerful turboboats came thumping through the darkness over Tranquil Bay.

Aboard the *Kalashnikov* a state of maximum alert prevailed. Keen-eyed revolutionary guards patrolled the decks, sub-machine-guns at the ready, peering eagerly into the night for things to shoot. Below, in the presidential stateroom, defence chiefs and the politburo were digesting the grave news from London. The mood was one of shock as much as anger. Engineer had led them to believe that their great leader was at the top of a short list of one, to be guest of honour at the Wopec inauguration ceremony. That that honour should have been given to British royalty without so much as a by-your-leave to Port Paradise beggared all belief. The more so now that genealogists at Paradise University had stumbled on evidence that Hudson Butcher could be a direct descendant of one of the oldest monarchies in the world.

Clearly, some sort of international imperialist conspiracy was at work – possibly at the instigation of the Great Satan in Washington DC, and unquestionably with the knowledge and connivance of the British government. National honour had been foully besmirched, and no civilised country could allow this flagrant violation of the accepted norms of protocol to pass without redress. The question, then, was not *whether* to retaliate but what form of retaliation would be most appropriate. Finance Minister Milton Proctor was already compiling a list of British-owned businesses on the islands for expropriation. The Chief of the Defence Staff, General Eldridge Hampton, was proposing the expulsion of the British High Commissioner. While the Interior Secretary, Colonel-General Stockminder, was calling for the arrest of a random sample of British expatriates on whatever charges the prosecutor-general could think of. One minister alone had not yet spoken: the Foreign Secretary, Great-Uncle Albert.

Hudson Butcher was lounging sullenly on his leopard-skin throne, threshing the air with a bamboo fly-swat. He glowered at Great-Uncle Albert. 'And what do you say, wise old one?'

'The shrewd hunter,' Great-Uncle Albert replied quietly, 'does not waste his energy baiting a toothless lion.'

Which was not at all what the fiery young President wished to hear. 'But if the toothless lion is still a menace to the people?'

'Then trap it,' said Great-Uncle Albert. 'But the shrewd hunter lets others dig the lion-pit.'

'What others?' said the President, irritated by all these tiresome old saws from jungle lore. 'Who would dig the lion-pit for us, old one?'

'Others with a grievance.' Great-Uncle Albert shrugged. 'People with a righteous cause, perhaps. An oppressed people. There are oppressed peoples everywhere. Some seek their liberation peacefully. Some resort to arms. And some would readily use an event like Wopec to advance their cause.'

The President lay back on his throne, slashing the air with the fly-swat as if he were flaying the flesh of some invisible incarnation of British imperialism. He brooded for a while on Great-Uncle Albert's wise words. To be seen by the world to take reprisals would be undignified, ignoble. Whereas, to suffer these slings and arrows without so much as a flicker of an eyelid would be judged as a mature, statesmanlike response, befitting the character of a true world leader. Besides, there was much to be said for the time-honoured antisocial maxim: if you can't join it, wreck it. He turned to his chief of intelligence, Brigadier Elisha Longfellow. 'Find me,' he commanded, 'an expert on oppressed peoples.'

It had been another successful day for SPIS, the Socialist People's Intelligence Service, whose agents had been hard at it since dawn, scouring the archipelago for plots against the state. Now all was moony-dark and cicada-quiet up at Joy of Socialist Labour Gaol, the old colonial prison on the snake-infested north side of the island, where thousands of unwitting counter-revolutionaries were lying tucked up in their chains, dreaming of new things to confess to on the morrow.

Next door, the lights were burning late at SPIS headquarters, where weary interrogators were mopping up the blood after another rewarding day's work, and the duty officer of Section

Five was still busy at his desk. Section Five was the most secret branch of SPIS. The mere mention of it put the fear of G**[*] into the hearts of every citizen. Section Five never stopped. They worked all day and all night, seven days a week. No one knew who they were or what they did. Not even the head of Section Five; and no one knew who *he* was either.

It was ten twenty-five when the telephone rang on the duty officer's desk that night. An anonymous hand picked up the receiver. An anonymous voice said: 'Section Five. Duty officer speaking.'

'Chief of SPIS here,' said the caller, 'Brigadier Longfellow. I'm on board the *Kalashnikov*. We need an expert on oppressed peoples.'

'Hostile to us or friendly?'

'Friendly.'

'Belligerent or pacifist?'

'Belligerent.'

'Active or dormant?'

'Active.'

'Religious oppression? Cultural? Racial? Or political?'

'All four,' said Longfellow, 'if possible.'

'Anything is possible.'

'Then anything will do.'

'Then expect Colonel Boatman.'

'How soon?'

'When he arrives.'

'Most grateful,' said Longfellow, hanging up and wondering who on earth he'd been speaking to.

Half an hour later a Chevrolet with blacked-out windows crept silently along the quay at Tranquil Bay towards the *Kalashnikov*. It pulled up in the shadows and a lean figure in a white safari suit and dark glasses climbed out and walked up the gangway. On board, the revolutionary guards had seen the number 5 on the Chevrolet's licence plate and now cringed back into the shadows, saluting and bowing. The colonel ignored them and went below. He entered the stateroom without knocking. The assembled ministers and defence chiefs observed him with a blend of fear and curiosity. He had a shaven skull and a hard,

* God. (Banned by presidential decree)

bony face. His dark glasses reflected like mirrors. Under his left arm he carried a snakeskin document case.

Hudson Butcher swished the air with his fly-swat, ill at ease. A man from Section Five was a rare sight. Everybody in the room owed his continuing good health to the indulgence of Section Five. 'You have something for me, Colonel?' he enquired.

'I have, Mr President,' said Boatman, and unzipped the document case. He took out a glossy white plastic file and presented it to Butcher like a salesman with the special offer of the month. 'I would most strongly recommend for your purposes the oppressed people of the state of Sandhustan.'

17

SEVERAL DAYS had elapsed since Jericho Engineer had telexed the bad tidings to Port Paradise and he was feeling better already. If the President was going to have him recalled and shot he would almost certainly have done so by now. Whatever his faults – and for the life of him, Jericho could not think of a single one – Hudson Butcher was certainly not slow off the mark when it came to exacting retribution. But just when he was beginning to convince himself that he was out of danger . . .

It was a Tuesday and he had spent an exhausting day motoring round Knightsbridge, mowing down cyclists and claiming diplomatic immunity. Returning to his Mayfair mansion at half past four, with a boot full of monogrammed silk underwear from Harrods, he retired to bed with his Antiguan masseuse. Divesting himself of half an acre of bathrobe, he was just lowering his twenty-two-stone bulk onto the steel-reinforced play-bed, when his valet phoned from downstairs to inform him that a Colonel Boatman had arrived and was waiting for him in the drawing-room. Staggered by the sheer impertinence of the man, Jericho reminded his valet that no one –but no one – was allowed to interrupt him in the middle of a massage and asked him to show scum Boatman, whoever he was, to the door and tell the uncouth slob to make an appointment in the proper manner in future. The valet telephoned again a moment later to say that Colonel Boatman refused to leave and that he was from Section Five or some such thing. Jericho froze. Section Five? Something like that, the valet replied. Jericho instructed him to make the good colonel as comfortable as possible and explain that the air vice-marshal was unavoidably detained on the telephone to the United Nations and would be down in two shakes. He then pushed his masseuse back into bed, hurried into his dressing room and pulled on a shirt and slacks. *Section Five*? Dear G** in heaven. Was this retribution time, after all? Termination, right there in the heart of Mayfair, in broad daylight? Would they dare? Yes, Section Five would dare. One bullet clean through the forehead. Or a dash of ricin in his pink gin. Or a quick poke in the leg with a sharp umbrella.

He wobbled downstairs as fast as his legs could tremble. Boatman was standing at ease by the drawing-room window, looking out into Park Street. Jericho began to bleat his apologies for keeping him waiting; but Boatman was not interested. So he began to bleat his apologies for the confusion over their royal highnesses; but the colonel was not interested in that either.

'Sit,' said Boatman.

Jericho dropped into a chair. Wasn't he even going to be given a chance to explain? He looked a nasty piece of work, this Boatman. Shiny black skull, hollow cheeks, dark glasses and a sinister little mouth. Jericho began to sweat. Section Five were capable of almost anything. 'Stray dogs' in any corner of the globe could disappear at the mere whim of men like Boatman – drugged, crated up and flown out with the diplomatic baggage. One minute Mayfair, next minute Paradise, in chains in Joy of Socialist Labour Gaol.

Boatman sank into an armchair, cool and relaxed. 'Unibore.'

'Colonel sir?'

'Wopec.'

'Colonel?'

'CLAC. You are a member of this committee, CLAC.'

'I am, sir, yes.'

'So you are intimately involved with the planning of the conference and privy to every detail of its organisation?'

'Well, I *would* be,' Jericho stressed, 'but nothing much in the way of detail has been decided yet.'

'Very well,' said Boatman, 'tell me what has been decided so far.'

'It'll be a five-day conference, Colonel sir,' Jericho replied, trying to swallow the quaver of panic in his voice. 'At Carnage Castle. Starting on Monday the twenty-sixth of June. With an inauguration ceremony on Saturday the twenty-fourth attended by their royal highnesses. There'll be speeches, a fête, a funfair, fireworks, a barbecue, and a banquet.'

'Banquet?' said Boatman.

'Yes, sir, Colonel sir. A private banquet given by Director-General Fabrizi and his wife.'

'For?'

'Four what, Colonel?'

'For whom? Who will be invited?'

'Just a few ambassadors and high commissioners. All personal friends of the Fabrizis. It's their farewell party for the diplomatic corps.'

Boatman looked interested. 'Which ambassadors in particular?'

'I've no idea, Colonel sir. I haven't seen a guest list. I don't think they've drawn one up yet.'

'I'd like to see a copy of it as soon as they have.'

'The minute I can lay hands on one,' Jericho promised.

'With a list of the delegates who will be attending the Wopec symposium,' added Boatman, 'and details of the schedule for inauguration day.'

'Very good, sir, Colonel sir.'

Boatman got up to go. 'Make touch when you have news.'

'May I ask the Colonel, sir,' said Jericho, rising, thankful still to be alive, 'what the section's special interest in Wopec might be? It might help me to provide you with additional information if I knew.'

Boatman observed him for a moment in silence. Then: 'Tell me, Air Vice-Marshal, what do you know about the Sandhustan People's Liberation Army?'

Jericho frowned. Sandhustan? He'd heard of that. Somewhere. 'Nothing, sir,' he confessed at length.

'Excellent,' said Boatman. 'Then you know everything you

need to know.' And with a flash of a smile, like the glint of a bayonet, he departed as suddenly and mysteriously as he'd arrived.

18

SANDHUBAD, CITY of myth and legend. Jewelled oasis in the arid central plains of Sandhustan province. Spiritual home of the ancient Sandhu people.

Night in the sacred inner city. The narrow, dusty streets lay dark and silent around the great walled temple of Shrahma the Magnificent, the holiest Sandhu shrine. Its minarets and lofty towers stood silhouetted majestically against the starry sky. Beggars in ragged dhotis lay curled up, shivering in the gutter, dreaming of a happier incarnation. Feral cats, torn and tattered, crept through the shadows in pursuit of vermin. A bored constable in khaki shorts strolled aimlessly along the lightless Street of a Thousand Sighs, a teak truncheon dangling from his belt, a tarry roll-up glowing at his lips. A solitary figure in a cowled black robe – the cloak of the Holy Warriors of Shrahma – hurried past him towards the west gate of the sacred temple.

This hooded warrior, Captain Sharaq of the Sandhustan People's Liberation Army, entered the hallowed Temple of Elders and descended into the Golden Sanctum of the Sage, where he prostrated himself before the high priest and seven wise elders of the temple. The high priest bade him rise and led him into the *sanctum sanctorum* beyond, into the most holy presence of Shraddath ba Shrahma, thirty-fourth reincarnation of Shrahma the Magnificent.

The Shraddath, in a turquoise robe, was sitting cross-legged on a large gold cushion, a tiny, fragile figure, ninety-three years on earth and almost blind. Sharaq knelt and kissed the hem of his robe.

'Your hour has come, Sharaq, faithful warrior,' the Shraddath croaked in a frail, reedy voice. 'May the Lord Shrahma go with you.'

Surrounded by the high priest and seven wise elders, he began to chant the valedictory prayer for those about to go to battle. Fighting back tears of pride, Sharaq muttered the responses and remained kneeling while the sacred scriptures were placed before the Shraddath. The venerable ancient, however, kept his fading eyes on Sharaq and recited the verses from memory:

'In the autumn of that year, the Lord Shrahma
Returned to Sandu with the vanquished armies of the mogul Kalliq Khan.
And the vanquished cast down their heads in fear and shame, waiting for the sword of vengeance.
But the sword of vengeance fell not upon the heads of the vanquished.
And the Lord Shrahma appeared before them, high upon the Tower of the Ancients at the great temple of the warrior-princes.
And the vanquished were blinded by a bright light, as if the sun shone from the face of the Lord Shrahma.

And the Lord Shrahma spake unto the vanquished, saying, "Go in peace and liberty. No man shall be the slave of Sandhu.
And Sandhu shall be the slave of none.
Go then in brotherhood. Return to your homelands and speak of the wonders you have seen, and tell of the power and love of the Lord Shrahma."

And the vanquished closed their eyes, so bright was the light that shone from the Lord Shrahma's face.
And when they opened their eyes again to see, the Lord Shrahma had ascended into the Ninth Temple, beyond the sight of mortals.
And the Lord Shrahma returned not until the seventh incarnation.'

The Shraddath pushed aside the sacred scriptures and placed his hands on Sharaq's head. 'The blessing of the Lord Shrahma go with you, Sharaq, faithful warrior. May His hand be always upon your sword and upon the swords of your valiant comrades. And may the strength of His omnipotent arm bear you safely across the skies to England.'

Two miles away, in the teeming slum quarter of the city, Golam Nanjik Nurg, a bony, undernourished lad of nineteen, was sitting on the rush floor of his one-room hovel, surrounded by grandmas, children, chickens and old curry pots, checking the contents of his suitcase in the light of a dying candle.

The suitcase was not his. No one in his family had ever owned a suitcase. It had been given to him by the Sandhustan People's Liberation Army. It was a fine case, made of processed cardboard, in two pieces, secured with a length of string. A fine length of string, also given to him by the SPLA, with a suit, some shirts, underwear and a pair of smart brown leather shoes. Nothing quite fitted; but no matter. They were fine clothes, and Nurg felt very proud.

He looked at his wristwatch – former British army, also provided by the SPLA. Only five more minutes to go. Then out into the chilly night to meet the truck on Slaughterhouse Street, and from there, the short drive to the airport. Nurg had never been abroad before. He had only been outside Sandhustan province in the course of federal military service. He felt a surge of pride and exhilaration. A Sandhu warrior flying into combat, into the unknown. He had no idea what he would have to do when he got to England. The mission was a military secret. Holy Sandhu warriors were sworn blindly to obey.

Two minutes to ten. He began his farewells. Mother, father, grannies, uncles, aunts, cousins, sisters, chickens. Finally, his young wife.

'When will you return again, Golam Nanjik, my master?' she whispered tearfully.

'When the Lord Shrahma wills,' Nurg replied.

'Then the Lord Shrahma be always with you.'

He kissed her on each cheek, hugged her tightly and hurried out into the crowded, rat-infested alleys.

Half a mile away, on the dark and desolate corner of Slaughterhouse Street and Freightyard Row, a rusty pick-up truck was waiting, parked in the shadows. At the wheel sat the district adjutant of Number One Commando, the Sandhustan People's

Liberation Army. Beside him, former army sergeant Guppi Pungal of the mechanical engineers.

'Right, one more time,' said the adjutant. 'In English, what are your travel orders?'

'We are taking twenty-three fifteen night flight to Banaghar,' replied Pungal. 'And there we change to good old British Airways, sir, and fly the flag.'

'You are arriving now in London. I am British immigration officer. What it is you are doing here in England, Mr Pungal, old boy?'

'I am here, sir, on religious visit. To honour the funeral of my poor old Uncle Hari who has just kicked the bucket in Ashton-under-Lyme.'

'How long you are staying?'

'One month or two, sir, until I have executed the last will and testament of Uncle Hari.'

'OK. You have passed through customs and immigration,' said the adjutant. 'Who is meeting you?'

'Dubbi Muktar, sir. Who will take us to a house in west of London. If I get lost or am ill I have emergency number to telephone.'

'And if you are arrested? If traitors have betrayed your mission?'

'I say only, sir, I am Pungal, Guppi. My rank is engineer-sergeant. And my number is Two. And I demand my rights as a prisoner of war under the terms of the Geneva Convention.'

He broke off as the spindly figure of Golam Nurg emerged from the shadows of an alley and ran towards them. The adjutant restarted the truck. Nurg scrambled onto the back with his cardboard suitcase, and the adjutant drove away down Slaughterhouse Street.

Sandhubad airport was seven miles from the city centre. It handled twelve flights a day and the twenty-three fifteen to Banaghar was the last one before dawn. A piston-engined Douglas Dakota of Sandhustan Provincial Airways was waiting on the apron, an engineer working on the undercarriage by the light of his bicycle lamp.

The adjutant set them down by the customs shed and bade farewell. Nurg and Pungal made their way to the check-in desk, where an old woman was weighing baggage on a pair of bathroom scales made by Salter of England. There were a dozen other passengers waiting to check in for the night flight to Banaghar, among them the lean, rangy figure of Captain Sharaq, officer commanding Number One Commando, now divested of his black cowled robes and dressed in a smart blue business suit.

At eleven o'clock they boarded the Dakota. At eleven-fifteen flight SP12 set off along the runway with a bronchial roar and trembled up into the starry sky, tickling the tree-tops a mile to the south and sending cascades of leafy timber raining down upon the shanty slums below.

It was a one-hour flight to Banaghar and a further fifteen hours to London. They landed at Heathrow at half past eleven the following morning and were met by the SPLA's liaison man in Britain, Dubbi Muktar. Nurg was overcome. He had seen Britain many times on the video screen at SPLA training centre. He had seen royal weddings and cup finals and Trooping the Colour. He had seen *Dad's Army*, *Come Dancing* and about two hundred mystifying episodes of *Minder* dubbed into Sandhu. Yet never in his wildest fantasies had he conceived of so many planes and motor cars and fine concrete tower-blocks.

Dubbi drove them to Southall in his battered yellow minicab and installed them in a top-floor flat above his family's all-night grocery store. It was to be their temporary billet until Dubbi and Sharaq had found a suitable field HQ somewhere in the English countryside.

That first night they had a visitor. Nurg had no idea who he was. Nor had Pungal. Sharaq introduced the stranger as 'the Very Reverend'. He did not look very reverend to Nurg, however. He was bald, with cadaverously hollow cheeks; and the scarred, misshapen landscape of his skull prompted in Nurg the image of a shell-holed battlefield at night. His handshake was moist but iron cold and he wore sunglasses, even in the dark. Sharaq took him into the living-room and closed the door to confer in private. Nurg and Pungal were left in the kitchen, straining to hear what they were saying. They were discussing a conference of some kind.

'. . . still three months away,' Nurg heard the Very Reverend say. ' . . . nothing arranged in detail, but . . .'

'We're in no hurry, Colonel,' Sharaq replied.

Nurg glanced questioningly at Pungal. A very reverend

colonel? A military churchman? An army chaplain? Pungal frowned and pressed his ear to the door.

'We have pleny of planning and preparation to keep us occupied,' Sharaq was saying.

Nurg drew closer to the door. The colonel was speaking now. Nurg heard him say something about a banquet and ambassadors.

'Forgive me asking, Colonel Boatman,' he heard Sharaq say, 'but how reliable is your source of information?'

Colonel-boatman? Nurg's eyes widened. Some sort of naval chaplain? Perhaps this was to be a maritime operation, which was why the SPLA had sent over their crack marine commando unit.

'My information,' the Very Reverend replied, 'comes from a source right at the heart of the conference organising committee itself. He is one hundred per cent reliable.'

'And what does he know of the security arrangements for Wopec?'

'Nothing as yet. The Unibore board have placed the American delegate, Byron Cleveland, in overall charge of conference security. He's an incompetent man, I'm assured, but his job is to liaise with the appropriate police departments, and they could prove a tougher nut to crack . . '

19

IT WAS ten past three in the afternoon, and at the Metropolitan Police Special Operations centre in Buckingham Gate, S.W.1, an élite squad of highly trained tea ladies – the envy of police forces throughout the world – were hard at work bringing sweet relief and biscuits to the hard-pressed forces of law and order. Upstairs in his first-floor office, Superintendent Norman Hatchard of the Royalty and Diplomatic Protection Group had just had an unilluminating telephone conversation with some half-wit called Cleveland.

'Unibore, Joyce,' he said to his tea lady. 'Heard of Unibore?'

Joyce was a fount of general knowledge – capital cities, metric conversions, scenic routes to Bognor, state of the going at Kempton Park, buys-of-the-month at Tesco's – a walking encyclopaedia of useful information 'Unibore . . . Unibore . . . Unibore . . .' She frowned at the floor, hands on hips. 'Rings a bell, dear.'

'Allshott?' enquired Hatchard hopefully.

'Allshott . . .' More frowning and shaking of head. 'No, dear, no. Not Allshott. *Alder*shot . . . Bagshott . . . Oxshott. But not Allshott, no. Sorry, dear.' She put an extra biscuit in his saucer as a consolation.

'How about Carnage Castle?'

'Carnage?' Joyce looked puzzled.

'As in slaughter. As in battle.'

She had another think. 'There's a Battle *Abbey*. Near Hastings.'

'No, this is definitely a castle.'

'Well, there's Hastings Castle.'

'Near Allshott?'

'Dunno, dear. Where's Allshott?'

'That's what I'm asking, Joyce. That's what I'm trying to find out.' He scratched his dandruff. 'Maybe this charlie's got it wrong.'

'Charlie 'oo, dear?'

'This Cleveland charlie from Unibore.'

'Cleveland's near Redcar,' said Joyce, 'if that's any help.'

It was not. Hatchard got up from his desk and marched to the door.

'Unibore . . . Unibore . . . Unibore . . .' muttered Joyce, gazing vacantly down into Buckingham Gate. 'I think that's where my hubby gets bits and pieces for the car.'

Hatchard was not listening, however. He was already half way down stairs. Breezing into the squad room below, he found a sergeant and two PCs up to their eyes in the *Daily Mail* crossword. 'Anybody here know where Carnage Castle is?' he demanded. Pause for thought. Furrowed brows. 'Allshott?' Shaking of heads. 'Well, the bloody place has got to be somewhere. Unibore are having a do there at the end of June. A big do.'

'What's Unibore, sir?' enquired Sergeant McEwan.

'Anybody heard of Unibore?' asked Hatchard.

Frowns, smacking of lips, pensive uhms.

'Marvellous,' muttered Hatchard. 'Bloody marvellous. We've got four hundred and fifty of the cleverest people in the universe arriving in three months' time, and we don't know who they are, what they're doing, where they're going, or why.'

'I have heard of 'em, sir,' said one PC Sweet. 'Something to do with the United Nations.'

'That much I know, son,' Hatchard retorted.

'Been on the telly lately,' Sweet added.

'There's a lot of things been on the telly lately, laddie,' said Sergeant McEwan scathingly.

'The Yanks have got the hump about it, I know that much,' said Sweet.

'That ties up,' said Hatchard. 'This Unibore charlie's a Yank.'

'Which charlie, guv?' asked McEwan.

'Name of Cleveland.'

'Cleveland's in Middlesbrough,' said Sweet.

'Is it, bollocks,' scoffed McEwan. 'Middlesbrough's in Cleveland, you daft jessie.'

'But this herbert I've been talking to is an *American*, for the ninety-ninth bleeding time,' said Hatchard.

'He'll be thinking of Cleveland, Ohio, then,' said Sweet.

'We're talking about Allshott, you prat,' said McEwan.

'Allshott, Ohio, then,' said Sweet. 'Stands to reason.'

'Doesn't stand to bloody reason at all,' Hatchard rejoined hotly. 'Allshott's in the Home Counties.'

'Ah, but I bet there's one in America as well, sir,' replied Sweet. 'There are hundreds of English places all over the States. Portsmouth, New Hampshire. Worcester, Massachusetts. London, Ontario. Paris, Texas. Richmond, Virginia . . .'

'Ontario's in Canada,' McEwan cut in scornfully. 'Nowhere near the States, laddie.'

'But where's sodding *Allshott*?' bellowed Hatchard. 'That's what I'm trying to find out.'

The door opened at that moment and a tea-trolley trundled in, towing omniscient Joyce.

'Know where Allshott is, Joyce?' asked McEwan.

'Funny,' said Joyce, 'you're the second person's asked me

that this afternoon. Can't say as I do, dear, no. There's *Alder*shot, Bagshott, Oxshott . . .'

'Marvellous,' muttered Hatchard, sloping back to his office with notebook and ulcer. 'Bloody marvellous.'

A bleak March morning at Warmacre Camp, the army's top-secret training ground, deep in the heart of nowhere. Icy rain was sweeping in from the Welsh Marches on a force eight north-westerly, and somewhere out there in the savage wild, a troop of aspirant young Special Air Service trainees were floundering around up to their teeth in mud, trying to throttle a rabbit for lunch. Indoors, in a small, drab admin office in D (for draughty) block, Major Chris Kilmore, officer commanding 2 Troop, T (for training) Squadron, was drying out a pair of sodden stockinged feet in front of his fire/electric/two-bar/ officers only, for the use of, and perusing the small ads in that month's *Quim International*. He had just come across a sad little *cri de coeur* from a playful crofter's daughter on the Outer Hebrides, when his telephone rang.

'Yup?'

'Major Kilmore?'

'Speaking.'

'Good morning to you. Superintendent Hatchard here. Metropolitan Police, Diplomatic Protection Group.'

'Ah yes, well done, old man. Had a call about you from Muddy Mildwater at the MoD. I gather you've got some sort of show on at Cardiff Castle.'

'Carnage, actually. Carnage Castle. Near Allshott.'

'Yah, that's the baby. Unilever or someone.'

'Bore. Uni*bore*. Something to do with the United Nations. They're having an international conference at the castle at the end of June.'

'Biggie?'

'About four hundred and fifty academics, a hefty dollop of diplomats, plus HRH and The Wife.'

'Going on for how long?' asked Kilmore, noting down 'biggie' and 'Bore' beside an advert for Rockard tumescence-enhancing cream.

'One week,' Hatchard replied. 'I'm having a preliminary briefing with their head of security next Monday. Colonel Mildwater thought you might want to sit in on it.'

'When you say *their* head of security, you mean . . . ?'
'Unibore's. Some doctor charlie, name of Cleveland.'
Kilmore scribbled 'Doctor Charlie Cleveland. Tues. Unilever' beside the advertisement for Rockard cream. 'R.v. when/where?'
'Two-thirty at Halcyon House.'
'And that's in Allshott, is it?'
'Pall Mall.'
'So what's in Allshott?'
'The conference. The do.'
'Ah ha. Comprendy. Getting the picture now.'
'Wouldn't happen to know where Allshott is, by any chance?' Hatchard enquired hopefully.
'Matter of fact, I do,' Kilmore replied. 'It's near a little place called Lydhurst. Old General Sterling-Pallgrave used to live down there.'
'And where,' said Hatchard, 'is Lydhurst?'
'Oh, sort of round your neck of the woods somewhere,' said Kilmore vaguely. 'Home Counties-ish, kind of thing.'
'Any particular Home County in mind?' asked Hatchard. 'There are a good dozen to choose from.'
'Haven't the foggiest, old man. Fenlander, myself, born and bred.'
'Marvellous,' said Hatchard. 'Bloody marvellous.'

Not far away, that icy rain was bucketing down on a dozen intrepid men of 2 Troop, T (for training) Squadron, clawing their way up a thirty-foot wall of sheer concrete with hundred-weight bags of sand strapped to their backs. At the foot of the wall, drenched to the skin and sinking gently into a quagmire of mud and sewage, Corporal Ron Bile was spurring his lads on with bloodcurdling screams of abuse. A Land Rover approached, squelching in and out of the gooey morass with violent, axle-bending lurches. It drew up beside Bile. The driver wound down his window and shouted over the howling wind: 'CO wants you, Corp'l! Right now!'
'As you are!' Bile screamed at his troopers. 'Any man moves an eyelid before I get back, I'll chop his bastard hands off!'
They remained frozen like gargoyles to the side of the wall, clinging to crevices with numb fingers and saturated boots, the rain driving into them like rivets. Bile climbed into the Land Rover and was driven back through the quagmire to D block,

where Kilmore was busy writing to the Surgeon General, trying to explain why so many men in 2 Troop had a habit of falling off thirty-foot walls with sandbags strapped to their backs. Bile knocked once and stormed in, leaving a trail of sludge in his wake. 'Sah!' he bellowed, saluting and kicking the door shut in one deft manoeuvre.

'Take a pew, old man.'

'Sah.' Bile sat (chair/one/folding/wooden).

'Something interesting in the wind.'

'War, sah?' said Bile hopefully.

'No, a big conflab at Carnage Castle,' Kilmore replied. 'Last week of June. Crowd of UN johnnies.'

'What sort of conflab, sah?'

'Something to do with peace, I gather.'

'Peace?' Bile didn't like the sound of that at all.

'According to Superintendent Hatchard, the diplomatic protection wallah at Scotland Yard.'

'What's it got to do with us, sah?'

'The MoD wants us to keep a watching brief on security. Colonel Mildwater thought it might make a useful anti-terrorist training exercise for T Squadron.'

'The woodentops won't like that, sah,' said Bile, who had a particularly strong disaffection for the police.

'Well, we don't have to get too closely involved. Just a training op. Ideal opportunity, I'd have thought.'

'Oh, agreed, sah, agreed,' said Bile, who was all in favour of treading on police toes wherever possible. 'Just what 2 Troop could use.'

'Incidentally, talking of 2 Troop . . .'

'Sah?'

Kilmore looked out of the window, through the tumbling rain, to the distant concrete wall where the troop was now down to just seven men, still clinging on like grim death.

'Are you sure they're all right? They've been dangling there for the past ten minutes.'

'Oh, they're fine, sah, fine,' said Bile confidently. 'Doin' 'em good. Makes 'em *hate*. Doin' 'em a power of good, that is.'

'Well, just checking, old man,' said Kilmore, reassured, as another three troopers plunged to earth. 'Just checking.'

20

NINA HAD not heard a peep out of Zlob since the day he arrived, and a whole week had gone by since then. They were now into the last week of March and time was fast running out if the Kremlin still wanted their sneak preview of everybody else's agenda submissions. Bearing in mind what Zlob had said about the incompetence of his superiors, she had begun to wonder if the operation had been cancelled altogether and Stoyan Kotsev had forgotten to inform her. But then, quite out of the blue, Zlob telephoned her office at ten o'clock one Thursday morning.

'That Kabanova N.R.?'

'Speaking.'

'It's old Zlobby 'ere.'

'Zlob?'

'Here . . . you don't half sound different on the phone.'

'Where have you been? What's happening?'

'You sound all foreign and peculiar.'

'Zlob,' she said irritably, 'where have you *been* for the past week?'

'Bloody Deutschland,' he grumbled. 'Some clever clogs at HQ decided I had a few days to spare, so they sent me over to Bonn to bug this block of flats. They don't half mess you about in this game, I can tell you.'

'I don't understand. This job was supposed to be urgent. What's happening?'

'Not a lot. Don't panic. Your mate Kotsev's just been on the phone. He wants those Wopec documents by six o'clock tonight.'

'*Tonight*?'

'That's what the man said. Got to catch the last Aeroflot cargo flight to Moscow tonight.'

'But there are thousands of pages! We can't get them all copied in that time.'

'Well, that's life,' said Zlob philosophically. 'They always expect the impossible.'

'Where are you now? Germany?'

'Can't tell you, I'm afraid. That's a military secret. But they're dropping me off at your offices at two o'clock this afternoon.'

'Who are?'

'That's a secret too. Meet me at the front door, just in case.'

'In case what?'

'In case I have any bother getting in.'

'Why should you? Just ask for me at Reception.'

'I can't. I don't speak English.'

'Zlob, you're not serious?'

'I am, you know.' Sniffle, snuffle. He added reflectively, 'I'm actually quite a serious person deep down, when you get to know me.'

Nina was waiting for him in the busy foyer at the front entrance shortly before two. He arrived ten minutes late, dressed in filthy green overalls and a baseball cap and lugging his Drouzhba Dynamos F.C. grip. He passed the security guards without being challenged and made straight for Nina, who pretended not to know him and stepped smartly into the nearest vacant lift. Zlob stumbled in behind her. She pressed the button for the fourth floor.

'What in God's name are you dressed up like that for?' she said angrily as the lift began to ascend. 'Are you trying to make an idiot of me?'

'What do you mean?' said Zlob indignantly. 'My photocopy service engineer's disguise, this is. I've used it dozens of times. Works a treat.'

'Well, don't ask me to meet you in the main reception hall next time.' She was wondering what it was that looked odd about the words 'RANK 3ERОЖ ENGINEER' emblazoned in gold across the left breast pocket of his overalls. 'Kotsev couldn't have picked a worse day to send you either. The police are going to be here all afternoon.'

'Police?' He looked alarmed. 'What for?'

'Byron Cleveland is having a meeting with the Diplomatic Protection Group from Scotland Yard.'

'Who's Byron Cleveland?'

'The United States delegate.'

'Get away? Someone been threatening him then?' He looked almost hopeful.

'It's not about protecting *him*. It's about protecting everyone at Wopec.'

'Oh.' Sniff.

The lift came to a halt at the fourth floor. Nina stepped out first and led him cautiously into the CLAC wing and down the purple corridor, past the main CLAC suite, the secretaries' rooms and wee Hugo McGuffy's office, to the agenda room at the far end of the corridor.

'You're lucky there's no CLAC meeting this afternoon,' she said, while he fished several bunches of keys out of his Drouzhba Dynamos bag and tried a few in the door lock. 'There would have been one but it was cancelled because of Byron's meeting with the police. So there'll only be the secretaries around, and they're a pretty dozy lot at the best of times.'

Zlob found a key that turned. They crept into the agenda room and closed the door. It was a small, bare room with four grey steel cabinets ranged along one wall. 'Piece of cake,' said Zlob contemptuously. He took another bunch of keys from his bag and tried some in the cabinet locks. He felt cheated. 'I don't know why they bothered sending me over. A kid of ten could have got into this lot with a hairpin.' He opened all four cabinets. Two were empty. The other two contained the member-governments' agenda submissions, neatly filed away in blue cardboard folders in alphabetical order. 'Get through this lot in a couple of hours, no problem. Where's the nearest photocopier?'

'Three doors along, in the secretaries' room,' said Nina, 'but we can't hog that all afternoon. It'll look suspicious. We'll use the one near my office on the second floor.'

'We'll need a trolley then.'

'What sort of trolley?'

'A porter's trolley.'

'What for?'

'Well, we can't carry all these files downstairs in our arms, now can we?'

'You're not going to take the whole lot downstairs in one go?'

'Why not? We'll waste half the afternoon traipsing up and down in the lift otherwise.'

'But supposing someone comes in here and sees that the cabinets are empty?'

'Supposing you just find me a trolley and stop worrying,' said Zlob. 'I've been doing this sort of thing for many years, you know. Trust in Zlob. You let old Zlobby take care of everything.'

'That's what Kotsev said,' she recalled drily.

'Wise man, Kotsev.' Zlob tapped the side of his nose with his index finger. 'Could go far.'

'Well, where am I supposed to find a trolley?'

'I don't know. They're your offices, not mine. Haven't you got a parcel room? A mailing office?'

'Yes, but I can't just stroll in and ask for a trolley. I'm the delegate of a foreign government, not the front hall porter.'

'Well, it's no use looking at *me*. I can't go. I don't speak the language, for starters.'

'But what do I say?'

'Don't say anything. Just walk in and nick it.'

'But I don't know where it is. I don't even know if they've got one.'

'You're not being very helpful, are you?' grumbled Zlob. 'And Kotsev told me you were the co-operative sort.'

'And Kotsev told *me* that you'd take care of everything,' she retorted huffily, and strode out of the room, still trying to work out what looked so odd about RANK ЗЕРОЖ ENGINEER.

Taking a lift to the basement, she found a storeman's trolley outside the foreman's office. It was painted a vivid orange and marked clearly: STORES. DO NOT REMOVE. Nobody was in the vicinity, so she trundled it back to the lift, got in and pressed the button for the fourth floor. The lift took off and stopped again at the ground floor, where, to her acute embarrassment, Byron Cleveland got in, accompanied by a large police officer and an army major. Byron, too, pressed for the fourth floor and the lift took off again. He said, 'Hi, Nina.'

Nina said, 'Hi, Byron,' and blushed and pretended that she hadn't noticed the trolley between them.

Byron, however, found nothing very remarkable in meeting Nina in the lift with a bright orange parcel trolley; for she was a woman of mystery and rumoured to have a taste for all kinds of eccentric things – like weight-lifting and prune and seaweed compote. He introduced her to Superintendent Hatchard and

Major Kilmore and enquired good-humouredly if she were in the process of moving.

She looked puzzled. 'Do what?'

He patted the trolley, as if complimenting her on an excellent choice of transport.

'Ah, this? No, no, no.' She giggled unconvincingly and struggled to think of a plausible explanation. 'No, I just left something in the, ah, boardroom.'

'Oh, right,' said Byron, wondering what she could possibly have left in the boardroom that would require a trolley to shift it.

The lift came to a halt at the fourth floor and the three men got out. Nina said, 'I hope you enjoy a productive and happy meeting,' conscious that she sounded vaguely like a good-luck telegram from the Soviet labour ministry, and continued on up to the sixth floor, where she got out and waited a few minutes before returning again to the fourth.

'Took your time,' grumbled Zlob, as she wheeled the trolley into the agenda room. 'We haven't got all day, you know.'

'I've just had a very nasty moment,' said Nina, leaning back against the wall to catch her breath. 'I met Byron Cleveland in the lift with the trolley.'

'What did *he* want it for?'

'*I* had the trolley, stupid. He was with a police superintendent and some major from the Ministry of Defence. They're using the CLAC room three doors down.'

Zlob began piling the folders onto the trolley. 'I thought you said there wouldn't be anyone around this afternoon.'

'Well, I was wrong. We'll have to be ultra careful between here and the lifts.'

'In that case,' said Zlob, 'I'd better wrap a few sheets of newspaper round this lot. No one'll look twice then.' While she stacked the rest of the files onto the trolley he took a copy of the *Stara Zagora Evening Post* from his Drouzhba Dynamos bag and began separating the pages.

'But that'll make *every*one look twice,' Nina protested.

Zlob's eyes registered that vacant wacky look she had noticed when he first appeared on her doorstep. 'Why?'

'Because the newspaper is printed in Bulgarian, cretin.'

'Well, of course it's in Bulgarian,' he retorted, tucking sheets of it around the files to make them look like small parcels. 'It's the *Stara Zagora Evening Post*. What do you expect it to be in? Ancient Greek?'

She decided not to argue. Trust in Zlob, Kotsev had said. Zlob will take care of everything.

When he had finished wrapping everything in newspaper he wheeled the trolley over to the door. 'I'll cart this lot down to the lifts. You close up and bring my bag, OK?'

'For heaven's sake be careful,' she said, opening the door very cautiously and peering down the empty corridor.

'I'm always careful,' Zlob replied, wheeling the trolley out and piloting it straight into wee Hugo McGuffy's door. 'Just stop panicking for two minutes.'

He trundled on down the corridor as McGuffy's furry ginger face appeared around the office door, like a dormouse peeping from its burrow.

'Eh, anybody wanting me?'

'No, no,' said Nina, caught straddled across the threshold of the agenda room. 'Just, just looking for the key to, to the . . .' She dried up in mid-flow and smiled sweetly.

'Oh, aye, fine, fine. Righty ho,' said McGuffy, and ducked gratefully back into his busy burrow to press on with more calculations.

Nina grabbed Zlob's bag, closed the agenda-room door behind her and hurried back down the corridor.

Zlob had arrived at the lift landing by this time and found himself face to face with one of Unibore's elderly security guards on routine plodabout. 'Looking for CLAC?' enquired the guard, assuming from that vacant, wacky look that the stranger was lost.

Zlob had no idea what the old fellow was talking about. He had been taught a few handy English colloquialisms, parrot fashion, for use in emergencies but had forgotten what they meant. 'Watcher, cock,' he ventured, hoping for the best. 'Nice droppa rain for der time of year.'

The security guard turned, bemused, to Nina who came scurrying to Zlob's rescue. 'He's Polish,' she explained, dismissing Zlob with a contemptuous flick of the wrist. 'He's come to fix the photocopier. We're out of paper.'

'Polski, eh?' said the guard, who had served with a Polish aircrew in the Second World War. He turned brightly to Zlob. '*Dzień dobry. Czy pan mówi po angielsku?*'

Zlob, who could not speak a word of Polish, blinked and nodded and patted his trolley soberly. '*Da, da*. Vixa votocopy, john. Outa piper.'

'He doesn't speak much English,' said Nina simpering apologetically.

'And I don't speak much Polish,' chuckled the guard, wondering why Rank Xerox had started wrapping their products in what appeared to be back-copies of *Pravda*. He gave them an air force salute, said '*Do widzenia*' to Zlob, and plodded on his way, trying to work out what it was that looked odd about RANK ЗEROЖ ENGINEER.

'How did I do?' said Zlob, as soon as he was out of sight.

'Not very well,' said Nina. 'You told him it was raining. The sun's been shining all day.'

'Reckon he noticed?'

'Unless he's blind. It hasn't rained since last week.'

'Been chucking it down in Bonn,' grumbled Zlob.

'It's incredible,' said Nina, as a lift arrived and Zlob manoeuvred the trolley inside. 'Don't they teach you *any* English?'

'Well, they have a go every now and again. But I can't get the hang of the Roman alphabet.'

'Then they should send me someone who can.'

'You think *you've* got problems,' he retorted. 'My mate Christov speaks fluent Mandarin, but they keep on bundling him off on jobs in Japan. You might as well be on the dark side of the moon for all the use Mandarin is on the Tokyo metro. He gets lost every time he goes there. Spends days on end going round and round in circles. Then they dock the poor sod's wages for low productivity.'

The lift came to a halt at the second floor. The doors opened and Nina peered out. There was no one in sight. She led Zlob down a corridor into the wing where all the Eastern bloc delegates were located. The photocopier was in a small room of its own, sandwiched between Helmut Meisinger's office and Academician Rhoskov's. Nina went in first and held the door open for him. Zlob negotiated the gap with awesome ineptitude, crashing first into one doorjamb, then into the other, and finally capsizing the trolley completely, spilling the files and their contents all over the floor.

'Doesn't matter if they get mixed up,' he said, gathering up whatever papers came to hand, 'as long as they all get copied.'

'Of *course* it matters,' said Nina furiously, scrabbling about on the carpet, trying to sort them back into the right files. 'What do you think they'll say when they come to copy and distribute this lot next week and find them all in a jumble?'

'Worry, worry, worry,' sighed Zlob, switching on the machine. 'I don't know. All you brainy types ever seem to do is worry. *Relax*. Trust in your old mate Zlobby.'

Upstairs on the fourth floor, seated round the enormous mahogany table in the CLAC room, Byron and his two security advisers were discussing the precise nature of an ontological congress. Despite Byron's lengthy explanation, it was still a mystery to Hatchard and Kilmore.

'When you talk about people wandering around all over the castle and grounds,' said Hatchard, 'do you mean the general public?'

'No, no, just the delegates,' Byron replied. 'The public will only be allowed in on Saturday, inauguration day. For the rest of Wopec week the estate will be closed to everyone except official delegates and authorised conference personnel . . . such as journalists, camera crews, ushers, secretaries, whatever.'

'And what sort of issues are they going to be discussing at this congress?' Kilmore enquired.

'Is that relevant, security-wise?'

'Highly relevant,' said Hatchard. 'Volatile issues attract volatile people with volatile methods.'

'Well, we haven't drawn up the actual agenda yet,' Byron replied. 'But most of the governments have sent in their submissions. If you'd excuse me for just a minute, I can get you a random selection of the kind of issues they'll be hoping to discuss.'

He got up and walked out of the room, down the corridor and into the office next door, where dozens of secretaries were hard at work, telephoning their fiancés and loved ones.

'Forgive me,' said Byron, loath to interrupt Cupid's good work, 'but would somebody very kindly bring me a few files from the agenda room? Anybody, please?'

'We haven't got the keys,' a tiny waif in pink replied apologetically. 'Miss Elphinstone keeps them.'

Freda Elphinstone was Otello Fabrizi's secretary – a sixty-one-year-old spinster of the old school (Rugby, probably,

Byron suspected) and built to last, like a Foden truck.

'Then would somebody very kindly go and find Mzzz Elphinstone,' said Byron, 'and beg her on bended knees, please, to let me have half a dozen agenda files at her earliest convenience?'

Down in the second-floor photocopy room, Zlob was working like a demon. He was already a quarter of the way through the stack of files, and forging ahead at the rate of a file a minute.

'All you need,' he explained to Nina, shouting above the whirr and clatter of the machine, 'is a good *system*. Got to organise yourself. These big fellows' (patting the rumbling, flashing giant affectionately on its pressed steel flanks) 'get through the work like a dose of salts . . . as long as you've got a good system. Old Stalin, now *he* understood the value of a good system.'

Nina was not really listening. She was busy collecting up the files he had finished with and disguising them in newspaper again. 'I'll take this lot back up to the agenda room,' she called out, 'and put them away in their proper order. It'll save time later on.'

'Very much a machine-minded man was Stalin,' Zlob rambled on, unaware that she had even spoken. 'A good technocrat at the helm, that's what the country needs.'

Clutching a pile of files that reached from her belly to her chin, Nina struggled out of the room unaided and walked briskly down the corridor to the landing. Stepping into the first lift to arrive, she found herself confronted by Freda Elphinstone, who was on her way back up to her seventh-floor office after a painful half-hour in the dentist's chair.

'Well, well, well,' Freda squawked suspiciously. 'You *are* carrying a lot of newspapers, Doctor Kabanova.'

'Aren't I just?'

Freda began to chortle with menace. 'Or are you just trying to hide something interesting under there?'

'Yes, I *am* hiding something as a matter of fact,' Nina confessed. 'I'm hiding a big pile of Wopec agenda files that I've been secretly copying for the Bulgarian foreign ministry.'

'Ho, ho, ho,' said Freda. 'Quite the comedienne, Doctor Kabanova. We shall have to get you doing a turn at the next annual general conference. If we ever *have* a next annual general conference, that is.'

'Faith, Miss Elphinstone,' said Nina, stepping out at the fourth floor. 'You must have faith.' She left her with a reassuring smile and hurried away down the purple corridor, where she collided head-on with Byron who was emerging from the CLAC room.

'Oh, Nina, you haven't seen Freda the Elephant, by any chance? I need the keys to the agenda room.'

'The what room? Why.'

'Superintendent Hatchet in there wants to take a look at some of the submissions.' He lowered his voice. 'Jesus, they're driving me nuts, those guys. They think we have a security problem in this place.'

'What, here?' said Nina. 'Are they crazy?'

'They're paranoid. All these security freaks are the same.'

'You just stay with them,' said Nina. 'I'll go and find Freda.'

'Thanks, Nina, I sure would appreciate that,' said Byron, and disappeared back into the CLAC room.

Nina scuttled down the corridor to the agenda room, dumped the files in the nearest cabinet and ran back to the landing, where she met Freda Elphinstone again, arriving hotly from the seventh floor.

'Where is Doctor Cleveland?' Freda demanded. 'He wants some Wopec files, I'm told.'

'He's in, ah, in the basement,' said Nina, pushing her back into the lift. 'In the mail-room.'

'I do have better things to do, you realise, than yo-yo up and down in the lifts all afternoon,' Freda muttered abrasively.

'Find Gladstone,' Nina advised. 'He always knows where Byron is.'

She got out at the second floor and Freda continued on down to the basement. Speeding back down the corridor and into the photocopy room, Nina found the place engulfed in dense black smoke with an acrid stench of burning rubber wafting its way around the second floor. Somewhere in the middle of the billowing mass Zlob was stumbling around, coughing his lungs inside out, trying to find the mains plug.

'Zlob!' shrieked Nina, standing in the open doorway trying to fan some of the smoke out into the corridor. 'Are you all right? What's happened? Are you hurt?'

'The poxy bitch!' he spluttered, dealing the crippled monster a vicious kick in the flanks. 'Going like the clappers, I was.

Then flash, bang!' He dealt it another kick. 'This cheap capitalist junk-heap blows up on me. Bastard!' He gave it one more kick for good measure.

'Well, give me the files, quickly! I must get them back upstairs.'

'The what?'

'The files, the files! Where are they?'

'God only knows.' His fumbling hands found the mains plug and wrenched it from the socket. 'Can't see a sodding thing.'

'Well, open the windows, idiot, before the smoke alarm goes off!'

'Before *who* goes off?' said Zlob, wiping the tears from his eyes, as a shrill two-tone bleeper began to warble throughout the building.

After a sulphurous exchange with Gladstone Shilling in the basement chauffeur's room, Freda Elphinstone returned to the fourth floor and stormed into the CLAC room with all the grace and charm of an armoured personnel carrier. However, she got no further than, 'Doctor Cleveland, I do have better things to do with my time than spend the afternoon yo-yoing up and down in the . . .' when the fire alarms began to *bloop-blarp* throughout the building.

Byron turned anxiously to Hatchard. 'What the hell's that, for Christ's sake?'

'I wouldn't know, would I, sir?' Hatchard replied calmly. 'You're the chief of security here. You tell me.'

Byron snatched up one of the many telephones in front of him and dialled the switchboard.

'*I'll* handle this,' said Freda, wresting the phone from his hand and all but dislocating his shoulder as she did so.

'Switchboard,' moaned Switchboard.

'This is Miss Elphinstone,' said Freda gravely, as if she were announcing the outbreak of war. 'What is that frightful noise?'

'Smoke alarm,' Switchboard replied. 'Second floor.'

'Why?'

'Dunno,' said Switchboard. 'Place is on fire, I suppose.' And sounded faintly bored by the prospect.

Freda rang off. 'The building's burning down,' she informed Byron coolly. 'The second floor's ablaze.'

'It can't be,' said Byron. 'This place is fire-proof.'

'They said that about the *Titanic*,' Freda snorted, making swiftly for the door. 'Evacuate the gels and follow me.'

Down in the photocopy room Nina was just piling the last few files onto the trolley when a security guard peered gingerly around the door with a walkie-talkie gibbering madly in his hand.

'It's OK, it's OK!' Nina shouted above the bleep of the alarm. 'There's no fire!'

'Yah, OK, john, OK,' echoed Zlob, stuffing the finished photocopies into his Drouzhba Dynamos bag.

'The machine's kaput, that's all,' said Nina, wheeling the laden trolley to the door. 'I'll call an engineer in the morning.'

'But he *is* an engineer,' said the security man, pointing at smoke-begrimed Zlob.

'*Da, da*,' said Zlob. 'Enzhineer, john. Mazhine kaboot.'

'No, he's just the maintenance guy,' said Nina. 'He services them, he doesn't mend them.'

'Well, what's he doing servicing *this* machine?' said the guard, wondering what it was that looked odd about RANK ЗЕROЖ ENGINEER. 'This ain't a Xerox.'

'It ain't?' said Nina.

'Unless my eyes are deceiving me,' said the security man. He pointed to the words KATSUBISHI MEGACOPIER 5000, embossed in large characters on a metal strip along the front of the machine, above MADE IN JAPAN.

'Ah, well, that explains it,' said Nina, manoeuvring the trolley safely out of the door and into the corridor beyond. 'It's Japanese.'

'Jabonese, huh?' said Zlob, dealing the machine one last vengeful kick and scuttling out behind Nina, his bag stuffed to bursting with photocopies.

The corridor outside was swarming with puzzled delegates and secretaries, wondering what all that blooping and blarping was supposed to mean. Nina pushed her way through them and clip-clopped down the corridor at a brisk trot to the lift landing, with dirty Zlob loping along in pursuit. As they reached the landing the alarm was switched off and the whole building fell deathly silent. Two lifts arrived simultaneously: one on the way up, the other on the way down. Zlob made straight for the one that was going down.

'Wrong one, idiot,' said Nina, beckoning him into the 'up' lift.

'Not bloody likely,' he retorted. 'I'm off while the going's good. It's a madhouse, this place.'

Nina was stunned by his cowardice. 'How am I supposed to lock up the agenda room if you run out on me now?' she hissed furiously, as the doors opened on the 'up' lift.

'That's your problem, comrade,' said Zlob, stepping into the 'down' lift but finding his path blocked by the emerging bulk of Freda Elphinstone, with Byron beside her like an obedient mongrel.

'You, man!' said Freda, advancing menacingly on Zlob. 'Where's the fire?'

'Uh, scusey, john,' muttered Zlob, cowering hastily into the 'up' lift with Nina. 'Enzhineer kaboot. Jabonese.' The lift doors closed and spared him further horrors.

'You're a bastard, Zlob,' said Nina bitterly.

'I know,' he said glumly. 'But life wasn't easy for a young woman after the war.'

Half the building had been evacuated by this time, on Freda Elphinstone's orders, and hundreds of people were cluttering up the pavements of Pall Mall, clinging resolutely to their afternoon tea and awaiting further instructions. Finding the whole of the fourth floor deserted, Nina and Zlob sped along to the agenda room, threw the files back into the cabinets, sorted them into some semblance of alphabetical order, locked up and sped back to the lifts.

'I'll take you down to the basement,' said Nina. 'You can go out the back way. You'll be less conspicuous. Where do you have to get to?'

Zlob shrugged. 'Dunno.'

'What do you mean, you don't know?'

'Kotsev said *you'd* know.'

'How should *I* know?'

'Don't ask me.'

'You'd better take them to Kotsev then.'

'Where's that?'

'Holland Park. Where I took you before.'

'I'll have to get a taxi. What's the address?'

A lift arrived. They stepped in and Nina pressed for the basement.

'Got a pen?'
He patted his pockets. 'Nope.'
'OK,' said Nina, 'repeat after me.' She enunciated in slow, precise English: 'Thirty-four . . .'
'Dirty-voor.'
'Holland Park Crescent . . .'
'Ollent Par Crescent.'
'W Eleven.'
'Darble-you leffen.'
'Got that?'
'Like a native,' said Zlob, and recited it back to her.
They arrived at the basement. She led him past the stores, the post room, the boiler house, the chauffeurs' room, and out into the car park. 'That leads through to St James's Square,' she said. 'You can pick up a taxi anywhere.'
'Righto,' said Zlob. 'Be seeing you then. Ta ra.' He lurched away across the car park with his bulging grip-bag, reciting 'Dirty-voor, Ollentparcrescent, darble-you leffen' over and over again, to the bewilderment of Les Nuttall, head car-washer, who was idly hosing down the director-general's Rolls-Royce nearby.
Nina was so relieved to have got the files safely back to the agenda room and to be rid of Zlob once and for all that she broke into song as she sauntered back to the lifts. On her melodious way she bumped into Gladstone Shilling emerging from the stores in high dudgeon.
'Hi, Gladstone.'
'Hi, Doc,' he grunted.
'You don't look happy.'
'To tell you the truth,' said Gladstone, 'I'm pretty damn mad.'
'Why? What's the matter?'
'Well, first of all, I'm down 'ere mindin' me own business, havin' me afternoon cuppa, and Miss Elphinstone come clumpin' in, lookin' for me governor. And she starts givin' me a right mouthful. Then, juss when I'm settlin' down for a quiet forty winks in me armchair, some clumsy herbert on the second floor sets off the fire alarm and we all have to evacuate the buildin'. And now I've got four crates of booze to load up for me governor and I juss discovered some thievin' beggar's made off with the parcel trolley.'

'With the what?' said Nina, who had a sneaking feeling there was something she and Zlob had forgotten.

'When I catch up with him he's goin' to get a right spankin', the mood I'm in, I tell you,' said Gladstone, stomping off towards the post room. 'Man, I feelin' right mad. Mad, mad, *mad* . . .'

Upstairs on the fourth floor, Freda Elphinstone had just unlocked the agenda room and was staring perplexed, at the vivid orange parcel trolley (STORES. DO NOT REMOVE) that had managed to find its way through a locked door and park itself very tidily on two sheets of the *Stara Zagora Evening Post*.

Less than a mile away, Zlob was clattering towards Hyde Park Corner in a black cab, anxiously checking the miserable contents of his wallet and wondering how to say 'Do you take roubles?' in English.

21

BY EASTER week, copies of every member-government's agenda submissions had been distributed to all the delegates at Halcyon House, and on Wednesday 12 April, with the first breath of spring in the air, the executive board met for their second unusual general session (UGS 2) to begin compiling the Wopec agenda.

The first question they had to consider was how many issues they could reasonably hope to debate in the course of the full five days; for if there was too little on the agenda the conference would lack international credibility, and if there was too much, Wopec could be accused of a purely superficial approach to world problems. So, after a morning's deliberation, they agreed that ten issues per day – fifty in the course of Wopec week overall – struck a reasonable balance. The member-governments, however, had submitted no fewer than three thousand, eight hundred and seventy-eight issues in total, covering over two thousand, five hundred pages of typescript. The second problem the board had to consider, then, was how to select just fifty of them to go on the final agenda.

At UGS 3 the following day, the Swiss delegate, Professor Sigismund Frankl, proposed that every issue should be discussed in turn, and its significance to world peace evaluated by merit points on a scale from one to ten. This seemed to most of his colleagues to be a somewhat laborious way of going about it, so Academician Rhoskov – who had been thoroughly briefed by the Kremlin that weekend – proposed a simpler and more democratic method of selection.

Firstly, Rhoskov explained, they should divide the world into five geographical zones: Europe, Africa, the Middle East, Asia and the Americas. Every single issue submitted by all one hundred and fifty-two member-governments should then be listed in its appropriate zone. Since by far the greater bulk of submissions consisted of duplications of issues that *other* member-governments were putting forward (the conflicts in South Africa and Palestine being the two most common examples), it was only just and democratic that the board should select those fifty issues – ten from each zone – that the majority of governments wished to discuss. Having sorted all the submissions into their geographical zones, said Rhoskov, they could then count the total number of governments proposing each individual issue, and draw up a 'top ten' for each zone – which, in turn, would automatically go onto the Wopec agenda. This would require a certain amount of secretarial assistance, he conceded, to cope with all the sorting, listing and counting; but once that initial work had been completed, all their agenda problems would be solved at a stroke.

That sounded eminently fair and sensible to the rest of the board; so after taking a formal vote of approval, Otello summoned Freda Elphinstone to the boardroom to estimate how long it would take the CLAC secretaries to do all the necessary sorting, listing and counting.

It did not, however, sound eminently fair or sensible to Freda. On the contrary, it sounded eminently unreasonable all round. Those dedicated young gels of hers, she protested, had been left sitting around for the past two months, eating yoghurt and booking their hols in Alicante, waiting for someone on the sixth floor to wake up and give them something to do. Now – just a few hours before Halcyon House closed down for Easter – the board suddenly wanted to saddle them with the twelve labours of Hercules, and expected everything to be done in Olympic time.

Not the twelve labours of Hercules, Otello replied placatingly, merely a little hard work . . . which was, after all, what they were paid to do.

That was as may be, Freda retorted, but her gels had only one pair of hands apiece and a job of that magnitude could take months, with all the retyping it would involve.

Perhaps then, Byron suggested, this was where all that expensive word processing equipment might come into its own. If she were to liaise with Melanie Boewater, who seemed to be fairly au fait with the miracles of modern technology . . .

It had nothing whatever to do with the public relations department, Freda interrupted testily. *She* was the senior secretary, not Melanie Boewater. And Britain had been doing perfectly well for the last thousand years or more, winning world wars and civilising the savages, without any help from floppy disks or nasty green v.d.u.s, thank you very much.

In that case, Otello suggested pleasantly, perhaps the senior secretary would care to give learned delegates a vague estimate of how long it might take her (happily) two-handed gels to do what the board were asking them to do?

Well, it was Maundy Thursday already, Freda replied, so nothing could possibly be started until after the Easter break. Then they would need at least three weeks to do all that sorting. Perhaps they could manage it by the first week of May, at a push.

Well, that, said Otello, was a significant improvement on *months* at any rate, and canvassed the opinions of the board. Delegates agreed that the first week of May – or even the second or third, for that matter – would still leave them ample time to sort the top fifty issues into a practicable timetable. Otello therefore asked Freda if she would be so good as to put the necessary work in hand at her earliest possible convenience.

That done, the board voted thirty-five–nil to congratulate themselves on another excellent week's work, gave themselves the rest of the day off and scampered away for their Easter holidays.

It would all end in tears, Freda predicted hopefully, as she kicked and elbowed her way onto the 16.12 home to Orpington that afternoon.

22

It was the warmest Easter Saturday on record according to Radio Four, but Byron was not easily fooled. While millions were out enjoying the traffic jams and sunning themselves on Hampstead Heath, he was at home in his apartment with the central heating on, tucking into a nourishing pile of Ben Bull's full-fat Meatiburgers and French fries, and trying to make sense of the washing machine.

Everyone was far too obsessed with health and fitness these days, in Byron's opinion. Too much health was not good for people, and that was a proven medical fact. One could hardly go for a drive round the park any more without finding some sweaty jogger gasping his last in the gutter or writhing about in the geraniums with a ruptured tendon. Squash players everywhere were pegging out with cardiac arrest, and millions of blissfully fat women the world over were starving themselves to asthenic misery in the faint hope of waking up one day with a body like Jane Fonda.

All this punishing physical activity and rabbit food was not only dangerous, Byron maintained, but totally unnecessary. He had been strenuously avoiding fresh air and physical exertion for over forty years now and could honestly claim that he had never felt healthy in his life. Besides, it was a well-known fact that the human body could get all the exercise it needed from plenty of good, regular sex. He personally was an adherent (lapsed, admittedly) to the gospel of aerobic fornication, whose foremost exegetist, Sherrilee Bloom, author of the international best-seller *Screwing for Health*, had revealed to the world the splendid news that the heart, lungs, intestines, and those other messy visceral bits and pieces essential to life could get all the exercise they needed from just half an hour's vigorous coition twice a day. This wisdom had been passed on to Byron by no less an authority than his own wife, Rosheen, who had been laid by a cast of thousands in her time and was still as peppy as a tigress at the ripe old age of thirty-three, and living testimony to its efficacy.

That said, Byron was not a perfect medical specimen, he was the first to admit. He suffered from a variety of serious nervous conditions, for a start. Those were brought on by stress, however, and stress was in the mind. And since Byron's mind was constantly operating at peak pressure he was prone to a large number of these serious nervous conditions, which manifested themselves in all kinds of fascinating ways. (They fascinated Byron, at any rate.) Sometimes they merely made his ankles swell, or brought on migraine, or triggered an attack of athlete's foot or a touch of urethritis. More commonly they gave him a selection of flatulence, dandruff, heartburn, haemorrhoids, tonsillitis, low blood pressure, earache, eczema, high blood pressure, constipation, bleeding gums or acne. They could even, upon occasion, leave him with a dull ache in the testes – which, confusingly enough, was also a symptom of lapsed adherence to the gospel of aerobic fornication. To confirm the aetiology of all these absorbing maladies, Byron spent a small fortune on the finest Harley Street charlatan that Unibore's money could buy; although the only effective remedy, in his experience, was a strict regimen of rest, in close proximity to a television set, with a plentiful supply of Ben Bull's Meatiburgers, and as far apart from Rosheen as geographically possible. In fact, since she had cleared off and gone to live with the ageing Baron deBauchery in sufficiently faraway Mougins, he had suffered remarkably few attacks, and those had been triggered only by recent traumas of an exceptional nature involving Packard, SPACUNA and the State Department.

The only thing to be said for his minuscule apartment in Hamilton Grove was that it was moderately well equipped for doing nothing in. Rosheen had filled the sitting-room with lots of soft things to lounge about in and make love on, all stuffed with high fire risk poly-something-or-other and upholstered in a restful shade of mal-de-mer green. She had bought television sets and laser-controlled audio systems for every room, and packed the kitchen with all the labour-saving devices that technology had to offer. Last, but not least, she had found Mrs O'Nobblin.

Mrs O'Nobblin was their charlady, an industrious Connemara woman of sixty-two robust years whom Rosheen had discovered under a table at Bridey McPadden's bar in the Kilburn High Road one payday night. Mrs O'Nobblin was a treasure *sans pareil*, and all the more so now that Rosheen had decamped for France. For Byron was not the domesticated type. Running his own bath and sloshing a few Meatiburgers around in a pan full of spitting lard was about as much as he could manage.

It had hit him particularly hard, then, when Mrs O'Nobblin had been taken ill that winter and had had to go into hospital for 'tests'. Byron was not privy to the precise nature of these 'tests' (and nor did he wish to be) but by Easter she had been in hospital for over two months and was obviously going to be there for some while longer. So *force majeure* had obliged him finally to turn a hand to housework and do something about the mess that had been accumulating remorselessly for the past two months. To his pleasant surprise, many of these domestic chores were not nearly as difficult as they first appeared. Shaking the duvet, for instance; washing up the frying pan; pushing the vacuum cleaner; all these and more could be mastered with just a little time and practice. The Supalectric Turbowasher, however, was something else altogether.

Washing day with a Supalectric Turbowasher was supposed to be fun. And *so* simple. Indeed, until now Byron had always found it to be so. After all, what could be simpler and more fun than leaving one's dirty washing strewn all over the place for somebody else to pick up and stuff into the all-capable Turbowasher? But with Mrs O'Nobblin away, the system had come to a standstill, and by Easter weekend he had virtually nothing left to wear. He had run out of socks and underwear some time ago, naturally, but had been buying fresh supplies every week to make up the deficiency. However, there was a limit to the amount of new underwear one could go on buying (even at Unibore's expense). Besides, the heaps of soiled laundry accumulating around the flat in strategic stockpiles were reaching unmanageable proportions and beginning to smell. So, rather than open a window and risk letting fresh air into the place, Byron had decided – much against his better judgement – to do battle with the Supalectric Turbowasher.

Byron was a metaphysicist, pure and simple, and neither understood nor cared very much for things electrical or mechanical. They, in turn, it had to be said, did not care greatly for him. Nevertheless, sophisticated though the Supalectric Turbowasher was, certain basic features of it were obvious even to a man blessed with Byron's advanced lack of expertise. It took him barely ten minutes, for example, to work out how to stuff its fat tinny guts with socks and underpants and tip a kilo of soap powder down the appropriate chute. But that was the easy part. From there on the thing needed programming; which involved doing something intelligent with a keyboard of twenty-two push-buttons, six dials and a Piccadilly Circus of bright lights.

The Supalectric Turbowasher was yet another miracle of Japanese technology, and according to the handbook the lucky owner would find that programming the machine was a 'labour of happiest ease'. All that was required was to follow the simple illustrated instructions. Making sense of the simple illustrated instructions, however, was *not* a labour of happiest ease. The handbook itself was still reasonably legible, though somewhat faded, after Mrs O'Nobblin had inadvertently given it a prewash at forty centigrade and seven minutes in the tumble drier; but it appeared to Byron to have been written in some arcane Anglo-Saxon patois known only to the manufacturing classes in Tokyo.

> 'Ease of washing simplicity may leave the housewife joy of freedom. Set the controls desirably at all times and get hot if wished. Prewash facility may easily be expressed. To make happen step-by-step the programme functions, see table 6, page 9.'

However, Byron could not find a table 6. There was a table 5 concerning water temperatures, and a table 7 suggesting recommended drying times; but no table 6. There was, indeed, a page 9. In fact, there were *two* pages 9 when one came to look more carefully. But nowhere in the entire handbook was there a table to make happen step-by-step the programme functions.

Byron therefore tried to make happen step-by-step his own programme functions. He pressed all the buttons in various combinations and twiddled the six dials. All to no avail.

Piccadilly Circus remained obstinately dark. Not a murmur of sound came from within. Not a dribble of water.

He tried telephoning the manufacturer's service department in Slough, but merely got a pre-recorded message wishing him a happy Easter. He then phoned an electrician in Kilburn, but the electrician told him he ought to call a plumber. So he rang the plumber and spoke to Mrs plumber, who said that Mr plumber and all the little plumbers were at Loftus Road, watching QPR take another thrashing, and suggested that he should try an electrician instead. As a last resort he rang Mrs O'Nobblin at the Royal Free Hospital; but all he got was *Mr* O'Nobblin, who said his wife was coming on a treat and had just dozed off for her afternoon nap.

This was not a good start to his Easter holiday. Ease of washing simplicity was not leaving him very much joy of freedom. So, at six o'clock, he gave the machine up as a dead loss, cooked himself another plateful of Meatiburgers and settled down to a relaxing evening's television. A quick glance at his handy, chuck-away *Guardian* TV guide revealed the usual feast of Easter family fun across all four channels:

BBC 1: *The Battle of the Minjh*
Film. World War Two Pacific naval bloodbath spectacular. (Repeat.)

BBC 2: *L'Agonie et l'Horreur*
Film. Harrowing saga of French opera star dying slowly of throat cancer. Subtitles. (Repeat.)

ITV: *I Married a Ghoul*
Film. True story of mass sex murderer and sadist, Herbie 'The Clown' Hernandez. (Repeat.)

CHANNEL 4: *Fifty Years of Worker Cooperatives in Latin America*
Film. Epic 4-hour Cuban documentary. Winner of the *Izvestia* Silver Plough award for truth at the 1977 Angolan film festival. Essential viewing. Subtitles. (First showing on British television.)

He was ten minutes into *L'Agonie et l'Horreur* when Annabelle telephoned from Salvation to wish him a happy Easter and give him the exciting news.

'What news, honey?'
'You'll never guess.'
'Then I give in.'
'I'll give you one clue: Pan Am.'
'Ah . . . Pan Am. Pan Am, Pan Am . . .' That rang a faint bell. 'Give me another clue.'
'June the twenty-fourth.'
That sounded ominously like Rosheen's birthday. No, that was on the twenty-first. 'June the twenty-fourth Pan Am?'
'Right.'
'I don't know, baby, I give in.'
'No, no, no, you've got to guess.'
'Well, make it easy for me, I've had a hard week.'
'OK, another clue: Noah . . . me . . . castle.'
Which sounded to Byron like French or Spanish, and he spoke neither.
'No . . . ami . . . qua . . . sol?'
'Right.'
'Ah . . . No, friend . . . by which . . . sun?'
'*Byron*!'
'Sweetheart?'
'You're so pathetic.'
'I am?'
'Noah and I are coming over to England for Wopec Day!'
'You are?'
'We just decided.'
'Baby, that's *won*derful!'
'We won't be able to stay very long. I mean, like Friday through Wednesday maybe. They're giving me a few days off school as it's such a special occasion.'
'Still, that's nearly a week. This is the best news I've had in ages.'
'Well, you're quite a personality in Salvation now, you know. You being a Southern boy and all, and taking over Unibore when Otello retires. And everyone keeps asking me when you're coming over to visit and when we're getting married and where we're going to live and . . .'
'They do?'
'Well, you know what small-town talk is like.'
'And you're genuinely definitely coming over?'

'To be with you on your big day. We wouldn't miss it for the world.'

'Well, that really has brightened up a lousy Easter, sweet-heart.'

'Why? What's happened? The State Department giving you a hard time?'

'No, no, no. It's just the washing machine.'

'The what?'

'My Supalectric Turbowasher.' He recounted the saga thus far, up to and including the fruitless telephone call to the slumbering Mrs O'Nobblin.

'You did check it was plugged in?' Annabelle presumed . . . a trifle rashly perhaps.

'What do you mean?'

'There should be a flex trailing out of the back with three brass prongs on the end. It goes into a socket on the wall.'

'Honey, I know what a plug is, for Christ's sake. Sure I checked it was plugged in.'

'And switched on?'

'Angel, what do you take me for?'

She didn't say.

As soon as she had rung off, Byron crept furtively back to the kitchen and peered behind the Turbowasher, where he found a length of flex and three brass prongs dangling limply to the floor. He picked it up, plugged it in and switched on. *Still* nothing happened.

Fed up with the sight of the thing, he poured himself a large Scotch, retired to the sitting-room and caught the last forty minutes of *I Married a Ghoul*, which could yet prove to be his epitaph, he reflected. Cupid certainly lacked imagination; he should have matched Herbie 'The Clown' Hernandez with Rosheen 'The Scream' O'Halloran. Herbie wouldn't have lasted the night.

Still, the weekend had brought its compensations. On the plus side, Annabelle was coming over for Wopec Day. Though on the minus side, he had promised to talk about nitty-gritty matters like matrimony the next time they were together. Then again, on the plus side, Rosheen had at least conceded the *possibility* of a quick divorce, and now it was merely a question of haggling her down in price from a figure approaching the federal trade deficit to a few thousand dollars' worth of lawyers fees. That being the case, he was thinking in bed that night, there could be no real harm, surely, in sharing the secret (that he was still married) with Annabelle? After all, she was such a kind and understanding Christian soul, and it was not necessary for Noah to be told.

He awoke the following day, Easter Sunday, feeling spiritually refreshed and refortified by his decision to confess all to his beloved, and spent the morning full of the joys of spring, contemplating the most tactful way of broaching the subject and trying to make the Supalectric Turbowasher do something. He did not much care *what* it did by this time, if it would just do *some*thing. Yet still it defied every combination of dial-twiddling and button-pushing that he could think of and remained perversely lifeless. He even tried phoning Mrs O'Nobblin again at the hospital, but she was still asleep, a nurse informed him. He had the disquieting notion that she had been asleep ever since Good Friday and wondered if someone ought not to bring that to the attention of a doctor. With some reluctance he decided finally to let sleeping chars lie; he had quite enough to worry about as it was, without provoking an even bigger crisis in the National Health Service.

The answer, it occurred to him in one of those blinding flashes of genius to which he was so prone, was to call Rosheen. He had not heard a squeak out of her since March – not so much as one small obscenity. The obvious way to hurry this divorce along without aggravating her unduly was to call her on some apparently unrelated pretext . . . such as how to make happen the programme functions of his Supastatic Turbowasher. It was she who had bought the damn thing in the first place, anyway.

23

IT WAS a filthy grey day all over the Côte d'Azur, and fine rain was drizzling down on the Château Montcalme, where Rosheen and her housemaid were tucked up in bed trying to find their J-Zones.

The J-Zone was a tiny hyper-erogenous spot on the female body, many times more sensitive than all the other erogenous zones put together. Its existence had recently been revealed to the world by that renowned sexologist, Sherrilee Bloom (author of *Screwing for Health*) in her latest best-selling opus: *Your J-Zone*.

The J (for joy) Zone was not a new discovery. On the contrary, it had been known for many centuries to the Shocataw Indians, who had called it the *teeheepaca* – literally, 'tee-hee spot'. Sadly the Shocataw nation had become extinct by the eighteenth century (possibly, Ms Bloom conjectured, because all the squaws had aroused themselves to such heights of libidinous desire with their teeheepacas that they had left a whole generation of virile braves shagged out beyond repair) and the secret of the amazing J-Zone had died with them.

Happily for womankind, however, Sherrilee Bloom – former go-go dancer, croupier and mother of several from Reno, Nevada – had rediscovered the secret in the course of one of her many scientific expeditions in Central America. Strolling through the mountainous rainforests of Oaxaca in southern Mexico one morning, she had happened upon a remote cave in the foothills of the Sierra Madre del Sur, where a toothless old mestizo crone sat stirring a pot of broth over a wood fire. This shrivelled ancient – who, by happy chance, spoke excellent English – had shared with Ms Bloom the long-forgotten wisdom of her ancestors, the Shocataws, and the secret of the teeheepaca. Now, motivated solely by a selfless desire to enhance the sexual pleasure of all women everywhere, and without the remotest interest in the millions of dollars that were forcing their way into her many bank accounts, Ms Bloom was sharing her treasury of knowledge with the world in two hundred and forty-five easy-to-read pages at a price that any fool could afford.

The J-Zone was a remarkable little thing. Every woman had one, but only one, and it was very, very small. Which was probably as well for the future of humankind, bearing in mind the fate of the Shocataw Indians. The zone could be almost anywhere on the body, its precise location varying enormously from woman to woman, and, having been dormant in most races for thousands of years, it had to be found and gently reawakened – which was half the fun of the thing, according to Ms Bloom.

Fun notwithstanding, the J-Zone was frustratingly elusive. After several weeks of exhaustive bodily probing, Rosheen reluctantly had to admit, in all frankness, that she had not even come within smiling distance of her teeheepaca. So she sent for her new housemaid, Chantal, and asked her to see if she could find *her* teeheepaca. Chantal, a strapping young wench from the Auvergne, built like a Charollais and frisky as a colt, spent several days and nights exploring the formidable rolling land mass of her body. But all to no avail.

So, that cold grey Easter Sunday, while monsieur le baron sat cooped up in his study, working on his latest academic treatise, *Une Histoire Ontologique du Troilisme au 14ème Siècle*, Rosheen and Chantal withdrew to the boudoir for the afternoon, to go through every last detail of Sherrilee Bloom's fun-packed text to see if some vital nugget of information might yet have eluded them. They had just discovered an illuminating little footnote that they had not seen before, when the telephone began to ring . . . and went on ringing and ringing until Rosheen was sufficiently exasperated to answer it.

'*Oui*, allo?'

'Hi, sweetie.'

'Byron?'

'You saw through my disguise.'

'How is it you always manage to ring me at the worst possible time?'

'Sheer practice. Why? Are you in the middle of lunch?'

'No, I'm in bed.'

'Why? Are you sick?'

'Don't sound so hopeful. I'm busy.'

'Doing what?'

'Looking for my J-Zone, if you must know.'

'Why?'

'Byron, will you quit saying "why"? I'm looking for it because I want to find it, that's why.'

'Well, is it so urgent? Do you have to find it right now, this minute?'

'If I didn't want to find it, I wouldn't be looking for it, would I?'

'Well, where did you leave it?'
'I didn't leave it anywhere. My *J-Zone*, dummy.'
'OK, OK. I'm only trying to help. Where did you lose it?'
'I haven't lost it.'
'Then why are you looking for it?'
'You can't lose your J-Zone, asshole.'
'So how come you can't find it?'
'Look, just shut up about it, OK?'
'Why? What's the problem?'
'Byron, if you say "why" one more time I'm going to hang up on you.'
'Ah . . . *pourquoi*? I mean, what did I say wrong?'
'Byron — '
'What is Jayzone, anyhow? Is that the stuff you pour down the can at night?'
'Byron?'
'Honey?'
'If you're trying to get me mad, you're wasting your time.'
'You sound just a little mad, sweetie. What's the matter?'
'I'm not mad at all. Matter of fact, I'm really mellow right now.'
'You don't sound all that mellow.'
'Well, I feel it.'
'You sound a little truculent.'
'Byron, will you just say what you want, then ring off. I'm really very busy right now.'
'It's about the washing machine.'
'The what?'
'The washer. You know, that Turbolectric Supaheap. The one they had to hoist in through the window on a crane.'
'What are you talking about? It came up in the elevator like everything else.'
'You sure?'
'Sure.'
Pause.
'Well, what came in through the dining-room window?'
'The piano.'
'Are you absolutely positive?'
'The crane driver was Pat, the day was Tuesday, the weather was pissing. What else do you want to know?'
'How does it work?'

'What do you mean, how does it work?'
'Well, what do I press, push, kick, whatever? What makes what do what?'
'Are you putting me on? Blacks are sharps, whites are naturals. The left pedal's soft —'
'I'm talking about the washer, sweetie, not the Bechstein.'
'What do you want to fool around with that for?'
'Mrs O'Nobblin's off sick.'
'What's wrong with her?'
'She's in hospital.'
'That's not what I asked.'
'Something to do with her gall bladder, or thyroid, or round that area anyhow.'
'Byron, the gall bladder is not remotely near the thyroid.'
'Well, that could be her problem then.'
'The thyroid is in the neck.'
'Well, what's near the gall bladder?'
'The liver.'
'Liver doesn't begin with a T, honey.'
'I know that, dogbrain. I agree I'm not Einstein but I do know that liver does not begin with a T.'
'Well, whatever she's got begins with a T.'
'So how do you get gall bladder?'
'How the hell should I know? I'm not a doctor. Maybe from a virus, or too much gin or something. Anyhow, whatever she's got, she's been away the past couple of months and the laundry's piling up. So I figured I'd better give the old Turbowasher a workout. But the handbook doesn't make any sense. It's written in a kind of roundeye-speak-with-forked-tongue language.'
'Hold on. You're ringing me all the way from London just to ask me how to work the Turbowasher?'
'Right.'
'You've got to be kidding?'
'No, no, this is for real. I'm right out of clean underwear and it's Easter weekend.'
'Byron, it's a whole year since I worked that thing, I don't remember the first thing about it.'
'You don't?'
'I don't even remember what it looks like.'
'You want me to describe it to you?'

'If this is your idea of a joke, calling me up in the middle of the afternoon just to ask about the washer, I'm hanging up.'

'Well, hang on, don't you even want to talk about the divorce while I'm on the line?'

'No. If you've got anything new to say you can tell me face to face on Wopec Day. So long. Happy Laundromat.'

'Face to face on *what* did you just say?'

'Guy and I are going to be in England for Wopec Day. If you want to talk, you can talk then.'

'What does Guy want to come to Wopec Day for?'

'He wants to see all his old friends again.'

'Again? But he's only just retired.'

'So? Everybody likes an annual reunion from time to time.'

'But he only left twelve months ago.'

'Well, how often do you have an annual reunion, schmucko?'

'Rosheen, I'm sorry, but it doesn't seem quite right. The retired French delegate turning up at a prestigious royal occasion with the ex-wife of the new director-general.'

'*Wife*, Byron. I'm still your wife. Don't ex me yet.'

'Well, wife then. That's even worse. My wife turning up with the retired French delegate. Jesus.'

'On the contrary. I think it's charming. It shows there are no hard feelings between us.'

'But sweetheart, there are a *lot* of hard feelings. That is being very hypocritical.'

'Why? And since we're on the subject, who are *you* going to be with?'

'No one special.'

'The director-general-elect will be attending this prestigious royal occasion without a consort?'

'Well, since you mention it, I did have one but she snuck off with a geriatric Frog.'

'Leave Guy out of this.'

'I'd love to, honey, but I can't. He's turning up on Wopec Day with my wife.'

'*Ex*-wife, angel, ex-wife. Don't start giving me all that schmaltzy 'wifey' shit.'

'Well, if I'm going to be there on my own I think Guy might at least have the decency to come on his own as well.'

'Why? Why should I miss out just because you're going

through a dignity crisis? I want to meet HRH, same as the rest of them.'

'You? Meet HRH? Are you out of your mind? You don't *meet* HRHs, you get presented to them. What the hell makes you think *you'd* ever get presented?'

'Guy is one of the last descendants of Louis the Sixteenth. HRH will be damn glad to have a kindred spirit around. Europe's running out of royals. These bluebloods have to stick together.'

'And what do you think HRH is going to make of it? Louis the Sixteenth's six-times great-nephew, twice removed and probably illegitimate, turning up with my own lousy wife.'

'*Ex*-wife, Byron baby, your own lousy ex-wife, for the thousandth time.'

'Well, if you're so keen on being my ex-wife, where's my goddam divorce?'

'My, my, my. Me, me, me. Really, Byron, all you ever seem to think about these days is yourself. You were such a giving, caring man when I first married you . . .'

24

BYRON FELT ill for the rest of the day. Rosheen and Annabelle face to face at Wopec Day . . . in front of their royal highnesses and the whole world's press, television cameras and all. It didn't bear thinking about. Rosheen saw no point in attending any grand social event unless there was a sporting chance of wrecking it or making a public spectacle of herself. If she was in the mood she could hit Wopec like an MX missile.

He went to bed early with a case of Bourbon and a serious nervous condition. Maybe he could persuade Annabelle to change her mind. Or maybe Guy would drive off a corniche in the next few weeks . . . but just a *little* one, or there'd be nothing left of him to keep Rosheen safely out of harm's way down there at the château deBauchery.

He eventually worried himself to sleep and had a monstrous dream about a nursery school where a tiny tot in studded leather diapers set fire to her teacher's dress. The tiny tot was Rosheen; the teacher was Annabelle. He awoke just after midnight in a much sweat and got up to turn down the central heating. As he tottered sleepily along the hall passage he became conscious of a rhythmic whining noise in his ears. Presuming it to be an interesting new symptom of his latest serious nervous condition, he tottered into the kitchen to find himself ankle-deep in warm soap suds. The Supalectric Turbowasher had come miraculously to life at last. Quite what he had done to make happen step-by-step the programme functions he had no idea, but six week's supply of socks, shirts and underwear were now splish-sploshing happily about in an abundance of rich white later, an ever greater abundance of which was spewing forth through the soap hatch and pouring down all over the floor in a copious and ever deepening snowscape. Byron left the whole thing to its own diabolical devices, switched off the heating and paddled back to bed.

He awoke again at six to the full horrors of sunrise and the dawn chorus. Somewhere in the just-audible distance he could still hear that same rhythmic whining noise. Getting up and fumbling his semi-somnambulant way to the kitchen to investigate, he found the place knee-deep in foam, and Piccadilly Circus a blaze of winking lights. Somewhere inside the Turbomonster his socks and shirts and underwear were still splish-sploshing about to their hearts' content. Byron crept back to bed. It was all a passing nightmare. Any minute now he would wake up and find himself safe and snug under the duvet on a nice wet bank-holiday Monday, with not a single living bird within a mile of St John's Wood, and none of this would have happened.

Sure enough, he awoke at half past nine on Easter Monday, safe and snug under the duvet . . . With the starlings screeching a cantata in the eaves, and the apartment in the grip of a baby earthquake. Venturing into the kitchen with a deepening sense of foreboding, Byron found the Turboführer on the rampage. After ten hours of relentless washing, his clothes were now being spun with demoniacal fury. The machine was jigging up and down in a frenetic war dance. Having decided to go walkabout, constrained only by the leash of its hoses, it was transmitting powerful tremors right through the apartment . . . and probably half way down Hamilton Grove, for all he knew. Estimates of force four or five on the Richter scale flashed through Byron's troubled mind.

He peered despairingly into the port-hole for a while, in the hope of catching one last glimpse of the remains of his laundry, then abandoned the kitchen, broke the habit of a lifetime and went to Brighton for the day.

25

BENEATH THE dim light of a single grease- and filth-encrusted bulb, the officers and men of Number One Commando, the Sandhustan People's Liberation Army, were seated round the kitchen table in the attic flat above Muktar's all-night grocery store in Southall, studying an Esso road map of southern England.

'This,' said Dubbi, drawing a red cross on the map, 'is Allshott. About forty miles from here.'

'What is it?' asked Sharaq. 'A town?'

'A small village,' Dubbi replied, 'in what the English call the *commuter belt*.'

'What is *commuter*?' enquired Pungal.

'A commuter,' said Dubbi, with the authority of one who had once spent several months sweeping the platforms at Holborn Viaduct, 'is a person who lives in a place like Allshott and travels to work in London every day in silence, with an umbrella and a small case containing the *Daily Telegraph*.'

Pungal nodded, none the wiser.

'And Carnage Castle?' said Sharaq.

'Is two miles from the village.' Dubbi pointed to it with his pen. 'The boat for your escape to France is berthed at a place called Clympton-on-Solent, about two hours' drive away.' He pointed to another red cross on the Hampshire coast. 'So the ideal location for your field headquarters would be somewhere between the two.'

Sharaq agreed. 'So what have you found?'

'A farm in secluded countryside, just here, near Chipton Oxfold.' Dubbi pointed to a village he had ringed on the map. 'About five miles from the town of Hodditon St Mary.'

'How big is this farm?' said Sharaq.

'About fifty hectares. But there's a smallholding in one corner of it, at a spot called Oxfold Woods. Just a few fields and some derelict buildings. The whole property is to be sold at auction in the autumn, but the agents would consider letting the smallholding on short lease if they thought you were genuinely interested in bidding for the lot.'

'But are there no people farming on the rest of the land?' asked Pungal.

'No. It has been abandoned,' said Dubbi. 'The place is quite deserted.'

'Abandoned?' Sharaq was taken aback. At home in Sandhustan every square metre of fertile land was put to productive use. 'Why? Is there a water shortage?'

Dubbi shook his head. 'EEC.'

'What is EEC?' asked Pungal. 'A disease?'

'A sort of disease,' said Dubbi. 'EEC is a great puzzle to everyone. It's a kind of bank that gives away millions of pounds that nobody can afford, to pay farmers to produce the largest possible quantity of food that nobody will ever want, at the highest possible price.'

Pungal wondered if this was some sort of obscure English riddle. 'What do they do with it, if nobody wants it?'

'This is the great mystery,' said Dubbi. 'They hide it.'

'Hide it?' said Pungal. 'Where?'

'All over the place. There are secret mountains of butter and beef. Great lakes full of milk and wine. Underground warehouses packed with cheese and grain. All hidden away out of sight, so that everyone can pretend it isn't there.'

'What for?' said Sharaq.

Dubbi shrugged. 'No one seems to know.'

'And is that all that happens in EEC, Mr Muktar, sir?' enquired Nurg, who had been half starved since birth and took it as a fact of life that the higher castes would always hoard the fat of the land.

'Not quite,' said Dubbi. 'It gets curiouser still. Once a year everyone in EEC goes potty.'

'What do they do?' asked Pungal, who thought that everyone sounded quite potty enough as it was.

'All the farmers start pouring their milk down the drain, and throwing their meat into the sea, and dumping their eggs on the public highway, and burning other people's lorries. And they go on doing that until the big wise men who control EEC agree to pay them even more money that nobody can afford, to produce even more food that nobody will ever want, at an even more ridiculous price.'

'Then what?' said Pungal, who didn't believe a word of it.

'Then the minister of agriculture appears on television and tells everyone that it's a victory for common sense.'

'In that case,' said Sharaq, who had heard all sorts of bewildering tales about this EEC, 'why has everyone abandoned the farm at Chipton Oxfold?'

'Because EEC has run out of lakes in which to hide all the milk that nobody will ever want. So the farmers are selling up and turning instead to good old DHSS.'

'And what, Mr Muktar, sir,' enquired Nurg, 'is DHSS?'

'Ah now, DHSS,' said Dubbi gleefully, 'is another amazing British cash-dispensing institution . . .'

It was lunchtime on market day in the historic country town of Hodditon St Mary, famous for its old ladies, curdled cream and retired naval commanders. Dubbi parked his scruffy Cortina amongst an armada of dented cattle trucks on Market Street. A hundred yards away, down a quiet cobbled lane, he and Sharaq came upon the premises of Ratblat, Steed and Brooks, auctioneers, valuers and estate agents. Entering, they found the sole occupant, Edwin Ratblat F.S.V.A, up to his eyes in the *Sporting Life*, checking the runners and riders at Kempton Park.

'A very good morning to you, sir,' Dubbi greeted him. 'We are down from London. Perhaps you can assist us.'

Taking them to be a pair of foreign tourists, lost in a strange country and in need of help, Ratblat said: 'Sorry, squire, closed for lunch,' and showed them the door.

'No, no, sir,' said Dubbi. 'We have come concerning the farm at Chipton Oxfold. I telephoned your good Mr Brooks last week. Smith's the name. Harry Smith.'

Ratblat frowned vaguely recalling the enquiry. 'Ahhh, yes. Some kind of religious outfit, if memory serves.'

'Indeed, sir,' said Dubbi, 'but if you are closed for lunch . . .'

'Christ no,' said Ratblat, who hadn't managed to sell so much as a garden shed all year. 'Never touch the stuff.' He pushed them into a pair of comfortable armchairs and continued: 'What sort of farming are you interested in then, gents?'

'We are not farming as such,' Sharaq replied. 'Not yet. We are looking for a site for a new ashram, here in the south of England. Farming may come later.'

'Ashram?' said Ratblat – prompted by an immediate association of ideas to start scavenging round the office for a cigarette.

'A holy retreat,' explained Sharaq. 'We are devoted followers of His Divine Grace, Swami Dabhulatra.'

Ratblat rescued a dog-end from his wastebin and singed the hairs of his nostrils trying to light it. 'From that Harry Krishny mob, are you?' he enquired – though not unpleasantly, for, from what he had heard, Harry Krishny had a different Roller for every day of the week and devoured real estate like cornflakes.

'We are all seeking Krishna consciousness, friend,' said Sharaq. 'But we are not who you are thinking of. We are disciples of another swami.'

'And what sort of accommodation would you require, then?' asked Ratblat, wondering if he could persuade them to buy an even bigger dump in even worse condition than Lower Oxfold Farm. Ratblat, Steed and Brooks had a fine portfolio of freehold ruins available at a variety of extortionate prices.

'We have few material needs,' replied Sharaq. 'A roof over our heads. A little land to grow vegetables. Peace and quiet. Seclusion. And perhaps some sort of cowshed or barn to keep our people in.'

'Keep *who* in?' said Ratblat, choking on his dog-end and dunking it to death in the dregs of his mid-morning tea.

'Our disciples, our young followers,' said Sharaq. 'We need some kind of outbuilding that we could convert into a dormitory for them.'

'Then look no further, gents,' said Ratblat, savouring the prospect of a long and fruitful association with the great Harry Krishny. 'We have the very property you and your Mr K have been dreaming of . . .'

About seven miles from Hodditon St Mary, Ratblat swung his Hillman Husky off the winding country lane and drove along a deeply potholed cart track through Oxfold Woods. Ploughing on for half a mile through a bonnet-high overgrowth of weeds and brambles, they came eventually to a derelict farmyard with a stagnant duckpond, a clutch of crumbling outbuildings and a tumbledown farmhouse.

'A deceptively spacious character residence,' said Ratblat, drawing up in front of a vermin-infested pile that looked like something the Royal Artillery had been playing with. 'Offering ample scope for further improvement. Barns. Sheds. Commodious piggery in excellent order and ideal for conversion to residential purposes. All in all, a rare opportunity, gents, which my clients would be prepared to lease for six months, prior to auction, with full use of five acres of prime bog and woodland, at the giveaway consideration of five thousand pounds, to include all rates and services, payable cash in advance.'

'Truly a gem of potential, my friend,' agreed Sharaq, climbing out of the Husky and putting his foot through a rotting sheep's carcase. 'And well off the beaten track.'

'A trifle on the secluded side,' conceded Ratblat. 'But I'm sure that would be no problem to a resourceful man like your Mr Krishny.'

'Indeed not,' said Sharaq. 'Our transport officers are in London attending to such matters at this very time.'

Seventy miles away, in the east London breaker's yard of Horace Shadbarge and Son, scrap metal merchants, Engineer-Sergeant Guppi Pungal was lying flat on his back inspecting the underside of a thirty-two-year-old pantechnicon – whilom workhorse for Pickfords Removals Limited, and subsequently thrashed several times around the clock by a succession of loving cowboys.

'Genuine forty-six thousand miles,' said swarthy Shadbarge to bony Nurg. 'Museum piece. Concours condition.'

Nurg nodded, very impressed. Certainly a fine conveyance. It was unusual in his experience to see a lorry with a tyre on every wheel.

'One titled owner,' Shadbarge went on, pushing his luck. 'Been in his lordship's private collection since 1962. Hardly touched the Queen's highway. Stand on me.'

Pungal emerged from beneath the cab and brushed the grit off his overalls. 'Five hundred,' he offered Shadbarge.

Shadbarge looked staggered. 'Five *'undred*? Are you getting me at it? That's a collector's item, a genuine Pickfords original. One of the last surviving. Fifteen 'undred, and that's a bleedin' giveaway.'

'Six hundred,' said Pungal, not impressed.

'Leave it out,' scoffed Shadbarge. 'That's not a truck, mate, that's a gilt-edged investment. The price can only rocket with the passing of time. The sky's the limit. Twelve 'undred, my final offer.'

Pungal shook his head. 'Six.'

'Twelve 'undred, that is,' Shadbarge continued, 'less your buyer's wholesale vending discount . . . Eleven twenty-five, and that's rock bottom.'

'Six fifty. That's all I have, my friend.'

'Eleven twenty-five . . . less your first purchase premium rebate . . . works out at ten fifty. Call it a round grand.'

'Not worth a penny over seven hundred,' said Pungal resolutely. 'I am army vehicle expert, my friend. I know all about these trucks, I assure you.'

'Ah, well, that's ten per cent off for trade then,' said Shadbarge. 'To you, nine 'undred.'

'Eight.'

'Eight and a half with derv in the tank. And I'm a fool to meself.'

'Eight twenty-five, cash on the nail,' said Pungal.

'You strike a bloody 'ard bargain, chief,' said Shadbarge, clasping Pungal's outstretched hand. 'Eight and a quarter it is, then.'

'And the guarantee?' asked Pungal.

'Every vehicle,' Shadbarge assured him, 'comes with a full week's unwritten guarantee, exclusive parts and labour.'

'Then it's a deal, my friend.' Pungal took a wad of banknotes from a pocket in his overalls.

'A decision you'll never regret, pal,' said Shadbarge, holding out an oily palm for Pungal's grubby tenners.

'So much for smartarse cockneys,' snickered Pungal, as they drove out of the yard and turned south towards East India Dock Road.

'Why?' said Nurg. 'How much money do we really have?'

'Twelve hundred pounds!' crowed gleeful Pungal. 'And I knocked him down from fifteen to eight twenty-five!'

'Sergeant Pungal, sir, you are truly a master of business!' exclaimed Nurg, as the near-side door fell off and he disappeared from the cab in a flurry of spindly limbs.

'Strange,' mused Pungal, as the truck gathered speed when he crushed the brake pedal to the floor.

26

JERICHO ENGINEER had been having the devil's own time trying to make contact with the dreaded Boatman. 'Make touch' was all he had said; he had not said *how*. Jericho had tried everything. He had telexed SPIS headquarters at Joy of Socialist Labour Gaol. He had telephoned the Interior Ministry in Port Paradise. He had even cabled the chief of intelligence, Brigadier Elisha Longfellow, in person. But nobody seemed to know who Colonel Boatman was.

After a time he had begun to wonder whether Boatman existed any more. He could easily have been liquidated and no one would have been any the wiser. After all, these were tough times for the hawk-eyed men of SPIS. Deviationist scum were everywhere, according to the party daily, *Pure Truth*, pullulating like bacteria, disseminating their vile creed of revisionism and counter-revolution. They could infect anyone at any time. Remorseless purgation was essential to keep society clean and healthy. Liquidation was the golden key to a pure and beautiful new world. Vigilance was vital. No one – not even Colonel Boatman – could be above suspicion. But Boatman was from Section Five; and Section Five did all the liquidating. So, if no one was above suspicion, who then liquidated Section Five, Jericho wondered? Perhaps Colonel Boatman had liquidated himself as a wise precaution.

Then, late one Friday afternoon at the end of April, Jericho arrived home at his Mayfair mansion after an arduous day's work with CLAC, and there was the colonel looking as mean and bald as ever. He was waiting in the drawing-room, standing by the window, gazing out into the twilight in his customary safari suit and sunglasses, hands clasped behind his back and fingers drubbing impatiently on an invisible drum.

'My dear Colonel, sir!' Jericho greeted him joyfully, as if he had been longing for this moment for every waking second of the last three weeks.

'You made touch,' said Boatman, without turning.

'The CLAC committee have finalised the arrangements for Wopec Day, Colonel sir. You asked for the details as soon as they were ready.'

'Specify.'

'The papers are in my study, Colonel sir.'

'Produce.'

'Sir, Colonel sir.' Jericho bowed rapidly several times and waddled away at speed to his study. Opening a small safe hidden behind an early Degas on the chimney breast, he removed a dossier of papers from among the fat bundles of hard currency, bearer bonds and open-dated tickets to Rio de Janeiro, and hurried back to the drawing room. He found Boatman sitting bolt upright in a chair by the garden window. He was as still as a waxwork, and with his dark glasses on it was even possible to hope that he might have just expired.

'I have here,' said Jericho, tiptoeing towards Boatman for fear that the slightest unnecessary sound might bring him back to life, 'a list of all the guests who have been sent personal invitations to Wopec Day.'

'Quantify,' said Boatman.

'About ten thousand, worldwide.' Jericho handed him an eighty-six page schedule of distinguished names. 'But we expect less than half that number to attend.'

Boatman flipped idly through the schedule. 'And when do the official ceremonies begin?'

'At about two o'clock, when their royal highnesses arrive, Colonel sir.'

'Expatiate.'

'After the board of Unibore and other important persons have been presented to the royals, everyone will assemble on the south terrace of the castle. There will then be about half an hour of speeches, beginning at half past two. Otello Fabrizi will speak first and tell everyone what the Wopec congress is all about. Then the UN secretary-general will get up and tell everyone what a fine director-general Professor Fabrizi has been and present him with a surprise farewell gift from the United Nations. And finally, HRH will make the inaugural speech and declare the congress open. After that, everyone will walk across the south lawns to a special hole in the ground and HRH will plant an olive tree for world peace to commemorate the occasion.'

'And all this has been agreed with the palace?'

'With Blah-blah, sir, Colonel sir.'

'Blah-blah?' said Boatman. 'What is Blah-blah?'

'A person, sir. A very small person. Some palace menial.'

Blah-blah, in fact, was a bustling, jolly little chap who was responsible for making sure that HRH did not end up on a plane for Caracas when he was due to open a maternity clinic in Aberystwyth, or learn 'welcome to England' in Gujarati when he was about to meet the chief minister of the Turks and Caicos Islands. He spoke very quickly and without opening his jaws, and no one at Halcyon House had managed to catch his name. But he answered to Blah-blah (as in Blaire-Blaire) so Blah-blah he had become.

'And after the planting of the olive tree?' Boatman enquired.

'The HRHs will go on a walkabout in the castle grounds,' said Jericho, 'where there will be a fête, folk dancing, children's games, sporting contests, and sundry entertainments. At about four o'clock they will take tea on the south terrace with the Wopec delegates and international VIPs. And they are expected to leave at about half past five.'

'And what security arrangements have been made?'

'Special Branch will be taking care of the HRHs, Colonel. Scotland Yard's Diplomatic Protection Group will be looking after the VIPs. And the local county police will handle the rest.'

'Will they all be on duty in the evening as well?'

'No, sir. Special Branch will go when the royals go. And most of the DPG men will knock off when the VIPs leave. Four officers will be on duty in the castle for the director-general's banquet. And the local Lydhurst police will be covering the public barbecue and fireworks display. But that won't start until later and there will be no distinguished guests as far as we know.'

'And the banquet?'

'I have a copy of the full guest-list here. Seventeen ambassadors, seven high commissioners, their wives/consorts, and the

Fabrizis. Fifty in all. The HRHs will not be attending.' Jericho handed him the list. 'They'll be arriving from eight o'clock onwards. There'll be cocktails in the grand drawing-room and dinner will be in the great eating room at nine.'

'And what about staff?' said Boatman. 'There are no servants living at the castle any more, are there?'

'Only one,' said Jericho. 'A drudge called Aubrey Wormslow, batman to the late General Sir Sackville Sterling-Pallgrave. But his brother Vernon runs a company called Rent-a-Footman Limited, which hires out butlers and waiters and suchlike. Professor Fabrizi has booked fifteen of them for the evening.'

'And the food?'

'The Department of the Environment has installed modern kitchens in the castle, Colonel sir, and the Fabrizis have engaged an Italian chef by the name of Fariscagni. You'll find all the information on this special banquet supplement here which Fabrizi has prepared for the CLAC committee.' He passed a photocopy of it to Boatman.

Boatman read it through from beginning to end. Jericho waited nervously for his reaction. 'Good,' said Boatman finally. He looked up, and for one disconcerting moment Jericho thought the man was actually going to smile. 'Excellent. Well done, Squadron Leader.'

Jericho beamed with gratitude, sweating buckets and loath to spoil the magic of the moment by pointing out that Hudson Butcher had promoted him to air vice-marshal since that daring air raid on the public conveniences in Port Paradise.

'Could there be any changes to these arrangements?' Boatman asked.

'Possibly in matters of minor detail, Colonel sir. But the main schedule of events has been agreed by CLAC and the executive board, and cleared with the DoE and the palace.'

'If there are any changes at all — '

'You'll be the first to know, Colonel sir.'

'Excellent.' Boatman collected all the papers together and had one last thought. 'Just one final matter. The Wopec agenda.'

'Colonel sir?'

'You will have noticed that foreign minister Albert Butcher has included the issue of Sandhustani independence among his submissions to Halcyon House.'

'I did see that, sir. But we're still waiting for the secretaries to finish sorting all the issues into zones.'

'And then?'

'The board will take the ten most popular issues in each zone and arrange them into a practicable agenda.'

'And we can rely on you, can we not, Squadron Leader, to ensure that Sandhustani independence is among those issues?'

'Colonel sir,' said Jericho uneasily (had he been secretly demoted or something?), 'that depends on how many member-governments have included Sandhustan in their submissions.'

'It is the President's wish,' said Boatman, not in the least concerned with trivialities like democracy or binding resolutions, 'that Sandhustan appears on the Wopec agenda.'

'But Colonel sir,' said Jericho, taking his life in both hands, 'if the issue is not popular enough to qualify for the top ten in that zone — '

'It is a party directive,' Boatman interrupted. 'It *will* be on the Wopec agenda, Squadron Leader.'

'I'm sure it will, Colonel sir,' said Jericho tremulously.

'Be quite sure, Mr Engineer,' Boatman advised him. 'Be very sure indeed.'

'I will, sir, Colonel sir.'

'Excellent.' Boatman got up to leave. 'The President knew you'd understand.' He raised a hand in farewell, palm out, Red Indian fashion. 'Peace and friendship, comrade.'

'Peace and friendship, Colonel,' echoed Jericho with a despairing smile.

Five thousand miles away in Paradise, in the cargo sheds of Hudson Butcher International Airport, agents of the Socialist People's Intelligence Service were hard at work, packing a bumper consignment of guns, ammunition and high explosives, labelled DIPLOMATIC FREIGHT and addressed to the religious affairs attaché at the Paradise Islands' High Commission in Belgrave Square, London.

27

TWILIGHT OVER Lower Oxfold Farm, and in the kitchen of their new, tumbledown headquarters the men of Number One Commando, the SPLA, were gathered round a table by the greenish-white light of hurricane lamps, digesting a tasty pigeon vindaloo and toying with some of the good things that their honoured guest, the Very Reverend Mogador Boatman, had brought them that day from Stansted airport – AK47 automatic rifles, Skorpion machine pistols, detonators, explosives, ammunition, walkie-talkie sets and combat fatigues.

'What will your fighting strength be on the night?' asked Boatman.

'Seven,' said Sharaq, 'not counting our adjutant, Dubbi Muktar. He must remain in London as our linkman.'

'Where is he now?'

'In Sandhubad. Making arrangements for four more commandos to join us in June. The fewer we have over here for the time being, the less the security risk.'

'And these will be experienced, trained men?'

'Fresh out of the federal marines,' said Sharaq. 'As fully trained as we are.' (Which was being a trifle generous to Nurg, whose two years of military service had been fairly evenly divided between the parachute regiment and a succession of army hospitals, where he had been taken for repair at regular intervals, and left languishing in plaster of Paris for months on end.)

'You have two clear advantages in making the banquet your target,' said Boatman. 'Firstly, there will be a lot of drink flowing all evening and an atmosphere of revelry about the place. Secondly, security will be at its most lax after six o'clock. And if you attack at around sunset you will have the benefit of daylight at the moment you strike, and darkness to cover the final stages of your getaway.'

'You have the guest-list?' asked Sharaq.

Boatman opened his snakeskin document case and took out copies of the papers that Jericho had supplied. He flicked through them until he came to the banquet schedule. 'The ambassadors,' he read aloud, 'of the US, the USSR, France, Spain, West Germany, Italy, China, Brazil, Norway, Sweden, Japan, Mexico, Israel, Hungary, Egypt, Holland and Saudi Arabia. And the high commissioners of India, Pakistan, Canada, Jamaica, Kenya, Australia and Zambia.' He handed the list to Sharaq. 'And wives or husbands, of course. Plus the Fabrizis. That makes fifty in all. You could have a transport problem.'

'We're not interested in the women,' said Sharaq, 'so that makes it twenty-five. And that' (pointing out of the paneless window to the farmyard) 'is the solution to all our transport problems.'

Boatman peered through the dusk to where Pungal's bargain pantechnicon stood surrounded by the pieces of its own dismembered engine and gearbox, awaiting refurbishment and a heart transplant. 'A furniture truck?' Boatman chuckled – a rare moment of bourgeois self-indulgence. 'Ingenious. And where do you plan to accommodate your distinguished guests?'

'In the piggery,' said Sharaq.

Boatman enjoyed that even more. 'Most appropriate.'

Sharaq read through the remainder of the banquet schedule. 'How final are these arrangements?'

'The invitations have been sent, the chef commissioned and the domestic staff engaged. My inside sources will inform me of any alterations to the schedule, but we are expecting none. If you hear nothing further from me you can be confident that everything is going ahead as planned.'

'We shan't be seeing you again?' asked Sharaq.

'The intelligence authorities in this country can be irritatingly vigilant at times,' said Boatman. 'For security reasons – both your country's and mine – I cannot take unnecessary risks.'

Sharaq nodded. 'We understand.'

'If you have any problems you can always contact me through this London number.' He wrote down Jericho Engineer's home telephone number on a scrap of paper. 'Only call if it is absolutely essential. Leave a message and I will make touch. But I have it on very reliable authority that nothing is likely to upset these banqueting arrangements from here on.'

A smile crept across Pungal's half-shadowed face in the flickering light of the hurricane lamp. 'Except, perhaps . . . seven uninvited guests, Your Very Reverence.'

Midnight in Oxfold Woods. Outside in the pigsty, where he had volunteered to spend each night on guard duty, untouchable bondserf Nurg lay curled up on the straw muttering prayers of thanks to the Lord Shrahma for sending them the esteemed Reverend Boatman. A fine man. A loyal friend of Sandhustan. The very avatar of munificence.

An owl hooted somewhere in the trees nearby. A shiver danced down Nurg's spine. It could be a spooky place at night, that piggery. Pungal said there were evil spirits in the woods – ghosts of English swineherds driven to their deaths by EEC and come back to haunt the land. Nurg tried to banish such thoughts from his mind. Warriors of Sandhu were made of sterner stuff. How lucky he was to have been given this privileged job each night. Guarding the piggery was a task of crucial importance to their mission, and the bountiful Captain Sharaq had awarded him – unworthy slum-born Golam Nanjik – that signal honour. He muttered prayers of thanks to the Lord Shrahma for placing him under the command of the noble Captain Sharaq. A fine soldier. The very avatar of officerliness . . .

Back at the farmhouse, Sharaq and Pungal were tucked up, warm and snug, in the only two available beds, sound asleep and snoring like troopers.

28

THANKS ENTIRELY to new, miracle Adeptalogic-2, the executive board were able to meet for their seventh unusual general session in the first week of May to resume work on the Wopec agenda. Adeptalogic-2 was the latest prodigy from that nursery of technological *wunderkinder*, the Unibore computer room, and was being talked about with awe and wonder all over Halcyon House, from the chauffeurs' room to the director-general's suite. It was a unique Wopec software programme, custom-designed by the bearded wizards of the ground-floor computer room, to meet the needs of Melanie Boewater and the CLAC secretaries, and was proving almost limitless in its capabilities. It had, for example, worked out the most efficient and cost-effective itineraries for each one of the four hundred and fifty-six Wopec delegates and selected the necessary accommodation to suit all their individual requirements. Furthermore, it had gobbled up the details of hundreds of tenders from tradesmen and subcontractors and computed who should get which contract and why. Finally, compatible as it was with CLAC's splendid new range of word processing equipment, it had made scornfully short work of sorting those three thousand eight hundred and seventy-eight agenda submissions into geographical zones and reprinting them all in summary form in order of popularity.

In theory (it was Kremlin theory, at any rate) the compilation of the agenda should have been child's play from here on. All the board had to do was cream off the top ten issues in each zone and arrange them into a timetable that was acceptable to the membership. Neither the Kremlin nor anyone else, however, had foreseen the possibility that a multiplicity of different issues might occupy the same spot in any one 'top ten' – as was the case, it now transpired, in the Americo-Caribbean zone, where the tenth position was shared by forty-six issues, all proposed by exactly the same number of countries, and all concerning embittered border disputes of no relevance whatsoever to world peace.

It was beyond even the powers of miraculous new Adeptalogic-2 to find a way out of this impasse. The Swiss delegate, Professor Sigismund Frankl, resurrected the suggestion he had made before Easter and proposed that the board should discuss all forty-six issues in turn and choose the single most important one for the Wopec agenda. That found little favour with anyone and was totally unacceptable to the Cuban delegate, Buonaventura Martinez, who insisted that the board had made a solemn and binding agreement to take the ten most popular issues in each zone. Accordingly, he argued, if the number ten position happened to be occupied by forty-six equally popular issues then all forty-six should go onto the agenda. He was strongly supported in that view by the non-aligned bloc, most of whose delegates had dozens of equally trivial border quarrels that they, too, were anxious to thrash out at Wopec.

This however, was wholly unacceptable to the Western delegates, who maintained that if the entire Wopec agenda was to be restricted to just fifty issues, it would be palpably absurd to swamp it with forty-six trivial Central American frontier disputes at the very outset.

The United Kingdom delegate, Laurie Tappet, emeritus professor of peace studies at Rotherham Polytechnic, suggested that the ideal solution would be to call the whole thing an Especially Difficult Problem (EDP), shelve it for a rainy day and move straight on to other, less contentious zones.

Li Zhao Yang of China, however, came forward with an ingenious compromise. He proposed that the board should discuss the forty-six issues as Professor Frankl had suggested, and place the most important one on the agenda, while assigning all the remaining issues to a new 'supplementary' agenda, the precise nature and purpose of which could be agreed on at some later date. By that means, every issue would be guaranteed a place on an agenda of one sort or another, and none would be rejected.

The board agreed that that seemed an eminently pragmatic way of making an even more sophisticated fudge of the whole thing, voted thirty-five – nil in favour, and immediately got on with the job of thrashing out each issue and awarding it points on a merit scale of one to ten.

This went on all week, and would very probably have gone on all the following week as well if another unforeseen crisis had not blown up and spared them further boredom. In the middle of UGS 11 on Friday morning, Blah-blah telephoned Otello from the palace with the shattering news that HRH would not, after all, be able to attend Wopec Day.

'Someone's made a Horlicks of the travel arrangements,' Blah-blah explained apologetically. 'Their royal highnesses won't be getting back from Africa until lunchtime on Wopec Day. It's all a question of astrology, I'm afraid, and Queen Shiwaza Matumbi's coronation.'

'Queen who?' said Otello.

'Well, she's not a queen, strictly speaking. She's the Great She-Rhino. *In loco regis*, till the crown prince comes of age. Anyway, the coronation *was* to have been on the Tuesday before Wopec Day, but Sagittarius is in the wrong quincunx or something, so everything has had to be postponed until Thursday the twenty-second. Which means HRH can't be back in London till midday on Saturday at the very earliest. And there's no way he can get to Allshott by two o'clock . . . or even five o'clock, for that matter.'

'Well, this is all rather devastating,' said Otello, somewhat numbed with shock. 'I don't know what to say.'

'I can't tell you how sorry we are,' Blah-blah sympathised. 'Strictly *entre nous*, HRH is bally furious about it. Rockets galore have been going off all morning. But I'm afraid affairs of state simply have to take precedence. If Wopec Day had been on the Sunday, of course, there would have been no problem. But as it is, the schedule is just too tight.'

Otello spied a glimmer of hope. 'Do you mean that if we were able to postpone the public inauguration until Sunday the twenty-fifth, their royal highnesses might be able to attend as planned?'

That caught Blah-blah on the wrong foot. 'Well, that's a hypothesis that hasn't been considered, of course. But I'm sure HRH would do his very best to oblige if it were humanly possible.'

Otello asked him if he would, in that case, put that possibility to their royal highnesses for their gracious consideration, while he in turn consulted his executive board. Blah-blah said he would be only too happy to do so and promised to call Otello on Monday morning with the royal reply.

Otello then telephoned J. Hector Lammas (whom God preserve) at the DoE's historic buildings directorate in Savile Row and asked him if the department would have any objections to the proposed change of date. To which Lammas replied that as Unibore had hired Carnage Castle for the last two weeks of June it did not really make a dog's bit of difference to the DoE *when* the inauguration ceremony took place.

So that afternoon, Otello reconvened the executive board, informed them of the situation and proposed that – subject to the agreement of their royal highnesses – Wopec Day be switched to Sunday the twenty-fifth. Since all the delegations and VIPs were going to be in London by Friday the twenty-third in any case, the board agreed that it did not much matter whether Wopec Day was held on the Saturday or the Sunday, but ruled that as a matter of courtesy the proposal would have to be referred to a special general conference of all the delegates.

The only person who raised any objections was Air Vice-Marshal Engineer, who complained bitterly that he had been given an assurance that, in the event of their royal highnesses being unable to attend Wopec Day, President Hudson Butcher would be offered first refusal in their place. However, since – technically speaking – the royal couple had not yet confirmed that they would *not* be attending the inauguration, Jericho was overruled and outvoted by thirty-four to one. Otello then circulated a memorandum to all the delegates at Halcyon House, giving notice of an emergency general conference at eleven o'clock on Monday morning. As a final peace offering to the air vice-marshal, he agreed to put before the conference any counter-motion that Jericho cared to table recommending the issue of an invitation to President Butcher in the royal stead.

29

FROM THE telex room of the Paradise Islands' High Commission, Belgrave Square, London S.W.1, *Friday 15.10 BST:*

Air Vice-Marshal Engineer to Duty Officer, SPIS

URGENT. FOR ATTENTION OF COL. BOATMAN, SECTION 5. UNIBORE BOARD PROPOSING SWITCH WOPEC DAY TO SUNDAY 25 JUNE. DOES PRESIDENT WISH TO PERFORM INAUGURATION CEREMONY? PLEASE REPLY SOONEST.

Brigadier Elisha Longfellow, C-in-C SPIS to Engineer:

BOATMAN UNDER ARREST. REVISIONIST DEVIATIONIST COUNTER-REVOLUTIONARY CONSPIRACY.

Engineer to Longfellow:
MAYBE WE TALKING ABOUT DIFFERENT BOATMAN?

Longfellow to Engineer:
NEGATIVE. MOGADOR BOATMAN (COL), SCTN. 5, ARRESTED ON ARRIVAL AIRPORT WEDS 8 MAY. AWAITING EXECUTION PENDING TRIAL.

Engineer to Longfellow:
WISE PRECAUTION. ALWAYS THOUGHT LOOKED SHIFTY. KINDLY INFORM HEAD SCTN. 5 PROPOSED WOPEC DAY CHANGE. URGENT. THANK YOU.

Longfellow to Engineer:
HEAD SCTN. 5 ALSO UNDR ARRST. REVSNST DEVIATNST CNTR-REVLUTNRY CONSPRICY.

Engineer to Longfellow:
THEN KINDLY INFRM NEW HEAD SCTN. 5. THNK U.

Longfellow to Engineer:
ALL SCTN. 5 UNDR ARRST (REV DEV CNTR-REV CNSPRCY.)

Engineer to Longfellow:
SO WHO DOING WORK OF SCTN. 5?

Longfellow to Engineer:
INTERIOR SECRTRY, COL-GEN STOCKMINDER.

Engineer to Colonel-General Leviticus Stockminder, Secretary of the Interior:
URGNT: UNIBORE BOARD PROPOSE SWITCH WOPEC DAY TO SUN 25 JUNE. DOES PRESIDENT STILL WISH PERFORM INAUGURATION? PLSE ADVSE SOONST.

Stockminder to Engineer:
KINDLY REFER CHEF DE PROTOCOL.

Engineer to Stockminder:
WHO CHEF DE PROTOCOL?

Stockminder to Engineer:
BRIG. ELISHA LONGFELLOW.

Engineer to Longfellow:
ME AGAIN. PLSE ADVSE SOONST IF PRSDNT WISHES INAUGRTE WOPEC DAY, SUN 25 JUN. EXTRMLY URGNT.

Cleaner to Engineer.
EVRYONE CLOCKED OFF FOR WEEKND. TRY AGAIN MONDY.

Air Vice-Marshal Engineer to Brigadier Longfellow, C-in-C SPIS *Monday 09.35 BST:*
TOP PRIORITY: PLSE INSTRCT IMMDTLY RE PRESDNT/WOPEC DAY. UNIBORE DELEGATES MEETING EMRGNCY GENRL CONFRNCE 11.00 BST TODAY.

Colonel-General Stockminder, Secretary of the Interior, to Air Vice-Marshal Engineer. *Monday 12.25 BST:*
RE YOUR TELEX 09.35.: BRIG. ELISHA LONGFELLOW UNDR ARREST (REVSNST DEVIATNST COUNTR-REVLTNRY ETC ETC). WHAT WAS THAT QUESTION ABOUT WOPEC DAY?

30

BY LUNCHTIME on Monday the good news was all over Halcyon House that Wopec Day had been changed to Sunday the twenty-fifth of June and that their royal highnesses would be able to attend the inauguration ceremonies after all.

The only person who did not look upon it as good news (apart from Jericho Engineer, who had been stuck in Belgrave Square all morning awaiting instructions from Port Paradise and had missed the emergency general conference entirely) was Freda Elphinstone. Storming uninvited into a CLAC meeting on the fourth floor that afternoon, she enquired whether anyone had the vaguest conception of how much work this was going to entail for all her hard-pressed gels. Literally tens of thousands of people all over the world would have to be notified individually of the change of date. Legions of tradesmen and subcontractors. Taxi firms, caterers, hotels, British Rail . . .

Ah-ha, but *this*, Melanie interrupted chirpily, was where new, miracle Adeptalogic-2 came into its own. At the mere stroking of a few keys on any CLAC word processor, the details of every Wopec delegate throughout the world, every invited guest, every contractor, every conceivable person who had anything to do with the symposium, could be displayed across the secretaries' monitor screens. At the mere stroking of a few *more* keys, all this information could be printed out – in file form, for instant reference, or onto envelopes, address labels, or in whatever way Ms Elphinstone would find most convenient.

That, retorted Freda, would have to be seen to be believed.

So everybody trooped next door to the secretaries' room and gathered round a word processor. Carefully following the simple step-by-step instructions supplied by the bearded inventors of Adeptalogic-2, Melanie keyed in the word 'Access', followed by a file number and a codeword that looked like the name of a Welsh railway station.

There, she said, easy as pie. She pressed 'D' for display and waited. A few seconds later, twenty-eight lines of gobbledegook flashed up on the monitor screen, full of Xs and Zs and vaguely reminiscent of a Polish weather forecast. Freda was delighted.

Not to worry, said Melanie. Referring back to the simple instructions, she typed in a different file number and several more Welsh railway stations and conjured up an even worse Polish weather forecast. CLAC and the secretaries looked on, sympathetic but uncomprehending.

Obviously some minor oversight somewhere, said Melanie, quite undaunted, and telephoned down to the computer room for assistance. A few minutes later an amiable young programmer called Nick loped into the room in a sweaty polyester shirt and needlecord jeans and asked what all the fuss was about. Melanie explained what she was trying to do.

Dead cinch, said sweaty Nick, stroking a whole mapful of Cambrian railway stations into the keyboard with the self-assurance of a concert pianist. Then he pressed 'D' for display and sat back. Another twenty-eight lines of Baltic meteorology promptly flashed up on the monitor. Funny, said Nick, and phoned down to the ground floor for reinforcements.

More bearded maths graduates duly loped up to the fourth floor, whiffing of armpits and real ale, and listened studiously to the tale thus far. Suspecting a minor fault in the monitoring system, they suggested printing out a sample of the required data instead. Excellent idea, said Melanie. Whereupon they all set off for the ground-floor computer room, followed by a convoy of fascinated secretaries and Freda Elphinstone, *humph*ing with derisive glee all the way, like an old tugboat.

As soon as he got back to the computer room, sweaty Nick discovered that the Wopec master-file had recently been transferred from lots of separate floppy disks onto just one super hard disk. Ah, said the bearded wizards, well that explained everything. So Nick put the new super hard disk into the disk drive and played another natty little mazurka on the keyboard with both hands, and the printer began to chatter away cheerfully at thirty characters per second. There you go – cinch, said Nick triumphantly. Easy as pie, said grateful Melanie, as everyone gathered round and watched the printer churn out a beautifully folded Polish weather forecast, half a mile long.

For the next three days the bearded wizards sweated and frowned and muttered, poring over diagrams of Adeptalogic-2, checking every calculation and spending a small tranche of Unibore funds discussing it over jars of real ale. The only thing that they could say for sure, however, was that all CLAC's computerised files now contained nothing but Xs and Zs, with an unhelpful smattering of surnames and postcodes every now and again to lend variety. How this calamitous state of affairs could have come to pass, given the infallible brilliance of their software, they could not even begin to imagine. Nevertheless, the fact remained that Adeptalogic-2 had successfully obliterated practically every last trace of CLAC's records, and with only six weeks to go to Wopec Day, something in the region of thirteen thousand people all round the world had yet to be informed that the date had been changed.

The only recourse the secretaries now had was to their manual records, which were in an appalling mess; for, with the advent of miraculous new Adeptalogic-2, plain old-fashioned filing (of the kind that Freda Elphinstone believed had made

Britain great) had come to be regarded as an obsolete irrelevance. So by the middle of May the whole of the fourth floor was in a state of bedlam, with every CLAC office knee-deep in files, invoices, letters, contracts, order books, advice notes, carbon flimsies, address lists, receipts and memoranda, and dozens of harassed secretaries scurrying about trying to find out who was notifying whom and at which address. In consequence, half the world and his dog began receiving innumerable letters with every post from a variety of illegible signatories, all claiming to be *p.p. Director-General* and conveying precisely the same information.

Miraculously, the only people whom they failed to inform amidst all this chaos were the seventeen ambassadors and seven high commissioners whom Otello had invited to his farewell banquet. Fortunately, this was of little consequence, for they read the news for themselves in the national press and were blessed with secretaries who had the initiative to check the date on their behalf. Which was more than could be said for the men of Number One Commando, the Sandhustan People's Liberation Army, who – with Dubbi Muktar five thousand miles away in Sandhubad, and the Very Reverend Mogador Boatman languishing in Joy of Socialist Labour Gaol – had no contact whatsoever with the outside world; and consequently, had no idea that the director-general's banquet would now be taking place on Sunday the twenty-fifth.

But then, nobody had invited them anyway.

31

THE NEWS reached Corporal Bile at Warmacre Camp one warm Friday evening in the middle of May. He had just completed an invigorating fortnight's survival training in the local mosquito swamps and was about to thunder home for the weekend on his two thousand cc Norton Exterminator, when he was summoned abruptly to the CO's office.

'Just had Colonel Mildwater on the blower from the MoD,' said Kilmore.

'More bellyaching, sah?' said Bile, fed up to the back teeth with Labour MPs wingeing about the high proportion of 2 Troop who had succumbed to typhoid after eating coypu butties in the swamps in recent months.

'No. That Unibore shindig at Carnage. It's been put back to June the twenty-fifth. And there's been an interesting development. The MoD have been trying to think of something useful to do with Carnage Castle ever since the day they were lumbered with it.'

'Yes, sah.' Bile knew only too well. The army had organised a competition open to all ranks, offering a dream holiday for two on Diego Garcia for the best suggestion as to what might be done with the place. He had suggested flattening it with plastic explosive, and had taken months to get over the news that he had not won a prize.

'Well, some bright johnny in the under-secretary's office has come up with the idea of turning it into a permanent top-security venue for international conferences – SALT talks, NATO, all that sort of palaver. They're setting up a joint study group with the Home Office to look into the feasibility of it, and one of the things they need to know is how vulnerable the place is to a terrorist attack. So, as we were planning to use the Wopec conference as an anti-terrorist training exercise anyway, Muddy Mildwater wants us to assist the police in making a detailed security appraisal of the castle and grounds.'

Bile shifted uneasily in his chair. 'When you say *assist*, sah . . . ?'

'I mean co-operate with. They want us to work together as a team on this.'

'Co-*operate*,' said Bile, appalled. 'My lads, sah? My boys? 2 Troop? Work with woodentops?'

'Well, that's the general idea, yes,' said Kilmore, gently. He was well aware of how sensitive Bile was about the police. The mere sight of a uniform had been known to throw the poor chap off balance for days on end, though for the life of him Kilmore had never been able to fathom out why. 'It can't hurt just for a few days, old man, surely?'

'With respect, sah,' said Bile, flecks of white beginning to bubble at the corners of his mouth, 'there's two arms: the military and the civil. They're like fire and piss, sah. They don't mix. Mr Plod should stick to what he's good at – holding up the traffic.'

Bile's loathing for the men in blue was a legend throughout the Special Air Service. But it was a fact little known beyond the rarefied confines of the Bile family, that young Ron had not *always* despised the constabulary with such remorseless passion. On the contrary, the secret truth was that for the first eighteen years of his life the only thing he had ever wanted to be was a copper. Ever since the day he could toddle, little Ronnie pictured himself pounding the beat in a smart blue uniform, with a shiny silver whistle and a big fat truncheon. While other boys were out playing football and lifting up little girls' skirts, young Ron was busy dragging his classmates home for questioning and locking them up in the coal cellar. All he ever dreamt about was zooming round London in a Wolseley 4/44 with his bell clanging, bashing up the punters. He devoted the best years of his childhood to preparing for that proud day when they gave him his first warrant card and his very own pair of handcuffs.

But then Dame Nature sprang a vicious trick on him. At the age of seventeen he stopped growing, without a hint of warning, at a height of just five feet six; and there was not one constabulary in the United Kingdom that would take a man who was under five feet eight. One by one his application forms were returned by police forces throughout the length and breadth of Britain, stamped: 'Too short,' or 'Too small,' 'Undersize,' 'Physique: substandard,' or 'Build: inadequate.' These searing phrases branded themselves in his memory. Burning with humiliation, the baleful little Bile signed up with the Paras in a fit of pique, and swore to be avenged one day on his lofty tormentors in blue.

Kilmore, however, was not privy to any of this, and the reason for Bile's implacable animosity towards the British bobby was a total mystery to him. 'Well, I'm sorry, old man,' he said, though without the least hint of an apology. 'I'm not exactly wild about the idea of mixing the civil and the military arms either, but there are occasions when this sort of co-operation is deemed necessary.'

'Very good, sah,' said Bile stoically. 'Understood, sah.'

'I'm having a meeting next Tuesday with Superintendent

Hatchard and Inspector Lipman from the local nick to try and work out a joint approach to this security appraisal. So have a think about it over the weekend, and if you come up with any good ideas for constructive things T Squadron can do with the Lydhurst police, let me know on Monday.'

'Right, sah. Will do, sah,' said Bile, who could think of a number of things he would dearly like to do with the Lydhurst police, but none of them remotely constructive.

The whole idea was Doris's really. (Leastways, that was what Bile would plead at the court martial.) Doris did not often have ideas. Like the bamboo, they seemed to flower about once every ten years. But then, precious little managed to blossom in the Bile household.

Ron and Doris lived in a small redbrick house called The Trenches in the middle of an army estate in Herefordshire. They were surrounded on all sides by brightly painted homes, with flourishing gardens where goldfish swam contentedly in plastic ponds, and songbirds chirruped their little hearts out all day long. The one house on the estate where nothing flourished in the garden or sang its little heart out was The Trenches. As soon as he moved in, Bile painted the whole place khaki, and within a few months there was not a living thing left in the garden save a small, rust-brown patch of terminally sick grass. Everything else had been dug up, mown down, trampled to death, burnt, throttled, shot or eaten alive by his pack of killer Alsatians.

Bile was not often there, which was partly why Doris had married him. He had four weeks leave a year, which he liked to spend canoeing in the Weddell Sea or bivouacking in the Kalahari Desert. When he did come home – about one weekend in three – he spent most of the time abseiling down from the roof or hiding in the local woods disguised as a bush. The rest of the time Doris had no idea where he was, what he was doing or why. So on those rare occasions when he returned to the nest and shared his problems with her she liked to be able to offer some wifely comfort and advice.

'But you won't have to *talk* to them, Ron luvvy,' she said soothingly, over Saturday lunch. 'No one's asking you to be *nice* to the policemen.'

'Kilmore specifically asked for co-operation,' said Ron

luvvy, sick with disgust. 'Troopers and flatfoots don't mix. It's bloody degrading.'

'Well, sulking about it won't help.'

'Not sulking,' he muttered, picking at his roly-poly pudding and custard.

'T Squadron is a training squadron, after all.'

'They may be training but they're still a crack fighting unit. They shouldn't have to work with bastard woodentops. So humiliating.'

'Well, they've got to think of every contingency, haven't they?'

'What bleeding contingency?'

'*I* don't know, dear, I'm not your commanding officer, am I? Now eat up, there's a good boy. Your roly-poly puddin's getting cold.'

'Not 'ungry.'

'Yes you are.'

'Not.'

'Are really.'

'Bloody *not*!' raged Bile, and downed irons and sat back defiantly with his arms folded.

'You'll get horrid slimy skin on your custard.'

'Good.'

Time passed. Doris cleared away and washed up. Bile sat there, peevish and resolute, with his cold roly-poly pudding covered in slimy skinful custard. Doris got out the raisins and flour and butter and began to make a cake. Bile decided to clean his submachine-gun and dropped oil and four-by-two into the cake-mix.

'Oh, do be reasonable, Ron luvvy,' Doris pleaded, adding a few shakes of vanilla essence to neutralise the flavour. 'See it from the Home Office's point of view. They have to be prepared. What would happen if a gang of loony terrorists took over the castle in the middle of a world conference?'

'We'd storm the place,' he said, with relish. 'Annihilate 'em, bastard subversive scumshite.'

'All right then,' said Doris, 'why don't you practise storming it? You and the police. Have a siege.'

'A siege?' Ron luvvy liked the sound of that word. It smacked of widespread destruction. 'What do you mean, *siege*?'

'Well, like one of those mock attacks you have in NATO

exercises,' said Doris. 'After all, the best way to find out how secure Carnage Castle is, would be to get someone to attack it and someone else to defend it, surely?'

Bile thought about that. That made a lot of sense. A mock siege . . . with a bunch of terrorists seizing the castle and 2 Troop under orders to go in and beat the living daylights out of them. That was nothing short of a brainwave. How much closer co-operation could Whitehall ask for? 'With the woodentops,' he said, excitedly shovelling cold roly-poly pudding down his throat, skin, gun-oil and all, 'taking the part of the filthy subversive scumshite.'

'. . . with our good colleagues from Lydhurst police station,' Bile explained to the joint security meeting at Buckingham Gate the following Tuesday, 'playing the role of the undesirable alien intruders.'

'Sounds a reasonable idea,' said Hatchard, and turned to Inspector Lipman from the Lydhurst force.

Lipman was as anxious as anyone to prove that Carnage Castle was secure enough to be a major international conference venue. For, with the possible exception of the Isle of Mull, Lydhurst was arguably the deadest police patch in the UK, and a few world conferences a year would liven the place up no end. 'Sounds all right in theory,' he agreed, 'but what sort of scenario do you have in mind?' He addressed that question to Kilmore.

Kilmore turned hopefully to Bile. 'Scenario, old man?'

'Yes, sah,' said Bile, who had thought it out in some detail. 'Your *lockers classicus*: a mob of terrorists are holed up inside the building with hostages. We have to get 'em out. We have to get 'em all out, hostages and filth alike. But when we storm a building under these circumstances we don't know which are hostages and which are filth. So, for the sake of this exercise, the whole police detachment would have to be regarded simply as filth. And when I say *filth*, you understand,' (smiling reassuringly at Lipman) 'I do, of course, refer to *terrorist* filth and not Old Bill filth.'

'And how big a detachment did you have in mind?' asked Lipman.

'About fifteen to twenty men on each side,' Bile replied.

'All confined to one part of the castle?' said Hatchard.

'Yes, sah. Realistically speaking, they'd all hole up in one place, with sentries posted here and there to keep a lookout.'

'But you wouldn't have any idea where we were at the start?' said Lipman.

'No, sah. We'd have to get into the castle without being seen, isolate the enemy and winkle 'em out. The police would be free to choose whatever part of the castle they wished and to make it as hard as they could for the attacking force. Our objective would be to get as close to the enemy as possible without being tumbled. So we'd have to have umpires, and troopers would have to be numbered for identification. The police would have to log every sighting of a trooper, and the results of the exercise could be analysed fully at a joint debriefing.'

'And did you have a specific date in mind for this exercise?' Lipman enquired.

'Well, we feel,' replied Kilmore, 'that there's no point in conducting it under anything other than conference conditions. At the moment Carnage Castle is practically empty. But it'll be packed with extra furniture, lighting and God knows what by the time the Wopec talks get under way, and those are the conditions that the place would be in were a terrorist incident of this kind to take place. So I'm suggesting that we should run the exercise a day or so before Wopec opens. That's now been put back to Sunday the twenty-fifth of June, so I'd have thought that the Friday or Saturday would have been the ideal choice.'

Lipman and Hatchard flipped through their diaries. 'Midsummer's Day,' observed Hatchard. 'Fair enough. It would give us about six weeks to organise everything.'

'Subject, of course, to the agreement of the Home Office and the MoD,' said Kilmore. 'But if you gentlemen are broadly in favour of the idea we could take matters one stage further and sound out feelings in Whitehall.'

It is difficult to conceive of any sane person, the Home Secretary wrote to the Metropolitan Police Commissioner on the twenty-third of May, giving his formal assent to Operation Midsummer Night, *taking hostages and electing to hold out in a medieval fortress like Carnage Castle. But, regrettably, we have to face the fact that there is always somebody somewhere in the world these days who is crackers enough to try anything once.*

32

RAIN FELL on Chipton Oxfold, a refreshing May shower that sweetened the bog-scented air around Lower Oxfold Woods and leaked *splatt splatt* through the holes in the piggery roof above Nurg's head. Below, sitting cross-legged in his favourite pigsty, Golam Nanjik was trying to put together the twelve easy-to-assemble pieces of his Skorpion machine pistol, with the aid of a pictorial maintenance manual written entirely in easy-to-read Czech.

Thanks to the SPLA and his two limb-fracturing years of compulsory military service with 58th Airborne Division, Nurg had acquired many useful skills that would otherwise have been beyond the educational aspirations of one of his unspeakably low caste. He could speak English, read a prismatic compass, tell the time, fall out of an aeroplane upside down and drive a Jeep clean through a brick wall in broad daylight. Even so, he had never quite got the hang of stripping firearms and reassembling them again in the right order. This was no small handicap at the best of times, but to complicate things still further, the esteemed and bountiful Reverend Boatman had brought these sophisticated little Skorpions from Czechoslovakia that Nurg had never seen before.

Sharaq had issued an order that every man should be able to strip and reassemble these new weapons blindfold in sixty seconds. Those who could not, he had decreed, would have to practise in their spare time. Sharaq, however, was not very generous when it came to allocating spare time. He was a stickler for training, discipline and hard work. Reveille was at dawn, followed by prayers, half an hour of rigorous physical exercise, three kilometres of road running, cold showers (bucket of pond water over head), breakfast and domestic chores. The rest of the morning was given over to weapons-training and fieldcraft. After lunch they had English language practice; then map reading, signals and telecommunications training, tactics lectures and manual labour (fortifying piggery in preparation for esteemed guests). Then more buckets of cold pondwater over head (*mens sana in corpore frigido* etc. – the CO being Captain Sharaq MA Oxon, no less) and supper. That left them with just one hour's leisure time before prayers. After which Nurg retired, totally knackered, to his pigsty each night and slept soundly till dawn.

Today, however, there had been a welcome and unexpected change in the routine. Dubbi Muktar, safely returned from Sandhubad, had taken Sharaq down to the Hampshire coast to inspect the getaway boat that was to carry them safely across the sea to France. Guppi Pungal, meantime, had taken his refurbished pantechnicon out onto the public highway, after weeks of sweated labour, for its first major road test. Leaving Nurg alone at the farm to guard the armoury and stores, with express orders to employ the time fruitfully and perfect his competence at stripping and reassembling the Skorpion machine pistol. Which implied a touching degree of faith on Sharaq's part that there was at least a modicum of competence there to begin with (a rash assumption, but some consolation, nonetheless, to the diffident Nurg). After many hours of trial and error with the aid of his illustrated Czech maintenance manual, he had indeed made some sort of visible progress. His machine pistol was no longer in twelve easy-to-assemble pieces . . . it was now in twenty-six even smaller easy-to-assemble pieces. And the rain was *splatt-splatting* ever harder on his head through the holes in the piggery roof.

Sharaq and Dubbi, meanwhile, had arrived at the quiet seaside resort of Clympton-on-Solent – made famous throughout every consumer complaints bureau in the land by Sir Charlie Codlin, that renowned vulgarian and misanthrope, who first cloned the advantages of group vacationing with the economic principles of the *Konzentrationslager*, and unleashed upon humankind Codlin's of Clympton, the nonpareil of holiday camps.

Notable for its uncommonly high incidence of dysentery, due to the close proximity of beach and sewage farm, Clympton-on-Solent boasted one of the cheapest yachting marinas in the world. So cheap, in fact, that the Clympton Yacht Club was almost prepared to pay people a small allowance to berth their craft there. Amongst the many members who had taken advantage of the generous rates was Dubbi's wealthy godfather,

Oqtar Tanqeddi, who kept a twelve-metre motor yacht, the *Amphitrite*, tied up there amidst the becalmed flotsam of driftwood, old condoms and Fairy Liquid containers.

Tanqeddi, who came from a landlocked nation-state and had never set foot on a boat in his life before, had purchased the *Amphitrite* some three years earlier with vague ambitions of sailing to the Channel Islands at weekends and returning laden to the gunwales with illicit hooch, illegal immigrants and VAT-free Krugerrands. But after several unnerving and near-calamitous attempts to sail her out into open water, Tanqeddi had quickly gone off the whole idea and invested in bootleg videos instead. Ever since, the *Amphitrite* had moved barely a boathook's length from the quayside, and only now, with this opportunity of contributing discreetly to the Sandhustani liberation struggle had Tanqeddi found a worthy use for her . . . although he wanted nothing to do with the SPLA himself and had left her in the unnautical hands of Dubbi Muktar.

'You know anything about boats?' asked Dubbi, as he and Sharaq climbed aboard.

'I read Hornblower when I was a boy,' Sharaq replied, as though it were the sailor's bible and he was just a little rusty when it came to chapter and verse.

'It has a very good engine,' said Dubbi, 'so you won't have to bother shoving up the sails or anything.'

'*She*,' said Sharaq, expanding his lungs with ozone. 'Not *it*.'

Dubbi did not argue. 'Mind you, I don't think she's been driven as far as France before.'

'Boats don't *drive* to places. They steam or sail.'

Perhaps it had something to do with coming from a landlocked country, but Sharaq – it was plain to Dubbi – was obviously picturing himself at the helm already, with a salty, barnacled expression on his face and a peaked cap, with anchor motif, perched above. Quite what steam had to do with a marine diesel engine was beyond Dubbi, but he shrugged in mute deference to his captain's scholarly knowledge of Hornblower and led the way below.

'You must make sure that she's well stocked,' said Sharaq, inspecting the four-berth cabin. 'A full tank of butane for the cooker, plenty of drinking water and enough food for a week.'

'A *week*?' said Dubbi. 'But surely it won't take that long to drive . . . sail . . . steam across to France, will it?'

'One night at most,' Sharaq replied. 'But I have to be prepared for every contingency – bad weather, fog, break-downs, berthing problems across the Channel. All kinds of things could delay us.'

'You'd try and cross by night?' said Dubbi, gazing unhappily through the port-hole towards the restless grey sea beyond the marina.

'Possibly,' said Sharaq. 'It might be more prudent to slip away under cover of darkness.'

'You can navigate at night?' Dubbi never ceased to marvel at Sharaq's multifarious talents.

'We have charts,' said Sharaq. 'And with a man like Guppi Pungal at the helm we can't go wrong. He was born with a compass between his ears. A prince among navigators . . .'

Having given his trusty furniture truck a thorough road test, Pungal was rattling across the Severn Bridge into Wales at that particular moment, leaving a trail of sloughed tyre rubber and half the exhaust system in his wake, and keeping a hopeful eye out for a signpost to Basingstoke.

Back at the piggery, Nurg had successfully broken his easy-to-fall-to-bits machine pistol into a grand total of forty-two easily-lost-in-the-straw pieces, and had given up all hope of ever putting them back together again. In the meantime he had been trying to work out which way round the bullets were supposed to go in the magazine of his AK47 assault carbine; and he was now lying flat on his belly in a pool of fresh rainwater, attempting to hit a dustbin lid at twenty paces.

33

BYRON KNEW instinctively that this was too good to last. While CLAC's shell-shocked secretaries were convalescing among the smoking ruins of their burnt-out typewriters in the aftermath of the Wopec Day/Adeptalogic-2 crisis, the executive board had been scything broad swathes of progress through the agenda jungle. This did not bode well. Progress was something that had always been looked upon as an undesirable and generally debilitating phenomenon at Halcyon House, and in Byron's experience broad swathes of the stuff could prove positively lethal.

The key to these rapid advances on the agenda front was a marvellous new fudging device called the EDP, or Especially Difficult Problem. The EDP was a wholly British invention, conceived by Professor Laurie Tappet on the lines of the 'special case' – that time-honoured trick of Whitehall leger-demain by which cabinet ministers and Whitehall mandarins have justified every kind of blatant electoral lie, broken pledge and political U-turn since time immemorial. The beauty of it was its sheer simplicity. Any agenda issue over which the board could not agree was immediately designated an EDP and shoved to one side for a 'special enquiry' or a rainy day. By this means, the board had been getting through the outstanding mountain of agenda submissions at a phenomenal rate . . . creating, as they did so, an entirely new mountain of EDPs, of course; but that was beside the point. Progress was progress.

However, the board were not accustomed to getting through anything at a phenomenal rate, and they were finding it all rather unsettling and exhausting. So most of them were secretly quite thankful when all this progress came to an abrupt halt at UGS 18, on the twenty-third of May, with the introduction of the Sandhustani independence issue.

None of the Western delegates cared twopence about Sandhustan if truth were told, but as it was one of eighteen issues that were vying for ninth place in the Asio-Pacific zone, its eligibility to appear on the Wopec agenda had to be assessed on its merits. Many Third World delegates held strong views about Sandhustan, however, and when Doctor Rolv Erlendsson of Norway moved that the issue be ruled ineligible because it was the internal affair of a sovereign independent government, the board were hopelessly divided yet again. At which point Professor Laurie Tappet got up and proposed that the whole thing be declared yet another Especially Difficult Problem and added to the Everest of EDPs already outstanding.

At this there was an invigorating outburst of foul temper

from the Australian delegate, Doctor Isobel Maddox, who livened up the tedium no end by thumping her table with both fists and inadvertently elbowing a stack of dirty coffee cups onto the floor, where they obligingly smashed into a thousand pieces. No bloody way, she stormed. Enough was enough. There'd been far too much fudge and mudge already. No more EDPs. It was high time they started thrashing out these time-wasting pisspot trivialities once and for all. Forcing it to a vote, she carried the overwhelming majority of the board with her, rejecting by twenty-nine votes to six any proposal to bypass the Sandhustan issue and move on to the next.

Air Vice-Marshal Engineer proposed that in that case, they should now affirm positively that Sandhustan *was* eligible for the Wopec agenda and adjudge it on its merits accordingly. But that also split the board right down the middle and failed to win a two-thirds majority either way. Which effectively left them locked in a state of constitutional paralysis. Technically speaking, they could not discuss the issue, ignore the issue, place it on the agenda, keep it off the agenda or move on to any other business. All they could do was adjourn for lunch in the hope that fine wine and cordon-bleu diplomacy would succeed where reason and common sense had failed.

They reassembled shortly after three (almost in time to adjourn for tea, Byron noted thankfully) and Li Zhao Yang now put forward another of his famous Chinese compromises. Speaking through his interpreter – who had spent the entire lunchbreak trying to find *fudge and mudge* in an English–Mandarin dictionary – Li reminded them all of the 'supplementary' agenda that they had voted into being as long ago as UGS 7. Why not, he suggest, use it as a reservoir of supplementary issues that could be drawn upon to fill any unscheduled gaps in the *main* agenda? One or two gaps were bound to occur in even the most meticulously organised timetable, and if the board would agree to place Sandhustan at the top of this 'supplementary' agenda it would virtually be guaranteed discussion time at some point during the conference. Thus, technically speaking, it would be *on* the Wopec agenda, while at the same time – technically speaking – it would not . . . depending on how you chose to look at it.

Jericho did not know quite what to make of this. His instructions from the foreign ministry in Port Paradise had been predicated on the not unreasonable assumption that an issue was either *on* an agenda or *not* on it. The possibility that it could be both at once had not even been considered. After careful deliberation he decided to play safe and accept Li's compromise in principle.

Not so Isobel Maddox. Supplementary this and supplementary that, she scoffed. Just more fudge and mudge. An agenda was an agenda was an agenda, and that was that. No more weasel words. No more hollow compromises. The issue had to be thrashed out once and for all. A view that was strongly applauded by her neighbour, Zenia Schapiro of Israel, and the surrounding caucus of Western delegates.

Otello then put Li's resolution to the vote. Twenty-three arms went up in favour, eleven against. The motion was just one vote short of a two-thirds majority; but one delegate had not yet been accounted for. Puzzled, Otello enquired if there were any abstentions. A lone hand went up – Doctor Dermott Plunkett of Ireland. Surprised that anyone should wish to withhold his vote on such a crucial issue and at such a crucial time, Otello asked Dermott if he would like a moment or two to reconsider his position. No, Dermott replied amicably, Ireland was a neutral country, and as he had no strong feelings on the matter one way or the other he felt it would be quite wrong for him to cast the decisive vote.

Jericho – whose temper was considerably the worse for wear after a château-bottled luncheon at the Connaught and substantial quantities of cognac – rounded savagely on Dermott. If the reunification of the thirty-two counties was at issue, he ranted, spraying everyone in the vicinity with seventy-proof spittle, the world would not hear so much as a whisper about Irish neutrality.

But Ireland, Otello interceded gently, was *not* at issue. And learned delegates were not helping an already difficult situation by raising their voices at their colleagues. This was a time for cool heads and reasoned argument.

Jericho rose unsteadily to his feet in a froth of righteous indignation. He was not raising his voice, he thundered, fiery-eyed. *He* was the one who was being reasonable, trying to reach a compromise. And that was more than could be said for the director-general. What had happened to the so-called neutrality of the chair?

With that, he seized a heap of documents from his table and hurled them defiantly across the room towards Otello's podium. Papers flew everywhere, like a flock of startled birds. The Dutch and West German delegates protested angrily; Dermott Plunkett appealed for calm. Rolv Erlendsson moved that the Air Vice-Marshal be suspended from the session for being drunk and disorderly. Jericho advised him to withdraw that slanderous accusation or take the consequences. Tancredo Ferreira of Brazil told him to go home and sober up. Jericho advanced menacingly on Ferreira, demanding satisfaction. Ingvar Lundstrom of Sweden and Nelson Bedekunwe of Zimbabwe leapt up to intervene, as Jericho threw a wild punch at Ferreira and fetched him a glancing blow on the nose. Ferreira staggered backwards, stammering in Portuguese, dabbing a handkerchief at the first dribble of blood that was already beginning to seep from his nostrils.

Lundstrom and Bedekunwe made a grab for the raging Air Vice-Marshal; Mohinder Banherjee of India sprang to their assistance. Otello thumped furiously on his table for order, with Isobel and Zenia shouting 'Shame!' The majority of delegates gazed on in silence, however, transfixed with disgust and speechless fascination as Jericho lost the last vestiges of his self-control. With Lundstrom round his neck, Bedekunwe round his waist, and little Mohinder clinging resolutely to his ankles, the valiant aviator threw himself headlong at the petrified figure of Tancredo Ferreira. Hopelessly overwhelmed, he lost his balance at the onset of the charge, and the entire scrummage, weighing the best part of half a ton, piled into the neutral table of Sigismund Frankl, the venerable old Swiss delegate. Frankl went flying; his chair went flying; while the table rose, as if by levitation, and capsized. Jericho tumbled to the floor like a felled rhinoceros, amidst a cascade of papers, water carafes and coffee cups, and the rest of the scrum collapsed in a heap on top of him.

Silence. Not a soul moved. Delegates sat and stared, bemused, incredulous, like passers-by gathered round a car smash. It was so still everywhere that, for one moment, all that could be heard was the sound of a telephone ringing somewhere, several floors below.

Finally, the ruck began to untangle itself. Dermott Plunkett eased the ancient Frankl to his feet and helped him to a chair.

Lundstrom and Bedekunwe got up, dusted themselves down, and extended helping hands to the prostrate Mohinder. Lastly, the Air Vice-Marshal – his left hand bleeding profusely from an intimate encounter with a shattered water carafe – arose, awash with sweat, and collapsed, dazed, into Erlendsson's vacant chair.

The room began to buzz with conversation once more. Dieter Landgrebe and Laurie Tappet started picking up the furniture. Dermott Plunkett applied a makeshift tourniquet to Jericho's bleeding palm, and Tancredo Ferreira sat gazing at the ceiling as Li Zhao Yang's interpreter tried to staunch the copious flow of blood from his injured nose. Such were the wages of progress, Byron reflected sadly, as Jericho tottered quietly out of the room, badly shaken, clutching his wounded paw to his breast like the dying body of a much-loved pet.

From that moment on, Wopec began to fall apart like a house of cards. Isobel Maddox and Zenia Schapiro announced straightaway that Australia and Israel would be taking no further part in the conference until the Air Vice-Marshal had apologised to the board. Rolv Erlendsson and Dieter Landgrebe of West Germany went one further and proposed a resolution to suspend Jericho from the board until that apology was forthcoming. Buonaventura Martinez protested that that was grossly unconstitutional; only a full delegate conference could suspend a board member. Otello agreed to put it to a vote. Whereupon the entire Soviet bloc and half their non-aligned colleagues got up and walked out. Otello decided that he could not now put the matter to a vote; so Doctors Erlendsson, Landgrebe, Maddox and Schapiro walked out in protest as well. Otello then terminated the session in the hope that when everyone reassembled in the morning for UGS 19 tempers would have cooled and moderation would prevail.

By the following day, however, news of the fracas had leaked out to Fleet Street and a full report of the Air Vice-Marshal's antics appeared in that morning's *Daily Express* under the headline *Blood Flows at Peace Talks*. How the *Express* had got hold of the story it declined to reveal, but it was ascribed to a very well-placed source, interviewed on her way to Australia House.

The minute Otello opened UGS 19 at ten o'clock that morning, furious Third World delegates called on him to suspend Isobel Maddox from the board for such a flagrant breach of confidentiality. Otello replied that nobody could suspend a member merely for speaking to the press and declined to put it to a vote. So the non-aligned block got up *en masse* and stalked out of the chamber in protest. Western delegates then called on Otello to continue the business of UGS 19 without them . . . which the Soviet bloc stolidly refused to allow. At that, the Dutch, French and Japanese delegates walked out in protest too.

By this time the board no longer had a quorum (twenty) and had no constitutional authority to do anything any more. They could not propose motions, discuss them, amend them, adjourn the session, take a vote, read the minutes or address the chair. Technically speaking, they had ceased to exist, according to the strict letter of the Unibore charter, and could not even pack up and go home. So with only four weeks to go to Wopec Day and not so much as a comma on the final agenda, most delegates decided that the only useful thing they could do was to call a press conference and get their version of the story into print ahead of everybody else's.

By Thursday it was on breakfast tables all around the world:

Carnage Comes to Wopec — Washington Post
La Bataille de Jericho. Wopec Est Mort — Le Figaro
Engineer Puts Spanner in Works — Times of India
Paradise Envoy Turns Tables in Wopec Brawl — Guardian
Fists Fly at Peace Punch-up — Sydney Morning Herald
World Peace Dream Blitzed in Drunken Bloodbath Horror Orgy — Sun

Just to hammer home the final nail in Wopec's coffin, Blah-blah telephoned from the palace the following morning and informed Otello that in the light of all these unseemly and embarrassing goings-on at Halcyon House, and with the future of the conference now seriously in doubt, their royal highnesses no longer thought it politic for them to be associated with Wopec Day and the inauguration ceremony – assuming, of course, Blah-blah added (though not unkindly) that Unibore was still intending to try and hold one.

Nil desperandum, Otello exhorted his successor-elect over lunch that afternoon. It was the Spring Bank Holiday coming up and delegates would have plenty of time to relax and reflect on the unwisdom of their obduracy. Besides, if the worst came to the worst . . . well, he was retiring in six weeks' time, in any case.

Byron was also retiring, but only as far as St John's Wood, where he planned to spend the entire bank-holiday weekend in bed with a serious nervous condition.

Moscow alone remained strangely silent. *Izvestia* referred merely to a 'frank and businesslike exchange of views' at Halcyon House. *Pravda* did not mention it at all.

34

MOSCOW WAS silent because Moscow was mystified. The Kremlin had long since written off Hudson Butcher as a liability to world socialism, but they found it difficult to see what even *he* thought he stood to gain from wrecking the Wopec conference over an issue like Sandhustan. It was a God-given gift to Washington. Life was quite difficult enough as it was, with all that Moslem fundamentalism spreading across the East like forest fire, without renegades like him stoking the coals of religious nationalism. The only possible explanation was that he was waging some crazy vendetta of his own against someone or something. Or, conceivably, trying to make a bid for the leadership of the Third World. Either way, he would have to be diplomatically outmanoeuvred, the Kremlin had decided, and then discreetly blown out.

The immediate problem, however, was Wopec. To be or not to be. Whether to try and save the conference and maximise the embarrassment to Washington, or let it die an ignominious death and think up some way of blaming that on Uncle Sam as well. With these thoughts in mind, one fine summer's day – as Red Square echoed to the click of a thousand Nikon cameras, and bootleg reprints of *Your J-Zone* by Sherrilee Bloom changed hands up shady alleys everywhere at fifty roubles a copy – two ancient savants of the Soviet foreign ministry,

Andrei Feodorenko and Dimitri Chernikov, were sitting in a sun-drenched Kremlin courtyard, enjoying a quiet game of Moskopoly.

'Interesting,' reflected Andrei Nikolayevich, 'that Byron Cleveland undertook no initiative to try and stop the walk-outs at UGS 19.' He shook the dice, threw six and one, and moved his T-62 tank around the board from Dzerzhinsky Street to the Byelorussia railway station. Counting his dwindling treasury of toy banknotes, he decided reluctantly not to buy it.

'Perhaps he had instructions from the State Department to do nothing,' Dimitri Sergeyevich replied. 'Passive sabotage, I believe they call it.'

'Vitaly Semyonovich even wonders whether Washington might have secretly engineered the breakdown all along.'

A crack of a smile appeared in Dimitri Sergeyevich's crumbling concrete face. 'Engineered the Engineer?'

'Possible. If Wopec collapses now, the White House will be crowing about it all the way to election day.'

'Then we shall not let it collapse,' concluded Dimitri Sergeyevich.

'And that mountain of outstanding agenda problems?'

'When a bear cannot climb over a mountain, my dear friend, he simply goes round it.' Dimitri Sergeyevich shook the dice and threw five and four. He pushed his little red tractor round the board to *Chance?*, took the top card from the deck and read aloud: '*You have won an educational outing for high productivity. Advance to 25th October Gasworks.*'

'My property,' snapped Andrei Nikolayevich, with a glint of unseemly avarice in his tired old eyes. 'Four hundred and fifty roubles, old comrade.' Carefully watching him count out each note (for there was nothing that Andrei Nikolayevich despised more than a cheat) he went on: 'And how do you propose to circumvent this mountain?'

'Three of the five agenda zones have been agreed in principle – Europe, Africa and the Middle East. All the outstanding difficulties are in the Americo-Caribbean and Asio-Pacific zones.'

'Well?'

'If Unibore's executive board were to pass a resolution ruling that the conference should go ahead, whether the agendas for those two remaining zones are ready in time or not — '

'The Third World would never agree to that,' Andrei Nikolayevich interrupted. 'Out of the question.'

'What do they matter?' said Dimitri Sergeyevich. 'If we can be assured of support from the Western delegates, the non-aligned bloc will be out-voted.'

'You mean . . . a deal?' said Andrei Nikolayevich uneasily. 'Some sort of tacit agreement with them in advance?'

'Possibly. Through Byron Cleveland perhaps. He seems to have the most influence among his Western colleagues.'

Andrei Nikolayevich did not like making secret deals with the West. They had a nasty habit of coming unstuck at the seams and leaking – though, admittedly, the Americans were a far less leaky lot to deal with than the British. 'But if Byron Cleveland is following instructions from Washington — '

'*If*.'

' — he could lure us into a highly compromising position with the Third World.'

'Then we must arrange for Cleveland to initiate the whole thing.' Dimitri Sergeyevich smiled. 'Believe me, my dear Andrei, the man is fighting for his job. He's grasping at straws. He'll be extremely impressionable and open to suggestion.'

Andrei Nikolayevich still had reservations. 'Even so, we should monitor his communications with the State Department very carefully for the next few weeks. And we shall need someone with a very delicate touch to make the first approach.'

'We could take a chance on the Bulgarians again. Delegate Kabanova has a friendly working relationship with Cleveland, we're told.'

'That depends how friendly you wish her to be,' said Andrei Nikolayevich, throwing a double four and moving his T-62 tank around to *Kollektiv Chest*. 'Rhoskov reports that she is inclined to be rather frigid with men.'

'Rhoskov is a miserable old misogynist. What would he know?'

Andrei Nikolayevich took the top card from the *Kollektiv Chest*. It read: *You have been caught trading sable on the black market. Go to Lubianka Prison. Go straight to the Lubianka. Do not pass the State bank. Do not collect 5000 roubles*. 'I have won a ploughing competition,' he said brightly, slipping the card back into the middle of the pack. 'The bank pays me one thousand roubles.' And while Dimitri Sergeyevich obligingly counted out his prize in hundred-rouble bills, he went on: 'There is just one serious flaw in what you propose, dear comrade. The Western delegates are refusing to discuss anything until Engineer apologises to the board.'

'Then we must persuade Hudson Butcher to *order* Engineer to apologise.'

'You can't reason with a man like Butcher.'

'If we can't appeal to his sense of reason then we must appeal to his vanity. As the Americans say: make him an offer he can't refuse.'

'You have something particular in mind?' enquired Andrei Nikolayevich with considerable scepticism. Hudson Butcher had already syphoned off vast tranches of foreign development aid into his bank accounts in Liechtenstein and Panama, so it was difficult to see how he could be susceptible to bribes of anything less than the contents of Fort Knox.

'Well, now that the British royals have decided not to attend Wopec Day,' Dimitri Sergeyevich replied, with a spark of mischief in his eyes, 'Unibore will be looking for another Extremely Famous Person, will they not?'

35

SUNDAY IN sunny Mougins, and the solitary, plangent tolling of a church bell echoed through the deserted steets, summoning the faithful to morning mass. A kilometre away at the Château Montcalme, those who were past all hope of salvation were sitting up in their four-poster bed, reading all the filth and lies they could find in the Sunday papers and waiting for Chantal to arrive with their breakfast.

If the Wopec conference is abandoned, as now seems inevitable, Rosheen was reading in her airmail edition of *The Sunday Times, the United States will almost certainly withdraw from Unibore before the presidential election campaign gets under way at the beginning of July.*' She stopped reading and turned to the baron. 'Hey, Guy? You see this?'

He was deeply engrossed in news of the latest regional government vice scandal in *Le Provençale* and checking how many of his friends and business partners had been named so far. '*Ma douce*?'

'You read this about Wopec?'

'What about it?'

'It's on the verge of collapse. They had a fight in the boardroom. That fat slob from the Paradise Islands started throwing tables around.'

'It was in Friday's *Le Monde*.'

'You knew already?'

'Ah hah.'

'Well, for Christ's sake, why didn't you tell me?'

Guy peered up from his *Provençale*. 'Why should I?'

'He's my husband, you callous pig. He could be out of a job by summer.'

'So?'

'So, what about my divorce settlement?'

The baron shrugged and went back to his newspaper. '*Je suis désolé*.'

'No good just sitting there saying you're *désolé*, you tête-de-merde. How am I going to get alimony out of the son-of-a-bitch if he's out of a job?'

'Does he have life insurance?'

'How should I know?'

'Shoot him and see.'

'You're really not being very helpful, Guy.'

'Well, I don't think your divorce settlement is any of my business, little wasp.'

'Don't be so selfish.'

'But he's not *my* husband.'

'I'm afraid I find that a very French kind of attitude.'

'Well, I'm a very French kind of person,' reasoned the baron.

Chantal lumbered into the room, brown as a barnyard, built like a blacksmith, bearing a tray laden with coffee, cups and croissants.

'What do you reckon that asshole started this boardroom bust-up deliberately?' said Rosheen, reading *The Sunday Times* article again.

'Who? The air vice-marshal?'

'No. Byron.'

'Why should he want to do a thing like that?'

'To wreck Wopec and give the US the excuse to pull clean out of Unibore and put himself out of a job.'

'Whatever for?'

'To stop me getting my goddam alimony!' said Rosheen angrily. 'That's whatever for.'

'Don't you think that's just a tiny bit implausible?'

'No, I do not. We're talking about a hundred thousand dollars. That mean son-of-a-bitch would kidnap his own mother for less.'

Chantal placed the tray on the bedside table next to Rosheen and clambered over her.

'Well, if that's how you feel,' said the baron, 'you'd better hurry over to London and sort something out while there's still time.'

'Exactly what I was thinking,' murmured Rosheen, bobbing about like a ketch in a squall as Chantal waded across the bed, sank like a whale and squashed her expansive leathery buttocks in between them.

36

OTELLO WAS about the only person at Halcyon House who had not yet given Wopec up for dead. Ever the unsinkable optimist, he had spent all Saturday on the telephone to foreign ministers around the world, most of Sunday relaxing in the bath with family and friends, and most of Bank-Holiday Monday having lunch. Byron, conversely, had spent the entire weekend in bed with *The Times Higher Educational Supplement*, looking for a new job. There was something touchingly childlike (or was it wilfully perverse?) about Otello's indestructible faith in human nature, he was thinking on Monday night, as he watched the imperturbable Sicilian on *Panorama*, trying to convince five million viewers that it was perfectly normal for air vice-marshals to throw furniture round the boardroom at Halcyon

House and slug Brazilian professors on the nose. Even the ignominious failure of his attempts to convene UGS 20 the following morning did nothing to shake his confidence, despite the fact that only nine delegates turned up and the session had to be abandoned after twenty minutes for lack of a quorum. Time was a great healer, he assured Byron, as they went their separate ways to lunch. All that was needed was a little patience and some quiet, determined diplomacy.

Convinced that all that was needed was a large dose of divine intervention and a stiff drink, Byron retreated despondently to his local wine bar in Jermyn Street, where, to his considerable surprise, he found Nina Kabanova wilting quietly in a corner with a face as long as the Berlin Wall. Byron could not recall ever having seen her in a drinking establishment before. But then she was a highly enigmatic woman, shy and secretive, with an air of dark Balkan mystery about her; and after some of the rumours he had heard about her penchant for weightlifting, and all the algae she was reputed to shovel down her gullet for breakfast every morning, he had begun to wonder if she were not ever so slightly unhinged. Unhinged, perhaps; but he found her a strangely alluring creature, with a sad, almost beautiful face, a cryptic smile and beguiling, sleepy, green eyes. And there was something instantly consoling about seeing her there, slumped miserably in a corner of the wine bar like a broken doll. If there was one thing that never failed to lift Byron's spirits in times of deep despair it was chancing upon someone who was even more fed up with life than he was.

'Hi, Nina.'

Curiously, she did not seem at all surprised to see him.

'Hello, Byron.'

'May I join you?'

She gave him a wan smile and offered him all three empty chairs around the table. 'Be my guest.'

He took off his jacket, draped it over the back of a chair and sat down. 'Where were your crowd this morning?'

'Consultations.' Her accent lent the word a languorous, almost sensual quality. *Con-zul-deh-zhuns*.

'You missed UGS 20.'

'I did?'

'You and twenty-five others.'

'Anything happen?'

'Coffee for nine.'

She nodded gloomily, as if that lived up fully to her expectations. 'Doesn't look so good, hah?'

'Rhoskov got any tricks up his sleeve?'

She shook her head. 'Everyone seems to have given up hope.'

'You too?'

'Well, what's the use?' She sighed – a deep, dark sigh, far older than her years. 'My first posting in the West. Eighteen months. Now it looks as though Unibore is finished and I'll have to go back to Sofia and . . .' She shrugged hopelessly. 'God knows what will become of me.'

'Hey, come on, come on,' said Byron. 'It can't be that bad. You're still a kid by Russian standards, you've got your whole career ahead of you.'

'As what? I'm an academic, not an apparatchik. There's no other posting in the West I'm qualified for. I'll end my days a spinster in the cobwebs of the state archive office . . . or worse.'

'Nina, that is ridiculous. You won't end up any such thing. You're far too clever. You're far too . . .' He took a breath. He was going to say 'attractive' but didn't want to risk giving her the wrong idea. 'Far too gifted,' he concluded lamely. 'You must know that.'

'You don't understand, Byron,' she said, but without resentment. 'How can you?'

'Nina, honey, believe me, I understand. If Washington pulls out of Unibore now I'm going to be the *first* one out of a job.'

'But you have freedom, Byron. The freedom to go where you want and do what you like, whenever you feel like it.'

'Well, I guess so, sure, but . . .' He struggled to think of some of the advantages of not being able to go where one wanted and do what one liked, but eventually gave up. Nina assumed the condition of a Thracian lament and sipped her hock in melancholy silence.

A breathless girl in pink rompers scuttled up to the table and gasped, ''Splease?' Byron ordered fish pâté and a glass of Chablis. Pink rompers scuttled away and 'spleased? somewhere else.

Never having enjoyed the privilege of an even faintly intimate conversation with Nina before, and never having encountered her in this depressed state, Byron did not know quite how to cope with the situation. He tried to look on the positive side. 'If it's your Alfa that's bothering you, I wouldn't worry. I'm sure David Schellenberg will let you ship it home on Unibore's account.'

Nina seemed confused. 'My what?'

'Your Alfa Romeo.'

'What about it?'

'I'm just saying, I'm sure Unibore will ship it back to Bulgaria for you, if that's what's bothering you.'

She looked saddened and slightly shocked. '*Et tu*, Byron?'

'I say something wrong?'

'And you were the one man in Halcyon House I thought I could talk to.'

'What do you mean? What did I say?'

'But you're just as superficial as the rest.'

'*Me*? Superficial?'

'Like everything and everybody else in the West. Nothing but Kentucky-fried superficiality everywhere you go.'

Byron was stung. If anyone understood what superficiality was, *he* did. He'd been married to an advanced prototype of it for the past twelve years. The one distinguishing feature that marked him out as a pariah among Rosheen and her cardboard cut-out cronies was that he had an attention span of more than three minutes and was able to hold a deep, meaningful, depressing conversation about anything at any time. 'Nina, that is grossly unfair,' he protested. 'I'm a very good listener. And a very *sympathetic* listener, believe me. If you want to talk, you talk.'

'Forget it, Byron.' She finished her hock. 'You and me, it's like we come from different planets.'

'Honey, that's just not true. We're two intelligent adult people. We're colleagues. We're friends. When it comes to saving Unibore we're all on the same side. Let me order you another glass of — '

'No, no, forget it,' she said wearily. Taking two pounds from her purse, she placed them beside the empty wine glass.

'No, I won't forget it,' Byron replied, coming back strongly. 'If you want to talk, let's talk, damn it. I insist we talk. There's not enough talk between East and West on a personal level. That's our whole problem. We've stopped thinking of each other as human beings, with the same human problems, the same human worries.'

Nina hesitated, as if weakening to some instinctive impulse, but then got up to go. 'I can't talk now, anyway. I've got another meeting at the embassy.'

'Well, OK, how about tea this afternoon?'

'I shan't be through till six.'

'All right, then why don't we meet up for a drink this evening?'

'This evening?' Nina looked troubled. 'I don't know. Maybe, I suppose — '

'I could stop by your place around, say, eight o'clock. We could find somewhere quiet, have a bite to eat maybe and talk the whole thing through.'

'But not my place.' She lowered her voice and peered nervously around the wine bar. 'There's constant surveillance. It could cause trouble. Somewhere else perhaps.'

'Anywhere you like,' said Byron. 'My place, if it makes it any easier.'

'Your place?'

'You know where I am? Twenty-two Hamilton Grove. Off Hamilton Terrace.'

She nodded. 'OK, I can look it up. Say eight – eight-fifteen?'

'Fine by me. Whenever.'

'And don't tell anyone,' she whispered. 'We're not supposed to meet Western delegates like this.'

'No, well I guess the CIA wouldn't go a bundle on it either,' said Byron. 'Don't worry. I won't breathe a word.'

'*A ce soir*, then.' She turned to go.

'Have a nice consultation. And don't get too depressed.'

'I'll try not to.' She gave him a forlorn smile, walked quickly out of the bar and disappeared among the lunchtime crowds in Jermyn Street.

Byron spent the rest of his lunch-hour deep in thought. Aside from the fact that she had played the damsel in distress and brought out the streak of St George in him, he could not quite work out why he was letting himself become involved in Nina's personal problems in this way. He was not at all sure he even *wanted* to get involved in Nina's personal problems. It was flattering to think that he was the one man in Halcyon House whom she felt she could talk to, but upon reflection, he could not think of anything that she could conceivably want to talk *about*. And upon maturer consideration she was absolutely right – they *did* come from different planets.

He returned to Halcyon House at two o'clock for Otello's second abortive attempt to convene UGS 20, twiddled his thumbs in the boardroom for half an hour and then awarded himself the afternoon off. Faintly discomfited by the strange encounter with Nina – and not at all convinced he was doing the right thing, inviting her to his apartment for the evening – he recounted the incident in full to Gladstone Shilling on the way home to St John's Wood.

Gladstone was highly sympathetic. He had come across this sort of thing before and was familiar with the symptoms.

'Symptoms?' said Byron, sniffing a rat. 'What symptoms?'

'Must've been the year before you came, Doc,' Gladstone recalled. 'The Polish delegate went jus' the same way.'

'No kidding? Which way?'

'Came over all strange and depressed, like. Then one dinner time he had some kind of secret meetin' with the American delegate, Mrs Arlene Baker-Dixon. Next morning he walked out of his apartment to go to work, same as usual, got in this US embassy car waitin' for him outside, drove to Mildenhall air force base, and next thing you know he was in Washin'ton DC, bein' given diplomatic asylum.'

'*Asylum?*' Byron swallowed the faint note of hysteria in his voice and said it again. 'Asylum?' This time he laughed. 'Gladstone, that's absurd. Nina? Defect?'

Gladstone nodded soberly. 'Thass what it sounds like to me, Doc.'

'Jesus, that's ridiculous.' The fish pâté heaved uneasily in Byron's belly. 'Nina? Defect Stateside? She couldn't do it. The Soviets would go screaming nuts. They'd have my director-generalship annulled.'

'More than likely,' said Gladstone.

'God almighty, you have to be kidding. I've got Wopec crashing down round my ears . . . I've got a whole professional future on the line . . . I've got a demented Visigoth of a wife I can't divorce . . . I've got a fiancée I can't marry . . . And now I've got a depressive Bulgarian health freak who wants me to — ' Byron broke off in despair. 'Well, what *does* she want me to do?'

Gladstone shrugged. 'Dunno, Doc. Fix up some kind of deal with the State Department, I s'pose.'

'I just can't believe it,' said Byron, who could, but simply did not wish to. 'Not Nina. She's the archetypal diehard Stalinist.

They say she still hasn't recovered from the Twentieth Party Congress.'

'Yip, right,' said Gladstone, as if that only served to confirm his diagnosis. 'Same with that Polish guy. He was a close mate of Brezhnev, by all accounts. Hero of Socialist Labour. Order of Lenin. You name it, he had it. Now he's over there, sunnin' hisself in Florida all year round and probbly campaignin' for the President's re-election.'

Byron wilted. The fish pâté churned over in open rebellion. Of course it made sense. It made perfect sense. Nina was precisely the type who *did* defect. The shy, silent type. The still waters. The party faithful. The loner who bottled up her resentment and frustration for just so long and then boiled over without a word of warning, pouring her troubles straight down the earhole of the nearest sympathetic American, and pleading to be bundled on the next available 747 to New York.

Byron arrived back at Hamilton Grove with all the makings of a promisingly acute migraine. He swallowed a shovelful of paracodeine tablets, turned the central heating up and retired to bed for the rest of the afternoon to panic. The exquisite beauty of life, he reflected, was that no matter how bad things were, they could always get worse, and frequently did. If the White House did not succeed in destroying him, then the Kremlin probably would. And if those two couldn't manage it, then the press most *certainly* would . . .

U.S. Envoy up to Fat Neck in Red Defection Plot.

New York Times

'My Torrid Nights With Byron.' Balkan Beauty Reveals All

Daily News

'Betrayed by a Red Defector-loving Bigamist Monster.' Heart-broken Annabelle Speaks Out

Salvation Herald-Examiner

He drifted off to sleep at last. The next thing he knew, it was quarter past six and there was a woman standing by his bed. She had a vaguely familiar shape. He sat up, eyes foggy with sleep, expecting Nina to swim into focus with all her worldly possessions and a crisp new copy of *America on Twenty Dollars a Day*.

'Hi, sweetie.'

It was Rosheen.

37

ZLOB ARRIVED at Nina's apartment at half past six, with a fresh crop of pustules all over his face and a cheap-looking plastic attaché case in his hand.

Nina had spent half the afternoon doing herself up for her date with Byron. 'How do I look?' she said, and danced a pirouette in the middle of the sitting-room to show off a new Balenciaga dress in eau-de-nil satin.

'All right,' moaned Zlob. 'Why? Don't you feel so good?'

Nina stopped pirouetting and offered him a drink.

'Wouldn't say no. Ta.'

She went out to the kitchen to pour him a vodka. When she came back she found him standing in front of a mirror on the wall, squeezing a creamy eruption on his neck. He'd left one of his malodorous army-issue cigarettes smouldering in an antique Meissen nut-bowl – a much-treasured memento of a whirlwind romance with an East German air force general. She tossed the cigarette out of the window. 'Are you married, Zlob?' she enquired testily. She found it impossible to visualise, but stranger things did happen.

'Nope.' He took the vodka, sniffed, said 'Ta' and knocked back half of it in one shot. 'I did have a girlfriend once, though. Back home in Stara Zagora. We met at the Ninth of September bricklaying competition.'

'Romantic.'

'Not really. She gave me the elbow next day.'

'How old was she?'

'Eleven.'

'*Eleven*?'

'Well, ten and half actually, but she called it eleven. I was only nine. So I suppose it mightn't have worked out in the long run.' He knocked back the rest of the vodka and opened his attaché case. 'I brought a little something for you.'

'Sweet of you. But you needn't have troubled.'

'No trouble.' He handed her an egg of sticky black putty.
'What's this?'
'Black stuff.'
'I can see that.'
'I call it gunk.'
'Well, what do *I* want it for?'
'To jam the lock so I can get into this brainy Yank's flat tonight.'
'Are you sure you know what you're doing this time?'
He looked indignant. 'Of course I'm sure. This sort of thing is my speciality.'
'What did Kotsev tell you?'
'Not much. Bug this Yankee know-all's gaff. Then bug the castle.'
'Castle?' Kotsev had not mentioned that to Nina.
'The castle where you're having this war conference.'
'Peace conference.'
'Same difference.'
'So what am I supposed to do with this black gunk?'
'Bung it in the lock hole in his front door before you go out.'
'Before *I* go out?'
'Before you both go out.'
'Go out where?'
'Don't ask me. I don't know London from the South Pole. That's up to you.'
'But we haven't planned to go anywhere.'
'Well, you'll just have to, I'm afraid. I can't do my stuff with him there, can I? He might get suspicious seeing me crawling about under the furniture with a boxful of micro-transmitters.'
'But suppose he doesn't *want* to go out?'
'Then you'll have to insist.'
'All right, let's say I insist. What am I supposed to do with the gunk?'
'I'll show you.' He took her out into the hallway and opened her front door. 'Just before you leave, secretly open his front door, thus . . .'
'What if he sees me?'
'Sees you what?'
'Secretly opening his front door.'
'Well, wait till he's in the toilet or something.'

'Suppose he doesn't go?'
'Where?'
'To the toilet.'
'Of course he goes to the toilet. Don't be daft, everyone goes to the toilet at some time or other.'
'But suppose he doesn't want to go while I'm there?'
'Blimey, you brainy types really do look on the cheerful side, don't you? Suppose, suppose, suppose. Give him plenty to drink, then he'll *have* to go. Use some initiative.'
'Oh, very well,' sighed Nina, not in the least happy with all these blasé presumptions but having no time to argue. 'So I've secretly opened his front door while he's in another room. Now what do I do?'
'You take small gob of gunk, thus,' (breaking off a piece) 'And bung in latch hole, thus. Place this tiny copper striker plate on top of gunk, so it lies flush with door jamb, thus. So that when you go out and shut the front door behind you, the latch won't click home properly. Watch.' He closed the door to demonstrate what he meant. Perversely, it swung straight open again. Zlob was unperturbed. 'If it won't stay shut, all you have to do is press a few gobs of the magic gunk elsewhere on the jamb, thus. And as an extra precaution make sure that *you* close the door when you go out, and not him.'
'And suppose,' said Nina, 'he double locks the door when he goes out?'
'Why should he?' Burglary being nothing like as fashionable in Stara Zagora as it was in St John's Wood, Zlob had never heard of people having two locks on their front doors.
'Well, in an area like that,' said Nina, 'he's bound to have a mortice lock as well.'
'A what?'
'I thought you were an expert? Haven't you come across Chubb locks before?'
'Czubloks?' Zlob frowned and gnawed his lower lip. 'Can't say as I have. Is he KGB or GRU?'

Rosheen was lying sprawled across the sofa in French paratrooper's trousers, bulging bra-less out of a vivid ochre tank-top and knocking back a tequila sunrise. She would be thirty-four on the twenty-first of the month, and considering the legions of people she had been intimate with over the years, still looked remarkably spry and nubile, if just a little bandy at the knees. Byron had not seen her since her departure to Mougins the previous spring. She had been a redhead at the time; now she was a frizzy blonde. Strange, but he could not remember what she was originally.

'It's not that I'm suspicious, sweetheart,' he said, 'but you just turn up out of the blue like this, when I've been asking for a divorce pretty well since before we were married . . . I mean, how come you've changed your mind so suddenly?'

'To be honest,' said Rosheen, 'I've finally seen the light. I realise that you've been right all along. It *is* best to finish everything quickly, quietly and cleanly. You want a divorce? OK, honey, you've got it. No strings. Finito. Let's wrap the whole thing up.'

Byron was trying not to get too excited about this. 'Why? Are you and Guy getting married or something?'

'Maybe. Some day. Who knows?'

'Sweetie, that's terrific. I'm so proud. My own wife marrying a real live descendant of Louis the Sixteenth.'

'I'm not saying we *are*, I'm just saying we might. But that's not the point, angel. The point is, we are very close friends, you and me. And friends shouldn't fight like animals over a divorce. My sister Siobhan in Trenton tells me I ought to screw you for all the alimony I can get. She asks me, what have I got to show for all those years of marriage? What did I get out of it? Like it was a fruit machine. Now isn't that sick? Isn't that a terrible endearment of our society?'

'*Dict*ment.'

'Right. I mean, what a sordid attitude of mind. Just because she's knocking forty and still single and no one wants to jump her any more. I tell her: what I have got to show for all those long, happy years of wedded bliss is a very beautiful, deep, undying friendship.'

'Absolutely.'

'And that is worth more than all the gold in the world.'

'Sweetie, you're so right. Just so right.'

'But these mercenary assholes today don't even know the meaning of the word.'

'The age we live in, honey. It's all shallowness, insincerity, Kentucky-fried superficiality — '

'I tell Siobhan, Christ, you know friendship is just *galaxies* above temporal effeminate things like . . . I don't mean effeminate, baby, what do I mean?'

'Ephemeral.'

'Ephemeral, right. Ephemeral. God, it's it's it's . . . What was my point?'

'That love may come and love may go, but friendship is a true enduring thing. Like gold. It wasteth not away, nor rusteth not.'

'The Bible say that?'

'Pretty much.'

'That's a really beautiful way of putting it.'

'Isn't it? Isn't it just?'

'I mean, I don't know what the Bible says about love, but . . . Could you please pour me another one of these, treasure? But I mean, for Christ's sake, what is love? You know, any jerk can love someone. All you need is a bed or a car seat or a back alley, whatever. But friendship is like cheese, you know? It takes time to mature and ripen to its full richness, right?'

Byron got up to mix her another tequila sunrise. 'I guess so. I hadn't thought of it that way before.'

'Maybe the Bible says it better. But the point is we don't get divorced very often in this life, so it's a kind of special occasion. Like the apotheosis – is that the right word? – the apotheosis of our marriage. So I'd like it to be an event we can look back on when we're old and grey, and remember with affection, and tell our grandchildren all about. In short, who wants to foul up a beautiful friendship with fat greedy lawyers and court hearings and maintenance orders?'

'Rosheen, can I tell you something, very, very sincerely?'

'Sure.'

'You have grown into a very, very beautiful person, you know. A very *real* person, a very . . .'

'Oh, shit, no, not really, just . . . just, you know . . .'

'You have, sweetie, you have . . . really matured into a wonderful, caring human being. I mean, we'd never have talked like this ten years ago.'

'Well, I think being with Guy has taught me a lot. He's very worldly-wise and philosophical.'

'I guess so. Must be like living with your grandpa.' Byron handed her a fresh tequila sunrise and sat down again.

'The point is, what I'm getting round to saying is, let's have a quick, quiet, friendly divorce now. No cross-petitions, no alimony claims, nothing.'

'Nothing?'

'Absolutely nothing. Fat zero. Zilch. Except, of course, just some token once-for-all cash payment to cover my expenses, the various little inconveniences, compensation for furthering your career, so on, so forth.'

Byron had rather suspected that some sort of token cash sum might come into it somewhere. 'How much did you have in mind?'

'Oh, I don't know. Say . . . a hundred grand.'

'A hundred *grand*?'

'Something in that area, you know, I haven't really given it a lot of — '

'Are you out of your mind?'

'Oh, now come on, angel, be reasonable.'

'*Me* be reasonable?'

'What's a hundred thousand dollars to a guy in your position? Siobhan says I should sue you for fifty grand a year for life. But I say, no way, Siobhan. Byron and I have something very special between us . . . a friendship that is worth more than all the gold that rusteth away and wasteth and, you know, all that Bible crap.'

'Rosheen, that's way *way* over the top. I just don't *have* that kind of money.'

'It's OK. I understand. Things are a little difficult for you right now. I'll settle for, say, twenty down and the rest in instalments.'

'Besides, I don't actually see why I have to pay you anything in the first place, to be perfectly honest.'

'You don't?'

'Frankly, no.'

Pause.

'Well, I find that really quite extraordinary.'

'Sweetheart, you're living with one of the richest men in France.'

'What has that got to do with anything?'

'He's supporting you. And in very fine style. You're living like a princess out there.'

'Darling, how can you be so unfeeling? You are my husband. Are you *proud* of the fact that your wife is being kept like a princess by another man? Don't you want her to be independent, to be able to pay her own way?'

'Aw, now come on, honey, be fair. Who left whom?'

'What the hell kind of argument is that?'

'No, no, come on, fair's fair. Who ran off with Moses "The Rod" McRory and the Cincinnati Cyclones in the first place?'

'Oh Byron, Christ, that is *old*, sweetie, that is ancient history.'

'Just because it happened a few years ago — '

'Byron, come on, hell. True friends don't rake up that kind of tired old horseshit. True friends let bygones by bygones.'

'So how come true friend is demanding a hundred thousand bucks off me?'

'I'm not demanding *any*thing, Byron darling. I'm simply asking. Nicely. That's all.'

'Well, I'm telling you equally nicely that your request is quite unreasonable. Who deserted the family home? *Twice*?'

'Byron, that really is pathetic. That is childish. Two weeny infidelities. Two measly guys. A footballer and a Frog. How can you be so — '

'It's not just the two guys you ran off with, sweetie, it's the four or five hundred you had in between.'

'Jesus, that's out*rageous* — '

'A judge would take them all into account, you know.'

'I never made it with five hundred guys in my whole life twice over, let alone ten years of marriage. That's the most ridiculous thing I ever heard. And I suppose you're trying to tell me you've been some kind of monk the last fifteen months? Sitting all alone here like little boy blue waiting for some chick to come blow up your horn. Who are you trying to kid?'

The telephone began to ring.

'I'm not trying to kid anybody. I'm just saying that I didn't walk out on our marriage, that's all.'

'What do you mean you didn't walk out on our . . . You went to live in the summerhouse!'

'The summerhouse was in the garden. I didn't leave home.'

'*Ah-ha*, the home does not include the — '

'It does too.'

'Ah-ah, ah-ah, the house does *not* include — '

'The garden is part of the marital — '

'Ah-ah, bull*shit*, you can *not* go and live in the fucking garden and claim you — '

'Please, Rosheen, the Feinbaums. The walls are very thin — '

' . . . *claim you haven't left home*!'

'Will you just quit bawling?'

'And will you get that damn phone?'

'Sweetie, this is a respectable neighbourhood, not the Cincinnati Cyclones' locker room.'

'Don't change the subject.'

'The English are very sensitive about that kind of language.'

'Well, they should know, they invented it.'

'It might go down a treat with the Gauls but you're in a civilised country now.'

'Byron, will you get the phone, please? It's driving me nuts.'

'That'll be Nina, my defecting Bulgarian health freak.'

'I don't care who it is, just answer the thing. Tell her you're busy right now.'

'I can't. She's in a bad way.'

'Don't be so damn selfish. So is our marriage.'

Byron got up and crossed to the telephone: 'Hello? Seven, nine, double four.'

'Byron?' It was Annabelle.

'Oh hi, baby . . .' He turned his back on Rosheen. 'Surprise, surprise.'

Rosheen called over: 'Is that your commie health nut?'

Byron said, 'How are things?'

'Oh, we're fine,' said Annabelle. 'But how are things in London, more's the point?'

'Oh, fine, fine. That is, ah . . . OK, I guess. Well, you know, pretty lousy really. Say, where are you calling from?'

'The kitchen. Why?'

'You sound miles away.'

'Well, I guess I am.'

Rosheen called out: 'Is she phoning from Bulgaria?'

Byron shook his head.

Annabelle was saying, 'We've been reading about the big fight and all the Wopec trouble, darling. Is it really bad? What's happening?'

'No one's sure at the moment. There are just lots of consultations going on.'

'Only Noah doesn't know whether or not to confirm our travel reservations for the inauguration weekend.'

'Tell the bitch you're busy,' said Rosheen. 'Tell her your wife just got in from Mougins, France.' (Moojinz, Frants.)

Annabelle said, 'Byron, do you have someone there?'

'Just a colleague happened by, that's all.'

'Tell her it's Rosheen,' shouted Rosheen.

'Rosheen?' said Annabelle. 'Your new secretary?'

'That's right. Just a little business.'

'I'm sorry. I didn't mean to interrupt — '

'No, no, no, it's lovely to hear your voice, sweetheart. But if I could just call you back in a short while . . . ?'

'Sure. Any time. I'll be home all afternoon.'

'Byron, will you just tell the cow to piss off?' shouted Rosheen.

'Call you right back,' said Byron. 'Bye now.'

'Bye, darl — '

Byron slammed down the phone. 'Damn it, Rosheen, just watch your dirty mouth, will you?'

'Yeh? Why? Who was she, loverboy?'

'Like I told you. Nina, my manic-depressive Bulgarian. She's on her way over, so do me a favour and get lost, hah? This could get heavy.'

'You lying son of a bitch. That wasn't your commie defector. You called her *sweetheart*.'

'So? I happen to be very fond of Nina.'

'You call all the other communists at Unibore sweetheart?'

'Of course I don't. They're all men.'

'Fairies, hah? So what's going on between you and this fat Bulgarian fag-hag?'

'Nothing's going on between me and . . . Who the hell said anything about a fat fag-hag, anyhow? She's got a damn sight better figure than *you*. She works out, she eats seaweed, she's in terrific shape.'

'Been jumping her, hah?'

'Don't be so childish. She's a colleague who's going through a very bad time, that's all.'

'Bad time, my ass. You're shafting a communist. You're making it with a filthy lousy Russian.'

'She's Bulgarian, and *very* clean, and that is the most absurd thing I ever — '

'Screwing a lousy Russian Bulgarian then. And here's you trying to be all holier-than-thou, celibate as a monk, too pure and superior to get your rocks off, and all this time you've been fornicating with a communist.'

'Nina and I are *not* forni — '

'God, I am nauseated. I fly thousands of miles here all the way from Europe, wanting to make our divorce a really nice, happy occasion — '

'Oh, Jesus, spare my breaking heart, Rosheen, you hypocrite.'

'Something to remember all our lives . . . to tell our children about . . .'

'We don't *have* any children, duckbrain.'

'Well, I might just start having a few. So up you.'

'Yeah? With that geriatric paedophile down there in Mougins? Who are you kidding?'

'At least he doesn't shaft communists, you filthy degenerate. My God, and to think I flew all this way with my heart full of goodness and love to — '

'Extort a hundred thousand bucks out of this amazing true friend.'

'And that's cheap at the price.'

'It probably is. Most guys would pay the earth to be rid of you.'

'Listen, fuckhead, I'm doing you a favour. I could screw you in the courts for fifty thousand bucks a year, the rest of your life!'

'Will you just *quit shouting*? The Feinbaums can hear us. They're nice, decent sons-of-bitches.'

'If you mention the Feinbaums just *one* more time,' said Rosheen, hurling her tequila sunrise at him, 'I'm gonna get really good and mad.' Byron ducked and the glass shattered on the wall behind him. 'I didn't fly here ten thousand miles from the south of France to talk about the lousy Feinbaums.'

'My God, you really are a pathetic specimen, Rosheen. You ought to be in a cage, you know that? You ought to be in the Regent's Park Zoo. Except you're an insult to the animal kingdom.'

'Oh, I am, am I?' She reached over the back of the sofa and plucked a Charlie Mingus album from the record shelf behind her. 'So what are you planning to do about that, Einstein?' And she spun the record across the room at him like a frisbee. It missed by inches and hit the wall behind.

'That is just wanton vandalism, Rosheen,' he said wearily. 'If you're going to vandalise my home I'm going to have to put you outside in the gutter where you belong.'

'Aw, the big talkin' man.' She reached out and grabbed a handful of LPs. '*Wanton* vandalism, baby? OK, you've *gotten* vandalism.'

'Rosheen, you pack that in right now, or so help me God — ' Coleman Hawkins came scything through the air and caught him across the bridge of the nose. 'All right, OK, you've had fair warning, Gorgonella. This is it.' And with remarkable athleticism for one who preached that fitness was the curse of the technological age, he threw himself at the mal-de-mer green sofa with one feline leap and belly-flopped onto the semi-recumbent Rosheen. It was like landing on a dozing tigress. She was suddenly the Eumenides unleashed, all teeth and claws and spitting, savage fury. They tumbled out of the sofa onto the floor, locked together in a frenzy of threshing limbs. A table capsized; a lamp fell; pictures tumbled; bottles flew; and faintly, through the din of crashing glass, Byron heard the dull *thud-thud* of Leo Feinbaum protesting fistily on the wall next door.

Outside, some fifty yards up the street in her Bolshevik-red Alfa Romeo, Nina and the pustulous Zlob were sitting listening to this awesome cacophony of violence.

'Some poor sod's getting a right spanking,' said Zlob.

'Let's hope it's not coming from Byron's block. The police will be called if this goes on much longer, and they're the *last* people we want nosing around.'

Zlob lit up one of his mephitic yak-dung cigarettes. 'Maybe we'd better wait a few minutes till things quieten down.'

Having wreaked as much impromptu devastation as she could in the sitting-room, Rosheen retreated under heavy fire to the kitchen, where the prospects for vandalism were at their frangible richest.

'Yeh, you just go to court, Clarence Darrow!' she screamed, flinging open the crockery cupboard. 'And I'll tell the DA's office you've been shafting communists!'

'Yeh, you do that. You do that!' Byron shouted back, taking cover as she opened up with a barrage of cheap coffee mugs.

'And I'll tell the Friends of Hibernia League you've had more pussy than they've got in the New Jersey state cat sanctuary.'

'Yeh, and I'll tell the court how you put prussic acid in my yoghurt.'

'That was a new lemon and almond flavour, you dumb bitch.'

'That was *prussic acid*. I checked with Siobhan. She read it in Perry Mason.'

'And, oh boy,' said Byron, counter-attacking from a small arsenal of canned food, 'is that judge gonna just love you, firebaby, when he learns you set light to the summerhouse with me inside.'

'And who put a tarantula in my lingerie drawer? And who hid a baby alligator in my bidet on Christmas Eve?'

'That was a goddam garden spider come indoors to hibernate.'

'Bull*shit*. That was a goddam alligator. I know an alligator from a garden spider, for Christ's sake.' And hitting him plum in the middle of the forehead with a soup tureen: 'Aw *shot*, Sheenie baby! Right between the eyes.'

Byron's vision misted over and dissolved in ripples like a mirage. He collapsed back against the fridge, the floor seemed to melt beneath him and he sank gently into a dark, bottomless pit of oblivion.

Rosheen stood over him, hands on hips, hot and exhilarated, breasts heaving wetly behind the ochre tank-top. 'Had enough, wimp?' He was lying in an undignified heap, as still as a corpse. 'Byron?' She prodded him in the kidneys with her foot. 'Byron, you yellow-bellied creep. I know you're faking it. Get up, you spineless son-of-a-bitch.' She kicked him again. 'Up off your butt. The party's not over yet. C'mon, dickhead, get up.' How could he do it to her? How could he pass out on her at a moment like this? Just when things were starting to go so well between them. They hadn't had a fight like this in ages. It was like old times. It brought back happy memories of the best days of their marriage, when they used to wreck the whole house in the course of a single weekend. 'Byron!' She booted him in the buttock. 'Get up and fight, you feeble chickengut.' Not a murmur. Not a flicker of movement. Maybe he'd had a cardiac arrest or something? 'Byron, if you've gone and died on me I'll kill you, you bastard.' Yet not even the prospect of death after death could tempt him back to the fray.

Rosheen gave up, and feeling somewhat sandpapery of throat after all that exertion, returned to the sitting-room in search of liquor. But nothing stronger than sherry had survived. Everything else was still glistening on the walls or soaking into the carpet. The floor sparkled and crunched under foot with broken glass. The room reeked of some satanic, noxious cocktail. Disgusted – not by the stench or the mess, but by the fact that Byron hadn't had the decency to put a few bottles aside in a safe place in anticipation of hostilities like these – Rosheen exhumed her handbag from an avalanche of fallen books, grabbed her leather jacket and set off in search of a friendly local hostelry. Emerging from the flat, she collided with Leo Feinbaum who was about to hammer on Byron's door in protest.

'Hi, Leo, treasure. How are things?'

'Vot za hell's going on in zere?' he demanded, trying to recollect where he had seen that face before.

'Christ knows,' said Rosheen. 'I just called by to complain about the language.' And stepping into the lift, she descended to the ground floor, where she found a tall dark stranger in an eau-de-nil Balenciaga dress trying to get in through the front door. Rosheen opened it and saved her the trouble of using the Entriphone.

'Thank you,' said Nina, thinking that the face looked somehow familiar.

'My pleasure,' said Rosheen, thinking the same. She walked out into Hamilton Grove and away down the street towards Kilburn.

Nina got into the lift and travelled up to the third floor. Stepping out, she came face to face with Leo Feinbaum who had given up trying to get an answer from Byron's apartment. 'Don't bother,' he muttered, shuffling back into his own baroque hallway. 'His vife she just killed him.'

'Killed . . . ?' Nina stared after him, wondering if he was senile or just drunk.

'Ja,' said Feinbaum. 'Vis any luck.' He shooed his herd of fretting dachshunds back into the apartment and closed the door behind him.

Nina pressed Byron's bell. The door opened very slowly after the fifth ring and Byron peered cautiously out. He looked as if he'd just been hit by a wall. 'Oh, Nina, hi. Ah . . . come on in.'

'Are you OK?'

'Me? Sure. Why?'

'Your funny old neighbour just told me your wife killed you.'

'Well, if she has, I'm really pissed off with my reincarnation. Come on in. Excuse the mess.'

Nina stepped inside, took in the hallway strewn with books and records, and glanced down the passage to the kitchen, now blanched with shattered china, spilt milk, scattered pap-bread, and isolated snowfalls of flour and granulated sugar. The heat and the stench were overpowering.

'A small difference of opinion with a passing yeti,' Byron explained apologetically, 'bearing a strong resemblance to my *ci-devant* spouse.' Nina looked worried. 'It's OK, it's all clear now,' he assured her. 'She just left. Swung away into the trees.'

'I think maybe I passed her at the street door.'

'You can't miss her. Wears Asprey knuckledusters and talks fluent Anglo-Saxon.'

'What happened to your head?'

'She was trying to attract my attention with a cauldron.'

'Is it bleeding?'

'Maybe inside, I don't know. But what's a haematoma or two between friends?'

'You feel all right? You don't look too good.'

'Sure. I just need a drink, that's all. Look, this is very embarrassing for me, Nina, but there's nowhere to sit and nothing left to drink. Would you mind if we went out someplace? We can't have a civilised talk in here.'

'No, I don't mind at all. In fact, I think under the circumstances it might be a good idea. Your wife might come back.

'I doubt it. There's nothing left to wreck. I'll just go and get cleaned up. Pull up a broken chairleg and make yourself at home.'

'I'll pick up some of these things, if you don't mind. I hate to see books and records thrown about.'

'Me too, but that's what happens when you marry a Neanderthal,' said Byron, retiring to his bedroom.

As soon as the bedroom door was shut, Nina opened her handbag and took out the lump of tacky black gunk . . .

Zlob was sitting outside in the Alfa, waiting for Nina and Byron to leave and wishing that he was working with someone a lot less intelligent. In his experience, clever people could always be relied upon to cock up the simplest of tasks. Being possessed of an IQ of about three hundred, Comrade Brain would almost certainly have bunged the gunk into the wrong hole, and in full view of Byron Cleverclogs – though with any luck, he would be too intelligent to realise that anything suspicious was going on.

Stalin was absolutely right. It was thanks to the intelligentsia that the world was in such a mess. If Zlob had his way, they would boot all the clever people out of politics and the *apparat* and put idiots in charge of everything. Only morons of proven ineptitude would be given the top party posts, and all ministers would have to satisfy the central committee (an entirely *new* central committee, made up of real thickoes) that they were daft enough to sit on the politburo. Then maybe the human race would start to make progress.

Zlob's contemplations were interrupted at long last by the sight of Comrade Brain emerging from the block of flats, accompanied by a bespectacled shambles in a scruffy grey suit. They walked along to the main road, flagged down a taxi and disappeared from view. Zlob grabbed his plastic attaché case, got out of the car and hurried along to the apartment block. Wonder upon wonders, Comrade Brain had had the good sense not to let the front door lock properly. The lobby was deserted. He took the lift to the third floor. That too was deserted. He tiptoed across the landing to the door of number eight. It swung gently open. Well done, Comrade Brain. He stepped inside and peered around. 'Ullo?' Silence. He quickly prised the gunk out of the latch-hole, shut the door behind him and got down to work.

Rosheen had not gone far – just as far as the nearest Irish pub, McGilligan's Bar in the Kilburn High Road, where she had partaken of three glasses of Liam O'Hagen's finest bog whiskey and donated a purseful of centimes to a charity called 'Armalites for Erin'. And having given the matter at least ten minutes' careful consideration, she had decided, reluctantly, that she would have to return to the matrimonial home and pursue her one hundred thousand dollars in a more orthodox and civilised manner – i.e. in bed, where Byron was at his most excitable and therefore his most vulnerable.

Arriving back at the apartment, she pushed her doorkey

quietly into the lock and opened the door with extreme caution; even a peace freak like Byron could be a demon when roused.

'Byron?' she cooed sweetly. 'It's me-ee! Hon-ey . . . ?'

Having made a lightning survey of the premises, Zlob had decided to plant one of his tiny bugs inside each of the three telephones. Starting in the principal bedroom, he was about to open his box of dirty tricks when he heard a latchkey in the front door. Then, to his horror, a woman's voice called out: 'By-ron? It's me-ee! Hon-ey . . . ?' He glanced round frantically for somewhere to hide. There was no window recess and the curtains were too short. There was no space beneath the bed. But there was a fitted cupboard along one wall, with sliding doors. Zlob crept inside, squashed himself in amongst a rail of suits and overcoats, and slid the door shut, leaving just a tiny gap so that he could peer out.

A moment later the bedroom door opened and a frizzy blonde walked in. 'Byron . . . ?'

'Byron . . . ?' No Byron. Perhaps he was still lying on the kitchen floor, pretending to be unconscious? Rosheen walked out of the bedroom and down the hallway to the kitchen. No Byron there either. Perhaps he'd gone out for a drink with his defective Bulgarian. Or dinner even. Either way, they wouldn't be back for a couple of hours. Maybe, if she could clean the place up a bit in the meantime, it might help to mollify the old bastard . . .

Byron had brought Nina to the Tay Ninh Moon, a Vietnamese brasserie in Kentish Town, owned by a prolific family of Dhongs. The place was as steamy as the Mekong at monsoon, furnished in bamboo and rattan, and crowded with rubbery, homnivorous-looking jungle plants. Byron (it seemed to Byron) was the only customer they ever had; though whether that was due to the suffocating humidity, the oppressive flora or the high risk of contracting blackwater fever he did not care to guess. He ordered a very large Scotch, Broth of Many Fishies and something that sounded suspiciously like lizard pie. Nina settled for Perrier water and a plate of steamed vegetables.

Byron's head still ached fiercely from the impact of the soup tureen, and the whole trauma had temporarily derailed his train of thought. It was only now, as he began to recover from the general aftershock of hostilities, that he remembered what Nina was doing there. Although, for a woman who had sounded almost suicidal just a few hours earlier, she was looking remarkably serene and confident. Perhaps it was her special defector's appearance. After all, one would want to look one's alluring best for the State Department; it was not every day they got a top Bulgarian ontologist crossing over. He tried to think of a subtle way of broaching the subject, but gave up and plunged straight in at the deep end.

'Nina, honey, may I talk to you like a brother?'

'If you like.'

'You see, I know how you feel about the danger of Unibore going down the chute and your being sent home, but — '

'How can you know? Have you lived in the East?'

'No. But I can guess what it's like. And I can guess exactly what's going through your mind right now.'

'You can?'

'But think about your family back home in Sofia.'

'Plovdiv.'

'Pardon me?'

'Plovdiv. My family live in Plovdiv.'

'But think how they'd feel.'

'If Unibore were to shut down?'

'No. If you ran away.'

'Ran away?' Nina wondered if that soup tureen had done more damage than was immediately apparent. 'I don't follow, I'm sorry.'

'Don't misunderstand me. I'm simply trying to put myself in your position. That is to say, if you could see things from *my* side, you'd realise.'

'Realise what?'

'What it's really like over there.'

'What *what's* really like?'

'Life.'

'In Bulgaria?'

'No. In the US.'

Nina spoke American almost as well as Byron – though about two octaves lower, with an accent as broad as the Thracian Plain; but she was beginning to wonder if she had not missed some vital link in the chain of conversation. 'Byron, what are you trying to say?'

'I'm simply trying to put you wise before we both find ourselves involved in something that could have major diplomatic ramifications. You've only been in the West, what, eighteen months? It must all seem like some kind of Disneyland to you still. But it's really not all champagne and roses over there, you know.'

'It's not?'

'Oh, my God, no. There's unemployment, street crime, violence, racial bigotry, drug addiction, poverty. You name it, we've got it.'

'It must be very unpleasant for you,' Nina sympathised. 'But what has it got to do with me?'

'Well, I'm sure you'd find it a hell of a shock.'

'I might,' she agreed tonelessly, wondering what all this could be leading up to. After a brief silence, she said: 'Byron, may I ask you a straight question?'

'Please do. That's what I'm here for. To counsel and advise.'

'Well, what exactly are you talking about?'

Byron took a breath, glanced discreetly round the deserted clusters of bamboo and rattan, and murmured: 'Come on, honey. We both know damn well what I'm talking about. Let's cut the bullshit. I'm talking about defecting.' He knew at once that he had made an appalling mistake.

'Defecting?' Nina swallowed the last two syllables, so they were barely audible. Her eyes bulged a little and her voice plunged to a conspiratorial bass. 'You mean . . . political asylum? The whole damn thing?'

'Oh my God,' muttered Byron, aching with embarrassment. 'You must think I've gone stark staring cuckoo. This is the most *terrible* . . .'

'No, no, no!' cried Nina, reaching across the table for his hand. 'I don't think you're mad at all. There's nothing to be embarrassed about. It's not a mistake, Byron, believe me.'

'It isn't?' Byron took her hand and gripped it like a drowning man on a lifeline. 'You mean . . . I'm right?'

'But of *course* you're right!' said Nina, passionately crushing his feeble hand in both of hers. (This was going to be one of the most spectacular diplomatic coups for Sofia in over forty years of socialism. America's leading ontologist defecting to

Bulgaria.) 'You must have the courage of your convictions. Do not flinch, comrade. Do not hesitate. The White House has treated you shamefully. The State Department is prepared to stop at nothing to destroy your intellectual freedom. Don't think twice, Byron. You're doing the right thing. Trust in me.'

Resigning himself to the inevitability of Fate and accepting that this was just not meant to be one of his better weeks, Byron bore the agony of his crushed hand and tureen-dented skull with that same stoic American fortitude which his great-grandfathers had displayed at Gettysburg, and surrendered himself totally to the onset of another serious nervous condition.

Back at Hamilton Grove, Zlob was still trapped in the bedroom cupboard, evaporating slowly in the suffocating heat. He had been there for over forty minutes by this time, desperately willing the frizzy blonde, whoever she was, to disappear as abruptly as she had arrived.

Rosheen, however, had no intention of disappearing – or not until the morning at any rate. Having cleared up the worst of the mess and vacuum-cleaned the apartment – something it had long been gasping for in Mrs O'Nobblin's absence – she decided to freshen up for the coming night of venerean sport. Helping herself to a beer from the fridge, she returned to the bedroom to strip off for a shower and noticed the cheap-looking attaché case that was lying on the bed. Opening it, in the faint hope that it might contain something nasty and incriminating, like a latex gymslip, she discovered what looked encouragingly like rutting accessories of a deviant nature. But on closer inspection, they appeared to be nothing more than bits and pieces of electrical apparatus. What Byron could possibly want with anything so technical when he could not even change the batteries in a vibrator, was totally beyond her. However, as she was in a tidy frame of mind and the case seemed to be serving no useful purpose in the bedroom, she took it out to the hall closet and stowed it away among Mrs O'Nobblin's brooms and polishes, where all boring, practical things belonged. She then returned to the bedroom to get undressed.

Ten feet away in the clothes cupboard, Zlob was peeping wide-eyed through a crack in the sliding doors. *Now* what was she doing? Dressing up to go out? Would she slide the doors open at any second and find him there? What would she do? Go berserk? Scream the place down? Beat him up? His bowels gurgled mutinously at the prospect. Whoever had been responsible for wreaking all that havoc earlier on had been no pacifist. Who the devil *was* she? Comrade Brain had assured him that Doctor Cleverclogs lived alone. He hadn't bargained for this. And had the brazen wench no shame, divesting herself in front of a total stranger? He was absolutely disgusted. If he pressed his face hard enough to the crack between the doors he could see her entire naked body . . . hot, voluptuous and wanton . . .

Byron was feeling very much better. His headache had gone, he had cleared up the confusion over his imminent defection to the East, and after four large whiskies and a bottle of Mr Dhong's finest Algerian *vin de campagne* he was beginning to feel as if he could develop a deep, meaningful affection for Nina at any moment. Those beguiling green eyes, that sleepy, enigmatic smile, the delicate rasping of nylon as she uncrossed and recrossed those strong athletic thighs.

'Byron, are you listening to me?'

'Every word,' he replied gravely, trying to recollect what she was talking about. 'You said it's a crazy situation.'

'Well, don't you think so? Three out of the five agenda zones have been agreed. It's only the Asian and American zones that are causing all this trouble. And two-thirds of the board couldn't give a damn about a few hectares of rainforest or separatist movements in the armpit of nowhere.'

'Hell, you don't have to convince *me*,' said Byron. 'You go and tell that to your friends in the non-aligned bloc.'

'But you see how crazy that is?' Nina protested. 'If only East and West could agree on a motion to bypass this agenda deadlock, we could outvote the non-aligned delegates and it wouldn't matter *what* they thought.'

'Sure,' said Byron, 'and if dreams were horses, beggars would be in bloodstock. I mean, let's be realistic. What are your side and mine ever going to agree on?'

'You don't *want* Wopec to succeed?'

'You know damn well I do. My whole future hangs on it. But . . .'

'Washington's leaning on you?'

'Washington can go screw themselves. The White House

won't say or do anything that'll rock the election campaign. I was on the phone to the State Department last night and . . .' He broke off abruptly. Phone . . . States. 'Aaah, shhhh*oot*!' He thumped the table with his fist, and a couple of dozen Dhongs looked worried and reached for his bill.

'What's wrong?' said Nina.

'I just remembered, I forgot.'

'Remembered forgot?'

'To make a call to Mississippi before we came out . . .'

Rosheen had just stepped out of the shower when the telephone rang. She draped herself in a bath sheet, padded back to the bedroom and picked up the phone. 'Yup, hullo?'

'Oh, hello. Is Byron there, please?'

'I'm afraid not. Can I take a message?'

'Is that Rosheen?'

'It most certainly is.'

'Oh hi, Rosheen. We haven't met. My name's Annabelle. Annabelle Cartwright.'

'Well, hi there, Annabelle.' Rosheen parked herself on the edge of the bed. Now this sounded promising. An unmistakable hint of li'l ole Dixie in those honey-sweet tones.

'Byron's told me all about you.'

'He has?'

'But I got the idea you were English.'

'Me? No, I'm from Madison, New Jersey.'

'I'm from Salvation, Mississippi . . . But I guess Byron's told you all about that.'

'Matter of fact he hasn't, no.'

'Oh. Well, I guess you're only his secretary for Wopec, is that right? I mean, you're not taking over full-time from Louise?'

Rosheen threw off the bath sheet and spread herself out on the bed. This was getting interesting. 'Did Byron tell you I was his secretary?'

'Sure. He tells me everything. We have no secrets.'

'No kidding?'

'Well, I believe in total honesty in marriage. I don't believe that a woman should keep a small part of herself totally secret from her husband like some people say.'

'That's very interesting, Annabelle. Tell me, I didn't realise that you and Doctor Cleveland were actually . . . ?'

'No, I guess I shouldn't have put it quite that way. I mean, we're not officially engaged yet, so don't quote me.'

'Only, it's just that I had this funny old notion at the back of my head that he was married already.'

'Oh, sure, that's right, he was,' said Annabelle. 'To a truly *awful* creature.'

'You don't say? Oh, my.'

'Well, I shouldn't speak unkindly of a woman I've never met. But she was kind of sick in the head, I believe. Anyhow, they were divorced a long time ago.'

'Is that so? Well, well, well. You learn a little something new every day.'

'Anyway, I'd better go, I'm calling from Salvation. Will Byron be long, do you think?'

'I doubt it. He's dating a Russian keep-fit nut. He won't want to hang around too long in case he gets a dose of health.'

'A Russian *what*?'

'He'll tell you all about it, honey, no sweat.'

'Well, would you just say I called, please? And ask him to phone me about Wopec as soon as he can, so we can make our reservations.'

'You mean, you're coming over for the conference? Over *here*?'

'Didn't Byron tell you?'

'Well, no, as a matter of fact he didn't. But then he's being extremely secretive these days. It must be the strain.'

'I guess so. Well, it's been nice talking to you, Rosheen.'

'Likewise, Annabelle.'

'Maybe see you on Wopec Day.'

'Can't wait. Should be a riot.'

'Bye then.'

'Bye, Annabelle.' Rosheen put the phone down with a triumphant shriek, and yodelled a long and gleeful 'Yeeeeee-hah!' to the bedroom ceiling and the Mendelsohns above . . .

Zlob's shirt and jacket were now soaked with perspiration, and rivulets of sweat were running down the inside of the cupboard where his face was pressed to the doors. Blondie was lying flat out on her back, stark naked, with her knees raised and parted as if about to give birth, scratching herself in a most unseemly fashion. Whatever that phone call was about, it was very good news apparently. She was clapping her hands and whooping with glee and calling to somebody somewhere . . .

'Whah, Miss Annabelle!' Rosheen exclaimed to the mirror in a mock Southern drawl. 'Ah do declare, you bin messin' with mah own dear husband, fixin' to wed behind mah back an' all. Mah poor achin heart is just all broke up. Ah fear ah may have to shoot his li'l ole rocks off for this wicked indiscretion, and cleanse his sinful soul in the eyes of the Lord. Hal-eeee-lujah!'

Gradually it dawned on Zlob that there was nobody else in the room. She was prattling and whooping and yee-hahing away to nobody but herself. Which explained, perhaps, why a small bomb appeared to have hit the place that evening: the poor tart was obviously totally off her trolley.

'Now if we had a *socialist* delegate structure at Halcyon House,' said Nina, 'we wouldn't have this kind of problem. You would be delegated by the West. I would be delegated by the East. And the two of us would find a solution to the agenda deadlock,' (snapping her fingers) 'just like that.'

Byron ordered another Courvoisier (probably his fifth, he had lost count) and tried to coax her face into focus. 'Ah hah? And how?'

'Well, it can't be beyond the wit of two intelligent human beings to agree on some sort of simple bypass motion, surely?'

'So if it was all down to you and me,' said Byron, 'what would *you* propose?'

'Oh, I don't know,' said Nina vaguely, 'some sort of ultimatum to the Third World, perhaps. It's a five-day conference. There are five agenda zones. So why not pass a motion specifying that we debate Europe on Monday, Africa on Tuesday, the Middle East on Wednesday and so on? And that if any zone does not have an agreed agenda by Wopec Day, the conference will just proceed without one, and delegates will discuss any issues they want from any zone they choose.'

Byron was functioning mainly on auto-pilot after all that Scotch and Courvoisier and Mr Dhong's finest *vin de campagne*, and it took a while for the elementary logic of Nina's proposal to filter through his mental processes. 'Well, that sounds a pretty smart move to me,' he concluded at length. 'Why the hell didn't someone think of that before?'

'They probably did,' said Nina. 'But the Western allies

spend so much time bickering with each other that I don't suppose they'd agree to a proposal like that anyway.'

'Oh, hell, I'm sure they'd agree all right, no problem,' said Byron confidently. 'Everyone's sick to the teeth of these Mickey Mouse republics throwing their weight around at our expense and holding Wopec to ransom. But the problem is Jericho Engineer. To get a two-thirds vote we need every delegate we can scrape up, but there's no way that we'll get Isobel or Zenia or Rolv Erlendsson back to the boardroom until Fatso apologises. Which Fatso won't.'

'He could be forced to.'

'Only by that paranoid megalomaniac in Port Paradise.'

'Hudson Butcher has his weaknesses,' said Nina, with more than a hint of contempt. 'Like all men. I'm sure he won't allow trivialities like Sandhustan to come between him and his lust for glory.'

'So what do you want to do? Offer him the suzerainty of all Asia?'

'Invite him to be the new guest of honour at Wopec Day.'

'Hudson Butcher?' Byron would have burst out laughing if she had not looked quite so serious. 'Inaugurate Wopec? In place of HRH? Speak the speech? Plant the tree?'

'Byron,' said Nina, urgently seizing him by his already once-crushed hand, 'do you want Wopec to die? Do you want the US to pull out of Unibore? Don't you *want* to be director-general?'

'Nina, sweetie, I don't give a twopenny damn *who* opens Wopec. They can resurrect the ghost of Charlemagne for all I care. But the board won't buy it. It would be like the Pope canonising Genghis Khan for services to peace.'

'Every single delegate,' said Nina, mangling what was left of his hand once more, 'is fighting to save his job. No one really cares who opens Wopec or what's on the agenda, as long as Unibore survives.'

'But the *State Department*,' said Byron, closing his eyes and feeling the room spin like a gyroscope. 'Washington would go *ber-serk*. Jesus. Butcher of all people . . . opening the world's biggest ever, first only, academic peace congress.'

'OK, so what are they going to do?' countered Nina. 'Walk out of Wopec just one month before the presidential election campaign gets under way?'

A long, cognac-sipping silence.

'No, well, I guess not,' Byron conceded upon reflection. He had, after all, been trying to dream up ways of shafting the administration ever since that terrible morning when Eddison Packard had first darkened the portals of Halcyon House. He ordered more coffee and tried to think it through. As long as he didn't refer the matter to Washington beforehand – as long as it was genuinely a *secret* secret understanding with the East – there would be absolutely nothing they could do about it. By the time they had heard the news it would all be a *fait accompli*. But this was assuming, of course, that the East would go along with it. 'You reckon Rhoskov and the boys would buy it?'

'I can't speak for anyone else, you understand,' Nina replied. 'But as long as they felt confident that you were sincere in undertaking this initiative, I'm sure they would be willing to come to some sort of unspoken, unwritten, unofficial understanding.'

'What do you mean *me* take an initiative?' said Byron, who had the uncomfortable feeling that he was being outmanoeuvred somehow but was in no condition to work out how. 'Whose idea *is* this?'

'But, Byron, someone will have to propose this bypass resolution to the board,' Nina reasoned. 'And you know *I* can't.'

'Why not?'

'The Soviet allies cannot return to the boardroom as long as the non-aligned delegates are absent. And the non-aligned delegates won't come back until Otello agrees to accept a resolution censuring Isobel Maddox for talking to the *Daily Express*. Someone has to persuade Otello to put that to the vote. *Then* we can all come back to the boardroom and abstain on the censure resolution, so that will be lost. And *then* you can propose your resolution to bypass the agenda deadlock.'

Byron no longer had the feeling that he was being outmanoeuvred, he *knew* he was. 'Supposing I just say no, and to hell with it?'

Nina fondled the bunch of ground bone and gristle that was still – miraculously – attached to the end of his right arm. 'Then you're not half the man I took you for.'

A shaft of light broke briefly through the woolly grey clouds that were thickening gently, like fog in November, around the powerhouse of perceptive genius between Byron's silvering temples. 'Was this what all those con-zul-deh-zhuns were about today?'

'Consultations?' said Nina, and looked bewildered.

Byron raised his sixth/seventh/eighth glass of cognac to her in salutation. 'Nina, you know, if my heart didn't belong to Salvation you'd almost be worth defecting for.'

Nina raised her glass of Perrier water in return. 'And if you were in better shape, Byron, you'd almost be worth considering.'

The taxi pulled up outside Byron's apartment block in Hamilton Grove. 'How's about a nightcap?' he suggested as they got out. 'I've got a secret store of hooch that Queen Kong doesn't know about. It should have survived the blitz OK.' He paid the cab driver.

'Thank you,' Nina replied, 'but I've got a long, heavy day ahead. And you have too, come to that.'

'Not even coffee?'

'Thank you all the same.'

'And thank *you* for a very constructive evening. Here's hoping for tomorrow.' He gave her a diplomatic peck on each cheek. 'Night. Safe drive home.'

'And a safe night's sleep,' said Nina, glancing ominously at the windows of his third-floor sitting-room.

'No, that's OK,' said Byron, 'she won't be back. She'll be in some bar in Bethnal Green right now, tossing bricklayers through the window.'

'Sweet dreams then.' Nina blew him a kiss and walked away up the road to where her Alfa was parked. Seeing no sign of Zlob in the vicinity, she assumed that he had done whatever he had to do and had found his own way back to wherever he was staying. She drove once around the block, to make sure that he was not lurking in wait in the shadows, and then sped home to Bayswater.

Byron took the lift to the third floor and, emerging, met Leo Feinbaum taking his pack of querulous dachshunds for their late-night leak. He got as far as saying, 'Oh hi, Leo, look I'm sorry about all that, ah . . .' when Feinbaum roasted him with one searing glance and disappeared earthwards in the Waygood Otis, muttering to his dogs in toxic Viennese. Reflecting sadly on the demise of the spirit of good-neighbourliness in this technological age, Byron opened his front door, tripped over the doormat and fell in a heap on the hall floor. Somewhat the worse for wear after a long, enervating day he struggled clumsily to his feet, and found a French paratrooper observing him from the sitting room doorway.

'Drunk, huh?' said Rosheen.

'No, I am not,' he retorted indignantly. 'I just happened to fall over the damn carpet, that's all. And what the hell are you doing, trespassing on my property?'

'Clearing up the mess you made.'

Byron lurched into the sitting room. 'So I notice. And what do you mean, the mess *I* made?'

'OK, the mess *we* made,' said Rosheen agreeably. 'Husbands and wives should share responsibility for the marital home, that's fair.'

'They should, hah?' said Byron. 'Then I take it you'll be paying your share of the damage here tonight?'

'Sure. Just tot it up and knock it off the hundred and fifty.'

'What hundred and fifty?'

'The hundred and fifty thousand bucks you'll be paying me for a divorce.'

'That's fifty per cent inflation in three hours, Frau Shylock,' said Byron, amazed at his own agility of mind at that late hour. 'What the hell kind of bargain do you call that?'

'I call that the price of Salvation,' Rosheen replied.

The deeper meaning of which did not immediately register with Byron. 'Why don't you take an evening stroll out of the window? I'm going to make myself some coffee.' He set off down the hall passage to the kitchen, saying as he went: 'I would consider it a signal honour, Mrs Cleveland, if you would zip your pendulous and long-since-ceased-to-be-appetising mammaries away in that trashy little leather number you brought them in, and piss off back to your hotel. I have a long, busy day tomorrow.'

Rosheen followed him into the kitchen where he was tottering about in search of an unbroken cup. 'Well, darling, I'm so glad you still think of me as Mrs Cleveland, because I have just had the most extraordinary telephone conversation with Salvation, Mississippi.'

'Ah right!' said Byron, glad that someone had taken the

trouble to remind him. 'I *knew* there was something I had to do as soon as I got in.'

'She gave me the happy news.'

'Who did?'

'Annabelle, of course, who else?'

'Annabelle? What happy news?'

'That *she* is about to become Mrs Cleveland *too*.'

Byron stopped tottering and cup-searching and steadied himself against the Supalectric Turbowasher. 'She's about to what?'

'Or so, ha ha, she seems to think.'

'Annabelle told you that?'

'And, of course, I told her I thought you were married already – being the very attentive secretary that I am. But she said oh no, you were divorced ten years ago. Well, imagine what a shock it was to discover that I'd been living in sin with my own husband all that time. But when she described your ex-spouse as a truly awful creature who was sick in the head, I realised that she must have been talking about *another* Mrs Cleveland. Frankly, Byron, I had no idea how complicated your personal life really is. This night has been a revelation. I'm so glad I made the trip.'

Byron's mind would have been wonderfully concentrated at this moment had it not been half-submerged in a sea of brandy and vin de Dhong. He sank into a chair at the kitchen table and swatted away the central thrust of Rosheen's allegation with a carefree flick of the wrist. 'This is a very trivial misunderstanding, sweetie. Easily explained. It's just a stupid little mix-up, that's all.'

'Oh, you don't need to explain a thing, darling. Because I am a very understanding wife. I'm sorry to keep mentioning that naughty little four-letter word *wife*, but that is still what I am. Despite popular belief. And I think that is something that Mrs Cleveland the Second really ought to be told. Very soon. For all our sakes. Because it's against the law, as I'm sure you know, to have two Mrs Clevelands at one time, and you wouldn't want to spend the next forty years in the Virginia state penitentiary, now would you?'

'OK, Rosheen . . .' Byron leant his elbow on the kitchen table. It slipped straight off again. 'What do you want?'

'Want?'

'You want to break the kid's heart?'

'*Me* break her heart? Have *I* proposed marriage to her? Have *I* cheated on her? Have *I* lied to her?'

'She's twenty-four years old. A small-town schoolteacher. She never hurt a living thing. She's sweet and kind and gentle, and we're very much in love, OK? Right? Now I've levelled with you. That's all there is. There's nothing more to it. For all I know she's still a virgin. So what do you want to do, tear her in pieces?'

'You're kidding me?'

'No. I'm not kidding you, I'm just talking way out of your depth. I'm talking about a woman who's decent and good-natured and who writes me silly twenty-five-page love letters, and believes in God, and still thinks KY Jelly is something kids have with ice cream and trifle.'

'Jesus, has teacher got an education coming her way.'

'So what are you going to do, hah? Destroy that little bit of purity and innocence? Smash up our happiness just like you have to smash up every other fucking thing you get your hands on?'

'Language, husband, *please* . . . The Feinbaums . . . These walls are so very thin, you know . . .'

'Rosheen, what do you *want*?'

'Please don't shout, dearest. You truly want to marry this kid?'

'I'm going to marry her, even if I have to bury you alive in fifty feet of wet concrete.'

'You want to get off the hook?'

'What's it to you?'

'I told you once already. A hundred and fifty thousand dollars. Pay it any way you like, anyhow you want. But a hundred and fifty grand and you're a free man.'

'Screw yourself.'

'Thirty days, honeybunch.'

'Which is a lot less than the judge will give you when I file for criminal extortion.'

'Thirty days, and then I file for divorce . . . citing your sweet, kind, gentle, innocent schoolteacher as co-respondent.'

'You wouldn't dare.'

'Try me.'

'Not in a thousand million years.'

'You're the one with the reputation, Mr Director-General, not me. You've got it all to lose. I've got it all to come.'

'Rosheen, I give you fair warning — '

'And by the time I walk out of that courthouse, you're not going to have *any* kind of a reputation. The truth about you is going to be over every newspaper and radio station from coast to coast.'

'Blackmail me, would you?' Byron reached out and flung the last surviving cup at her. It missed and shattered against the wall.

'*Please* . . . husband of mine, a little self control. One does so deplore violence in the home.'

'Sully and putrefy every decent thing you can get your claws into, huh?' Rising unsteadily to his feet, he hurled the tea caddy across the room. That also missed her, showering Fortnum's finest Darjeeling all over the Supalectric Turbowasher.

'Byron, that really is no way to treat your wife.'

'You're not a wife,' he raged, throwing open the food cupboard. 'You're a sick, perverted animal.'

'Now, husband, please . . . If you persist in throwing things at me in this uncivil manner I shall, with the very greatest regret, feel obliged to open this freezer chest and defend myself with its contents.'

A can of mulligatawny soup caught her in the solar plexus. 'Ow! Jesus! Byron, that *hurt*, you bastard!'

'Good. I hope you get a perforated gut and choke on your own haemorrhage.'

'All right, OK,' she bawled, throwing open the freezer and seizing a brick-hard pack of Ben Bull's full-fat Meatiburgers. 'If that's the way you want it . . .'

Zlob dreaded to imagine what was going on in that kitchen, and had not the slightest desire to stay and find out. Poking his nose nervously out of the bedroom, he crept down the hall passage to the front door, opened it as quietly as he could and stepped out onto the landing, where he bumped into Leo Feinbaum returning home with his pack of yapping sausages.

'My Gott,' muttered Feinbaum, hearing the sounds of distant mayhem. 'Is she killing him again so soon?'

'Uh, scusey, john,' mumbled Zlob apologetically. 'Cuppa tea. Why because.'

He fled down the stairs in blind panic and rushed out into the blessed cool air of evening . . . only to discover that the Alfa had gone. Comrade Megabrain, in her bountiful wisdom, had driven away and abandoned him – with no money in his pocket and not the faintest idea where he was, apart from the fact that he was in north London and had to get back to *south* London. Luckily, he was thinking to himself as he peered up at the cloudless heavens in search of the Pole Star, he had paid careful attention to the navigation lectures during his air force basic training.

It was not until he was striding along the M1 motorway, well on the way to Birmingham, that he realised he had left his box of dirty tricks behind in Doctor Cleverclogs' apartment.

38

Mystery Talks in Paradise. Red Envoy Flies in

Johannesburg Star

Bulgarian Adviser on Goodwill Visit.

Pure Truth (incorporating the Paradise Morning Post)

Butcher Denies Secret Pact With Sofia

The Times of India

Engineer Grovels: 'Wopec On,' Says U.N. Chief

Sydney Morning Herald

U.S. Breaks Wopec Deadlock. Soviet Support Shocks Third World

Guardian

Superpower Stitch-up, Says Third World

Daily Express

Moscow Denies Secret Deal. 'A Vote For Peace,' Says Envoy Rhoskov

Morning Star

Formal Invite to Butcher. Washington Silent

Financial Times

Butcher Accepts. Carnage Awaits

The Scotsman

Peace Bombshell: White House Fury Denied

The Observer

'I Am World's Prince of Peace,' Says Butcher

Daily Mail

'Queen Need Not Meet My Plane,' Says Prince Butcher

Daily Mirror

Hudson Butcher: Colossus of Honour, Principle and Justice

Pure Truth

39

THE NEWS that their great president had finally bowed to popular demand and agreed to honour the world with his presence at Carnage Castle on the twenty-fifth of June was greeted with scenes of unrestrained euphoria all over the Paradise Islands. Right across the archipelago, in every town and village, spontaneous demonstrations of proletarian joy were hastily organised by the secret police, and in Port Paradise itself ecstatic, cheering thousands gathered in Karl Marx Square with BUTCHER FOR EMPEROR placards in their hands and submachine-guns in their backs.

To commemorate the great occasion, the President had declared the whole of Wopec week a public holiday. Street carnivals and all-night festivities had been authorised by the Interior Secretary, Colonel-General Leviticus Stockminder, and Radio Paradise was preparing a deeply moving ten-episode serial of Hudson Butcher's lifelong struggle for peace and universal brotherhood. The President had already started work on the first volume of his memoirs, entitled *Hudson: the Epiphany Years*, to be published by the Paradise University Press in November. And (oh, the people's cornucopia of joy overfloweth) the Minister of Culture, Rear Admiral Josiah Kettle, had announced a prize of one thousand roubles for the best poem entitled *Pax Hudsonica*; entries to be submitted by Wopec Day and judged by a wholly independent panel of experts chaired by the President's sister, Gladys.

Accustomed though he was to making important public appearances and having a major impact on world affairs, the President was taking no chances with Wopec. A squad of speech-writers, hand-picked from the ranks of the most illustrious literary mercenaries in Europe, had been flown to Port Paradise to confect a feast of eloquence and wisdom for the undernourished souls of the attendant masses on Wopec Day. The finest military couturiers from Paris and Rome had been commissioned to design a new field-marshal's wardrobe especially for the occasion. And a full-dress rehearsal with the Unibore board at Carnage Castle had been arranged for the afternoon of Saturday the twenty-fourth.

One solitary doubt lingered in the minds of the President's advisers, one smudge on the roseate landscape, like something the dog had left behind on a carpet of freshly fallen snow: somebody, somewhere in the late, unlamented ranks of Section Five, had been stirring up some sort of trouble with somebody, somewhere, in Sandhustan. But nobody knew exactly what, or where, or with whom, or why. The answer had either been shot, along with most of Section Five, or burnt to ashes with their secret files. Or possibly, consumed by sharks in Archangel Bay, into whose perilous waters the treacherous Mogador Boatman and his co-conspirators had plunged one night, in a desperate break-out from Joy of Socialist Labour Gaol.

But whatever had become of Boatman and his secret plots, it was the unanimous opinion of the politburo that nothing concerning Sandhustan could possibly affect the smooth running of the Wopec conference. The mere suggestion that a pack of ragged starvelings from a primitive wilderness like Sandhustan might have the audacity – let alone the capability – to disrupt an international conference five thousand miles from home and in an advanced, security-conscious country like Britain, was too ludicrous even to contemplate.

40

Refreshed by a good night's sleep, after their long flight from Sandhubad, the four SPLA reinforcements trooped into the farmhouse kitchen and seated themselves on ammunition boxes in front of Sharaq's table for their first operational briefing. Sharaq felt greatly heartened by the sight of them. They were tough, aggressive young tigers, fresh out of military service, fired with the spirit of Sandhu liberation and Shrahmaic religious zeal.

'Welcome to Lower Oxfold,' he began. 'I am Captain Sharaq. Sergeant Pungal you've already met. And Corporal Nurg, of course.'

Nurg's face burned with pride. Lance-corporal. A field promotion. How proud his family would be – their worthless, slum-born bondserf, Golam Nanjik, a lance-corporal! Sadly, lines of supply to such far-flung field headquarters left something to be desired (they were barely sixty minutes' motoring from the front line, after all) and QM stores did not run to a brace of lance-corporal's stripes. But no matter; ever a master of improvisation, Nurg had drawn the chevrons on the sleeves of his combat fatigues with white chalk.

'Adjutant Muktar,' continued Sharaq, 'has already told you something about the Wopec conference, to be opened officially on the afternoon of Saturday the twenty-fourth of June. *Our* concern is only with the events of that evening, when twenty-four high-ranking diplomats and their wives will be attending a banquet at Carnage Castle as the private guests of Unibore's director-general. Our targets are those diplomats. Our task is codenamed Operation Thunder. This morning I shall give you a brief outline of the plan for Operation Thunder, and tomorrow we shall visit Carnage Castle as tourists and begin a detailed reconnaissance of the place. You will be issued with an official guidebook to the castle and a map of the estate. For the purposes of this briefing, however, you can refer to the sketch-plan that Corporal Nurg will now pass round.'

Nurg gave each of the new commandos a copy of the outline map that Sharaq had drawn and Dubbi Muktar had photocopied.

'You will see two diagrams,' said Sharaq. 'One of the ground floor of the castle, and one of the dungeons that lie beneath it. Security at the castle is expected to be very thorough, so we shall arrive there first thing in the morning and gain access to the building posing as workmen, with identity papers that Adjutant Muktar will be having printed for us in London. We shall then spend the day underground in the dungeons, emerging finally in the evening when the banquet is under way, and seizing our hostages from inside the building.'

The four commandos studied their outline maps.

'We shall leave here at oh eight hundred hours on the Saturday morning,' Sharaq continued, 'and travel to Carnage in the removal truck. This will also be used to convey our hostages back here after the operation. You will be wearing workmen's overalls on top of your combat fatigues and carrying plain canvas toolbags containing your weapons, ammunition, rations, flashlight and warm clothing. We shall arrive at Carnage at approximately oh nine hundred. Sergeant Pungal will drop us at the car park, as shown on your sketch-map, and then return here to guard our field headquarters. We shall walk from the car park to the gatehouse, across the north courtyard and enter the castle through the main front door, which leads into the great hall. From there we make our way eastwards towards the keep tower, where we find the public entrance to the dungeons.

'Sergeant Pungal and I have been into the dungeons on our recce and I can tell you that it's very cold down there, and apart from the electric lights – which we must assume will be switched off throughout Wopec Day – it's as black as pitch. As you can see from your maps there are five main chambers underground, running roughly in a line from east to west, with a warren of catacombs leading off them in all directions. It is easy to get lost in this maze of passages, and essential that we keep together at all times. You will see, running off chamber three, a passage that leads to what they call "ye olde chaymbre of torture", which is now a museum full of plastic skeletons and medieval torture devices. We shall base ourselves in a small cell to the west of this room and remain there all day.

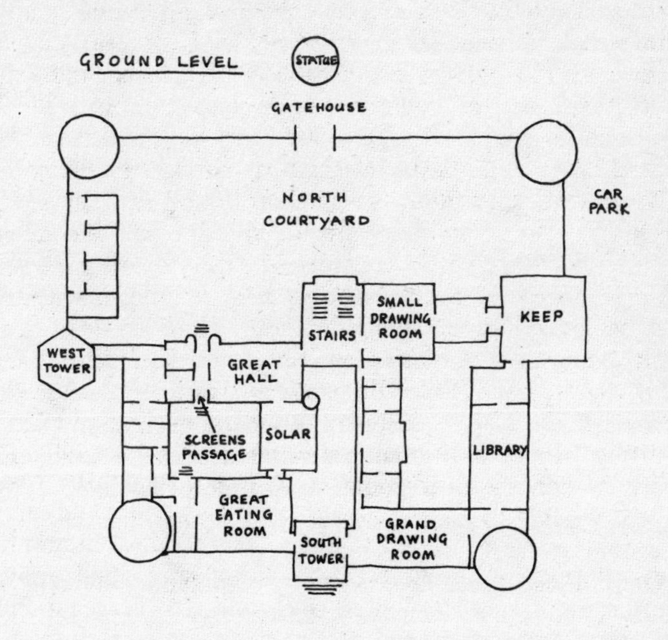
GROUND LEVEL
STATUE
GATEHOUSE
NORTH COURTYARD
CAR PARK
KEEP
SMALL DRAWING ROOM
STAIRS
WEST TOWER
GREAT HALL
SCREENS PASSAGE
SOLAR
LIBRARY
GREAT EATING ROOM
GRAND DRAWING ROOM
SOUTH TOWER

DUNGEONS

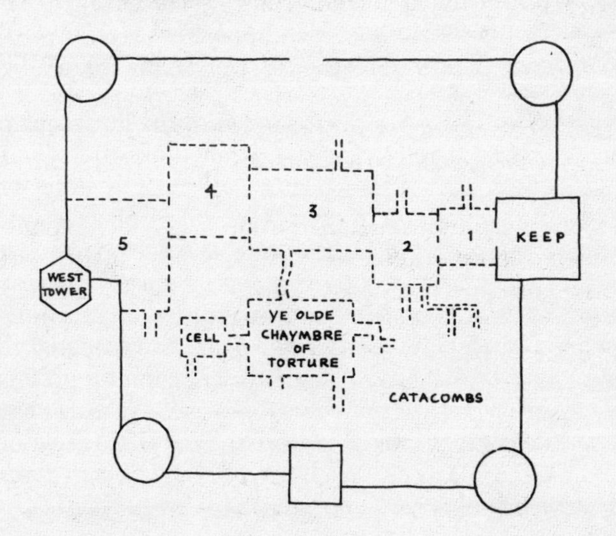
4
3
2
1
KEEP
5
WEST TOWER
CELL
YE OLDE CHAYMBRE OF TORTURE
CATACOMBS

'The ambassadors will start arriving at twenty hundred hours. They will be shown into the grand drawing-room for drinks. By that time Sergeant Pungal will have returned to the castle and will be waiting in the car park in constant radio contact with us. His codename is Fireball. Ours is Tiger. We shall emerge from the dungeons at twenty hundred and move to second base, in the keep tower. At twenty-thirty Pungal will drive the truck through the gatehouse, and as soon as he is safely into the north courtyard he will give us the codeword *Thunder Roll*. We shall then storm the drawing-room, seize as many hostages as we can and bring them back here, where they will be locked in the piggery under guard while Adjutant Muktar and intermediaries negotiate with the federal government on our behalf. Our demands are: one, the release of all Sandhustani political prisoners in federal gaols; and two, the granting of unconditional independence under UN supervision. When the time comes to abandon this camp, a boat will be waiting to take us across the Channel to France. Any questions so far?'

One of the fresh-faced young commandos put up his hand. 'Captain sir, what if the federal government refuses to negotiate?'

'Then they will have to be taught that we mean business,' Sharaq replied coldly. 'The hard way. One hostage at a time.'

Nurg's toes twitched uncomfortably in his new, slightly-too-large combat boots. He hoped and prayed that this would not end in violence or anything unpleasant. He still hadn't worked out how to put his machine pistol back together again and didn't have the nerve to tell Sharaq. Perhaps, if he asked very nicely, one of these fly young squaddies would help him out on the quiet.

A second fly young squaddie put up his hand. 'Captain, sir, how much opposition can we expect to meet at the castle?'

'I have it on expert authority,' Sharaq replied, 'that there will be no more than a token force of police officers on duty that night.'

41

'AND WHAT exactly do you mean by a *token* force?' enquired Edwina suspiciously, as if the phrase might mean anything up to a regiment of infantry and half an armoured division.

They were seated like a tribunal round the desk in Edwina Sheffield's bulging medieval office: Edwina, Aubrey Wormslow, Clarence Brownjohn and smelly dog Walpole. In front of them, like a defendant in the witness box, sat Superintendent Norman Hatchard who – ever mindful of the need for improved public relations – had taken the time and trouble to travel down to Carnage Castle to deliver the glad tidings about Operation Midsummer Night and all the inconvenience it was going to cause, in the hope of securing everybody's willing co-operation all round. But negotiations were not going at all well and he was beginning to wish that he had left everything in the hands of the Ministry of Defence.

'Well, *two* token forces, madam, to be precise,' he confessed. 'Eighteen troopers under the command of a corporal will be attacking. And a similar number of police officers from the local station at Lydhurst will be defending. They'll be under the command of Inspector Lipman. And Major Kilmore and I will be on hand throughout as umpires.'

'Well, it's deplorably ill-timed, the whole thing,' Edwina protested. She had fundamental objections anyway to letting security forces play cowboys and Indians in one of the nation's finest historic buildings. 'I realise you want to stage this exercise under proper conference conditions, but on *Saturday* of all days. You couldn't have picked a more inconvenient time if you'd tried.' She glanced out of her office window to the north courtyard. 'You can see for yourself the chaos we're in . . . and this is only Monday!'

Wopec had hit Carnage like a cyclone, and the whole estate had begun to take on the appearance of a disaster relief co-ordination centre. There was still a week to go before the start of the conference, but already the castle was under siege – and not at all the kind of siege that Doris Bile had had in mind when she had first put the idea for Operation Midsummer Night into Ron-luvvy's bullet-proof head. Armies of invading workmen had descended, wave upon wave of them: scaffolders, sparks, chippies, plumbers, caterers, cleaners, drivers, labourers, fork-lift operators, loaders, packers, chargehands, foremen . . . Wandering, muttering, shouting, grumbling, pointing, arguing, head-shaking, smoke-puffing, tea-drinking, list-checking, pencil-licking, bum-scratching and offering no end of expert advice to all and sundry. Queues of vehicles – vans, pick-ups, artics, rigids, tractors, trailers, dumper trucks – tailed back from the car park to the Allshott road. Stuff was everywhere; heaps of stuff, mountains of stuff. In every room, doorway, passage and courtyard. Strewn over all the pathways and terraces and flower beds. Piled up in the car park and right down the avenue to the main gates. Draped over walls, propped up against trees, stacked on the lawns. Five marquees and seventeen tents for the Wopec Day fête. One hundred and fifty catering tables; chairs: five hundred stacking and four thousand folding; seven hundredweight of crockery and cutlery; fifty thousand cardboard plates and plastic knives and forks. Five hundred kilowatts of auxiliary lighting and power. Two thousand metres of wire and cable. A dozen pantechnicon loads of chairs and tables from Period Furniture Hire (Films and Exhibitions) Limited. Eight Portaloo trailers. One British Telecom mobile telephone exchange. Sixty kilos of Brasswick's brightest and best fireworks. A truckful of Wopec sweatshirts, coffee mugs, ballpens and bikini briefs from Metaxis Leisure Enterprises (Camden Town). And somewhere in the midst of it all, a lost tribe of television people in Hush Puppies looking for the nearest pub.

'What it's going to be like by Saturday one dreads to imagine,' said Edwina. 'We're going to be rushing about like loonies all day long as it is, trying to get everything finished in time. And now you tell me you want the entire estate evacuated by six o'clock!'

'I didn't say *quite* that, madam,' Hatchard replied pleasantly. 'I was merely asking you when it would be convenient for everybody to vacate the premises, and suggesting six p.m. as an example.'

'Well, I'm sorry, but that's quite out of the question,' said Edwina firmly. 'I doubt if even the workmen will be finished by then, and Unibore are going to be here till seven.' She consulted the typewritten schedule that had arrived by post that morning from Freda Elphinstone. 'President Butcher is due to fly in at half past eight on Saturday morning. He goes straight to his hotel in London and is due here at four o'clock for the dress rehearsal with the CLAC committee. There'll be a final tour of inspection between five and six. Then Professor Fabrizi and his wife have a meeting with their *maître de cuisine* and the staff from Rent-a-Footman, to go over all the banqueting arrangements. They estimate they'll be finished by seven. And my staff will need at least an hour to clear up after they've all gone.'

'Very well,' said Hatchard patiently. 'Why don't we make that an hour and a half? Then I can advise Major Kilmore that the place will be ours from half past eight onwards.'

'And that's *another* point,' said Edwina. 'Mr Wormslow and I live on the premises. Certain areas are going to have to be out of bounds. The west and south-west towers, for a start.'

'Well, we can go over the whole castle, madam,' Hatchard replied, 'and agree between ourselves which areas should be roped off on the night.'

'And suppose some clumsy bugger puts his foot through a window?' said Brownjohn. 'Have the MoD thought about that? There's a lot of valuable glass in this place, you know. Pillaged from the old monasteries.'

'I believe the ministry are fully aware of that, sir,' said Hatchard. 'It is their property, after all.'

'No one's disputing that,' said Edwina, feeling increasingly put out about the whole thing. 'But we *live* here, Superintendent.'

'I do appreciate that, madam.'

'We have rights too, you know. If we *have* to be confined to quarters for a whole night we should at least be told who exactly is going to be running riot here, fighting and screaming and shooting the place up while the rest of us are trying to get some sleep.'

'No one is going to be running riot, madam,' Hatchard assured her, a trifle wearily. 'Or fighting or screaming or shooting the place up. This is going to be a perfectly peaceful exercise in friendly co-operation between local police officers and a small team of highly-trained professional soldiers . . .'

42

'THE SECRET of a good night op is *hate*,' said Bile. 'Haitch, a, tee-hee, *hate*.' He paused and surveyed the seventeen stubble-pated troopers seated before him in the lecture room. 'Now unfortunately, the powers-that-be have refused to let us use live ammunition against Mr Plod, in case we damage the medieval plasterwork or stained-glass windows. So we're restricted to smoke, concussion grenades and blanks. But that does not prevent you from employing all the maximum possible physical violence you consider reasonably necessary in the heat of the moment to ensure the safe apprehension of the enemy. So then . . .' Bile crossed to a blackboard on which he had chalked a ground plan of Carnage Castle. 'Situation: a mob of terrorist scumshite is somewhere inside the castle. They have hostages. All attempts to negotiate with them have failed and we have to go in and get them poor bastard hostages out alive. At first glance it looks a bit tasty. Anyone 'oled up in there could see us coming a mile off, whether we legged it across country or come in by chopper or tried a waterborne landing upriver. By the time we got there, they'd have shot every bugger dead or blown theirselves to kingdom come.

'Why then, you may ask, is the MoD, in its infinite wisdom, contemplating turning this useless pile of medieval history into a permanent, top-security conference centre? Because they know something you don't. And that something I will now impart to you, you lucky bleeders. An underground passage exists, a secret tunnel, running from the dungeons on the east side beneath the keep tower, for about half a mile, and terminating in the cellar beneath the ruins of a gamekeeper's lodge in the East Woods. This tunnel was an escape route, dug way back in the days of Ethelred the Lionheart or whoever, in case the place ever fell to invading French scumturds from across the water. The tunnel still exists today and is still what is known in army parlance as *negotiable*. That is to say, it's two feet deep in piss and shite and bursting with sewer rats.' (Which warmed the cockles of every trooper's heart and brought back fond memories of dining by moonlight on fricassee of coypu in the fetid swamps around Warmacre Camp.)

'Our plan of attack then,' Bile continued. 'The enemy will r.v. at the castle at twenty thirty and take up their chosen positions, all in one room – we have no idea where, but anywhere on the three floors. We have until midnight to find 'em. Logic will tell 'em to expect us to wait until nightfall and attack under cover of darkness. So we're going to do the logical thing and take the bastards out in broad daylight while they're off guard. It's midsummer night and the sun sets at twenty-one twenty. We r.v. at the TA depot in Oldingham, twenty miles away, at sixteen forty-five, travel to Allshott village in a fleet of one-tonners, and leg it across the East Woods to the game-keeper's cottage. We then descend into the underground passage and wade through the tunnel until we reach the dungeons. We start searching the castle at around twenty-thirty. Work solo, spread out, and radio back if and when you rumble the enemy. We then regroup and storm the bastards. Smoke, flashbangs, blanks and plenty of haitch, a, tee-hee. Bag 'em, 'andcuff 'em, sling 'em in the transport, and straight back to Lydhurst nick for debrief and a good piss-up. I want a pint in each hand by sundown, so God help you poor sods if you don't get your fingers out.'

'Watcher mean "bag 'em", Corp'al?' asked one Trooper Stoatley.

'I mean the black bag,' said Bile with relish. 'I mean the 'ood.' He took a black, cotton drawstring bag from the table in front of him and held it up. 'Exhibit One: one 'ood, for interrogation, black, subversive scumfilth heads for the covering of. Disorientation, that's the name of the game. Bags of disorientation. And this bag disorientationalises the bastards like there's no tomorrer. And don't just bag 'em, lads . . . whirl 'em out like spinning tops. Spin, spin, spin. All the way outside and into the wagons. Disorientation, that's the stuff. By the time that pack of squealing scumshite hit the van deck they won't know if it's Saturday night or Shepton Mallet. *But* . . . one word of caution: do not, repeat not, handcuff, spin or clump an umpire. Partly because there'll be a fifty-fifty chance you'll be clobbering your commanding officer, but also because umpires in general do not take kindly to being hooded, spun or clumped. And never forget: this is not just an exercise to save hostages. You are being trained to save civilisation. Do you know what civilisation is, Trooper Doyle?'

'No, Corp'l,' said Doyle, fairly confident of that.

'I'll tell you what it is, son. It's fragile. That's what it is. Awful fragile. Civilisation is delicate as a moth's wing. Fine as gossamer. Thin as a sheet of Andrex. And this cruel world is full of raving nutters who'll stop at nothing to shove a finger through it. Get that, Doyle?'

'Corp'l.'

'So don't go into this exercise thinking it's just a game of hide and seek with the woodentops. Don't let your minds slither down that slippery slope of delusion that tells you to go easy because it's only Old Bill. Because that way madness lies. Start telling yourself he's only the friendly local bobby with long legs and big feet, and Christ only knows where it could all end. When you go into that castle they are your *enemy*. No more, no less. Don't think of your cheery, timetelling, kneesbending, whistleblowing, I'm-over-five-foot-eight-so-fuck-you-shortarse PC Plod.' Bile's face was now taking on a raspberry hue, veins like purple worms beginning to bulge at his temples and spots of white froth appearing at the corners of his mouth. 'Think, instead, of them poor, poor hostages. Think of it as if they was holding your own son in there . . . your baby daughter . . . your bastard bleeding missis. In there, frightened, lonely, helpless . . .' Bile's eyes began to glaze over, like a clairvoyant making contact with another world, beyond the grim attentive faces seated before him. Recalling faintly some meagre scraps of once-remembered, force fed, classroom Shakespeare, he went on proudly: 'So let 'em call you pint size. Midget. Pygmy. What's in a name, lads, eh? A rose by any other name stinks just the same. For there's a tide in the affairs of man, which, when we take arms against a sea of troubles, leads on to the flood. And *then* they change their tune . . . Oh, my Christ, do they ever? Did long legs matter at Dunkirk?' (Voice quavering with passion.) 'Did height matter on the Normandy beaches? When we stood alone – we few, we happy few, we band of brothers – Göring's Dorniers bombing almighty fuck out of Coventry,' (Bile now raging frothily) 'did they turn away recruits because they wasn't *five feet eight sodding inches tall*?' He seized Trooper Stoatley by the lapels, lifted him clean off the bench and shook him like a pair of marimbas. 'Did they?' he demanded. 'Well, *did* they? *Did* they, you ignorant, long-legged toe-rag?'

'No, Gorp'l,' gargled blue-turning long-legged Stoatley.

'No, Gorp'l,' echoed Bile, gazing foggy-eyed into nowhere. Slowly his grip slackened and Stoatley slumped back onto the bench, pale as semolina. Bile snuffled, struggled to refocus his vision, and punished tear-damp cheeks harshly with a tattooed forearm. He stood swaying for a moment, trying to recall who they were and what they were doing there.

'As I was saying,' he resumed quietly, and then paused for thought. He frowned and turned to Trooper Doyle. 'What was I sayin', son?'

'You was saying that civilisation is like Andrex,' said Doyle gently. 'And that this world is full of raving nutters who'll stop at nothing to shove a finger through it.'

'Ah, so I was, lad, so I was,' sighed Bile, feeling the consoling warmth of a much-loved and oft-quoted text flow like ambrosia through his weary soul.

43

WEDNESDAY JUNE the twenty-first was Rosheen's thirty-fourth birthday and it was just *full* of surprises.

'Surprise! Surprise!' the baron exclaimed, wakening her that morning with a magnum of spuming Taittinger and a gift-wrapped package the size of a Turbowasheur Supalectrique.

Anticipating at the very least a Pissarro or a small Ferrari, Rosheen leapt out of bed and pounced on the package like a hungry panther. Tearing away its gold-paper flesh with powerful swipes of her greedy paws, she uncovered a set of pigskin luggage – four suitcases, a valise, a matching shoulder-bag, grip and passport wallet. She gave them an indignant once-over and estimated that the whole lot could not have set him back one measly centime over ten thousand francs.

'Terrific,' she said tonelessly. 'Baggage. Thanks a billion, Guy. Just what I always . . .'

'*Et surprise! Surprise*!' exclaimed the baron once more, as Chantal came rumbling into the bedroom, steady as a freight train, beaming from ear to ear.

'Appee burfdee,' she cooed, plonking her slug-moist lips on Rosheen's cheeks. She held out a small pink package, a trifle coyly, like a piece of Meissen she had just smashed in the dishwasher.

'Oh, Chantal, you really *shouldn't* have,' said Rosheen, smarting fiercely over her heap of pigskin non-Ferraris. She tore off the pink paper and opened the box inside. 'A clock . . . an alarm clock . . . a *travelling* alarm clock.'

'A *pigskin* travelling alarm clock,' the baron pointed out, delirious with joy and pouring three goblets of champagne. 'To match your suitcases, little cobra!'

'*Merci bien*, Chantal,' said Rosheen, wondering why everybody seemed to think she was going somewhere all of a sudden. 'A pigskin clock, just what I always . . .' And pressed her lips to Chantal's rawhide cheeks.

She spent the rest of that day brooding over Guy's niggardly gift. Why luggage? Why a travelling alarm clock? Were they going somewhere? Were there yet *more* surprises in store then? Like a three-month cruise on the QE2?'

Evening came, but still no more surprises. She took a bath before dinner and was quietly soaking away her resentment when suddenly . . . 'Surprise! Surprise!' exclaimed the baron, sailing into the bathroom in a tuxedo and a cloud of cologne. And plucking her from the Badedas, zipped her into Dior and whisked her outside to le Roller, where Chantal was waiting, a blaze of fuchsia organdie, exuding a pungent blend of Rochas and strong exocrine secretions. Patrice, the chauffeur, sped them away through Mougins and into Cannes.

'Guy, sweetie,' said Rosheen, sensing imminent bacchanalia, 'where are we going?'

'Surprise! Surprise!' said the baron, as Patrice drew up outside Le Club des Satyrs.

'Le Club des Satyrs!' Rosheen shrieked. 'Oh . . . *too-oo . . . much*!'

Which indeed it was, costing as it did an arm and a leg to get in, the other arm and leg to get out, and a king's ransom to do pretty well anything in between. Le Club des Satyrs was the *plus chic* stamping ground of the deviant super-rich and the most notorious nightspot on the Côte d'Azur.

Rosheen was to remember virtually nothing of her thirty-fourth birthday party. She regained consciousness some hours later, back at the Château Montcalme, and found herself in bed with Guy and Chantal. A whiff of cognac and the sweet scent of hashish came wafting her way.

'Want dwinkie,' she mumbled in the little girl's voice in which she always sought sanctuary when the world started getting out of hand. Chantal passed her a glass of cognac. 'Want puff-puff.' Chantal passed her a fat spliff.

'*Bienvenue, chérie*,' said the baron, adrift somewhere on a cloud of sublime insouciance. 'Just in time for your last surprise, surprise! Chantal and I — '

'Got bwain pain.'

' — are getting married.'

'Got windypops.' Rosheen released a warm, satisfying blast.

'We wanted you to be the first to know, my little mongoose.'

'Mongoose go shleepybies,' gurgled Rosheen.

'Nothing personal, you understand, but Chantal is expecting our first baby in the new year.'

'Bebbeeee,' Rosheen echoed sleepily. And after a moment: 'But we don't have no *bebbees, stupide*.'

'But happily,' said the baron, 'Chantal has just learnt that she is with child.'

'Naughty, naughty . . .' Rosheen cuddled up to the calving Chantal and caressed her swelling belly. 'Who bin a careless puddy-tat then?'

'I'd hate you to think that we don't want you any more,' the baron went on sympathetically, 'but now that we're starting a family — '

'No womb at the inn,' Rosheen burbled, nestling up to Chantal's sprawling, gelatinous dugs. 'Mmmmmmm . . . Wosheen feel sickypoos.'

' — we feel that in the interests of propriety, it would be better all round if you made alternative arrangements.'

Rosheen began to sing: 'A womb with a view . . . and you . . . and no one to dum-di-dum, dah dah di-dah di-dah . . .'

When she awoke the next morning she was lying naked on the bed, alone and roasting gently in the punishing white blaze of the Mediterranean sun, with a jackhammer working away inside her head and a mouth like soiled cat litter.

Solange, the cook, prepared a citron pressé, croissants and fresh coffee, and Patrice carried the tray out to the pool where monsieur le baron was floating almost motionless on an airbed, composing the guest-list for his wedding.

Rosheen slipped and slurped and chewed for a while in jackhammering silence. Then: 'Guy?'

'My little ferret?'

'Did I dream it, or did you tell me Chantal was pregnant last night?'

'You didn't dream it.'

'She is?'

'She is.'

Rosheen broke two paracetamol tablets into little bits and swallowed the fragments with the last of the citron pressé. Then: 'Guy?'

'Mm-hm?'

'Did you say something about you and Chantal getting married?'

'In September.'

'September?'

'Mm-hm.'

'Funny. That's what I thought you said.' She finished her coffee in silence. Then: 'Guy?'

'Sweet scorpion?'

'You can't be serious.'

'Serious?'

'You are really and truly thinking of marrying that baby ox?'

'That's not a very nice way to speak of a servant.'

'But she's *my* playmate, not yours.'

'And it's not a very nice way to speak of a playmate either.'

'But I found her, you thieving son of a bitch!' The jackhammer started up again with a vengeance. 'Jesus, my head. Guy,' she said weakly, 'Guy, listen to me, you can't do this.'

'Do what?'

'Marry a hog farmer's daughter from the Auvergne.'

'Why not?'

'Because, Christ, you're one of the last surviving descendants of Louis the Sixteenth. Probably. You can't miscegenate with a barnyard peasant like her.'

'Why not? There are centuries of pure Gallic blood in those fecund loins. Without heirs, remember, I might be the *very* last surviving descendant of Louis the Sixteenth. Do you want to be responsible for exterminating the French monarchy?'

'But you can't just . . . just . . .' Rosheen clutched her pounding head, too weak even to shout. 'I mean, how can you be so . . . After all we've been through together . . . I mean, Christ, don't I even get a *thought*? Am I not even being considered?'

'*Mais bien sûr, ma douce,*' said the baron, displaying an inordinately long schedule of wedding guests. 'You're at the very top of my list. Do you and Byron want separate invitations, or can I give you just the one to take back to Hamilton Grove for both of you?'

'God, this cannot be for real . . .'

'Please, don't think I'm trying to skimp on the postage or anything, but . . .'

'It's got to be a joke, Guy,' Rosheen bleated. 'Tell me it's a put-on. You can't go through with this.'

The baron shrugged regretfully. 'But I have to, little hornet. Chantal has already told her family, and they're volatile people up there in the Auvergne. Besides, it'll be in all the papers by tomorrow . . .'

44

BYRON READ about it the following morning, slouched at the kitchen table in his bathrobe, with a plate of goodness-free wheat toasties and that day's edition of the *International Herald*

Tribune. It was tucked away on an inside page under the headline *Bourbon wedding*, which caught Byron's eye only because it seemed to presage some major dynastic reshuffle among the great Southern whiskey families.

Nice, June 22nd,

The distinguished French ontologist Baron Guy de Montcalme-Challois, who claims to be a direct descendant of Louis XVI, is to marry again in September. His previous marriage to his fifth wife, Natalya Feodorovna Romanov, who thought she was a grand-daughter of Tsar Nicholas II, was annulled in 1978 on grounds of insanity.

Incredulous, Byron read it through again. There must have been some mistake. A transmission error perhaps between Nice and the *Tribune*'s Paris office. A drunken compositor even.

The minute he arrived at Halcyon House he rushed up to Otello's office to ask whether he had read or heard anything about this alleged wedding. Otello had not only read about it (in that morning's *La Stampa*), he had just received a telegram from the baron himself, which he translated from the French for Byron's benefit:

REGRET IMMINENCE WEDDING AND DOMESTIC UPHEAVALS PREVENT ATTENDANCE WOPEC. ALL GOOD WISHES FOR FUTURE AND CONGRATULATIONS YOUR SUCCESSFUL QUINQUENNIUM UNIBORE. HOPE YOU AND MIRELLA WILL BE HERE WEDDING. GUY.

Suddenly it all made sense to Byron at last, in as much as anything Rosheen ever did made sense. So that was why she had turned up out of the blue just a couple of weeks ago wanting a lightning divorce. But now the truth was out, the scheming bitch would have to agree to a divorce on *any* terms. Practically airborne with euphoria, he sent a telegram of congratulations at once to the Château Montcalme:

MILLIARDS DE FÉLICITATIONS. OVER THE MOON FOR YOU BOTH. ALL HAPPINESS. BYRON.

An hour later Gladstone loped into his office with the mid-morning mail. A telegram had just arrived from Salvation.

FLYING NEW ORLEANS-LONDON, ARRIVING GATWICK 12.00 SATURDAY. BOOKED WEEKEND LOCAL HOTEL. CAN WE MEET EVENING? ALL LOVE, ANNABELLE.

With a whoop of joy, Byron ripped the telegram to shreds and tossed the pieces over his head like confetti. 'Gladstone, old buddy,' he said, 'you being a good church-going Christian and all, I want you to be the first to hear the glad tidings.'

'Yeh? Whassat, Doc?'

'The new director-general of Unibore, a devout, practising pagan these last forty-two years, is about to become affianced to Annabelle Laura, only daughter of the Reverend Noah and the late Mrs Evelyn Cartwright of Salvation, Mississippi . . .'

Five hundred miles away, Rosheen Rynagh Bridget, fifth daughter of Eamon and Rosaline O'Halloran of Madison, New Jersey, was at the Air France office in Nice, booking a seat on the 10.05 flight to London on Saturday morning.

45

SUNDOWN, MIDSUMMER'S EVE. A warm night and a gentle breeze. Carnage Castle lay like some stately warship briefly becalmed in the stormy waters of Wopec. Around her lapped a silent sea of shifting grey canvas; flags of every nation stirred restlessly on their masts along the battlements.

High up in her bathroom in the west tower, like an officer of the watch, Edwina Sheffield gazed across the medieval roofs to the Tudor south wing, where a pale light burned in the Hapsburg chamber.

'He's in the General's bedroom again,' she murmured.

Brownjohn was stretched out in a foot of scummy water, with a Wills' Gold Flake in one hand and a brown ale in the other. 'Who? Aubrey?'

'What does he *do* in there every night?'

'Gawd knows.'

'I sometimes think this Wopec business has begun to turn his mind. He actually seems *glad* the army are moving in tomorrow night.'

Over in the Hapsburg chamber, lonely Wormslow laid out the

General's best tunic and breeches, and flicked a yellow duster over the gleaming brass buttons.

'It'll be nice to see some troops around the place again, eh sir?' he muttered happily. 'They'll be sorry you can't be there to welcome them in person. But we know you'll be with us all in spirit.'

A warm breeze drifted through the room and teased the curtains. Wormslow took a few discreet sniffs and thought for one magic moment that he caught the leathery-salt tang of horses in the air. The General was in good humour, right enough.

He placed his master's cavalry boots at the foot of the bed and paused to gaze proudly at his own reflection in the leather. 'The old boots come up a treat then, sir,' he said to the empty bed. 'Three weeks' spit and Kiwi done the trick.'

He worked a clothes brush smartly round the crown of the General's peaked hat and placed it on the bed beside his Sam Browne belt and pistol holster. Picking up the old man's favourite long-barrelled .45 revolver, he aimed it at the United Nations' flag outside, and added with a hint of relish: 'You'll be needing this as well, sir. That Wopec rabble could take a bit of shifting, I think you'll find.'

Part Three

MIDSUMMER NIGHT

46

SUNRISE, MIDSUMMER'S DAY. A clear sky and a light mist on the meadows. Nurg was lying wide awake in his pigsty, listening to the dawn chorus in Oxfold Woods and contemplating a whole kaleidoscope of disasters that could befall Operation Thunder that day. He had hardly slept a wink all night for worrying. What if Pungal's truck broke down? What if they were searched as they tried to enter the castle? What if the dungeons had been locked up for the weekend? Or, worse still, what if someone locked the doors with Number One Commando trapped inside? And what if the ambassadors *refused* to be kidnapped? Suppose some of them got bolshy and began to biff him in the eye? Nurg had been biffed in the eye before and it was no joke.

Pungal came crashing into the piggery at ten to six, vibrant with vigour, crow-black hair still glistening from a dawn plunge in the duck pond. He walked the length of the shed, banging on the pigsty doors to waken the commandos. Nurg tottered out into the farmyard in his underpants – one of the few items of clothing on which he had not yet drawn a lance corporal's stripe – and called the young commandos out for p.e. They lined up beside him in their boxer shorts and singlets for Sharaq's rigorous morning work-out. Sinewy bodies soon began to shine with sweat. Chests expanded, muscles bulged. Spindly Nurg alone shivered in the early morning chill as his joints creaked reluctantly to life.

The sun was climbing into a clear blue sky, shining palely on the dew-drenched meadows. Pigeons were warbling in the chestnut trees nearby. Somewhere a cock was crowing. Following his sergeant's lead, Nurg plunged bravely into the icy pond to set a good example to his men. The young commandos watched him emerge, draped in green slime and quaking with cold, and promptly trooped off to a nice warm bathroom in the farmhouse.

They assembled for breakfast at seven. Nurg wolfed down

three large bowlfuls of porridge to pack some calories into his frozen body. At quarter to eight they lined up beside the truck in their blue boilersuits for kit inspection. Each commando had a canvas toolbag packed with a woollen sweater, machine pistol, ammunition, hand grenades, flashlight, gloves, Balaclava helmet and army backpack. Pungal carried one extra bag of rations.

After the inspection, Sharaq delivered a final, morale-boosting exhortation and gave the order to embark. Pungal opened the tailgates and lowered the ramp, and Nurg led the eager young commandos into the empty belly of the truck. Sharaq and Pungal closed the tailgates and climbed into the cab. Pungal pressed the starter. Arthritic pistons ground up and down in their carbon-caked cylinders. The engine clattered reluctantly to life and shot sulphurous black blasts into the dew-sweet air. With a crunch of gears and a fierce lurch, the aged behemoth bumped away down the track towards Chipton Oxfold.

It was an hour and twenty minutes' drive to Allshott. Carnage was already swarming with workmen when they arrived, and no one looked twice at the seven dark strangers who emerged from the scruffy truck in the shadow of the east wall and made their way at a workmanlike trudge across the car park towards the gatehouse.

Nurg looked up at the statue of General Sterling-Pallgrave as they passed.

'Imperial British warlord,' Pungal murmured darkly. 'Mighty scourge of our federal oppressors.'

Nurg nodded with respect and approval. Anyone who scourged the oppressors of Sandhustan must indeed have been a mighty warlord.

They entered the gatehouse and were confronted by two Aceguards on loan from Halcyon House, in pale blue uniforms and expensive sunglasses.

'Chippie,' said Sharaq, and waved a handful of official-looking papers that Dubbi Muktar's uncle had forged for them on his printing press in London.

The Aceguards waved them past. Sharaq led the way across the north courtyard, in through the front door of the great hall, down the screens passage and into the hall, where electricians were busy rigging auxiliary lights.

'You the chippie?' asked the sparks foreman.

'Plumber,' said Sharaq.

''Kin 'ell,' grumbled the foreman. 'Where's that chippie got to then?'

'Dunno,' said Sharaq.

''Kin 'ell,' said the foreman, turning to Nurg, hoping *he* might know.

''Kin 'ell,' said Nurg, assuming that it was some sort of colloquial labourer's greeting.

They trooped across the great hall, through the doors at the dais end, into the Tudor north wing, past the main staircase and the small drawing-room, through the ante-room and into the keep – a fifty-foot square tower, empty, musty, and lit by a single shaft of brilliant sunlight through an arched window fifteen feet above the ground. Sharaq led them down the dungeon steps, opened the oak door at the bottom and entered the chilly black void beyond. The commandos followed in single file, through the first and second vaults, into the third and then down the passage to Ye Olde Chaymbre of Torture. Nurg flashed his torch around the room. Moisture glistened on the rough-hewn limestone walls. A skeleton lay crushed in a medieval iron body press. Another dangled from the ceiling in a cocoon of spikes. A third was spit-roasting over a blacksmith's forge. Nurg shivered.

'Haunted,' Pungal whispered in his ear.

Nurg stopped in his tracks. 'This place?'

Pungal nodded. 'By the spirits of the tortured dead.'

Nurg grinned foolishly. 'You're having me on.'

'Never mock the unquiet spirits,' whispered Pungal, drawing a warning finger across his gullet. 'They're all around us.'

Nurg swallowed hard. 'Wasn't mocking, Guppi.'

'Beware the ghost of the Imperial Warlord, General Sterling-Thing. He haunts these dungeons, seeking vengeance on the unbeliever.'

'Oh, I believe, Guppi,' murmured fearful Nurg. 'I really do believe.'

'You just better had,' Pungal warned him.

Next door to the torture chamber was a small cell where Sharaq set up quarters for the day. He took the spare bag of rations from Pungal. 'Be back here by nineteen forty-five, remember. And make radio contact as soon as you're standing by in the car park.'

'Will do,' Pungal replied. 'The Lord Shrahma be with you.' He shook hands with Sharaq and each of the commandos in turn, and then hurried back through the darkness to the keep tower.

Nurg watched the torchlight fade away and felt a twinge of envy. Lucky Pungal, spending the day in the sunshine back at Lower Oxfold Farm, while they had to wait entombed in those freezing black catacombs, with the ghost of the Imperial British Warlord, and the unquiet spirits all around them.

Air Vice-Marshal Engineer had been up since the crack of dawn too, and with Hudson Butcher and his party due to land at Heathrow at eight twenty-five he had been in as acute a state of anxiety all night as Golam Nurg.

Jericho had been preparing for this great day for some considerable time. Taking it for granted that everyone at the Paradise Islands' High Commission – and the cream of the British Foreign Office to boot – would be there at the airport to greet the Prince of Peace, he had made a supreme effort to look his sartorial finest for the occasion. He had a resplendent new air vice-marshal's uniform, tailored by Meyer and Mortimer of Sackville Street; new boots, handlasted by James Taylor of Paddington Street; and a chestful of assorted medals for extreme valour, exclusively minted from genuine original copies by Demosthenes Metaxis (Sunwear and Funwear) of Camden Town. Having been pushed, squeezed, laced, buttoned and zipped into this lot, he was transported downstairs by four strong servants, eased into the back of his reinforced Mercedes, squeaking and tinkling like a glockenspiel, and whisked away to Heathrow.

He arrived at Terminal Three in a flurry of flapping pennants with half an hour to spare, and barged his way into the VIP lounge, where he found one solitary clerk from the High Commission and the most insignificant Foreign Office dogsbody that protocol would permit Whitehall to send. Everybody else – with the vital exception of the Prince of Peace and his retinue – had already been and gone. The President was stranded temporarily in Athens, the dogsbody explained to Jericho. A terrorist bomb alert had closed Athens airport, and all flights out – including Equatorial Airways flight QR514, on which His Almighty Peacefulness was travelling – had been suspended until nine a.m. London time. As it was a four-hour flight from Athens to London, the vast welcoming party that had been assembled at Heathrow since seven o'clock had decided to go home and come back at lunchtime.

Furious at having been turfed out of bed at the ungodly hour of five a.m. for no good purpose (but consoled somewhat by the prospect of being able to make a second spectacular arrival at Heathrow later in the day) Jericho returned to Mayfair for a slap-up breakfast, and spent the rest of the morning posing importantly in Harrods – where, to his further vexation, he was mistaken for a commissionaire and importuned by thousands of foreign rabble looking for the escalators.

Nina Kabanova had also been up since the crack of dawn, anticipating the early arrival of Zlob. (But then she was always up at the crack of dawn, up-pressing and chest expanding and sprinting round Kensington Gardens.) Zlob, however, had *not* been anticipating the early arrival of Zlob and did not turn up until midday. And he most certainly had *not* been up since dawn; he had been up since twenty-five past eleven. Which had given him just enough time to wash the few parts of his body that showed, behead a few pustules with his mark-IV army-issur razor and scoot over to Bayswater for a late elevenses with Comrade Brain. He arrived at her apartment breathless and flatulent, wearing a beige summerweight suit and carrying an aluminium photographer's case. He asked for five sugars in the coffee she had not offered him and joined her in the kitchen while she prepared it.

'Dead clever those Russians,' he said, laying the case down on the table and opening it to reveal a thirty-five-millimetre camera, a selection of lenses, and a box purporting to contain thirty rolls of colour film. Opening the box he took out a microtransmitter half the size of his thumb. 'Neat, eh?' He passed it to her for approval.

'What is it?' She examined it. 'A bug?'

He nodded proudly. 'I helped to develop that. It's got a range of fifteen kilometres.'

'How many have you brought?'

'Twenty. Should be enough.'

'It's a big castle. Where are you going to put them?'

'Dunno yet.' He sniffed and wiped his nose with his fingers. 'Have to see when we get there.'

'And what's the camera for?'

'That's my cover.'

'Cover?'

'Dimiter Vulchanov, press photographer.' He showed her an international press card in that name, with his maudlin acne-speckled mugshot affixed. 'So I can go in and out of the castle all week unsuspected, and keep an eye on me bugs. Dimiter Vulchanov, the dapper snapper from Stara Zagora. Neat, eh?'

'And how long do you think it'll take you to plant them all?'

He shrugged. 'An hour, maybe. Dunno. The sooner we get there, the sooner I'll be done.'

'Well, there's no desperate rush. Didn't you hear the news this morning?'

'No. Can't get Radio Sofia on my tranny. Why? Anything interesting happened?'

'There's been a terrorist incident at Athens airport.'

'No kidding?' He brightened a little.

'Hudson Butcher's flight has been delayed.'

'Hudson Butcher?' Zlob frowned. 'Now don't tell me . . . don't tell me. Know the name . . . Hudson . . . Hudson . . .'

Dubbi Muktar, at home in Southall, had only just heard the news too. He had been feeling uneasy ever since breakfast when he opened the *Daily Express* and saw pictures of the VIPs arriving in London for Wopec Day '. . . on *Sunday*.' He had put that down to a misprint at first. But then he switched on the radio for the midday news bulletin and heard the newsreader say quite clearly that President Butcher had been delayed in Athens '. . . *on his way to London to open the Wopec conference at Carnage Castle on Sunday*.'

Dubbi sat stupefied. It was not possible – the BBC and the *Express* couldn't *both* be wrong. But how could the SPLA have made such a disastrous and fundamental error? Had Unibore changed the date? Wouldn't he have read about it in the daily papers or seen it on the television news? Unless, of course, it had happened while he was away in Sandhubad in mid-May. But then, surely Colonel Boatman would have let them know? He phoned Carnage Castle. No one there seemed to know what he was talking about. Wopec Day was on Sunday. Wopec Day had always been on Sunday as far as they knew. Nothing was happening on Saturday – no speeches, no fête, no fireworks. And certainly no director-general's banquet.

Dubbi sat down, refused to panic, and calmly considered his options. There were another eight hours to go before Operation Thunder was due to start. That was more than enough time to rescue Sharaq and the commandos from the castle dungeons and get them safely back to the farm. No harm had been done and there was nothing to stop them remounting the operation, exactly according to plan, the next day. It was no more than an hour and three-quarters' drive to Chipton Oxfold; if he put his foot down he could be there by two o'clock. He and Pungal would have plenty of time to plan an orderly rescue mission. With luck the whole team would be safely back at the farm by six o'clock.

Whilst Dubbi was speeding south towards the M3 in his shabby yellow minicab, Jericho Engineer was arriving at Heathrow airport for the second time that day to greet the Prince of Peace. Entering Terminal Three shortly before one o'clock, he found the VIP lounge full of oil sheikhs and boy rock stars in summer dresses. Seeing no sign of anyone from the High Commission – and not even *one* insignificant dogsmess from the Foreign Office – he waddled up to the nearest information desk to enquire what had happened to Equatorial Airways flight QR514 from Nairobi. A highly efficient Miss Information obligingly poked a question into a computer keyboard and came up with the news that QR514 had only just taken off from Athens and would not reach London before four o'clock at the earliest. Mindful of the fact that the President was due at Carnage Castle at four o'clock for a dress rehearsal, Jericho protested that that was just not good enough and enquired if she had even the faintest notion of who was travelling on that flight. Miss Information said she was terribly sorry, no, she didn't have access to passenger lists, but if sir wanted to know if his friends or relatives had caught the plane on time sir could always try asking at the Equatorial Airways desk.

Much put out, Jericho repaired to the nearest cafeteria for a plate of doughnuts.

While Jericho was stuffing his face with carbohydrate, passengers off Air France flight AF812, were passing through customs a few hundred yards away at Terminal Two, where Rosheen was confidently trundling through the 'nothing to declare' gate with all her worldly possessions and three trolley-loads of contraband, pornography and booty she had pillaged from the Château Montcalme. Mowing a swathe clean through a dithering flock of sweet old ladies returning from Lourdes, she ploughed her way to the taxi rank outside and – oblivious of the queue – began piling her caravan of goodies into the first cab that came along, yelling 'St John's Wood, Sundance' at the driver and '*Va te faire foutre*' at anyone who took exception.

Thirty miles away to the south-east, a Boeing 747 from New Orleans was just descending on final approach to Gatwick airport.

Byron had been in a frenzy of activity for the past twenty-four hours, galvanised by the hectic pace of events at Halcyon House and the imminent arrival of the Cartwrights. He had spent all Friday afternoon making lists (lists of things to buy, lists of things to do, lists of things to wear, lists of things to tell Annabelle, and so on ad dementiam), all Friday night tidying up the apartment, and all Saturday morning steaming up and down the Kilburn High Road, looking for cheap crockery, so that he could at the very least entertain his future wife and father-in-law to a cup of tea. Rosheen had left him with scarcely an eggcup in one piece, and negotiations with Leo Feinbaum for the loan of a few plates had not gone well. After a lengthy search he stumbled upon Mukherjee's Megamart on Cricklewood Broadway and invested in a heap of nasty-looking rose-spotted boneware as an emergency stopgap. (He could always give it to Guy and Rosheen as a wedding present afterwards.)

There being no end to this midsummer madness, he even opened several windows in honour of the occasion. Now happily restored to rude health, Mrs O'Nobblin had implied – none too subtly – that the flat was beginning to smell. (*Pong* was the actual word she had used.) So, as it was one of the hottest weeks of the year and one of the most important weeks in his life, Byron threw all caution to the winds, switched off the central heating, unscrewed the casements and surrendered the place to the ravages of fresh air.

The only thing he had not managed to do so far was find out where the Cartwrights were staying. Annabelle's telegram had said something about the local hotel (though since he had torn it up like confetti he had no record of her exact words). But there was nowhere in the vicinity of Hamilton Grove that could be described as a *local* hotel. There wasn't even a local pub within walking distance; leastways, not what Byron called walking distance, which was about as far as the nearest bus-stop. Not that it much mattered, he supposed, for she would either phone him as soon as she got to London, or call in on her way from the airport. However, he had completely forgotten what time her plane was scheduled to arrive. By quarter past two that afternoon he was on the verge of calling Gatwick airport to find out, when he heard three short, sharp buzzes on the Entriphone. Wondering if that could be Annabelle, or just Gladstone fifteen minutes early, he hurried down the hallway and picked up the receiver.

'Hello?'

'Hi, sweetie. Guess who.'

Byron gazed stupefied at the Entriphone. '*Rosheen* . . . ?'

'My doorkeys are buried somewhere in my baggage.'

'What the hell are *you* doing here?'

'Just got in. Press the tit, honey. It's ninety in the shade out here and I'm gasping for a beer.'

Byron rocked back against the hall wall. 'Rosheen, have you gone nuts or something? What do you want?'

'Just a hand up with the baggage, baby. Oh, and twenty-two fifty for the cab fare.'

'Twenty-two *what*?'

'Better make it twenty-five with the gratuity. Sorry, angel, but all I've got are lousy francs.'

Zlob had had a wretched journey down to Allshott. Cars, like aircraft, made him violently sick, and Nina – who saw no point in having an Alfa if you didn't drive it like a Ferrari – had had to stop half a dozen times along the way to let him heave into the hedgerow. He arrived at Carnage an unnerving shade of post-mortem ecru, vowing never to set foot in a car with her again.

She drove into the castle car park and parked among the contractors' vehicles alongside the east wall. Gangs of workmen were lying on the grass, stripped to the waist in the blazing sun, eating ice creams, pulling on cans of beer, waiting for instructions, the bulk of their labour now finished.

'I should be through by six,' said Nina, glancing at her watch. 'So you've got about four hours.'

'A doddle,' said Zlob confidently, taking his aluminium case from the back seat. 'Piece of cake. I'll be finished by half three, no problem.' He opened the door. 'And remember, if anyone asks who I am, I'm Dimiter . . . Dimiter . . . Someone or other. Who did I say I was?'

'Vulchanov.'

'Vulchanov. That's the boy. So don't forget.'

'Are you quite sure you know where you're going?'

'Course I'm sure.'

'Got your guidebook and map?'

'Think I'm daft or something?' Without waiting for an answer, he got out of the car, slammed the door and walked across to the gatehouse, where he was confronted by the two Aceguards who had stopped Sharaq earlier in the day.

'Squire?' said the first.

Zlob flashed his international press card. 'Vulchovsky, Dimiter. VOPEK votograver. Okey, john?'

The guard took the card and examined it. 'Russki?'

'*Ne*. Bulgarski.'

Aceguard Two pointed to the case. 'Open *sie, dankeschön*.' Zlob obliged. Both guards glanced at the contents. Aceguard One handed back the press card, muttered 'Cheers, mate,' and nodded him through.

'Cheers, john,' said Zlob, and strolled on through the north courtyard.

Aceguard Two was looking baffled. 'If he's a press photographer, how come he's got a box full of 126 film for a 35 mill camera?'

Aceguard One had a little think about that. 'Good question.'

'What's his name?'

'Dunno. Tchaikovsky or something.'

Aceguard Two set off across the courtyard in pursuit of the distant Zlob, calling: 'Oi! *Bitteschön*! Herr Tchaikovsky!'

Zlob heard the shouting but kept walking and quickened his pace. He entered the castle and hurried down the screens passage into the great hall, where a team of workmen were unrolling a red carpet for the Prince of Peace. Zlob glanced out of the window. Aceguard Two was still marching briskly across the courtyard towards him, Oying and Tchaikovskying. Zlob decided to make himself scarce for a while. Tramping a trail of dust and gravel across the pristine red carpet and ignoring cries of "Kin 'ell!' from the workmen, he scuttled through the hall to the Tudor north wing, past the main staircase and small drawing-room, through an ante-room and into the keep tower. Finding nowhere to hide there, he proceeded cautiously down the flight of stone steps to the dungeons. Opening the heavy oak door at the bottom, he stood for a moment contemplating the cold black void beyond. The catacombs, he presumed. Comrade Brain had told him about the catacombs and Ye Olde Chaymbre of Torture. The perfect place to lie low for twenty minutes or so and shake off that security guard. Using a box of Bulgarian army matches to light his way, he ventured warily into the yawning darkness ahead and closed the great oak door behind him.

Dubbi Muktar, meanwhile, was making excellent time for Chipton Oxfold. For a car in such an appalling condition, his minicab had a remarkable turn of speed, and he was rattling down the M3, gobbling up the miles at a voracious rate. At what rate precisely, he had no idea; for his speedometer had long since given up the ghost. But as luck would have it, he was being pursued by two very obliging young police officers in a white Range Rover.

It seemed surprising to these two Samaritans of the Hampshire Constabulary that Dubbi had not noticed them sitting on his tail for the past ten miles. Littered as they were with flashing blue lights and the letters P, O, L, I, C and E, they could hardly have been accused of being inconspicuous. But sadly, Dubbi's rear-view mirror had lately parted company with its mountings and was now hiding under the driver's seat, busily reflecting the carpet. So his first intimation of trouble came when he noticed a police officer gliding sedately past his window at a hundred and ten miles per hour, jabbing a hostile finger at the hard shoulder.

The Range Rover pulled up three-quarters of a mile further on – apparently under the misapprehension that the scruffy Cortina would do likewise. Dubbi's brake linings had seen better days, however, and were no more capable of stopping his rusting heap in three-quarters of a mile than Dubbi himself was of vanishing into thin air. Which was precisely what he wished to do when he eventually slewed to a halt some two thousand yards nearer Southampton.

All of which might have been viewed less seriously by the Hampshire Constabulary if there had been the slightest trace of tread left on any of his tyres . . . or the merest scrap of road tax on his windscreen . . . or a glimpse of an MoT certificate about his person . . . or even so much as a cover note from his insurance company . . .

47

THE COMMANDO's lot was not a happy one, Nurg reflected miserably as he sat shivering in the dark, waiting for the endless hours to drag by. After his sleepless night his jaws had begun to ache with yawning, but it was too cold and uncomfortable down there in the dungeon to take a nap. He thought of the crowds assembling outside in the bright sunshine, the VIPs, their royal highnesses. Or was it raining perhaps? There could have been a typhoon raging out there for all they knew. He looked for the hundred thousandth time at the luminous characters of his army watch. Half past two. Six more hours to go.

He felt a tap on his shoulder and heard Sharaq murmur: 'They'll be starting the speeches up there now. It should be safe to stretch your legs and take a breather in the keep tower, if you want.'

'Shrahma be praised,' muttered Nurg, pining for a glimpse of daylight and a sniff of fresh air.

'We'll take ten minutes each,' said Sharaq. 'You go first. Keep your eyes and ears open. Vigilance at all times.'

Nurg scrambled to his feet, switched on his torch and padded away into the darkness, through Ye Olde Chaymbre of Torture and down the narrow passage into the vault beyond. Turning towards the keep, he walked through to the adjacent chamber and was startled by two brilliant yellow-green jewels reflected in the light of his torch: the eyes of a large brown rat. He leapt back with a stifled shriek and the torch slipped out of his hand. It clattered onto the stone floor and the light died instantly. Nurg felt a twinge of panic. He dropped to his knees and groped about in the dark. He found the torch and tried the switch. Not a glimmer of light. It was totally dead. As dead as . . . an unquiet spirit. He struggled to banish such foolish thoughts from his mind and tried to gather his bearings. But he had lost his sense of direction. He fumbled his way forwards . . . or was it backwards? Was he returning the way he had come or heading towards the keep? He collided with a wall. But which wall? He edged his way along it until he came to an opening that led into the next chamber . . . or was it the previous chamber? Or was he in the labyrinth, the warren of passages that went on round and round in a never-ending maze, where Guppi Pungal had told him men had been known to wander for years and years and never be seen again.

'*Haunted*,' he could hear Pungal whispering. '*By the spirits of the tortured dead.*' A shiver snaked its way down Nurg's spine. 'Captain Sharaq, sir!' he hissed, as loudly as he dared. 'It's Nurg, sir! Corporal Nurg! Where are you Captain sir?' There was no reply. He tried again a little louder; but all he heard was the echo of his own voice, and Pungal whispering: '*Beware the ghost of the Imperial Warlord.*'

Calm, Golam Nanjik, he told himself. Calm. He edged his way forwards again, like a swimmer breaststroking his way through a sea of black ink. *Calm.* There are no spirits of the tortured dead down here. No ghost of any Mighty British Warlord. Pungal is a liar. Pungal is a trickster.

At that second he collided with something large, bony and diabolically alive. Seized with blind terror, Nurg began flailing his arms about in all directions and inadvertently fetched the thing a cracking right-hander, which did Nurg's knobbly fist a power of harm and loosed all the demons of hell upon him. Blows hammered into him from all sides with merciless ferocity, accompanied by some wild gibberish the like of which Nurg had never heard human utter. Throwing himself to his knees and curling up in a protective ball, he began wailing a holy chant of Sandhu: 'Oh, Shrahma Omnipotent, my spirit is departing this mortal incarnation . . .' Which put the fear of god into The Thing who leapt back in panic, spitting blood and shards of smashed denture in all directions. Fumbling blindly for the door to the keep tower he fell straight over the wailing Nurg and tumbled headlong, screaming volubly in foulest Bulgarian.

'Rosheen, just what the *hell* is this?' said Byron, staggered by the mountain of luggage that was now piled up in the hallway.

'Baggage, sweetheart.'

'I can see that, I'm not blind. But what's it doing here?'

'Baby's back,' Rosheen replied gaily, breezing into the kitchen for a beer. 'I'm home to stay, angel.'

'Stay?' said Byron, chasing after her. 'What are you talking about? You can't stay here. You're a newly married woman . . . almost. It's not decent. What would the Feinbaums think? What would Guy think, come to that? I mean, Jesus — '

'Don't mention that name,' Rosheen cut in bitterly, taking two cans of Carlsberg Special Brew from the fridge.

'Jesus?'

'Guy.' She tossed one can to Byron and opened the other for herself. 'Son-of-a-bitch.'

'Why? What's happened? Where is he?'

She guzzled a few mouthfuls of beer. 'How should I know? Didn't you hear about the wedding?'

'Sure I heard. It was in the *Herald Tribune*. Didn't you get my wire?'

'Isn't it just the most incredible thing you ever heard?' Guzzle, guzzle, guzzle.

'Incredible. I'm proud of you, baby, I truly am. To think, if it hadn't been for Robespierre you might have been the next queen of France.'

'You realise the bastard only did it to get even.'

'Robespierre?'

'Guy.'

'Did what?'

'Asked the slut to marry him, what do you think?'

'Asked who?'

'Chantal.'

'Who's Chantal?'

'Nineteen and built like a boxcar. Her old man keeps hogs in the Auvergne. Rumour has it she took a bronze at the

Clermont-Ferrand fatstock show last summer. She's expecting a calf next January. Pathetic, hah?' Guzzle, guzzle, guzzle.

'Are you trying to tell me that Guy is going to *marry* this, this, this hog farmer's daughter?'

'You betcha sweet ass.' Rosheen eructed reverberantly. 'On the rebound, you see. That's what it does to a guy. Like a hurt child. Hysterical over-reaction. Soon as I gave him the news.'

'What news?'

'About our reconciliation. Broke the poor bastard up.' She crumpled the empty beer can in her fist and tossed it into the waste bin. 'Honey, if you don't want that other beer, chuck it this aways, I've got a throat like an emery board. It's a hundred and three in the shade at Heathrow, the pilot said and — '

'Rosheen, will you just shut up a minute?' said Byron, tossing her the other can of Special Brew. 'I don't know what the hell you're talking about. I'm not interested in hog farmers or Chantal or any of this reconciliation shit. If you and Guy have had a row that's your problem. You're his responsibility from now on.'

'Angel, you don't seem to understand,' said Rosheen patiently, tugging back the ring to open the beer can and spraying him with a wild jet of foam. 'That's all in the past. It's all history now. Guy and I — '

She was interrupted by a buzz on the Entriphone.

'OK, I'll get it,' she said, throwing him a dishcloth. 'You relax and dry off.'

But Byron scampered down the hall passage ahead of her. Not Annabelle, *please God*, don't let it be Annabelle. He snatched up the phone. 'Yup? Hullo?'

'Hi, Doc. 'S Gladstone.'

'Gladstone, thank God. What time do you have?'

'Twenty-five to three.'

'OK, I'll be right down. No, no, no . . . second thoughts, you'd better come up. We've got a ton and a half of baggage to shift out of here.'

'Right, Doc.'

Byron pressed the button to open the street door, hung up and hurried back to the kitchen. 'Rosheen, I have to go now. We'll drop you off at a ho — ' No Rosheen. 'Rosheen? Rosheen!'

'In here!' she called from the bedroom.

He walked in and found her stark naked. 'Oh God, what the hell are you doing now?'

'Taking a shower.'

'A shower? Are you out of your mind? I've got to be at Carnage Castle in an hour for the dress rehearsal.'

'Well, I feel all clammy and soiled,' she said, padding out of the bedroom and into the bathroom. 'Like a bus ticket that's been in some kid's hand all day. You realise it's a hundred and thirteen in the shade at Heathrow?'

'Rosheen, for Christ's sake . . .' Byron pursued her into the bathroom. 'I am going to be late for a very important dress rehearsal with the President of the Paradise Islands. Will you get your ass out of that shower right now? Gladstone and I will drop you and your small juggernaut of luggage at a hotel someplace.'

'Oh no, darling. I'm coming to the rehearsal with you.'

'Just get out of the shower, hah?'

'Because if I'm going to be there by your side tomorrow, wife of the new director-general and all, I'm going to need a rehearsal too.'

'Rosheen, there is no way you're going to be by my side tomorrow. And no way are you staying here.'

'Byron, husband, please, don't be difficult. I am, after all, the new first lady of Unibore . . . in a manner of speaking. Unless, of course, you were fixing to have someone *else* at your side tomorrow . . . like that strumpet of yours from Missouri.'

'Mississippi. And that's a ridiculous thing to suggest. She's five thousand miles away right now.'

'She told me she was coming to England for Wopec Day.'

'Well, she changed her mind. She couldn't get time off school.'

'Figures, I guess. What is she in? Fourth grade?'

'Oh, very funny.' The doorbell chimed. 'That'll be Gladstone. I can't wait any longer.'

'OK, sweetheart, if it's that urgent, you just run along. We'll discuss it later. You'd better leave me some money before you go. A hundred should see me through to Monday all right.'

'Rosheen, for the last time, you are *not . . . coming* . . to *Wopec*! Get it? And you are not staying here. I don't care what you do or where you go, but I want your ass out of this apartment by the time I get back tonight.' The doorbell rang again. He hurried out of the bathroom and back to the bedroom, shouting, 'Be right with you, Gladstone.' Stripping off his beer-wet clothes, he put on a clean shirt and trousers, grabbed his chequebook, credit cards and anything else that Rosheen could conceivably try to negotiate for cash, shouted a final, 'You've had your last warning, kiddo,' at the bathroom door and stormed out of the flat.

'Trouble, Doc?' asked Gladstone as they drove away.

'Damn right I've got trouble,' Byron replied. 'Rosheen showed up half an hour ago with everything she possesses. She's had some kind of bust-up with Guy. But I can't find out where Annabelle's staying, so I've got no way of warning her not to phone the apartment . . .'

If Byron had given the matter a little lateral thought and not been in the habit of shredding his telegrams the moment they arrived, he would have deduced exactly where Annabelle was staying – where she *said* she was staying: at the local hotel. Though not, as Byron had assumed, local to St John's Wood, but local to Carnage Castle. In fact, just as he and Gladstone were leaving Hamilton Grove, she and her father were arriving at the Carnage Arms, Allshott (free house, AA three stars) in their hired Ford Escort, looking forward to a quiet siesta after their long tiring flight.

Back at the castle, Sharaq and his commandos, alerted by Nurg's deathly wailing, had grabbed their weapons and rushed to the rescue of their beleaguered lance corporal only to find him threshing about on his own on the dungeon floor in a frenzy of abject terror. About thirty feet away, a lanky shambles in a grubby beige suit was stumbling around trying to retrieve his photographic case. Dazzled by their flashlights, the shambles drew back, shielding his eyes and shouting: 'Prezz, john! Vopek votograver! Vulchitsky, Dimiter Vulchitsky.'

Sharaq pulled Nurg to his feet. 'Oh, sir, sir,' gasped Nurg, quaking so much he could hardly speak, 'this madman, raving madman, attacked me in the dark. Son of the devil! Has eyes like a tiger!'

'Bulgarski,' Zlob pleaded, believing that he had fallen into the hands of a British army patrol. 'Bulgarski, john. Prezz votograver. Vopek.'

One of the commandos rummaged through the aluminium

case. Sharaq searched Zlob's pockets and found the international press card. 'Newspaper cameraman,' he murmured to Nurg. 'What's he doing down here?'

Nurg was too shocked to reply . . . even if he had known the answer.

Sharaq turned to Zlob. 'Do you speak English?'

'English, *da da*.' Zlob nodded and shook his head. 'Ullo, john. Me Vopek votograving, klik-klik. Vulchanov, Dimiter. OK, cock?'

Sharaq turned to his men. 'Two of you go with Corporal Nurg. Take this wog back to the torture chamber and tie him up with detonator wire. You other two help me search this place. There may be someone else down here.' He gave Nurg his automatic pistol. 'If he tries to run for it, blow his head off.'

'I will, sir,' whispered obedient Nurg, trembling so much he would have been hard put to it to hit the Great Wall of China at ten paces.

Outside in the car park, three more members of the CLAC committee had just arrived for the President's dress rehearsal – Otello and Mirella in the Silver Shadow, Melanie Boewater in her latest aquamarine parachute suit and matching BMW, and wee fluffy McGuffy in his much Plastic-Padded Morris Minor. Byron and Gladstone were still on their way. No one had the faintest idea what had happened to Jericho Engineer.

Jericho, in fact, was arriving at Heathrow at that moment, for the third time, to welcome The Most Important Person In The World. The Most Important Person In The World, however, was in Paris, knocking back arrack and inveighing passionately against the wickedness of international terrorism to a hastily-assembled press conference. Due to the excessive number of long-delayed aircraft stacked aloft and waiting to land at Heathrow, flight QR514 had been diverted to Orly for an unscheduled rest. It was not due to take off for another two hours, Miss Information told the Air Vice-Marshal.

Well, that was wholly unacceptable, Jericho retorted heatedly. Field-Marshal Butcher was supposed to be at Carnage Castle by four o'clock for a dress rehearsal of one of the most significant events in modern history. He insisted on seeing the head of air traffic control at once.

That, Miss Information replied very sweetly, would not get sir anywhere. Nor would it get Field-Marshal Butcher anywhere, more to the point. QR514 was now hopelessly off schedule and had to be reallocated landing and servicing time. Planes could not be allowed to go jetting around ad lib all day long or they'd be whanging into each other like dodgem cars.

When, in that case, Jericho enquired, could one reasonably expect QR514 to reach London? By midnight? The end of the month? The first Sunday in Advent?

No, replied the unflappable Miss Information, QR514 was scheduled to take off again at 17.30. As it was a one-hour flight to London, it would obviously, therefore, *arrive* at 17.30. The logic of which was not immediately apparent to the air vice-marshal, who had never fathomed the mysteries of international time zones, but he took her word for it, elbowed his way to the nearest payphone and relayed the information direct to Carnage Castle.

Upon hearing that His Theophanic Omnipotence was unlikely to reach Allshott much before seven, CLAC decided to put the time to good use and stage an unscheduled dress rehearsal of the dress rehearsal, to iron out any practical difficulties before the President arrived. Clarence Brownjohn gamely agreed to stand in for the great man, and spent the next twenty minutes clumping round the north courtyard, shaking hands with CLAC and dozens of bemused workmen who had been roped in to play sundry dignitaries. The whole party then traipsed through the castle, into the grand drawing-room and out onto the south terrace, where Brownjohn mounted a purple-carpeted dais and barked, 'My lords, ladies and gentlemen,' several times into a bouquet of microphones, which carried beautifully to the commuter semis in the purlieus of Lydhurst a good league distant, but was totally incomprehensible to anyone within a half-mile radius of Carnage Castle.

While worried sound engineers were adjusting the p.a. system and everybody else stood around making unhelpful suggestions, Nina slipped away to look for Zlob, who had been missing now for almost two hours.

Zlob had been trussed hand and foot and was lying in the dark in a spiky metal contraption in Ye Olde Chaymbre of Torture, shaking with cold and petrified witless, wondering what was going to happen to him next.

Close by, on sentry duty, lonely Nurg sat clutching his machine pistol for comfort and thinking of Dubbi Muktar, waiting patiently at his home in Southall for Operation Thunder to begin . . .

Dubbi *was* waiting. But in Basingstoke, not Southall. Waiting for his solicitor. Having driven a coach and horses (not to mention a lethal minicab) through about forty-three sections of the Road Traffic Act, and being unable to offer any persuasive explanation as to why he should have been travelling along the M3 at over a hundred miles per hour without tax or insurance, Dubbi had been charged (with so many things he'd lost count) and locked up in the cells at Basingstoke police station, where he now languished, waiting for his lawyer to return home from the test match at the Oval and negotiate his bail. With barely two hours to go before Pungal set off on his return journey to Carnage Castle – with heaven only knew what disastrous consequences – Dubbi could only hope and pray that Guppi was listening to the radio that day and had heard a news bulletin.

Guppi *had* been listening to the radio, as it happened, and still was; but listening to virtually the only programme that was not interrupted by irritating irrelevances like world news – the cricket commentary on Radio Three. And while Dubbi was chanting silent prayers to Shrahma in the cells at Basingstoke police station, Pungal was lying spreadeagled in the sun at Lower Oxfold Farm, enjoying the sorry saga of yet another English middle-order collapse.

Annabelle had been fast asleep on her bed at the Carnage Arms Hotel all afternoon and had not heard the news either. Awaking from her siesta at ten past five, much refreshed, she decided to telephone Hamilton Grove to see whether Byron had returned from the dress rehearsal yet . . .

Back at château Cleveland, Rosheen had spent the afternoon unpacking all her worldly goods and chattels and trying to pawn Byron's Piaget wristwatch to the publicans of Kilburn for a hundred pounds. It had been hot, thirsty (and ultimately futile) work and she had consumed countless pints of Guinness in the course of it, and was well into a fresh six-pack of Carlsberg Special Brew by quarter past five when the telephone rang. Presuming it to be her doting spouse calling to see if she had fallen headfirst out of the window or contracted a rare terminal disease by any chance, she picked up one of the many handsets that she found shimmering on the kitchen wall and said: 'Hi, dickhead. If you're on your way home, stop by a McDonalds, will you? I could eat the ass off an elephant right now.'

A puzzled silence. Then: 'Oh.' (Not Dickhead.) 'Is that, ah . . . that Rosheen?'

'Could be.' Those delicate Southern tones sounded faintly familiar. 'Whoozat?'

'It's Annabelle.'

'Hey . . . Not Annabelle Carthorse? From li'l ole Salvation, Mizz'ippi?'

'That's right. Nice to talk to you again. How are you?'

'Me? Oh, I'm on toppa the world,' burbled Rosheen, sliding gently down the kitchen wall. 'How's things in Cabbageville?'

Accustomed to coping with women with acute alcohol problems in the course of her father's good works, Annabelle replied pleasantly, 'Well, I'm over *here* right now, which is why I'm phoning. Is Byron there, please?'

'No, he's had a meeting with that Butcher jerk from Paradise. He'll be on his way home now, I guess.'

'Only, I don't think he knows where we're staying.'

'We?'

'My father and I. We're spending the weekend here in Allshott.'

'Orleshot, Mizz'ippi?'

'No, no. Allshott, England.'

'Where the hellzat?'

'England?'

'I know where England is, you dumb klutz. Where's Orleshot?'

'Right down the road from Carnage Castle. We're staying at the Carnage Arms Hotel.'

'You mean you're over *here*?'

'Didn't Byron tell you we were coming?'

'No, he damn well did not. Sonvabitch told me you couldn't make it.'

'He did? Well, I can't imagine why he thought that. Didn't he get my telegram?'

'No.'

'I wired him we'd be arriving at twelve o'clock. I was hoping we'd be able to meet tonight.'

'Tonight?'

'If he's not — '

'Aw, thazza *shame*. He's all tied up tonight. We're having dinner someplace else.'

'Well, would you ask him to call me at the Carnage Arms Hotel if he has time?'

'I most definitely will. Don't you worry your sweet head about a thing, Loulabelle, sugar. Juzz sit tight like a good li'l puddy-tat and let Rosheen take care of everything.'

'Thank you, Rosheen, I sure appreciate it. I'm really looking forward to meeting you at inauguration day tomorrow.'

'Pleasure's gonna be all mine, treasure, believe me.'

'Bye then.'

'Stay loose.' Rosheen hung up and ferreted about in the kitchen closet for the S to Z phone book. (T for trains.) Conspiracy, huh? Some sweet, kind, virgin schoolma'am she turned out to be. So much for KY Jelly and ice cream. Treacherous tramp thought she could sneak into the country behind the back of the first unsuspecting wife she found and check into a motel for a night of filthy, torrid passion, did she? Well, if teacher was looking for action, teacher sure had come to the right person . . .

48

A FINE shroud of haze had begun to filter the warmth from the sun by late afternoon. A breeze was stirring gently in the south-west as shadows lengthened across the Carnage estate, and an early evening stillness had already settled on the East Woods by half past five . . . when the rural peace for miles around was abruptly shattered by the arrival of five olive-green vans (infantry/one-ton/personnel/for the conveyance of), which shot straight through Allshott at two-and-a-half times the permitted speed, and skidded violently down a narrow lane off the Lydhurst Road, past Clarence Brownjohn's dark, satanic hovel.

'Right! Right! *Right*!' screamed Bile, in the leading van, whipped into a frenzy of demonic anticipation by this time.

The van slewed round through ninety degrees, bounced a short way down a narrow bridle path and crashed clean through a rotting five-barred gate (*Ministry of Defence, KEEP OUT*), into the East Woods.

Ron-luvvy's bomb-proof skull thudded into the roof, and troopers were tossed about in the back of the van like tumbleweed in a storm.

''Kinbloody raving' *mad*man!' Bile shrieked at the driver, more in approbation than in anger.

The driver took it as a compliment and accelerated on into the woods. Petrified birds took to the sky in their thousands, as the convoy careered on blindly through a protected nature reserve, leaving swathes of death and destruction across acres of rare flora, and crushing dozens of happy, unsuspecting voles. Emerging finally into a small clearing, the five vans pulled up in front of a derelict cottage – the old gamekeeper's lodge, a roofless ruin, empty since the Great War and frequented now only by bats, lice, slugs, snakes, hornets and the likes of Ron Bile.

The lads of 2 Troop leapt from the vans and plunged eagerly into the dense clumps of wild briar and stinging nettles that surrounded the cottage. Face working with hatred, Bile destroyed what remained of the front door with one kick and stormed into the building. Terrified fauna scurried and slithered into the sanctuary of dark corners. Smashing his way through to what remained of the kitchen, Bile heaved open a rotting wooden hatch-cover in the floor and peered down into a black pit, twelve feet deep. The troopers gathered round and shone their torches into the void. A fetid stench of death and decay wafted up. Bile jumped first, plunging *splat* into fifteen inches of icy feculent sludge.

'Fair whiff of God's good methane down 'ere, boys,' he bellowed up, drawing the miasma deep into his lungs like soothing balsam. 'Like Clacton in August. Let's be havin' you, then: Doyle, Stoatley, Higgins . . .'

One by one the troopers leapt down into the pit and began to squelch their way forwards through the treacle-thick mud into the narrow tunnel that led to the dungeons of Carnage Castle.

The estate was looking strangely deserted by this time. Most of the workmen had gone home, and pending the arrival of Hudson Butcher, CLAC had run out of useful things to do. Otello was awaiting the arrival of Aubrey Wormslow's brother, Vernon, with his colleagues from Rent-a-Footman. Mirella was awaiting the arrival of her chef, Enrico Fariscagni. Nina was still looking for Zlob. And Byron was on the telephone in Edwina Sheffield's office, ringing his own number in Hamilton Grove in the faint hope that there would be no reply – indicating that Rosheen might have chickened out for once in her life and cleared off back to Nice to marry the hog farmer. There *was* no reply, as it happened; but only because the line was engaged . . .

It was engaged because Rosheen was conducting a heated dialogue with the British Rail information office at Waterloo.

'Not *Alder*shot, for Christ's sake. *Orle*shot.'

'Never 'eard of it,' said Waterloo. 'How about *Ox*shott?'

'I don't want Oxshott.'

'Sure you don't mean Ox*ted*?'

'If I wanted Oxted, I'd *say* Oxted. I want O-r-l-e-s-h-o-t, Orleshot.'

'There's Bagshot. And Grayshott, change at Haslemere — '

'*Orleshot*. It's right down the road from Carnage Castle. You *must*'ve heard of Carnage. Jesus — '

'Carnage Castle?' said Waterloo. 'I'd give that a miss for the next couple of weeks, if I was you. There's a world conference going on. How about Penshurst Place? That's a nice trip out for the — '

'I know . . . there's a world . . . conference . . . going . . . on,' replied Rosheen, tight jawed. 'My husband's running the goddam thing.'

'He should know how to get there then,' reasoned Waterloo.

'You want Lydhurst Junction. Twenty minutes past the hour from Charing Cross. Last train twenty-three twelve.'

'Hallelujah,' said Rosheen, scrawling that information across the kitchen wall with a felt-tipped pen. 'Come back Amtrak, all is forgiven.' She hung up and was about to call for a cab when the phone rang almost at once. She snatched it up again. 'Yeh, hello?'

'Still there, hah?' said Byron.

'No, this is a recorded message. And if you're on your way home, pick me up a hamburger. I can't last out till dinner.'

'I'm not on my way home. I'm still here.'

'Where's here?'

'Carnage. Waiting for Hudson Butcher. It could be a long night.'

'Yeh, I'll just bet.'

'And what the hell are you doing in my apartment, please? I told you to be out of there by six o'clock.'

'Well, if you didn't expect me to be here, dogbrain, what are you phoning for? Hoping somebody else might answer? Like that tramp of yours from Mississippi?'

'Leave Annabelle out of this. I told you, she's not over here.'

'I know. I just talked with her.'

'Annabelle? You mean she phoned?'

'Twenty minutes ago.'

'Did she leave a message? Where was she calling from?'

'Uh . . . Tupelo, I think she said.'

'*Tupelo*?'

'Yup. Tupelo county hospital.'

'What do you mean? What the hell is she doing phoning from Tupelo? She's supposed to be in — ' Byron broke off, suddenly registering what Rosheen had just said.

'Did you say *hospital*?'

'Yup. But she says you're not to worry. Daddy's gonna be just fine.'

'Noah? Her old man? What about him?'

'No problem. He should be out of intensive care in no time.'

'Rosheen, what in God's name are you talking about?'

'You didn't hear about the truck . . .?'

At ten minutes past six, just nine and three quarter hours behind schedule, flight QR514 from Nairobi touched down at

Heathrow and Hudson Montgomery Butcher, statesman and scholar, set foot on British soil for the first time in his life. After an official welcome from junior ministers of state and Foreign Office flunkeys, he climbed into Jericho Engineer's bomb-proof Mercedes and, to the cheering of several thousand stoned adolescents who thought he was part of a reggae band that had just flown in from Trinidad, sped away to Allshott, hotly pursued by an anxious bodyguard, Great-Uncle Albert, Colonel-General Stockminder and Brigadier Claybuck, chief of SPIS.

Vernon Wormslow and his fifteen rentable footmen had arrived at Carnage by this time and were lined up for inspection in the great eating room, immaculately attired in tail coats, wing collars and snow-white gloves, receiving detailed instructions from Otello. Mirella was in the kitchen with her chef, Enrico Fariscagni. Melanie and McGuffy had slipped away to the Carnage Arms for a few gins. And Byron was in Edwina's office, calling Gatwick airport to enquire whether anyone called Cartwright had flown in from New Orleans that day.

Nina had finally given up looking for Zlob and had come to the conclusion that he must have finished his work long since and returned to London by train. It struck her as somewhat boorish to disappear like that without even leaving a note on her windscreen; but then, he was a boorish sort of fellow. And he had, after all, vowed passionately (between fierce ventral heaves in a layby near Biggin Hill) never to get into a car with her again.

Zlob, at that very moment, would happily have agreed to spend the rest of his life and much of the hereafter in a car with Comrade Brain if it would have got him out of that freezing dungeon and back to Stara Zagora in one piece. He had managed to wriggle his wrists free, but he was still suspended in the spiky torture contraption six feet above the ground, and had no idea what had become of his captors. They seemed to have disappeared into thin air . . .

Sharaq and his commandos had not disappeared anywhere. They were in the adjacent cell, tucking into an early supper of tinned soup and hard tack, and thinking about Guppi Pungal speeding along the road out of Chipton Oxfold at that moment, on his heroic journey back to Carnage for Thunder Hour.

Pungal, however, was not speeding anywhere. He was lying flat on his back beneath the cab of the truck in some god-forsaken country lane, trying to mend a broken throttle cable and spitting curses upon the whole house of Horace Shadbarge, scrap metal merchant and vehicle breaker to the gentry.

Some miles to the north, three white Mercedes saloons bearing the flag of the Paradise Islands were shooting straight through a set of red traffic lights in the comatose commuter town of Leatherhead (welcomes careful drivers), scaring the living daylight out of thousands of perfectly decent, Volvo-owning Tories.

While, on the other side of London, in Hamilton Grove N.W.8, Rosheen was falling into the back of a cab, dressed to slaughter in black leather from head to toe, and armed with a fresh, life-saving six-pack of Special Brew to see her safely through to the next watering hole at the Carnage Arms.

Noah and Annabelle, meantime, were sitting down to dinner and contemplating the prospect of a gentle evening stroll up to the castle before sundown.

49

THE CLOCK of St Clement's parish church, Allshott, was just striking eight. Down in the dungeons of Carnage Castle, Sharaq and his commandos, in full combat fig, their *bleu de travail* stuffed into military backpacks, were beginning their advance to second base in the keep tower. Pausing for a moment in Ye Olde Chaymbre of Torture, Sharaq shone his torch beam over the shivering Zlob.

'What shall we do with him, sir?' asked anxious Nurg. Enemy or no enemy, he was not happy about abandoning the poor chap to the mercy of the imperial ghostly warlord and all those unquiet spirits.

'Leave him,' said Sharaq, moving on along the passage to the main vaults. 'He'll get free eventually.'

They followed Sharaq in single file, listening, watching, machine pistols at the ready . . .

Twenty feet below them, Bile and the boys had reached the end of the tunnel at long last. After two and a quarter agonising hours, bent double, knee deep in sludge, they had arrived at the foundations of the keep tower and were splashing wearily up the flight of stone steps that led into the dungeons . . .

Sharaq opened the door that led up to the keep, paused and listened. Hearing nothing, he ventured cautiously up to the top of the steps and peered around. The tower was empty. Beckoning to Nurg and the others to follow, he squatted on the steps and took out his radio transceiver to call up Guppi Pungal. The commandos crept up the stairs and squatted down beside him. Thankful just to be out of that evil charnel pit, Nurg closed the heavy oak door behind them and breathed a deep sigh of relief . . .

. . . as an identical arched doorway swung open not twenty feet away, and Bile emerged from the tunnel into the dungeons, dripping a trail of slime and rat's blood. One by one the troopers staggered up the steps, luxuriating in the freedom to unbend their tortured spines.

Bile consulted his watch. 'Fifty minutes to kill, boys.' The word *kill* brought a cheer to their flagging spirits. 'Time for a brew up.'

Without waiting for further orders, Trooper Stoatley took the butane burner from his backpack, Doyle the coffee, and Higgins the rum.

Above them in the keep, Sharaq was murmuring anxiously into his radio set, trying to get through to Pungal, who should have been standing by in the car park since a quarter to eight: 'Tiger to Fireball, Tiger to Fireball, come in Fireball.' But there was not so much as a crackle of response. 'Tiger to Fireball, Tiger to Fireball, come in Fireball . . .'

Ball-of-fire Pungal was not responding because ball-of-fire Pungal was not receiving, because he was way behind schedule and still out of range. It had taken forty minutes and five years off his life to botch together the broken throttle cable and get the pantechnicon back on the road again, and he was only now grinding along towards Allshott at twenty-five miles per hour, cursing the eyes of Shrahma's mother.

Seven miles away in the opposite direction, the nineteen twelve from Charing Cross had just pulled into Lydhurst Junction, where Rosheen was weaving a serpentine course along the platform, clutching her last surviving can of Special Brew and searching for the way out. Two blocks away, on the other side of the tracks, three blue minibuses packed with police officers in mufti were pulling out of the rear yard of Lydhurst police station and setting off along the road to Allshott.

Everyone at Carnage Castle had given President Butcher up for lost by this time, and Otello had just invited Edwina, Brownjohn and the rentable footmen to join CLAC for an informal drink in the drawing-room, when Gladstone rushed in with the news that Jericho's Mercedes was turning into the north courtyard at that very moment, followed by two limousines full of harassed-looking VIPs.

Otello and Byron hastened outside to greet the party, and having been presented to the President and shaken hands with his entourage, led the way back inside to the drawing-room to introduce them to the CLAC committee.

After his long, exhausting flight the President was gratified to discover that Unibore had had the common decency to lay on a quiet cocktail party to welcome him to Carnage, and peremptorily instructed Vernon Wormslow to bring a magnum of iced champagne. Otello hastily explained to Jericho Engineer that the footmen were there to rehearse for the banquet and not to serve at a cocktail party, but Great-Uncle Albert had already despatched another hireling to fetch a *pina colada* for himself and a *mai tai* for Brigadier Claybuck. Seeing that everybody seemed to be getting into a party mood and there was enough liquor in store to sink a battleship, Melanie Boewater sent another obliging young man away to freshen up her gin and tonic, Byron and McGuffy ordered more Scotch, and Brownjohn clumped off to the kitchen to see if there was any keg bitter going.

'Nice place you got here,' said Colonel-General Stockminder to Nina, thinking that he could do with a retreat like this to retire to after the next coup d'état.

Outside, three police minibuses were turning into the north courtyard.

Unable to see anything from the keep, where the lowest window was fifteen feet above the ground, the SPLA commandos assumed that all those vehicles they could hear, and the distant hubbub of lively chatter, signified the arrival of the banquet guests. But all that Sharaq wanted to hear at that moment was the lively chatter of Guppi Pungal . . .

Twenty minutes overdue, Pungal swung the gasping pantechnicon through the gates of Carnage and began the long winding climb up to the car park. At last, Sharaq's frantic signals began to gargle their way through the ether: '. . . Iger oo Ireball! Tiger ahhhhh ball! Come in Ire all!'

Pungal snatched up his radio handset: 'Fireball to Tiger, Fireball to Tiger. Receiving you faint and breaking.'

'Air ah oo I aw? Over.'

'Breaking badly, Tiger. Repeat, breaking badly.'

'Tiger to Fireball, *where . . . are . . . you?* Over.'

'Turning into car park, Tiger. Minor technical hitch, but all OK now. Read me, Tiger? Over.'

'Loud and clear, Fireball,' Sharaq replied, and immediately lapsed into another thirty seconds of Japanese and rice crispies.

Pungal ignored him while he swung the truck into the car park and pulled up.

'Tiger to Fireball, Tiger to Fireball,' Sharaq was screaming. 'In God's name, *Fireball* . . . !'

'Yeh, yeh, yeh, receiving strength nine!' Pungal shouted back. 'Take it easy, Tiger, everything's OK now. Over.'

'What's going on out there, Fireball? We can't see a damn thing in here, over.'

Pungal glanced around the car park and over to the fields behind, where Gladstone and the chauffeurs from the Paradise Islands' High Commission were killing time with a cricket bat and a few tennis balls. 'Nothing going on out here, Tiger. All quiet. Hardly a soul in sight . . .'

*

There was quite a party going on in the drawing-room by now. Delighted to learn that all these scruffy coppers from Lydhurst were on night manoeuvres with the British army for his personal protection, Hudson Butcher had invited them to join him for a drink before going about their business. Reluctant to disoblige a visiting head of state – particularly when it involved free drinks – Hatchard and Kilmore had gratefully accepted the invitation; and one drink was leading to another . . .

Down in Ye Olde Chaymbre of Torture, Zlob had finally wriggled his hands free and untied his feet. But in trying to unhitch himself from the medieval torture contraption, he upset a delicate mechanical structure above his head and brought half a hundredweight of chains and plate steel crashing down around his ears. The din reverberated right through the dungeons, from the west tower to the keep.

Some thirty yards away, Bile sprang to his feet like a startled cat. 'Whuzzat?' he hissed.

The troopers stopped sipping their coffee and listened.

'Rats, Corp'l?' whispered Doyle.

'Yeh, a rat in tin boots,' scoffed Higgins.

'A bleedin' rat copper, more like,' muttered Bile. 'Sneaky, snidey bastard.'

They listened again. Back in Ye Olde Chaymbre of falling ironmongery, Zlob was stumbling about in a sea of clattering steel.

'He's close, wherever he is,' said Bile. 'Some clumsy flatfoot come down here snoopin' on us. Soon mark his card, *no* problem. Teach the whelp to come spying. Doyle, Lewis, cover this door. The rest of you, grab your torches and spread out.'

Immediately above them, Number One Commando were pulling on their balaclava helmets and checking their weapons. Sharaq looked at his watch and picked up the radio: 'Tiger to Fireball, Tiger to Fireball . . .'

'Fireball receiving.'

'Ninety seconds.'

'Check, Tiger.'

'Clear out there?'

'All clear.'

'Stand by.' Sharaq turned to his men. 'No one moves till we get *Starfire* from Pungal, understand? Not a sound.' He brought the handset to his mouth again: 'Tiger to Fireball, stand by to Thunder Roll. One minute and counting . . .'

Outside in the car park, Pungal wiped his clammy hands on his combat trousers, brushed the sweat off his brow and began revving up the engine.

Two miles away in Allshott village, Rosheen had just fallen out of the back of a taxi and into the saloon bar of the Carnage Arms Hotel, in search of Annabelle – little realising that she had passed her barely a mile back down the road. On being informed by the hotel manager that the Cartwrights had taken a gentle evening stroll up to the castle, she knocked back a quick Schlitz to slake her thirst and set off in hot pursuit.

Pungal's stomach was churning as he waited – clutch pedal pressed to the floor – while Sharaq's husky voice counted down the last few seconds: '. . . eight . . . seven . . . six . . .five . . .' (Pungal muttering one final prayer to Shrahma the Magnificent) '. . .four . . . three . . . two . . . one . . . and *Thunder Roll*!'

'Thunder rolling!' Pungal shouted into his handset, flooring the throttle and releasing the clutch. With a great shudder that shook it from axles to roof, the weary beast lurched out of the car park and grumbled round the gravel circus, past the statue of General Sir Sackville Sterling-Pallgrave, towards the medieval gatehouse.

Inside the keep, cursing the genius who had had the bright idea of installing windows fifteen feet above the ground, Sharaq crouched with the radio pressed to his ear. Beside him, in a puddle of cold sweat, Nurg waited, bowels shifting timorously, for *Starfire*.

Pungal was also awash with cold sweat, as he tried to straighten up the pantechnicon to squeeze it through the narrow gatheouse and suddenly remembered that no one had bothered to check the width of the thing. Gritting his teeth and pleading with Almighty Shrahma, he drove on regardless. For one blessed moment he thought his nearside wing was going to clear the wall by a shaving of paint. Then, with a sickening crunch, a few square inches of vintage Bedford bodywork met eight hundred years of unyielding Kentish limestone, and the truck stopped dead and stalled. Screaming abominations upon the whole family of Shrahma the Execrable, Pungal restarted the engine and backed erratically out of the gatehouse as far as he could go, until another sickening crunch warned him that his rear end had become intimate with General Sir Sackville. Edging the truck backwards and forwards with much grinding of gears and squealing of brakes, he lined it up and tried once more. This time, Shrahma be praised, he entered the gatehouse with a yard to spare on either side. Grabbing the radio, he was about to shout *Starfire*! when – with an even more appalling crunch than before – the truck juddered to a halt and stalled yet again.

Pungal leapt down from the cab, ran through to the courtyard and peered up. A row of iron spikes, extending across the arch of the gatehouse, had embedded themselves into the roof of the truck and clawed back the aluminium sheeting like the lid of a sardine tin. Pungal ran back to the cab, restarted the engine and tried to reverse out.

Unable to see what was going on, but hearing all this crunching and grinding, Sharaq was growing increasingly desperate. 'Tiger to Fireball, Tiger to Fireball,' he gabbled into his radio, 'do we have *Starfire*? Do we have *Starfire*?'

'No, no, no!' Pungal screamed back. 'I'm stuck in the bloody gatehouse!' With much squealing of tortured metal, he backed slowly out onto the circus once more, turned the truck around, jumped out, let about twenty pounds of air out of each tyre, and tried reversing into the courtyard.

'Tiger to Fireball, Tiger to Fireball,' Sharaq was jabbering, 'I must have *Starfire*. Do I have *Starfire*?'

With the rear half of the truck just clearing the spiked archway through to the north courtyard at last, Pungal screeched into his radio: 'Roger, Tiger! *Starfire*! *Starfire*!' But even as he spoke, the spikes snared the crumpled aluminium that was flapping about at the cab end of the truck and embedded themselves a second time. Yet again the hapless truck came to an abrupt halt and stalled.

'Fireball to Tiger, Fireball to Tiger!' Pungal shrieked into his radio.

Too late. Sharaq had already switched off his receiver and stuffed it into an ammunition pouch. Grabbing his machine pistol and beckoning his men forwards, he darted across to the keep door, opened it and glanced out into the ante-room beyond. It was deserted. It struck him how strangely quiet the castle seemed . . .

It was quiet because the impromptu cocktail party had broken up by this time and everybody who was anybody – from colonel-generals to smelly mongrels – was a hundred yards away across the south lawns watching Hudson Butcher inspect the freshly dug hole in which he was to plant the Unibore olive tree for world peace, on the morrow.

The only people left in the drawing-room when Sharaq and his commandos came storming in were Vernon Wormslow and his fifteen colleagues from Rent-a-Footman, who were clearing away the dirty glasses.

Whilst Wormslow was not actually *expecting* half a dozen balaclava-helmeted soldiers to charge in waving submachine-guns and shouting 'Out! Out! Out!' he knew that everybody was supposed to be off the premises by half past eight for a military exercise and assumed that this was merely the SAS's high-spirited way of pointing out that they had overstayed their welcome. Even so, there was such a thing as saying *please* . . .

'This is really quite unnecessary, dear,' Wormslow protested, pink and flustered, as they were hustled at gun point across the great hall and down the screens passage. 'You only have to ask nicely and we'll — '

'Shut your face and keep moving,' barked Sharaq, who was already beginning to suspect that something had gone seriously wrong here. Where were the rest of the party? Where were the women? Where were the police? But worse was to come as he emerged from the screens passage into the north courtyard: where was the bloody *truck*?

He stared across the courtyard to the gatehouse, sixty yards away, where Pungal was leaping up and down beside the jammed pantechnicon, beckoning frantically.

'I think he's stuck, dear,' said Wormslow, trying to be helpful.

Precious seconds ticked away while Sharaq stood paralysed with indecision. But it was too late to abort the mission now. There was no alternative but to leg it across the courtyard to the waiting transport.

'OK, let's go!' he shouted, jamming the muzzle of his gun into Wormslow's ribs. 'Everybody run, run, *run*!'

Indoors, Vernon's brother Aubrey returned to the drawing-room from the kitchen and found the place strangely deserted. Wandering around the house wondering what had happened to everyone, he peered out of the window in the great hall, just in time to see Vernon and his colleagues disappearing into the back of a removal truck with a squad of armed soldiers. Whilst Aubrey knew that his brother harboured something of a passion for the military, this did strike him as carrying elopement just a little too far. He rapped frantically on the delicate Tudor window panes, shrieking 'Oi! Oi! Oi!' But not a soul could hear him. He scuttled down the screens passage and out into the courtyard. 'Oi!' he yelled. 'What's going on?'

Pungal and Sharaq were already bolting shut the tailgates. At the sound of Aubrey's voice they abandoned the job, scrambled round to the front of the truck and jumped in.

'That's my brother!' Aubrey screamed, running across the courtyard. 'They're civvies, you stupid prats!'

Sharaq wound down the cab window and prepared to fire a warning burst. Pungal stamped on the throttle, and with more agonised squealing and grinding of tortured metal, the truck tore itself free from the spikes, ripping off some sixty square feet of roof in the process, and leaving twists of mangled aluminium dangling from the gatehouse roof like grotesque mobiles.

Aubrey gave up the chase and gaped in wonder at the wreckage, as the truck coughed its bronchial way down the avenue towards the main gates and Gladstone came wandering over from the car park to find out what was going on.

'Hey, man, whass all this racket about?'

'The bloody army!' bleated Aubrey, twitching with rage and disbelief. 'They just hijacked my brother!' He turned and scurried back inside to the great hall, where CLAC and the presidential party were getting ready to leave, and Inspector Lipman's unit were on their way upstairs to deploy themselves in the long gallery for Operation Midsummer Night.

'Your death-or-glory mob,' Aubrey screeched at Kilmore. 'Just bagged the wrong bloody lot! They've kidnapped my brother and his mates!'

The news went off like a hand grenade. A dozen busy conversations collapsed and died. Police officers froze in mid step on the staircase. Hatchard sniffed the air for subversion.

'What the hell do you mean?' said Kilmore.

Aubrey blurted out his story, pointing dramatically out of the window to the evidence still dangling from the gatehouse arch and lying scattered about over the gravel. Everyone – police, CLAC, Prince of Peace, smelly dog Walpole – hurried outside to the gatehouse, where Gladstone added his two-penn'orth to the story.

For the life of him Kilmore could not imagine how Bile – even *Bile* – could conceivably have mistaken sixteen footmen in tail coats for eighteen police officers . . . of whom six, he knew in advance, were women. Nor was it immediately clear what he was doing with an old furniture truck when transport corps had laid on a fleet of one-ton vans. Embarrassing though it was – and the more so in front of these visiting dignitaries from the Paradise Islands – Kilmore could only suggest to Hatchard that they abandon the exercise forthwith and return to Lydhurst police station to liberate the footmen and establish what had gone so disastrously wrong. So, cock-a-hoop at this stupendous army bungle, the entire police detachment climbed aboard their minibuses once more and set off back to Lydhurst, while the presidential party, hugely entertained by the whole débacle, retired to the drawing-room for further refreshment.

Half a mile away, Noah and Annabelle had just walked in through the main gates, and were strolling up the avenue, wondering if the black Jaguar in the car park could possibly belong to Byron.

Down in the dungeons, meanwhile, unaware of all this mayhem erupting above, Bile and the boys had been assiduously searching for the mysterious maker of crashing noises, and now stumbled on the quaking Zlob, practically blue with hypothermia, fumbling his way deeper and deeper into a maze of dead-end passages.

'Freeze!' screamed Bile. (Which was all that Zlob had been doing with any degree of success for the past five or six hours.)

Blinded by their torch beams, Zlob cringed back into the shadows, shielding his eyes.

'Oo are you, you 'orrible little whelp'?' Bile demanded. 'Police?'

'Poleez!' exclaimed Zlob, believing that deliverance had come at last.

'I bloody knew it,' said Bile jubilantly. 'Dirty spying bastard.'

At that, the luckless Zlob was set upon from all sides, trussed up with army string, and dumped back in Ye Olde Chaymbre of Heath Robinson ironmongery.

Much refreshed by that invigorating little limber-up, Bile and the boys returned to where they had left their kit, packed away their tin mugs and moved quietly up into the keep tower to prepare for the attack.

Outside by the gatehouse, Annabelle and her father were introducing themselves to Gladstone Shilling, who – having heard so much about them, and knowing how anxious Byron was to make contact with his beloved – politely insisted on ushering them indoors to the grand drawing-room, where drinks were flowing freely once more and everyone was having a whale of a time.

Byron had no more swallowed Rosheen's story about the phone call from Tupelo county hospital than he'd swallowed the one about Guy marrying a swineherd from Clermont-Ferrand; and by the time Gladstone appeared in the drawing-room doorway, with Annabelle and Noah trailing sheepishly behind, he had knocked back sufficient Scotch and champagne to have forgotten all about it anyway. Overjoyed to see them suddenly materialise out of nowhere – and without the slightest regard for protocol – he introduced them first to Otello and Mirella, then to his CLAC colleagues, and finally to Hudson Butcher – who was three sheets in the wind himself by this time and congratulated Noah on being blessed with such a beautiful wife.

'Not my wife, sir,' said Noah, amused but flattered. 'My daughter.'

'Then she must be *your* wife,' said Butcher, turning to Byron. (For, having been married to a considerable number of women himself, he took it for granted that Annabelle had to be *some*body's wife.)

'Well, not exactly,' said Byron, 'not quite, ah . . . Not, not quite — '

'Not quite yet,' Annabelle chimed in, blushing a furious pink. 'We're just . . . just, you know . . .'

'Engaged,' concluded Butcher, who – despite his predilection for keeping the proletariat permanently in fear and chains – was not immune to the occasional attack of romantic sentimentalism. 'My dear children, my very warmest congratulations to you both.' And to Byron's acute embarrassment, the great man actually began to applaud them, as if they were the star turn at a royal variety performance. To make matters worse, Jericho Engineer and Colonel-General Stockminder loyally began to clap as well, followed by Great-Uncle Albert, Brigadier Claybuck, Brownjohn, Edwina, and gradually the entire room.

The news of Byron and Annabelle's engagement was as much of a surprise to Noah as it was to Byron's CLAC colleagues, who had not realised that he had managed to rid himself of the *first* Mrs Cleveland yet, let alone find a second. Feeling that this called for a special celebration, Otello despatched Aubrey Wormslow to the kitchen to fetch more champagne, and asked Gladstone to invite the chauffeurs in to join them and toast the happy couple.

Gladstone obligingly set off across the north courtyard to summon Sid Tideyman and the three drivers from the Paradise Islands' High Commission, who were in the car park, watching television in the director-general's Silver Shadow. Emerging from the gatehouse, he was hailed by a black-leather blonde, steaming ferociously towards him past General Sterling-Pallgrave.

'Hey, Mac!' she called out. 'Anyone called Cartwright in there?'

Taking her to be a friend of Annabelle's, Gladstone called back: 'In the drawin'-room with Doc Cleveland. Through the hall . . . first left . . . past the stairs . . . first right . . . straight down the end.'

'Gotcher,' said Rosheen, steaming on through the gatehouse.

Funny, Gladstone was thinking . . . face is familiar . . . voice rings a bell . . .

In the keep, meantime, Bile's reconnaissance patrol had returned from a furtive sortie with welcome news. Bile had expected the police to deploy themselves in a part of the castle that it would be almost impossible to take by surprise. He was delighted to learn, then, that they had elected to ensconce themselves in the grand drawing-room, of all places. And to judge from the amount of noise they were making, they were not anticipating an attack before nightfall.

Bile studied his wristwatch and turned to the troop: 'Sixty seconds.'

They pulled on their Balaclava helmets and snapped blank-filled magazines into the submachine-guns.

Bile picked up his radio handset: 'Oscar One from Delta Bravo . . .'

Half a mile away in a secluded lay-by, five olive-green Bedford vans started up, pulled out onto the Allshott road with a screech of rubber, and screamed away towards the gates of Carnage.

Regardless of Gladstone's directions to the drawing-room, Rosheen walked in through the front door, down the entire length of the screens passage and straight out at the other end. Crossing the south-west courtyard, she re-entered the castle through an ante-chamber between the dining-room and the south-west tower, and collided with Aubrey Wormslow, who was hurrying back to the drawing-room with a magnum of Krug in each hand.

'Just watch who you're shoving round, fellah,' she snarled. 'I'm the director-general's wife. Where the hell is he?'

'Through here, madam,' sighed flustered Wormslow, and hurried on through the great eating room and the south tower beyond, and into the drawing-room, where Hudson Butcher was about to propose a toast to the happy couple.

'To Byron and Annabelle,' said the great one, raising his champagne glass, as Rosheen blundered in through the south door.

'Byron and Annabelle,' everybody chorused.

'By-ron and *whoooooo*?' wailed Rosheen, with the mellifluousness of an air-raid siren. 'Oh, *ex*cuse *me*, King Kong,' (barging her way through to Hudson Butcher) 'but I don't think I caught the name of the unlucky bitch.' She aimed a menacing finger at Annabelle's face. 'Who d'ya say this miserable streak of Dixie chickenshit was?'

Accustomed to having people boiled in oil for less, Butcher gazed stupefied at Rosheen's hot, damp bosom heaving insolently behind her unzipped leather top, and waited for somebody to shoot her or drag her away in irons.

'This is my daughter, young lady,' said Noah, who was quite used to dealing with drunks, harlots and persons of unsound mind. 'And who, pray, are you?'

'I, pray,' Rosheen declaimed operatically, 'am Mrs Byron Cleveland, pray. For the past twelve years, lawful wedded wife of that bumbling fuckwit beside you, who's been bedding your adulterous little whore of a daughter since Christ knows how long.'

'Byron,' said Noah, who would age four-score years and ten in the next minute or two, 'do you know this young woman?'

'Know her?' squeaked Byron pathetically, as the first concussion grenades and two cans of smoke came flying in from the south-east tower.

Precisely what happened next, nobody in the room could ever clearly recall.

50

HEARING THE explosions and the sound of automatic gunfire, Gladstone and his fellow chauffeurs came running back from the car park, just as five army vans hurtled out of the gatehouse, full of armed men in Balaclava helmets. They stood and watched, bewildered, as the convoy skidded respectfully around General Sterling-Pallgrave and sped away down the avenue through a spray of dust and gravel. Sprinting indoors, only to find the place full of smoke and reeking of cordite, Gladstone began to search the castle for a telephone to call the police.

*

All hell was breaking loose at Lydhurst police station by this time. Kilmore and Hatchard had returned with Inspector Lipman and his officers, only to discover that nobody there knew anything about any rentable footmen or roofless pantechnicons, and that nothing had been seen or heard of Corporal Bile all evening. A call to Oldingham TA depot, furthermore, confirmed that 2 Troop had definitely set out for Allshott in a fleet of one-ton vans.

At that point, the army GOC, South-East District, was informed; and just as he was ordering an air-ground search for the missing SAS men, news reached New Scotland Yard that President Butcher and seventeen others had been violently abducted from Carnage Castle. Within minutes, Special Branch were notifying every port and airfield in the country, and by sunset the first of the search-and-rescue helicopters was chattering eastwards from Army Air Corps headquarters, Middle Wallop. Then at twenty-five past nine, with dusk approaching and every anti-terrorist unit from Plymouth to Glasgow standing by on red alert, five olive-green vans came screeching into the rear yard of Lydhurst police station.

Kilmore hurried outside as Bile leapt down from the leading van.

'Beat the clock, sah!' Bile announced triumphantly. 'Caught the idle bastards on the 'op. Twelve men and six tarts, all present and accounted for.'

One by one, the victims were dragged feet-first from the back of the vans and dumped unceremoniously on terra firma. Kilmore looked on, mortified, as they were released from their handcuffs and black, drawstring hoods . . . One Engineer, two Cartwrights, a director-general and his deputy, their wives, Brownjohn, McGuffy, Nina, Edwina, Melanie, suddenly bald Wormslow, a brigadier, a colonel-general, a terrified bodyguard, a foreign minister and a visiting head of state.

The look on Kilmore's face was the first intimation Bile had that something might have gone awry. 'Problem, sah?' he enquired.

Superintendent Hatchard, meanwhile, was totally unaware of all this melodrama unfolding outside; for he had just been summoned to the CID room, where an urgent telex message was coming through from his commander at Buckingham Gate, who had not yet heard about President Butcher's abduction and was dealing with an entirely different crisis, news of which had only just come in from the Foreign Office.

Outside, kindly WPCs were dispensing sweet tea and soothing words to the bewildered victims, who were wandering round the station yard like dazed survivors from some terrible natural disaster, clutching at one another for comfort and reassurance. Colonel-General Stockminder was weeping quietly into Jericho's capacious peaked hat. Rosheen was regurgitating several litres of Special Brew down the side of a police car. And bald Wormslow was hunting frantically for his missing toupee.

The only victim of Operation Midsummer Night who had remained cool, calm and collected throughout was President Hudson Butcher himself. As one who had fought his way up through the ranks from lance-sergeant to field-marshal at the age of only forty-three, it took more than a corporal and seventeen troopers to shake *his* cast-iron military composure. Having ascertained that no serious harm had befallen his entourage, he summarily requisitioned Lipman's office, convened an impromptu assembly of police and military, and like the conquerors of ancient times dealing retribution to the vanquished, pronounced sentence on the British nation.

'At eleven o'clock tomorrow morning,' he informed them – really rather cordially, considering the circumstances, 'I shall hold a press conference at the Dorchester Hotel and give the world a very full and precise account of everything that has happened here this evening. It will also give me very great pleasure to repeat the story for the television cameras at the Wopec inauguration ceremony tomorrow afternoon. And by the time I've finished, this contemptible little country, with its miserable little army and its pathetic, bungling police force, will be the biggest laughing stock on earth. And every man in this room is going to wish to God he'd never been born.'

With that, he smiled, looked around the silent, poker-faced assembly and began to laugh – a faint snigger that gradually grew into a cackle of contempt, gaining steadily in pitch and volume until it acquired a note of incipient hysteria, and tears rolled down the great one's cheeks.

At a loss to see the joke, but finding these falsetto peals irresistibly infectious, Great-Uncle Albert started laughing too . . . Which promptly set off Colonel-General Stockminder and

Jericho Engineer – whose elephantine trumps of mirth were too much even for the dour-faced Brigadier Claybuck and the witless bodyguard. They too began to laugh; and the more the great one laughed, the more *they* laughed. Until, eventually, with the entire presidential party almost on the floor in hysterics, even Superintendent Hatchard and Major Kilmore began to laugh. And the more they laughed, so Corporal Bile began to laugh; Inspector Lipman; the station sergeant; and so on through the ranks, until every police officer and trooper in the room was all but doubled up in stitches, with tears coursing down his cheeks in torrents . . . As, one by one, they passed around the telex that had just come in for Norman Hatchard from his commander at Royalty and Diplomatic Protection Group Headquarters, Buckingham Gate:

ATTENTION SUPT. HATCHARD MP/DPG. MAX PRIORITY. FOREIGN OFFICE CONFIRMS MILITARY COUP, PARADISE ISLANDS, DAWN TODAY. COL MOGADOR BOATMAN NEW CHIEF OF JUNTA. EXTRADITION WARRANTS IN TRANSIT FOR L/SGT BUTCHER, CPL STOCKMINDER, PRIVATE CLAYBUCK AND OTHERS. DIPLOMATIC STATUS WITHDRAWN AS OF 18.00 BST TODAY. DETAIN IN PROTECTIVE CUSTODY PENDING DEPORTATION.

51

NIGHT FELL. A barn owl hooted and a farm dog barked at the melancholy moon. Somewhere down a dark country lane, deep in the heart of Sussex, a crippled pantechnicon stood, still and silent, in the shadows of a lay-by, a broken throttle cable dangling from its engine. Locked safely inside its capacious womb, Vernon Wormslow and fifteen immaculately groomed footmen were gazing thoughtfully through the gash in the roof at the starry sky above, wondering why everything had gone so deathly quiet and what was going to happen next.

A few miles further on, the full complement of Number One

Commando, the Sandhustan People's Liberation Army, were yomping along the road for all they were worth, trying to make it to Clympton-on-Solent by daybreak.

Deep in the bowels of Carnage Castle, where day and night were all one, frozen Zlob had spent a painful and exhausting hour wriggling free from his bonds a second time. Stumbling through the darkness, pausing every few moments to illuminate the way with a box of finest Bulgarian army matches, he succeeded finally in reaching the east wall of the dungeon. Weak from cold and hunger, he swung open the heavy oak door that he hoped, in desperation, would lead him upstairs to the keep tower and to freedom, and found himself at the top of the steps that led down to Bile's rat-infested tunnel, far below.

Prolonged darkness and hypothermia can have bizarre effects upon the mind. For one fleeting moment, as he stood there in the flickering light of his last dying match, Zlob thought he glimpsed the ghostly figure of an aged cavalry general, with thick moustaches – not unlike his late, unlamented hero, Josef Stalin. In that second, he felt a strange and horrible sensation, as if a powerful, unseen hand were pushing him into the yawning black void behind. Stranger still, as he tumbled backwards off the steps and plunged thirty feet down into the pool of feculent sludge beneath, he could have sworn he heard the sound of belly laughter echoing madly round the dungeons . . .

EPILOGUE

No Accord at Wopec. Threat of Peace Recedes
Sunday Telegraph 2 July

Wopec Talks End But Kidpan Gang Hunt Goes On
Guardian 3 July

Kidnap Gang Riddle Deepens. Yard Chiefs Baffled
Daily Express 3 July

'Not Us' Say I.R.A.
Liverpool Daily Post 4 July

Police Quiz Libyans
Daily Mirror 5 July

Red Brigades Theory
International Herald Tribune 6 July

Baader-Meinhof Links Probe
Irish Times 7 July

P.L.O. Terror Jackal Ghoul Hunt
Sun 8 July

South African Plot, Says Ex-M15 Mole
The Sunday Times 9 July

Belgrano Connexion, Claims Labour M.P.
The Observer 9 July

Lord Lucan File Reopened
News of the World 9 July

A fine Sunday morning in July and a grand day to be adrift in the Atlantic, where, after several weeks at sea, the motor yacht *Amphitrite* was still bobbing about in search of France, with green Nurg slung over the taffrail like an old raincoat, heaving relentlessly into the surging brine.

'Sure that's Guernsey?' said worried Sharaq, as they passed the Azores.

'Aye, Skip. Should sight the coast of Brittany any minute,' replied navigator Pungal, as they drifted gently on towards the West Indies.

High in the sky and far away, a Tupolev 134 of Balkan-Bulgarian Airways, en route from London to Sofia, was crossing the Austrian frontier and beginning its slow descent towards Vienna's international airport.

Alone in her tourist-class window-seat, Bulgaria's erstwhile delegate to Unibore – newly promoted to the post of assistant clerk in the musty catacombs of the State Archive Office in Sofia – sat munching a rice-and-seaweed cookie, nervously trying to remember what 'political asylum' was in German, and wondering whether Byron would accept a transfer-charge call from the American embassy in Vienna to Salvation, Mississippi.

Five thousand miles away in Dixie, the new director-general of Unibore was spending a lazy Sunday morning in bed with his bride-to-be and the Sunday papers.

'I wonder how Daddy's making out,' murmured Annabelle, underlining a significant passage in her new copy of *Your J-Zone* by Sherrilee Bloom. 'It's not like him to be away this long.'

'Well, the Lord's work taketh time,' Byron replied, skimming idly through the job vacancies in the *Salvation Herald-Examiner*. 'Remember: there is more joy in heaven over one sinner that repenteth than in ninety and nine just persons . . .'

In a tiny ecumenical chapel in Madison, New Jersey, a humble penitent in a smock of coarse Irish linen was on her knees before the altar of God.

'Jesus loves *every*one, my dear,' said Noah soothingly

'Even Rosheen?' blubbed born-again Rosheen.

'Most especially Rosheen.'

'Oh, shit,' wailed Rosheen. 'That's just too beautiful . . .'

August came, bringing bleak and bitter winter to the south Atlantic. A vicious gale, keen as a razor, swept in from the Antarctic, slashing mercilessly across the face of the barren island of South Georgia, where a pair of stoic British troopers were just beginning a lonely two-year vigil.

'The secret of survival out 'ere, sah,' said Bile, helping Kilmore to a plateful of freshly fried penguin, 'is *hate*. Plenty of haitch-a-tee-hee . . .'